Y0-AAU-247

DUTCH TREAT

ALSO BY ELMORE LEONARD

HOMBRE
THE MOONSHINE WAR
VALDEZ IS COMING
FORTY LASHES LESS ONE
FIFTY-TWO PICKUP
3:10 TO YUMA
SWAG
THE HUNTED
MR. MAJESTYK
UNKNOWN MAN NO. 89
THE SWITCH
GUNSIGHTS
GOLD COAST
CITY PRIMEVAL: HIGH NOON IN DETROIT
SPLIT IMAGES
CAT CHASER
STICK
LaBRAVA
GLITZ

3 NOVELS
THE HUNTED
SWAG
MR. MAJESTYK

ELMORE LEONARD'S
DUTCH TREAT

INTRODUCTION BY GEORGE F. WILL

ARBOR HOUSE
NEW YORK

Manufactured in the United States of America

10 9 8 7 6 5 4 3 2 1

Library of Congress Cataloging in Publication Data

Leonard, Elmore, 1925–
Elmore Leonard's Dutch treat.

Contents: The hunted—Swag—Mr. Majestyk.
I. Title. II. Title: Dutch treat.
PS3562.E55A6 1985   813'.54   85-11246
ISBN: 0-87795-768-1

A limited first edition of this book has been published by The
Mysterious Press.

CONTENTS

Introduction by George F. Will
ix

THE HUNTED
1

SWAG
211

MR. MAJESTYK
429

INTRODUCTION

In the 1950s, when Elmore "Dutch" Leonard was plugging away at writing novels but was keeping the wolf from his door by writing advertising copy for Chevrolet trucks, he would go out among the truckers and listen to them talk. Leonard asked one trucker to say what he liked best about his truck. The fellow replied, "You can't wear that sonofabitch out, you just get tired of looking at it and buy a new one."

Those words have a ring of authenticity rarely found in testimonials, and I will wager dollars against donuts that if Detroit had listened as carefully to Leonard as Leonard listened to the truckers, today we would not so often find ourselves driving behind pick-up trucks with the word *Toyota* on their tailgates. But Detroit's loss was literature's gain. Thirty years later there is a thick shelf of Leonard works, three of which are collected in this volume, which is a kind of club sandwich for the many thousands of us who have robust appetites for Leonard's work.

Leonard got his nickname—Dutch—when he was a boy and there was a major league baseball player named Emil "Dutch" Leonard. Emil Leonard was the sort of player the boys in the press box call a "journeyman." He broke into the big leagues in 1933 and pitched for twenty seasons, generally with teams (the Brooklyn Dodgers, Washington Senators, Philadelphia Phillies, Chicago Cubs) that rarely rose to mediocrity. He had one sensational season, going 20-8 in 1939. He finished his career with 191 wins and 181 losses, which was not at all bad. In fact, late in his career baseball people came to realize that his record was remarkably good, considering that in his two decades of toil, only two of his teams had seasons in which they won more games than they lost.

Elmore Leonard's career has been bit a like that. Appreciation has come late. But the appreciation must be all the more satisfying to him because it is coming from readers who, like the boys in the bleachers and press boxes, are real aficionados, not just people whose attention is attracted only by a noisy splash. Elmore Leonard is not a journeyman anymore. He is an all-star.

Emil Leonard relied a lot on his knuckle ball. Most breaking pitches derive their motion from the speed and spin the pitcher imparts to the ball. A knuckle ball is slow and, ideally, has no spin. The slowness makes it tantalizing to hitters, but the lack of spin gives it an erratic motion that makes it effective. (It is elusive to catchers as well as hitters. One catcher, asked how to catch a knuckle ball, said, "You wait until it stops rolling, then pick it up.")

Elmore Leonard's novels are like that—like literary knuckle balls. Their effectiveness derives from their realism. The realism is in the elusive path of the narrative. This might be the place for me to wax metaphysical, to say that life is like a knuckle ball because . . . But Leonard is the least metaphysical of writers. He deals in small, telling details, not the Big Picture. However, he knows that if you gather enough of the right details, you have, at the end of the day, a picture, and a true one.

A knuckle ball pitcher is apt to last, as Emil Leonard did. He is apt to have his mind on the long haul, and to plan to make it with something other than a spectacular—and perishable—fast ball. He survives on nuance, not speed. Sportswriters specialize in picking precisely the right adjectives, and the one they prefer for knuckle ballers is *crafty*.

Elmore Leonard is like that—crafty—in several senses. His stories come at you sideways; often he portrays the world as it looks when just glimpsed, as a motion or shadow, out of the corner of the mind's eye. He also is crafty in the sense that he brings to the business of writing novels the discipline of a craftsman. There are few flourishes and no wasted motion.

Two years ago I bought my first Elmore Leonard novel, in Cleveland, in his kind of place. Cleveland, an elemental place, is not long on flourishes. Since then I have read thirteen more of his novels. Recently, while eating lunch where I work (at home), I read a newspaper story reporting the publication of a new Leonard novel. I put down my sandwich and drove directly to a bookstore. It was a peanut butter and pickle sandwich I abandoned, so you know Leonard is good.

After publishing twenty-three novels in thirty-two years, he finally made the *New York Times* best-seller list with *Glitz*. His good luck is good news because luck had nothing to do with it. Craftsmanship has been rewarded. The reading public has come to its senses and made the gratifying discovery that a fine talent has been on hand for a long time.

Leonard lives in Birmingham, Michigan, a suburb of Detroit, where some of his stories are set. The description of Detroit as "Cleveland without the glitter" could come from one of his novels. Detroit is not Bloomsbury, but then Leonard, with his gray beard and a wardrobe consisting mainly of a tweed jacket and cloth cap, says he is not an artist, he is just an entertainer. *Just?* As though it is not a complex art to be as entertaining as he is.

His books are not exactly crime novels, although crimes occur and guns go off. But the guns do not go off often enough for the sort of people who cannot be entertained by anything more subtle than a train wreck. Hollywood took a splendid Leonard novel, *Stick*, and made a dreadful movie of it. Hollywood accomplished this by souping up the story with lots of machine guns. Moviemakers, like all hyperkinetic children, cannot stand a measured pace. Leonard is not for children.

By the way, the title of *Stick* comes from the name of one of Leonard's most memorable, and in an odd way admirable, characters, Ernest Stickley, Jr. He is admirable because he has talent without being a blowhard. He, too, does well what he does, and does it without playing to the grandstand. Of course you expect a sort of, shall we say, reserve from people whose chosen profession is stealing cars and sticking up stores. Mr. Stickley first appears in *Swag*, which is included in this collection. In that novel you will learn more than nice boys and girls should know about the science and art of armed robbery.

Leonard's novels are about marginal people, small people incompetent at even petty crime; or his novels are about quiet professionals who, like Leonard, are underestimated for a long time. Leonard uses no verbal pyrotechnics. Yet his style is as strong and personal as Van Gogh's brushstrokes. You could snip four square inches from any Van Gogh canvas, put the patch in front of almost anyone, and the person would instantly identify the painter. Leonard's readers could do something like that with any passage from his novels. He has perfect pitch for the street talk you might hear on some of America's mean streets.

Leonard errs on the side of underexplaining himself. He knows how easy it is to suffer overinterpretation at the hands of others. Assistant professors being what they are (incorrigible, for starters), there are thick volumes full of turgid essays clogged with coagulated passages about crime novels as sublimations of the class struggle. I recently read (well, started to) an essay that lays down this law: Detective stories are popular because secret crime and subsequent discovery are associated in the reader's subconsciousness with (I am not making this up; I could not) the "primal scene." What is that? That is a pyschoanalytic term referring to a child's imagining of sexual intercourse between his or her parents.

Leonard, too, has suffered semiacademic attention. A reviewer once said of him, "The aesthetic sub-text of his work is the systematic exposure of artistic pretension." Leonard retaliated. In his novel *LaBrava*, the protagonist, a photographer, refers to an exhibition of his pictures: "The review in the paper said, 'The aesthetic sub-text of his work is the systematic exposure of artistic pretension.' I thought I was just taking pictures."

Leonard's insistence that he is just a storyteller expresses pride, not humility. He has a craftsman's pride that being a fine craftsman is good enough, thank you.

He sold his first fiction in 1951, to *Argosy* magazine, and his first novel, a Western, in 1953. His mother wishes he were still writing Westerns because the language would be less gamy. Until he sold to Hollywood his novel *Hombre* (voted one of the twenty-five best Westerns of all time by the Western Writers of America), he had to work full-time writing advertising copy. Well, Wallace Stevens worked in an insurance office, T. S. Eliot at a bank, Anthony Trollope at the post office.

After *Hombre*, Leonard stopped writing Westerns and started making books the way a custom cobbler makes shoes: steadily. He writes from 9:30 A.M. to 6:00 P.M. He has been called the Dickens of Detroit because of the colorful characters he creates from the seamier side of life. But he reminds me of Trollope. This is not, Lord knows, because of his subjects, but because of his approach to his craft.

Trollope kept a meticulous diary of the pages he wrote. He noted that such discipline is considered beneath a man of genius. But, he said cheerfully, not being a genius, he had to be disciplined. You say that anyone who works with his imagination should wait for inspiration? Trollope said it would be just as absurd to say that a shoemaker should wait for inspiration. Writers, he said, should sit themselves at their desks as though they were clerks, and should sit until their daily writing quota is filled. If they adopt his quota, they will produce a book in four months.

Leonard's "sudden" success—he is an "overnight sensation" after more than thirty years of hard plugging—is a tribute to

INTRODUCTION

America. Here people are not homogenized, and cream rises. If you want a sip of the cream, start with these three novels, and then read *Stick*. Then, if you are not hooked, go watch television. It will serve you right.

GEORGE F. WILL
June 1985

THE HUNTED

"There are other ways to get home before your tour is up. You can get shipped home in a body bag, or you can pull a hat trick and get three Purple Hearts. If you think it's worth it."

—In a letter from Michael Cerre, formerly second lieutenant, 1st Recon Battalion, 1st Marine Division; postmarked December 3, 1970, Da Nang, Vietnam

1

This is the news story that appeared the next day, in the Sunday edition of the *Detroit Free Press*, page one:

FOUR TOURISTS DIE
IN ISRAELI HOTEL FIRE

TEL AVIV, March 20 (AP)—A predawn fire gutted an eight-story resort hotel Saturday, killing four tourists and injuring 46 others, including guests who leaped from upper-story windows to escape the flames. No Americans were killed, but two were reported injured, including an Ohio woman who jumped from a fourth-floor window.

The blaze swept through the 200-room Park Hotel in Netanya, a Mediterranean resort city about 20 miles north of Tel Aviv.

About 20 Americans escaped from the fire, an American Embassy official said, including a tour group of 17 who arrived in Israel a week ago from Columbus, Ohio.

According to a state radio report, the Park's management had recently considered closing the building after receiving threats from protection racketeers who had failed to extort payments from the hotel's owners.

Firemen extinguished the flames after a seven-hour battle.

In a six-column picture on the news-photo page of the *Free Press*, several elderly tourists who had escaped the fire were gathered in a group on the street, holding blankets around hunched shoulders. It was raining and they looked wet and cold. A dark, bearded man wearing white trousers, his chest and feet bare, stood apart from the group, somewhat in the background, and seemed to have been moving away when the picture was taken. The bearded man, glancing over his shoulder, was caught in that moment with a startled, open-mouthed expression.

The picture caption repeated most of the facts from the page-one story and quoted Mr. Nathan Fine, leader of the Columbus tour group, as saying, "It's a miracle we're alive. There was somebody went up and down the halls banging on doors, getting people out, telling them to put wet towels over their heads and follow him—crawl along the hall to the outside stairway in back. He must have saved the lives of twenty people. It was lucky, I'll tell you, those stairs were outside, or nobody would be here now."

The man who had gone up and down the halls banging on doors was not identified by name. Outside the hotel that rainy Saturday morning, no one seemed to know who he was or where he had gone.

2

Rosen first noticed the tourist lady on Friday, the day before the fire. He saw her and said to himself, New York.

She had the look—a trim forty-year-old who kept herself together: stylish in a quiet way, neatly combed dark hair and sunglasses; tailored beige sundress, about a size eight or ten; expensive cane-trimmed handbag hanging from her shoulder; nothing overdone, no camera case, no tourist lapel badge that said "Kiss Me, I'm Jewish." Rosen, watching her walk past the café, liked her thin legs, her high can, and her sensible breasts.

In Netanya the main street came in from the Haifa Road, crossed railroad tracks, and passed through crowded blocks of shops and business places before reaching an open parkway of shrubs and scattered palm trees—Netanya's promenade. Beyond were the beach road and the sea. Looking down on the park were hotels and flat-faced apartment buildings. On the ground level of these buildings were shops that sold oriental rugs and jewelry to tourists, and open-air cafés with striped awnings. One of the cafés, on the north side of the park, was the Acapulco. There Rosen had his midmorning coffee with hot milk, and there he was sitting when he first noticed the trim, New York–looking tourist lady.

He saw her again that evening at a quarter of ten in a beige pantsuit and red Arab jewelry, with red earrings dangling below neatly combed dark hair. He imagined she would smell of bath powder.

She pretended to be interested in looking at things—at signs, at the bill of fare on the stucco wall of the café—smiling a little now at the way "Bloody Mery" was spelled, and "Manhatan" and "te." She needed something to look at, Rosen decided, because she was self-conscious, feeling people at the tables looking at her and making judgments in Hebrew and in foreign languages. She maintained a pleasant expression, wanting people to like her.

Rosen never worried about what people thought. Years ago, developing confidence, yes, he'd used to say, "Fuck 'em." Now he didn't even think about people thinking. He felt good and he looked good, a new person: face deeply tanned, full beard with streaks of gray in it. Hair a little thin on top, but the way he combed it across on a slant, curling over his ears, his scalp didn't show. He never wore suits anymore. Dark blue knit shirt open to show the pale blue choker beads and some chest hair. Contrast was the key. The faded, washed-out safari jacket with short sleeves and the fifteen-hundred-dollar gold wristwatch. The outdoor look. The sun-blackened forearms and hands. Authentic casual. Off-white trousers, lined, seventy-five bucks in the U.S., and ten-dollar Israeli sandals. (There were other combinations: fifteen-dollar faded Levi's with two-hundred-dollar Swiss boots; cashmere sportcoat and French jeans. But no business or even leisure suits, no matching outfits.)

He felt that he looked *very* good, in fact, down to 149 from the 170 pounds he had carried for more than twenty years. He was also down to five-nine from the five-ten he had measured when he'd gotten out of the service, but that didn't bother him.

He still considered himself five-ten and tried to remember not to let his shoulders droop or his gut hang out.

He could hold himself up and in and still sit low, relaxed—the quiet man who knew where he was—a thumb hooked in a tight pants pocket and a pencil-thin Danneman cigar between the fingers of his hand on the metal table. The thumb remained hooked; he would use his cigar hand to raise the demitasse of Turkish coffee.

Rosen was always comfortable in his surroundings. A few days in a new place, like Netanya, and he was at home and would never be taken for a tourist. And after three years in Israel—three years next week—he felt he might even pass for a sabra. Rosen was forty-nine and had been forty-nine for the past year and a half. Sometimes he was younger. For the neat-looking tourist lady, if age came up, he would probably be around forty-six.

He did not change his position, but looked up and gave her the one, "Did you know that if you sit at the Acapulco Café in Netanya long enough everyone you know will pass by? How about a cup of coffee?"

Her smile was natural and she seemed relieved, saved, though she glanced around before sitting down in the chair Rosen offered.

"Are you meeting someone?"

"No, I was just . . . taking a walk." She smiled again, looking toward the open front of the café. "I've been wondering—why do you suppose this place is called the Acapulco? I can't figure it out."

"The owner," Rosen said, "is an immigrant, a Mexican Jew. He came here from Mexico." It was probably true.

"That's interesting. You don't think of Mexico." She hunched over the table, holding her arms. Good rings, a diamond, no wedding band. "I was reading; I think it's eighty-two different nationalities are represented in Israel. People who've come here to live."

"Eighty-three," Rosen said. "The latest figure."

"Really?" She believed him. "Do you, I mean, are you Israeli?"

"I live here. Actually, I live in Jerusalem about eight months—"

"I'm *dying* to see Jerusalem."

"About eight months out of the year. I spend some time up in the Golan, in the mountains. Usually a couple of months in the winter I go down to Eilat." Carefully, as he spoke, feeling her watching him, Rosen turned the demitasse upside down on the saucer. "It gets too cold in Jerusalem, so I go down to Eilat, the Red Sea area, do some skin-diving around Sharm el Sheikh." The names sounded good, they were coming out easily. "You been to the Sinai?"

"We just got here the day before yesterday. We've been to Tel Aviv, Jaffa—"

"And today was a rest day, huh?"

"Most of the people in the group are a little older. So they set the pace, you might say."

Rosen turned the demitasse cup upright and looked into it, the cup white and fragile in his brown hand. He said, somewhat surprised, "You're with a group?"

"Yes; from Columbus, Ohio. What are you doing?"

"Hadassah ladies?"

"No—"

"United Jewish Appeal."

"No, a group from our temple, B'nai Zion."

"But your husband's not along?"

"What are you doing? Tell me."

"Reading your fortune." He showed her the shapes formed by the wet chocolaty sludge, the residue of the Turkish grounds that had oozed down the insides of the cup while it was inverted. Their heads were close. Rosen caught a hint of perfume with the bath powder. He raised his eyes. Very nice skin, no blemishes. He didn't even see any pores.

"Hmmmm," Rosen said, looking down again. "You're with a group, huh?"

"Why, what do you see?"

"Are you in show business? An actress maybe, or a model?"

"God, no. I work in a medical lab."

"You're a nurse?"

"I used to be, before I was married."

"See that, right there, it looks like a statue? Like Venus, no arms but all the rest. That's you."

"It is?"

"Like you're posing or on a stage, all by yourself."

"I've got two teenaged daughters at home, and I'll tell you, that's not being all by myself."

"But no man around."

"We were divorced."

"How long ago?"

She hesitated. "Three years."

The next question in Rosen's mind—"You fool around?"—remained there. "I see the trip, all those thin lines there, but I don't see you with a group. I see you as sort of a loner."

"If it's your cup," the tourist lady said, looking at him now, "shouldn't it be your fortune?"

Rosen gave her a nice grin. "I didn't think you'd notice that."

"So it's not me who's the loner, it's you. Am I right?"

"Well, in some ways, maybe. But I'm very friendly and easy to get along with." He smiled and offered his brown hand. "Al Rosen."

And the nice-smelling divorced lady on a tour with an elderly group from Columbus, Ohio, was Edie Broder; in Israel for twenty-two days, her first vacation in three years, more interested in the life of the country today than in looking at old stones from biblical times, though she was dying to see Jerusalem.

And Rosen actually lived there?

Most of the time.

It must be tremendously exciting, *being* here with all that's going on. It must be fascinating.

"That's why I've stayed," Rosen said.

It was something she could already feel, the vitality of the people, their *purpose*.

"It's something, all right," Rosen said, thinking she should see them getting on a bus in Dizengoff Street.

When you consider all that's been accomplished since just '48. It's fan*tas*tic.

"Unbelievable," Rosen said. Maybe she'd have a cocktail?

Edie Broder hoped she didn't sound like a tourist. She couldn't help it. It was what she felt, being here, experiencing it in the light of Judaic history, witnessing the fulfillment of a four-thousand-year-old dream. And on and on for several minutes, Edie Broder from Columbus letting out what she'd been feeling about Israel for the past few days.

Rosen wasn't sure he followed all of it. He nodded, though, paying attention, seeming to enjoy her enthusiasm.

She was kind of sorry now she was stuck with the tour group, when there was *so* much to see.

Rosen followed that all right. He straightened in his chair, waiting.

She would like to see more of how the people *lived* and learn what they *thought*. Maybe even stay on a kibbutz for a few days, if that was possible. Talk to the *real* people.

"How about a drink?" Rosen said. "Or a glass of wine?"

"Israeli wine?"

"Of course." Rosen raised his cigar to the owner or manager, who was standing inside the café. "The Grenache rosé, Carmel. Nice and cold, huh?"

The manager came out to them. "Please, you want the rosé wine?"

"Car-mel Avdat," Rosen said, in front of the tourist lady. "Israeli wine."

"Yes please. For two?"

"For two," Rosen said, and he smiled. See? He was patient, very easy to get along with.

Edie Broder leaned toward him on the table again, holding her arms. "Do you speak Hebrew?"

"Oh, a little. Actually, there's only one word you have to know, at least when you're driving. *Meshugah.*"

"*Meshugah?*"

"That's it. It means 'idiot.' You yell it at the other drivers," Rosen said and smiled to show he was kidding. "You feel they have spirit, wait till you drive against them."

"Well, I won't have to worry about that," Edie said, almost with a sigh. "I'll be on the big red tour bus."

"I suppose it's comfortable," Rosen said, "but a little slow, huh? I mean a lot of waiting around."

10

"It takes them forever, the older folks, to get on the bus. But they're dear people and I love them."

"One of them slips and breaks a hip, you've got another delay," Rosen said. He eased lower in the hard chair, getting comfortable. "I think the way to see Israel is in an air-conditioned Mercedes. Start in the north, in the Galilee. There's a little town up there built on a cliff, Sefad, with a great artist colony. And a kibbutz near there, at Sasa. Come down to Tiberias, on the Sea of Galilee. Visit Jericho on the Dead Sea, the oldest city in the world. Hebron, the city of patriarchs, where Abraham's buried. Maybe Ramallah—"

"You make it sound fascinating." Giving him her full attention.

"Spend a week in Jerusalem, then drive through the Negev to the Red Sea, follow the Sinai coast to an oasis on the southernmost tip, Sharm el Sheikh." There, he'd gotten it in again. He paused and looked at her and said quietly, "Why don't you let me be your tour guide?"

She hesitated, knowing he wasn't kidding. "You're serious, aren't you?"

"Uh-huh."

"But you must be busy, have things to do," Edie said, staring back at him.

"Nothing I can't put off." He hoped she wouldn't laugh and say something dumb, like they hardly knew each other.

She didn't. She didn't say anything, in fact, but continued to look at him.

Rosen decided to push on. He said, "I've got an idea. I'm at the Four Seasons. Why don't we take the wine and go sit by the pool, get away from the commercial atmosphere?"

"I'm at the Park," Edie Broder said after a moment. "Why don't we go to my room instead?"

"Well now," Rosen said, straightening.

"I mean we aren't getting any younger," Edie Broder said.

In Room 507 of the Park Hotel, at 2:20 in the morning, Rosen said, "I'll tell you something. Nothing surprises me anymore. You know why? Because I'm never disappointed, no matter what happens."

11

"You weren't shocked?" A subdued voice coming from the bed. Rosen was over by the bank of dressers in the lamp glow, looking for cigarettes in his superbrief white Jockeys.

"No, I wasn't shocked. Not at all."

"I was," Edie said. "Hearing myself. I've never done that before in my life. But I thought, It's going to happen. I was sure it was because I felt comfortable with you. So I thought, why be coy about it? Like not kissing on the first date."

Rosen was feeling through the pockets of his safari jacket. Passport, sunglasses, a disposable lighter but no cigarettes. "Listen, I thought it was great, except for the last part—'We're not getting any younger.' Don't put yourself down like that."

"I'm facing facts," Edie said.

"Fine, but don't use facts as a putdown. We all have a birthday ever year, fine," Rosen said. "I'm forty-five and there's nothing I can do to change it, but so what? Why would I want to?" Rosen paused. "I've got a new theory and I don't know why—it's amazing—I never thought of it before. You want to hear it?"

"Sure."

"You believe in God?"

She took a moment. "I suppose I do."

"This has to do with God's will," Rosen said, "and you either get it right away, what I'm talking about, or you don't."

Edie pushed up on her elbow to look at Rosen in his Jockeys. "Are you a religious person?"

"No, I never was what you'd call religious."

"But you went to temple once in a while, you were Bar Mitzvahed."

"No, as a matter of fact I never was. But listen, living in Jerusalem three years—the Jewish, Christian, and Moslem religions all jammed together there in the Old City—all these holy places, everything directed to the worship of God— maybe some of it rubbed off on me. I started thinking about God and what it might do for me. Then I started thinking about God's will and how people referred to it. Somebody dies, it's God's will. Somebody gets wiped out in business—God's will. You find out you've got cancer or multiple sclerosis—you know what I'm saying?"

"I know," Edie said. "It's supposed to make it easier to accept those things when they happen."

Rosen was ready. "Fine, but nobody says, a person swings a million-dollar deal, it's God's will. It's always something *bad*. So I decided, wait a minute. Why can't the good things that happen to you also be God's will? Like making a couple hundred grand a year tax free."

Yes, and like scoring with stylish ladies who appreciated you and absolutely fucking loved it and knew you weren't going to spread it around or tell the folks back home in Columbus.

"Or like you and I running into each other." He paused, looking toward the open balcony. "Tomorrow evening we'll walk the wall of the Old City, past the Armenian Quarter, and see, across the rooftops, the Dome of the Mosque bathed in moonlight." He turned from the balcony. "No, I wasn't surprised, and not because I had you figured out in any way. But as you said, you knew it was going to happen. I did too, and I accepted it as God's will." Rosen picked up his trousers from the chair and felt the pockets. "I thought I brought some cigarettes."

"I don't know if I can handle that," Edie said, "bringing God into it. I can't say I was thinking about God at the time."

"You don't have to. See, what you do, you aim in the direction you want to go, or to get what you want. But you don't manipulate or force people to do anything. What I mean is, you have to be honest with yourself. You're not out to con anybody; you let things happen and you don't worry about it. That's the key—you don't worry. Something happens or it doesn't."

"What about when something bad happens?" Edie said.

"What's bad? A week later you're telling somebody about it; you're laughing."

"Like if you find out you have terminal cancer."

"Then you're fucked," Rosen said. "No, I'm kidding. There's nothing you can do about that, right? So why fight it? That's the secret. Accept what comes and don't worry about anything you know you can't change."

"It's that simple, huh?" Edie eased back down to the pillow. "Maybe for some people."

"For anybody," Rosen said. "Listen, you didn't know me before. I've learned to be patient. I've almost quit smoking. In fact, it looks like I have. I haven't had a Gelusil in almost a year. And now you and I've met and we're going to have a wonderful time together. . . . You don't smoke, huh?"

"I quit two years ago."

"You don't happen to have a mashed-up pack in the bottom of your purse?" Rosen went into the bathroom and closed the door to take a leak.

It was getting easier to explain his revolutionary Will of God theory. A few months ago it hadn't sounded as clear or foolproof when he'd brought it out in the open. Like the time he'd told the lady at the Jerusalem Hilton about it—in that big, active cocktail lounge—their second day together, and she'd said, "Jesus Christ, I was worried you were a gangster, and you turn out to be a religious freak." He had put down in his mind: *Never talk philosophy with tourist ladies.* Then qualified it later: *At least never talk philosophy with ladies who stay at the Hilton.*

And don't overdo it with any of them. Edie seemed content—why confuse her?—lying in bed with her bare arms and shoulders out of the sheet, watching him as he came from the bathroom into the lamplight again.

"Were you smoking in there?"

"No, I told you, I don't have any." He looked on the low bank of dressers again, catching his reflection in the mirror, the deeply tanned hard body—relatively hard for his age—against the brief white Jockeys.

"I thought I smelled cigarette smoke," Edie said. "Guess not. . . . Is there any wine left?"

"All gone." Rosen came over and she moved her hip to give him space to sit down. "We can call room service."

"I think it's too late."

"You don't want the waiter to see me. Listen, they've seen everything. You can't shock a room-service waiter."

"I really do think it's too late."

"I can get us a bottle somewhere." He was touching her face, letting his hand slide down to her bare shoulder.

"Isn't everything closed?"

"If you want more wine, I'll get it," Rosen said, though he had no idea where.

"Do we need it?"

Quietly, caressing her: "No, we don't need it." She looked ten years younger in bed, in the lamp glow from across the room. Her breasts were good, hardly any sag—right there under the sheet—and her thighs were firm, with no sign yet of dimples, and not likely to develop any during the next ten days.

Edie sniffed. "I still smell something."

"It's not me," Rosen said. "Must be somebody else."

"No, like smoke. Don't you smell it?"

Rosen sniffed. He got up from the bed and walked across the room sniffing. He stopped. "Yeah—like something burning." He walked through the short hallway to the door, opened it— "Christ!"—and was coughing, choking, as he slammed the door against the smoke billowing in from the fifth-floor hall.

"Christ, the place is on fire!"

He was coughing again, then seeing Edie Broder out of bed naked, seeing her terrified expression as she screamed.

3

Tuesday, 10:40 A.M.: Rosen was the Acapulco's only customer. He sat with his coffee and pack of cigarettes in the row of tables nearest the street, at the edge of the awning shade. Across the square, above the shrubs and palm trees, the façade of the Goldar Hotel showed its age in the sunlight. Some of the guests from the Park Hotel had been moved there. Others were at the King Solomon. Mr. Fine had taken Edie Broder and the rest of the Columbus group to the Pal Hotel in Tel Aviv, to be near the U.S. embassy and whatever attaché handled legal matters for American citizens.

It was getting complicated. Why go to Tel Aviv? She could move in with him at the Four Seasons. But Edie felt she should stay with the tour until they decided what they were going to do, and made sure she'd have a flight home if they left, and all that. Rosen said that was the tour leader's responsibility. Edie said yes, except all Mr. Fine talked about was suing the hotel. She'd be back Tuesday afternoon, promise, ready for Al Rosen's super five-star Mercedes tour of Israel.

Ordinarily the new Rosen would have accepted this quietly. If she came back, fine. If she didn't, that was all right too. But there was a problem. Edie had his short-sleeved safari jacket, with his passport and prescription sunglasses in the pocket. Up in 507, before getting the wet towels, he'd jammed his shirt and jacket into her suitcase, on top of her clothes, and sailed the suitcase from the balcony, out into the night and straight down five stories to the pavement. All she had lost were some bathroom articles and makeup. He'd lost his sandals.

He should have driven down to Tel Aviv yesterday and picked up his passport and stuff.

That's where most of the cars were still coming from—Tel Aviv, sightseers. The cars passed close to the café, following the circle around the parkway, then turned off on the beach road north and crept past the fire-gutted hotel, everybody gawking up at the honeycomb of empty balconies and at the places where the cement was singed black. Saturday, the Shabat, had been the big day, the cars bumper to bumper all around the square, coming and going.

There were relatively few cars this morning—now that he thought about it—coming from the street to the parkway. There were no cars standing along the curb by the café. It gave Rosen a nice view of the square.

Sunday he had read the account of the fire in the *Jerusalem Post* and looked through the Hebrew dailies, *Ma'ariv* and *Ha'arez*, for pictures. There had been photos in all three papers of firemen fighting the blaze, and "before" and "after" shots of the hotel. But no pictures of rescued tourists, or of Rosen walking around without a shirt. So he didn't have to worry about becoming a celebrity.

Still, he was keyed up, experiencing old anxieties, smoking again, into his third pack of cigarettes since Saturday morning. Getting away for a while with Edie felt like a good idea.

He saw the white sedan go past, moving toward the beach.

With an Arab driving? It was possible, but not something he was used to seeing. Arabs were usually walking along the road, old men wearing the head scarves, the *kaffiyeh*, and drab, thrown-away clothes, old suitcoats that had never been cleaned. The one in the car wore the traditional *kaffiyeh*—the white with black checkered lines that gave the cloth a grayish look, a doubled black band holding it to his head.

The white car turned left and crept around the circle to the other side of the parkway, the driver maybe looking for something or not knowing where he was going. Rosen could see the front end now on an angle, two vertical ovals on the grille. A BMW. The higher-priced model that would cost roughly thirty thousand in Israel, maybe more. An Arab driving an expensive German automobile around Netanya, an expensive resort town.

Rosen lit a cigarette, keeping an eye on the BMW, waiting for it to come around this end of the circle. When it went past he'd try to get a look at the Arab. He wasn't suspicious, he was curious; he had nothing better to do. He heard the BMW, across the parkway, downshift and pick up speed.

It would probably keep going now and duck into the main street, away from the beach.

But it didn't. The BMW was coming around the near end of the circle. In second gear. Rosen could hear the revs, the engine winding up. He heard the tires begin to screech, the BMW coming through the circle now toward the café, Rosen looking directly at the grille and the broad windshield, thinking that the Arab had better crank it *now,* and knowing in that moment that the dark face under the *kaffiyeh* looking at him through the windshield had no intention of making the curve. Rosen pushed the table as he lunged out of the chair. He saw the owner standing inside the café and the expression on his face, but Rosen did not turn to look around. He was to the walk space between the café and the tables when the BMW jumped the curb and plowed through the first row of tables and kept pushing, taking out part of the second row before the car jerked to a stop and the dark man in the *kaffiyeh* was out, throwing an end of the scarf around the lower part of his face and bringing the heavy Webley military revolver from beneath his coat, aiming it as the owner of the café dropped flat to the tile floor, aiming at Rosen, who was inside now, running toward the back of the place between the counter and a row of tables, and firing the heavy revolver, firing again down the aisle, steadying the outstretched revolver with his left hand and firing quickly now, three times, before Rosen banged through a doorway and the door slammed closed.

In the ringing silence the man with the Arab scarf across his face stared into the café, making up his mind. He looked down at the owner of the Acapulco on the floor, his face buried in his arms. The man with the Arab scarf turned and looked up the sidewalk in the direction of the shops that sold oriental rugs and jewelry, where the sidewalk passed beneath the arches of a street-front arcade, where people were standing now, watching him. He got into the BMW and backed out, dragging a chair that was hooked to the front bumper, braked hard, and mangled the chair as the BMW shot forward, engine winding, taking the curve into the business street east; and then it was gone.

The owner of the Acapulco got to his hands and knees and looked out toward the street for a moment, then scrambled to his feet and went to the phone behind the counter. No—he remembered the customer—the customer first, and he hurried to the back of the café and opened the door with the sign that said TOILET.

Rosen was standing in the small enclosure, his back to the wall. There was a sound of water, the toilet tank dripping.

"He's gone," the owner of the café said. Rosen stared at him, his eyes strange, and the owner of the café, frightened and bewildered, wasn't sure Rosen understood him. "That man, the Arab, he's gone now." He wanted to say more to Rosen and ask him things, but he could only think of the words in Hebrew. Finally he said, "Why did he want to do that to you? The Arab. Try to hurt you like that."

"He wasn't an Arab," Rosen said.

The owner of the café tried to speak to Rosen and tried to make him remain while he called the police. But that was all Rosen said before he walked out.

"He wasn't an Arab."

* * *

Edie Broder, with Rosen's shirt and jacket in her big suitcase and his passport in her tote—anxious, antsy, hardly able to sit still—took a taxi back to Netanya from Tel Aviv and paid 120 Israeli pounds, almost twenty dollars, for the ride.

It was worth it, arriving at the Four Seasons just a little after one o'clock, in time to have lunch with her new boyfriend, God, as eager as a twenty-year-old but not nearly as cool about it. Her daughters would die. They wouldn't understand a mother having this kind of a feeling. They'd like him, though. He was kind, he was gentle, he was funny. He wasn't nearly as patient as he thought he was. She had to smile, picturing him in his Jockey shorts looking for cigarettes, holding his stomach in and glancing at himself in the mirror. (Telling her he was forty-five when his passport said fifty.) Then very cool with the whole building on fire, knowing exactly what to do, keeping everyone calm as he led them through the smoke. He was great. He might even be perfect. She wouldn't look too far ahead, though, and began fantasizing about the future. No, as Al Rosen would say, relax and let things happen.

The doorman asked Edie if she was checking in. She told him just to put the bags somewhere, she'd let him know, and went to a house phone to call Rosen's room. There was no answer.

She made a quick run down to the corner of the lobby that looked out on the pool. He wasn't there. He wasn't at the bar, or, looking past the bar, in the dining room.

At the desk she asked if Mr. Rosen had left a message for a Mrs. Broder.

The desk clerk said, "Mr. Rosen—" As he started to turn away, an Israeli woman Edie recognized as a guide with Egged Tours reached the desk and said something in Hebrew. The clerk paused to reply. The tour guide had him now and gave the clerk a barrage of Hebrew, her voice rising, intense. When the clerk turned away again, Edie said, "Mr. Rosen. Did he leave a message—" The clerk walked down to the cashier's counter and came back with something, a sheet of paper, and began talking to the Egged tour guide, who seemed in a rage now and reached the point of almost shouting at the indifferent clerk. The Egged tour woman stopped abruptly and walked away.

"Mr. Rosen," Edie said, trying very hard to remain calm. "I want to know if he left a note for me, Mrs. Broder."

The clerk looked at her vacantly for a moment. "Mr. Rosen? Oh, Mr. Rosen," the clerk said. "He checked out. I believe about an hour ago."

4

Mel Bandy said to the good-looking Israeli girl in the jeans and white blouse and no bra, "Actually, the flight was ten minutes early coming into Ben Gurion. So what do they do, they take you off the 707 and pack you on a bus with everybody and you stand out there for *fifteen* minutes to make up for it. How'd you know I was Mr. Bandy?"

"I asked the air hostess," the girl said. "She point you out to me."

"And you're Atalia."

"Yes, or Tali I'm called." She smiled. Nice smile, nice eyes and freckles. "We write to each other sometime, now we meet."

"You got a cute accent," Mel Bandy said. "You're a cute

girl," looking down at the open neck of her blouse. Not much there at all, but very tender. Twenty-one years old, out of the Israeli Army, very bright but seemed innocent, spoke Arabic as well as Hebrew and English. She didn't look Jewish.

The guy with her didn't look Jewish either. He looked like an Arab, or Mel Bandy's idea of a young Arab, with the moustache and wild curly hair. The rest of him, the jeans dragging on the ground and the open vinyl jacket, was universal. His name was Mati Harari and he was a Yemenite, supposedly trustworthy. But Mel had seen the guy too many times in Detroit Recorder's Court. White, black, Yemenite, they all looked alike—arraigned on some kind of a hustle.

Mel was carrying an alligator attaché case. He pointed to his red-and-green-trimmed Gucci luggage coming into the terminal on the conveyor loop. The skinny Yemenite picked up the two bags, brushing the porters aside in Hebrew, and Tali smiled and said something to the two Israeli customs officials, who waved them past. Nothing to it. Mel was surprised. Outside, waiting in front of the terminal while Mati got the car, he said, "I thought it was tight security here."

"They know you are searched before you get here, in New York or Athens." Tali shrugged. "You know—only if they don't like the way you look."

"It's hot here."

"Yes, it's nice, isn't it?"

Mel was sweating in the lightweight gray suit. The next few days he'd take it easy on the booze and all that sour-cream kosher shit he didn't like much anyway, maybe drop about ten pounds. Goddamn shirt, sticking to him—he pulled his silver-gray silk tie down and unbuttoned the collar. Goddamn pants were too tight. He gave Tali his attaché case, took off his suit-coat, and, holding it in front of him, adjusted his crotch. What he'd like to lose was about twenty-five pounds. He hadn't thought it was going to be this hot. Shit, it had been snowing when he'd left Detroit.

The car was a gray Mercedes. Tali wanted Mr. Bandy to get in front so he could see better, but Mel arranged the seating: him and Tali in back. He'd see all he wanted with the girl next to him and also be able to talk to her without the Arab-looking guy listening. He waited, though, until they were out of the airport and passing through open country on the way to Tel Aviv.

"Have you heard from him since we talked on the phone?"

"He didn't call last night or this morning," the girl said. "I don't know where he could be."

Mel Bandy looked over—she sounded genuinely worried— wondering if Rosen was getting into her. Why not? She worked for him. Probably made more than any secretary in Israel. If that's what she was, a secretary.

"You can't call him?"

"I tried three places. He wasn't there."

"He knows when he's supposed to get his money?"

"Yes, of course. Tomorrow, the twenty-sixth of March. Always the twenty-sixth of March and the twenty-sixth of September."

"When'd you last see him?"

"It was . . . a week ago today in Netanya. He wanted to write letters."

"In Netanya. What was he doing there?"

"I don't know. Maybe to swim in the sea."

"Or chasing tail. Was he staying in that hotel?"

"No, another one. I don't know why he was in the hotel that burned," Tali said. She imagined the building on fire, people running out through the smoke. "Did you bring the newspaper with the picture?"

Mel pulled his attaché case from the floor to his lap, opened it, and handed Tali a file folder. "Our hero," Mel said. "See if you recognize him."

She brought the tear sheets out of the folder, glanced at the front-page story, unfolded the sheets, and stared at the photo page, at the figures wrapped in blankets and the bearded, shirtless man in the light-colored trousers.

"Yes, he looks like an Israeli there," Tali said, "but I can see it's Mr. Rosen. We don't have this picture here."

"Wire service," Mel Bandy said. "It was in the *Times*, the *Chicago Tribune*, the Detroit papers, it could've been in every paper in the country—Rosie showing off his body—and he doesn't know it."

"He called you from Netanya?"

"I think that's what he said. But he was—what should I say—upset, distraught? He was shit-scared is what he was. See, I already had my reservation. I told him hang on, call me late Wednesday afternoon at the Pal Hotel, Tel Aviv, we'd work it out together."

"Oh, you were coming here to see him?"

"I told him last month I'd be here sometime in March."

"I didn't know that," the girl said. She had thought Mr. Bandy, Mr. Rosen's lawyer, was here because someone had tried to kill Mr. Rosen. She didn't know of another reason for the lawyer to be here. She didn't want to ask him about it. He looked tired and hot, even in the air-conditioned car.

"It wasn't in the newspapers about a man shooting at anyone," Tali said. "I went to Netanya, but I didn't find out what coffeehouse it was that it happened at. Only that he checked out from the hotel."

Approaching a highway intersection, they followed the curving shortcut lane past a green sign with arrows and the names of towns in Hebrew and English—Peta Tiqva, Ramla, Tel Aviv—and past lines of soldiers waiting for rides: girls in mini uniform skirts and young bareheaded men, some of them armed with submachine guns.

"How far is it?" Mel said.

Tali looked at him. "Netanya? I don't think he's there anymore."

"Tel Aviv."

"Oh . . . twenty minutes more."

"How about the money? The guy get it yet?"

"He receive it yesterday," Tali said. "I call when we get to the hotel."

"Have him bring it over as soon as he can."

Tali hesitated, not sure if it was her place to ask questions. "You want to give it to Mr. Rosen yourself?"

"I'm thinking about it," Mel said. "We'll see how it goes."

* * *

25

The black guy, standing by the open trunk of the BMW, waved in quick come-on gestures to the two Americans walking out of the Ben Gurion terminal building, each carrying a suitcase and a small bag.

The older of the two men, who had the look of a retired professional football player, a line coach, was Gene Valenzuela. His gaze, squinted in the sunglare, moved from the white BMW to the right, to the flow of traffic leaving the airport, and back again to the BMW. Valenzuela had short hair and wore his sport shirt open, the collar tips pointing out to his shoulders, outside his checked sportcoat.

The younger one, Teddy Cass, had long hair he combed with his fingers. He had good shoulders and no hips, the cuffs of his green-and-gold print shirt turned up once. Teddy Cass was saying, "Shit, we could've brought it with us. Anything we want to use."

The black guy was waving at them. "Come on, throw it in. They already took off."

Reaching him, Valenzuela said, "You see their car?"

"Gray Mercedes. Chickie with the nice ass got in with him."

"So they're going the same way we are," Teddy Cass said.

"My man," the black guy said, "anyplace you are, they four ways to go. They could be going to Jerusalem. They could be going north or south. We got to know it."

In the BMW, driving away from the terminal, Teddy Cass still couldn't get over breezing through Customs without opening a bag.

Gene Valenzuela had the back seat to himself. He had a road map of Israel open on his lap. He would look out the window at the fields and the sun and then look at the map.

The black guy asked, "He see you on the plane?" Leaving it up to either one.

"He was in back with the rabbis and the tour groups," Valenzuela said. "I know what he did, the cheap fuck. The company buys him a first-class ticket and he trades it in on a coach. Makes about a grand. I don't know, maybe he saw us. It doesn't matter. He's gonna see us again."

"We could've brought anything we wanted," Teddy Cass

said. "*Any*thing. Shit, I thought it was gonna be so tight I didn't even bring any e-z wider."

"Paper's scarce, but nobody gives a shit. You get all the hash you want," the black guy said. "They say anything to you at Immigration?"

"That's what I'm talking about," Teddy Cass said.

"No, that's Customs. Immigration, the man who looked at your passport." The black guy was holding the BMW at seventy-five, passing cars and tour buses in effortless sweeps. "Man look at mine, he look at me. He look at the passport again. He say, 'Kamal Rashad.' I say, 'That's right.' He say, where was I born? I say, 'It's right there. Dalton, Georgia.' He say, where was my mother and daddy born? I say, 'Dalton, Georgia.' He say, where do I live? I say, 'Detroit, Michigan.' He want to see my ticket, make sure that's where I came from. He say, when was the last time I was in an Arab country? I say I never been to an Arab country. He say, 'But you an Arab.' I say, 'My man, I'm a Muslim. You don't have to be an Arab to be a Muslim.' "

Teddy Cass said, "Kamal Rashad, shit. Clarence Robinson out of Dalton, Detroit, the Wayne County jail, and Jackson Prison."

"A long way around," Rashad said. "And I ain't goin' back."

"You're not going anywhere, you blow another setup," Valenzuela said.

"Man saw me," Rashad said, looking at the rearview mirror. "He moved. I had five in this big old army piece, that's all. What was I supposed to do? Once I emptied it—see, there was people—I didn't have the time to load and go after him."

"So it doesn't sound like you prepared it," Valenzuela said.

"I didn't have *time*. I had to get a car. I had to buy a gun. I had to locate the man and kill him in like twenty-four hours."

"No you didn't," Valenzuela said. "You had to locate him. That's what I'm saying—you didn't prepare it. You wanted the quick shot and some points. Now the guy's flushed and we gotta find him again. We can assume, I think, he hasn't left the country. Otherwise Mr. Mel Bandy wouldn't be here to see him. That's the only thing we got going for us. But we lose him, you don't get on that Mercedes' ass pretty soon, we might as well go home and wait for another fire."

"We already on it," Rashad said. "Three, four cars ahead of us." Nice. He felt his timing coming back.

Valenzuela leaned forward to lay his arms on the back of the front seat and study the traffic ahead of them. After a moment he said, "You're gonna have to get another car. Christ, driving around in a white car with red paint all over the front end. Also, we gotta make a contact for guns where we've got a selection, not some rusty shit they picked up in a field."

"I already done it," Rashad said.

"We could've brought our own if somebody'd told us," Teddy Cass said. He was looking out the window as they approached a line of hitchhiking soldiers. He got excited seeing them. "Hey, shit, we could take theirs. You see that?" Teddy Cass twisted in his seat to look back. "What's that they're carrying, M-16s?"

"M-16s and Uzis, the submachine gun," Rashad said. "Fine little weapon. Holds thirty rounds in a banana clip. Fold the stock up on the Uzi, it fit in your briefcase. But you take one off a soldier—I'm told they roadblock the whole fucking country, get your ass in half an hour."

"I like it," Teddy Cass said. "I like the sound. Ouuuzi."

"Five bills on the black," Rashad said. "You want to pay that much. Nice Browning automatic, Beretta Parabellum, we can get for two each. Very popular."

"How about explosives?" Valenzuela said.

"I haven't priced none of that," Rashad said. "I figure that's Teddy's department." He slowed down as he saw the Mercedes, now two cars ahead of them, making a curving right into an intersecting highway. Rashad grinned. "Keeping it easy for us. They going to Tel Aviv."

The five-star hotels in Tel Aviv are all on the Mediterranean on a one-mile stretch of beach: the Dan, the Continental, the Plaza, the Hilton, and the Pal.

Mel Bandy could see the Hilton as they came south on Hayarkon and turned into the Pal. The Hilton looked newer, more modern. The Pal looked put together, its newest wing coming out from the front on pillars, with a parking area and the main entrance beneath. Tali said oh, yes, the Pal was an excellent hotel. Mel Bandy wasn't sure.

He got out of the Mercedes and entered the lobby, pulling at the trousers sticking to his can, and waited while Tali spoke to the desk people in Hebrew, sounding like she was arguing with them—good, not taking any shit—then brought out the manager, Mr. Shapira, who was delighted to meet Mr. Bandy from Detroit. Mel was surprised and felt a little better.

Moving to the elevator, he said, "We got a suite?"

Tali looked at the two keys she was holding. "I don't know. I think it's adjoining rooms."

"I told them I wanted a suite."

"Let me ask Mr. Shapira."

"Never mind," Mel said. "Get the bags upstairs and call the guy at the embassy. I'll look at the rooms. I don't like them, we'll have them changed."

Tali said, yes, of course. She didn't know if she liked this Mr. Bandy. He wasn't at all like Mr. Rosen.

The white BMW, motor idling, waited on Hayarkon in front of the Pal.

"Where's the Hilton from here?" Valenzuela was leaning forward again, looking through the windshield.

Rashad pointed. "The one right there. Independence Park in between. You can run it in two minutes."

"Looks better'n this place," Teddy Cass said.

But it was Valenzuela who'd decide. He said, "I don't like to run. I want to be close by, in the same place."

"How do I know where the man's going to stay?" Rashad said. "See, he didn't call me and let me know."

Valenzuela didn't bother to give him a look. He said to Teddy Cass, "Go in, tell them we got a reservation. Two rooms. Wait a minute, tell them you're a friend of Mr. Bandy's. And find out what room he's in."

Teddy Cass got out of the car and walked into the shade of the parking area beneath the new wing.

Valenzuela sat back in the seat, thoughtful. "Where's the gun contact? How far?"

"Cross town, over in the Hatikva Quarter."

"You and Teddy'll go there this afternoon. But you got to watch him. Teddy'll buy the fucking store."

"I'm supposed to meet the man tonight. Ain't somebody you call up and say make it three-forty-five instead."

"All right, this evening. How'd you find him?"

"You recall I came here with a name. Friend of a friend."

"Five for an Uzi, huh?"

"Going price yesterday. Subject to change."

"We're not going to worry about that. We're not gonna go crazy, but we're not gonna skimp either. How about shotguns?"

"I 'magine. Probably buy shotguns on a street corner. This man leans toward the more exotic weapons."

"Teddy wants dynamite or some plastic, C4. He was thinking they got everything here, with all the fucking wars."

"If he's got it in stock," Rashad said. "See, the man's been dealing over the border, in Lebanon, selling everything he can get his hands on."

"We'll make him a better offer," Valenzuela said.

When Teddy Cass came back they saw him nodding before he reached the car.

"Okay, Clarence-Rashad," Valenzuela said. "Check out and come back here. We'll show you how it's done."

5

The Marine behind the high counter that was like a judge's bench inside the front entrance of the United States embassy, Tel Aviv, was Gunnery Sergeant David E. Davis: Regulation haircut, white cover with the spit-shine peak straight over his eyes, blue dress trousers, and short-sleeved tan shirt, the collar open, "Charlie" uniform of the day. He wore four rows of ribbons: all the Vietnam colors, Combat Action Ribbon, Expeditionary Forces Medal, three Unit Citations, two Hearts and a Silver Star. Below the ribbons were an Expert Rifleman badge and the smaller crossed-rifles-on-a-wreath version that indicated "expert with a pistol."

Davis appeared squared away, but with a tarnished look about him: a scrub farmer in his good Sunday shirt and tie. Davis was thirty-four. He had been in the Marines sixteen years. He was getting out of the Corps in exactly twenty-seven days and he couldn't sleep thinking about it. It scared him.

He picked up the phone on the first ring and said, "Sergeant Davis, Post One. . . . Oh, how are you? . . . Yeah, I can bring it when I get off duty." There was a hint of a wearing-off southern accent in his voice. "I got to change first and do a few things, so it'll be about an hour and a half. That okay?" He listened to the girl's voice, staring at the round convex mirror above the front entrance. The mirror showed the area behind him all the way to the fenced-off stairway at the end of the lobby. When someone came down the stairs or wanted to go up, the watch-stander on Post One pressed a button and buzzed open the gate in the low metal fence.

He said, "Pal Hotel. What room? . . . Okay, I'll call you from the desk. Listen, I told you I was going on leave? . . . It's like a vacation. I got twenty days coming and I'm taking some before I go home. . . . No, what I'm trying to tell you, I'm going on leave as soon as I get off duty. But I'll drop the package off first. . . . Okay, I'll see you in a while."

His gaze lowered from the mirror to the front entrance and the Israeli security guard at his desk next to the glass doors that sealed out the street noises and the sun and the construction dust. The façade of the embassy reminded Davis of a five-story post office, with official U.S. seal, placed by mistake on the street of a Mediterranean city. Inside, the embassy reminded him of a bank—the lobby with the high ceiling, clean, air-conditioned. He was the bank guard. When someone wanted to see the manager he buzzed the gate open.

When someone had an appointment upstairs Davis would call up first before buzzing the person through the gate. Or he'd direct people to the reading lounge or to the visa office. Or explain to someone, very politely, no, you can't stop in and say hi to the ambassador unless you have an appointment. Some of the tourists came in and were surprised that the ambassador wasn't there to greet them.

Embassy security guard duty was considered good duty.

Eight-hour watches, here and at the ambassador's residence, divided among a complement of seven Marines under Master

Sergeant T. C. Cox of the Amarillo, Texas, twenty-two years in the Corps. Military training two days a week. A hundred hours of language school, Hebrew. (Davis knew about five words.) Deliver some papers to the consulate in Jerusalem. Pick somebody up at Ben Gurion. Recommended calisthenics and a three-mile run every morning out at the Marine House in Herzliya Pituah. (Sergeant Willard Mims of Indianapolis, Indiana, a former 1st Force Recon Marine, ran ten miles every morning, down to Afeka and back, wearing a flak jacket and combat boots. Davis would say, "As long as we got Willard, nobody's gonna fuck with us.") Good quarters. Each man with his own room in a pair of town house condominiums a block from the sea. Each room comfortable and personal. (Sergeant Grady Mason from Fort Smith, Arkansas, had Arab rugs, a brass waterpipe he didn't use, and a Day-Glo painting on black velvet of the Mosque of Omar. Stores included refrigerators full of Maccabee beer and several cases of vodka. Fried eggs, potatoes, bacon, and pancakes for breakfast. You didn't wear a uniform more than a couple of days a week. Three days off out of every eleven. Good duty.

All the Marines at the Marine House said it was. Davis had asked each of them once, at different times, if they'd ever had bad duty. Each one had thought about it and said no, he'd never had bad duty. Davis had said, What about BLT duty—Battalion Landing Team? No, it was all right; you got to see foreign capitals and get laid. He'd said, What about in Nam? They had all been there and each one of them had thought about it some more and said no, Nam was bad, but it wasn't bad duty, it was part of it. Part of what? Part of being in the Marines.

Master Sergeant T. C. Cox would look at Davis funny. How could Davis be in the Marines sixteen years and ask questions like that? Davis didn't know. For sixteen years he had been looking for good duty. (He had been to Parris Island, Lejeune, the supply center in Philly, on Med Cruise BLT duty, Gitmo, Barstow, California—Christ—MCB McTureous on Okinawa, and with the 3rd Marines in Vietnam.) Now he was at the end of his fourth tour and still hadn't found any.

Sergeant Mims, roving security guard today, stopped at the Post One desk.

"Top wants to see you before you shove off."

Davis nodded. "Where is he?"

"Down in the cafeteria."

He'd see "Top"—Master Sergeant T. C. Cox—have a cup of coffee with him, and tell him again, "Yeah, I've thought about shipping over, but . . ." Then say, "You want to know the truth? I don't want to stay in, but I don't want to get out either. Do you understand where I'm at? If you do, then explain it to me."

And before he left for good, he'd see about getting somebody to take his place—somebody willing to receive by APO mail every six months a package that contained one hundred thousand dollars in U.S. currency. You could look at it, make sure it was money and not dope or dirty books—there was nothing illegal about receiving money in the mail. Just so you didn't ask too many questions, like, what was the money for? The girl wouldn't tell you anyway. Good-looking girl, too, with a nice little can. He should've gotten to know her better.

A girl in a white bridal gown was having her picture taken in Independence Park, posed in an arbor of shelf rock and shrubbery.

"There's another one," Mel Bandy said. He stood at the bank of windows in the eighth-floor hotel room, looking down at the park. "What is this with the brides?"

"It's very popular for wedding pictures," Tali said, "with the trees and the flowers."

"And the dog walkers. They're having a convention over there, all the dogs, and the owners sitting around on the grass." Mel turned to look at Tali, who was standing between the two beds with the telephone in her hand. "You going to call the manager?"

"I'm thinking the concierge would be the person for something like this."

"I don't care who you call."

She began to dial the number.

"What time's the Marine coming?"

Tali pressed the button down to break the connection. "He said in about an hour and a half."

"You know this guy pretty well, huh?"

"No, I've seen him only sometimes."

"Three years you've been dealing with him, you don't go out together?"

"There was another Marine before him we used. The first one went home. This one, Davis, I believe it's the third time only he receive it."

"What do you give him?"

"A thousand lira."

"Lira?"

"Israeli pounds."

"That's what, about a hundred and a half?" Mel said. "To hand over a package. The Marine know what it is?"

"Oh, yes. Mr. Rosen said, 'Let him look. Show him what it is.' The first one, I believe he thought maybe the money was to buy hashish. I told him no, I wouldn't do something like that, against the law."

"What about the Marine?" Mel said. "What if he gets ideas?"

"No, Mr. Rosen trusts him. He said, 'How is he going to steal it? We know who he is. He works for the embassy.'"

"Does the Marine know who Rosen is?"

"No, I wouldn't tell him that."

"Have they met?"

Tali shook her head. "Mr. Rosen didn't think it was necessary."

"Or a good idea," Mel said. "You going to call the manager?"

"Yes, right now," Tali said. She dialed the concierge, waited, said, "*Shalom,*" and began speaking in Hebrew.

Mel Bandy watched her. "Tell him what you want. You don't have to explain anything."

Tali was listening now and nodding, saying, "*Ken . . . ken,*" then gesturing with her hand as she began speaking again in a stream of Hebrew.

"You don't *ask* him, you *tell* him," Mel said. He came over from the window and took the phone out of her hand.

"This is Mr. Bandy in 824. I want a couple of men up here to move some furniture around. I want a bed moved out and I want a couch brought in . . . a sofa, and a small office refrigerator. . . . No, I said furniture. I want some *furni*ture moved. You understand? One of the beds, the double bed in here, I want it take out. . . . No, *out.* I want to get rid of it. It takes up too much room. And I want a couch, a sofa, brought in. . . . Jesus Christ," Mel said. He handed the phone to Tali. "Tell them what we want."

Late afternoon; they were the only ones in the embassy cafeteria: Master Sergeant Cox stirring two sugars and cream in a fresh cup of coffee; Gunnery Sergeant Davis with a Heineken, sipping it out of the bottle and trying to explain where he was, which Cox would never understand.

They had already gone through his being nervous, Sergeant Cox saying that if short time scared him, then he had no business stepping down. What was the date of his RELACDU orders? Twenty April. That's all? Shit, Sergeant Cox said, Davis was so short he'd fart and get sand in his face. From today, twenty-seven and a wakeup and he'd be out of the Corps with his DD214. That kind of talk.

Well, Sergeant Cox supposed Davis knew what he was going to do when he got out.

"I don't have any plans, no. But I feel right now it's time. I know, 1 put in four more years, at least I get some retirement. . . ."

"Some? You get half pay the rest of your life," Sergeant Cox said. "Twelve more years, seventy-five percent for life."

"I know, but if I stay in any longer—this is how I feel—it'll be too late to do anything else."

"Like what?"

"I don't know. But I don't want to be a bank guard. That's the way I feel about it."

"What do you have to be a bank guard for?"

"I mean right now. That's what I feel like."

Sergeant Cox didn't understand that. He squinted at Davis, thinking. "What's your MOS, Administration? You can probably get into I and I."

"Shit, no, I've got an oh-three MOS," Davis said. "Oh-three sixty-nine, Infantry Unit Leader."

"I didn't know that." Sergeant Cox paused, giving it more thought. "Well, the way I see it, Davis, you maintain pretty good. Passable service record on MSG duty. Re-up and I'll recommend you to the RSO in Karachi. They'll give you a choice of embassies, depending on openings. I hear Seoul's pretty good duty."

Jesus Christ, Korea. Davis was shaking his head. "No, that's what I'm talking about. Sitting at a guard post, or sitting out at the Marine House shining my shoes, getting ready to sit at the post. You know what I'm saying? What the fuck are we doing here? We're bank guards."

Sergeant Cox was squinting at him again, irritated. "What do we do anywhere? It's what we *do*."

"That's what I'm saying," Davis said.

"You don't like it, then get back into your MOS. You picked it."

"Or get out," Davis said. "See, basically, I'm an infantryman. . . ."

"We all are," Sergeant Cox said. "You're no different."

"Okay, but I'm just speaking for myself, the way I see it. I'm an infantryman without a job. But I wouldn't want the fucking job again if it was to open up. So what am I doing waiting around?"

Sergeant Cox wasn't squinting now, but continued to stare at him. "I think you got a problem, Davis. Finding out where you belong."

Davis almost smiled, relieved. He wanted to, but he didn't. "I probably make it sound more complicated than it is."

"I'll agree with you there," Sergeant Cox said. "We talk about something, it seems like a fairly simple issue, then you start telling me how you *feel*. What's that got to do with it?"

"Well, I'm gonna go away and think about it." Davis did grin then. "I don't know. I'm liable to come back and ship over again, but I got to be certain what I want to do."

Sergeant Cox hesitated, but decided not to get in any deeper. "You have transportation?"

"I was gonna rent a car, but Raymond Garcia's letting me use his."

"Going hot-rodding, huh? Scare the shit out of the Israelites?"

"No, I'm gonna take it easy," Davis said. "Maybe go down into the Sinai and shoot some birds. Get off by myself and think. I haven't made any real plans."

"Maybe that's your trouble," Sergeant Cox said.

The previous night in the Hilton bar, Kamal Rashad had been talking to a couple of Canadian U.N. soldiers stationed at Ismailiya on the Canal. Couple of assholes from Guelph, Ontario, sitting at the bar drinking their Maccabees, not knowing shit about anything.

That's what Rashad thought Davis was—walking into the Pal Hotel lobby with his haircut and his canvas bag and carrying a brown-paper package the size of a shoe box—a U.N. soldier.

Going over to the house phones at the end of the desk, Davis passed close to the spot where Rashad was sitting. Rashad saw the USMC and insignia on the olive-green canvas bag. Man had to be something like that with his haircut and suntans: a soldier or a man who worked construction. Rashad was watching the entrance and the pair of elevators that served the new wing of the hotel. He didn't look over at the Marine again until he heard the Marine say to the operator, "Mr. Bandy—can you give me his room number, please? I forgot it."

You never knew, did you? Rashad watched the Marine now. He could've raised his voice a little and said, "Eight-two-four." He heard the Marine say, "Thank you," and watched him dial the number.

After a moment the Marine said, "It's me. I'm down in the lobby."

Yeah, it's you, Rashad was thinking. But who are you? He waited until the Marine crossed to the elevators, then went to the same house phone and dialed 518.

Teddy Cass answered. Rashad said, "Man look like a soldier boy went up to their room. Had a overnight bag and a package with him." Teddy Cass told him to hang on. When Teddy came back to the phone he said, "Val wants you to stay awake. The guy comes down, follow him. You got it?"

"If I can remember all that," Rashad said.

It looked like somebody was moving, all the furniture strung along the hall on the eighth floor. The doors of both 823 and 824 were open. Davis stepped aside as two hotel employees came out carrying parts of a bed. He saw Tali inside 823 and went in when the hallway was clear. She smiled at him as if he were an old friend.

Davis smiled back, handing her the brown-paper package with his name and address on it. "What's going on?"

She gave him a tired shrug. "I don't know. He wants more room for something."

"Who does?"

"Mr. Bandy. I told you, the lawyer who came from the States. He's in there." She nodded toward the open connecting doors.

Davis could hear him: "You bring the couch? . . . I said I wanted a *couch*. It goes right there against the wall. . . . Hey, and another chair like this one. And the refrigerator. I'm supposed to have a refrigerator. . . . *Tali!*"

"He's going to have a heart attack," Davis said.

"I hope so," Tali said.

Mel appeared in the connecting doorway. He was in his socks, his silver-gray tie pulled down, his appearance rumpled, coming apart.

"The hell you doing?"

"Trying to stay out of the way," Tali said. "Mr. Bandy, this is Sergeant Davis."

Mel only glanced at him and nodded, more interested in the package. "That's it, huh?" He came in, taking the package out of Tali's hands, and moved past the double beds to the coffee table by the windows. "Give me a knife or something and get the sergeant a drink. Sarge, what do you like?"

"It doesn't matter. Anything."

Mel was grimacing, pulling at the cord tied around the package. "Tali!"

"I'm here."

"You call room service?"

"They should be here soon. You want something else?"

"Fucking string—see if one of those guys has something to cut it with."

As Tali turned to go, Davis stopped her. He dug a clasp knife from his pants pocket, pried open the blade as he stepped over to where Mel was sitting, and cut the cord from the package.

"Never mind!" Mel called out.

Davis looked at Tali, who gave him a little shrug again. They watched as Mel tore the paper from a light metal box, opened it on his lap, and began taking out packets of U.S. currency, twenty of them, placing them on the coffee table and squaring them off evenly into two stacks.

"You ever see this much money before?" He glanced up at Davis.

"More 'n that," Davis said.

"Where?"

"Parris Island. On payday."

"That doesn't count," Mel said, looking at the currency again. "How much would you say is there?"

"I don't know. The other times, Tali said it was a hundred thousand. But that looks like more."

"How much more?"

"Probably two hundred thousand."

"On the nose," Mel said.

Tali was frowning. "Why is it more this time?"

But Mel was already talking. "Doesn't look like that much, does it? But they're all hundred-dollar bills. You ever wonder about it? Where it goes?"

"Not too much," Davis said. He was wasting time while the guy played with him, showing off. He said to Tali, "Did you want to pay me now? I've got to get going."

"Yes, let me get my purse." Tali went into the adjoining room.

Mel was still watching him. "Where you going?"

"I've got some leave coming," Davis said, "and I'm getting out pretty soon, for good. So I thought I better take it."

"How long you been in?"

"Sixteen years."

"Jesus," Mel said.

"That's about the way I feel," Davis said. He was going to be paid and get out, so he didn't mind talking a little now. The man asked him where he was going, if he'd be staying right around here. Davis said the country wasn't that big. Anywhere you went, you were still around, you might say. Tali came in with her purse and handed him an Israeli thousand-pound note.

"I wanted to mention," Davis said, "I'm borrowing a car from a friend of mine, Sergeant Raymond Garcia. He's the NCO in charge at the consulate in Jerusalem. I've been thinking he'd probably be willing to take over for me, have the package mailed to him. The only thing, he's in Jerusalem. I didn't know if that would make a difference."

He looked from Tali to the heavyset, rumpled guy in the chair, Mr. Bandy, not sure who was going to make the decision. Neither of them said anything.

"He's driving over this evening. I'm supposed to meet him at Norman's. He's got a girlfriend here he'll probably stay with and she'll drive him back." Davis waited.

Tali nodded finally and said, "Yes, I could speak with him."

"Or hold up on it for the time being," Mel said. "Sarge, why don't you let us think about it. What I would like you to do, if it's not too much trouble"—pulling himself, with an effort, out of the chair as he asked the favor—"is stay with Tali while she takes the money downstairs to the hotel safe. Would you do that for us?"

Davis said it wouldn't be any trouble at all. He waited while the guy stacked the money in the metal box, then took it out again and sent Tali to get his attaché case from the next room. He took time to glance at some papers while he emptied the attaché case and threw the papers on the bed. The guy didn't seem very organized. Didn't give a shit at all about other people, Davis decided. A room-service waiter came with a bottle of scotch and ice while they were still there, but the guy didn't offer a drink now. He'd forgotten about it. He didn't even say anything as they walked out.

* * *

In the elevator, Davis waited until the door closed. "What's the matter?"

Tali shook her head. "I don't know. Something is going on. Something strange, but I don't know what it is." She was tense, holding the attaché case at her side.

"And you can't tell me what's wrong."

"I don't see how I can."

"Come to Norman's with me and have a drink."

"I would like to, but I have to go back."

"You work for that guy? Mr. Bandy?"

"In a way I do, I suppose."

"Upstairs, you looked at the money, you said, 'Why is there more this time?' He didn't answer you."

"I don't think he heard me. Or didn't choose to tell me. He doesn't have to."

"What's Mr. Bandy do? Can I ask you that?"

"He's a lawyer."

"In Tel Aviv with two hundred thousand dollars and you don't know why," Davis said, "and you're not sure if you work for him, but you have to get back upstairs."

The elevator door opened. Walking out into the lobby he stopped her, taking her gently by the arm. "Why don't you put the money in the safe and come with me to Norman's? Or don't come with me, but get out of whatever you're in. Okay?"

She shook her head, looking past him, avoiding his eyes. "I can't do that."

"Why?"

"Really, it isn't something to worry about. It isn't even my business to know. You understand? So how can I tell you anything?"

"I'm worried about you," Davis said. "I hardly even know you and I'm worried."

"Don't, please. I'm sorry."

"I'll be at Norman's," Davis said. "If I'm not there later, leave word where you are. Okay?"

He liked the way she was looking at him now. He thought for a moment she might change her mind and come with him. But she said, "Thank you, David," and walked off toward the desk with the attaché case. He watched her, still hearing her voice, realizing it was the first time she had ever said his name.

Rashad was sitting next to Valenzuela. They had a good view of Davis and the girl. Teddy Cass was across the lobby, looking at a display case containing handmade leather goods.

"Look at him looking at her ass," Rashad said. "He saying, 'I wouldn't mind me some of that.' Man, I wouldn't either."

"That's the briefcase Bandy had on the plane," Valenzuela said. "What'd you say the guy was carrying?"

"Yeah, he doesn't have them now," Rashad said. "Left them upstairs. A brown-paper package and a bag say Marines on it, U-S-M-C. Don't he look like one?"

"He's leaving," Valenzuela said. "Get on him."

Rashad stood up. He waited until Davis was outside before following him. Valenzuela crossed the lobby to where Teddy Cass was looking at himself in the glass case, reflected among the sandals and handbags.

"See anything you like?"

"They're made out of camel hide, all this stuff here."

"No shit," Valenzuela said. "You through, we'll go up and talk to the lawyer."

6

Mel Bandy took his shower in 823. It would be his bedroom. When they got 824 fixed up with a couch and refrigerator, it would be his sitting room, with a single bed in there in case he wanted the girl handy. He didn't like a girl living in the same room with him or using his bathroom.

He had a scotch with him in the steamy bathroom and sipped it while he dried off and shaved, standing naked in front of the wall mirror. He could use some sun. Drop about twenty-five pounds right out of the middle, where he could grab a handful. He'd always tended to be a little heavy. But at thirty-eight, he told himself, he wasn't in any worse shape than half the guys at the Southfield Athletic Club. Slimmed down, though, or able to hold it in, it made your pecker look longer. He wondered if Rosie was making it with the Israeli girl. He wondered if the Israeli girl was an up-to-date-thinking-today girl about sex. So you didn't have to go through a lot of shit and waste time. Fucking jet lag. He'd get in bed. She'd come in. He'd play it from there. "You must be worn out, all the running around. Why don't you come take a little nappy?"

Mel walked out of the bathroom naked.

Two guys he had never seen before in his life were sitting in the chairs by the windows, each with a drink, the older of the two smoking a cigarette. The younger one, with the hair, grinning.

"Jesus Christ, I think somebody's got the wrong room. Huh? What is this?"

Standing there naked—not at the athletic club, where it was all right—in a hotel room. Wanting to show some poise, but wanting to cover himself.

"No, we got the right room," the older one said. "We've come to visit you."

"You've come to *visit*. You walk right in—I don't even know you." He was looking around for something. The clothes he had taken off were on the floor by his open suitcase.

"You know me," the older guy said. He waited, seeing Mel bending over the suitcase, aiming his white ass at them. "Gene Valenzuela, Mel." It was as though the named goosed him, the way Mel Bandy came up straight and hurried to get into his pants.

"Three years ago ..." Valenzuela was saying.

Turning, zipping up, Mel began to get himself together and effect a smile.

"... at the Federal Building in Detroit. I was down there with Harry Manza."

"Sure, I know your name, of course," Mel said. "But I don't believe we ever really met."

"No, as I recall your friend had somebody else representing him with the grand jury," Valenzuela said, "and I guess you handle his business legal work. Is that it?"

The man was being nice, soft-spoken. He knew all about Mel and Mel could feel it. He hoped the man continued to be polite. He hoped the man had a good ear and could sense when someone was telling the truth. He had never imagined himself being alone in an eighth-floor hotel room in this kind of situation. He didn't want to appear nervous. He wanted to calmly get right to the point, show them he wasn't hiding anything. Fortunately, at the moment, he didn't have anything to hide. He didn't have the answer to what they were going to ask him. But they had to realize he was telling the truth.

He didn't know whether to sit down or keep standing. On the dresser there was another room-service glass by the bottle of J&B and the ice. He fixed himself a drink, telling Gene Valenzuela yes, he'd been handling most of the company's legal work for the past several years.

"But the reason you're here," Mel said—after swallowing a good ounce of scotch and warming up—"you saw the picture in the paper, the fire. If I saw it, I assume you saw it too. So there's no sense in kidding around, is there? You believe I'm in contact with him, since I'm here and I'm his corporate lawyer. But I'll tell you the absolute God's truth, gentlemen—I have no idea where he is."

There. Like making a confession without telling anything. Mel took his drink over to the bed and sat down on the edge of it.

Valenzuela sipped his scotch. He said, "You come over to visit the Holy City, Mel? See the Wailing Wall?"

"No-no, I'm here on business. At least I came for business reasons. I'm not gonna try and tell you I'm a tourist. But I haven't heard from him and I haven't been able to contact him. So—I don't know—I'll probably be going back in a couple of days."

"Unless you hear from him."

"That's possible."

"I think you already did," Valenzuela said, "or you wouldn't be here."

"No, I swear I haven't."

"I mean since he almost got run over by a car. What was that? Four days ago."

"Well, yeah, we heard from him at that time. I didn't personally. He called his office."

"And they sent you?"

46

"Actually I was coming anyway. See if we could locate him and get some papers signed."

"See if you could locate him," Valenzuela said. "Come on, Mel. You didn't have a phone number?"

"Honest to God. Nobody, and I mean *nobody*, knows where he lives."

"What name's he using?"

Mel had known it was coming. He saw no choice but to tell them. As he said, "Rosen," both Valenzuela and the younger guy were looking up, away from him.

Tali came in through the connecting doors. She stopped and said, "Oh, excuse me," seeing the two visitors and Mr. Bandy sitting on the bed with his shirt off and his hair uncombed. And smiling at her. The first time she had seen him in a good mood since he'd arrived.

"Tali," Mel said, "you want to call room service? Get some more ice and some peanuts and shit, you know, something to nibble on. Use the phone in the other room."

"Not for us," Valenzuela said, looking at the girl. "Tali, you go sit over there by the desk."

She looked at Mel.

"Yeah, if you don't want anything," Mel said, "that's fine."

The desk was built into the row of dressers, at the end nearer the windows. The younger guy reached with his foot to pull the chair out and stared at Tali as she sat down, half turned from him, to face Mr. Bandy.

Valenzuela said, "What was the name again?"

Mel hesitated. "Rosen."

"Just Rosen?"

"Al Rosen. I think it's Albert."

"It's funny the names they take," Valenzuela said. "Al Rosen. Changes it from Ross to Rosen, like he doesn't want to change it too much and forget who he is. . . . What's he doing now?"

"I really don't have any idea," Mel said. "I haven't been in contact with him at all. In fact, this is the first time the company's asked me to do anything connected with him. I didn't even know where he was."

Tali watched Mr. Bandy, knowing he was lying. Why? She

47

had no idea who these men were. She jumped as she felt her chair jiggled.

Teddy Cass, his foot still on the rung, said, "How about Tali here? Hey, you ever hear of a man name of Rosen?"

"Do I know him?"

"I asked if you ever heard his name."

She was looking at Mr. Bandy and saw his eyes shift away, offering no help.

"I've heard the name, yes, from Mr. Bandy, but I don't know him."

"Tali's working for me while I'm here," Mel said. "She's called a few hotels asking for a Mr. Rosen. That's about it."

"What I'm wondering," Valenzuela said, "is what he's been living on. He bring some money with him?"

"He must've," Mel said. "Unless he's working."

Valenzuela shook his head. "That doesn't seem likely. There isn't any kind of work over here could support him. I was thinking his company must be sending him money."

"That might be," Mel said.

"But if that's the case," Valenzuela said, "I'd think they'd get tired of carrying him. Three years—what's he done for the company?"

"So maybe they're not carrying him," Mel said.

Valenzuela stared at him for a moment. "For a lawyer you're very agreeable, aren't you?"

Mel shrugged. "Why not? What you say makes sense."

"You look like a pile of white dog shit," Valenzuela said, "but you're agreeable." He got up out of the chair and walked over to the dresser to put his glass on the room-service tray.

Mel sat with his shoulders drooping, tired. He seemed to shrug. "What can I say? I'm on the wrong side. Guilt by association."

Tali felt the hand of the younger one move over her back as he got up to walk past her. His touch was frightening. The way they stood over Mr. Bandy was frightening. As though they might pick him up and hurt him and he'd do nothing to defend himself. She watched the younger one walk toward the door, hoping he was leaving. But he stooped to pick up a green canvas bag and dropped it on the bed.

Teddy Cass looked at Valenzuela. "Guy comes up with a bag and a package. Leaves without them."

Valenzuela said, "Mel, who's the guy? He work for you?"

"He's a friend of mine," Tali said. "Tell them, please, Mr. Bandy, he's a friend that came to see us. He left, he forgot his bag."

"Jesus Christ," Valenzuela said, "what is this? She winking at you? You keep your fingers crossed it's all right. Where's the package the guy brought?" Valenzuela turned, looking around the room.

"Yes, he brought something for us," Tali said. She got up and went to the dresser, Mr. Bandy and the older man watching her. The younger one was zipping open the canvas bag. "This," Tali said, picking up the J&B.

"He brought you a bottle of booze," Valenzuela said.

Tali nodded. "Yes, as a present for Mr. Bandy coming here. Because I work for him. He was being nice."

"Nothing much in here," Teddy Cass said. "Some dirty clothes." He held up a uniform shirt that had been worn. "Guy's a sergeant in the Marines. What's he doing in Tel Aviv?"

"He works at the embassy," Tali said. "I know him for a little while. We're friends. So he bring us this when my boss comes."

"It was wrapped like a package that'd been mailed," Valenzuela said.

"There was some paper on it." Tali shrugged her shoulders. "I don't know."

"You want the wrapping paper?" Mel said. "I think the room-service guy took it. Gene," he said then. "You mind if I call you Gene? You mind if I suggest you're getting this all out of proportion? You want Ross. Okay. Looking at it from your standpoint I accept that, I understand. But I came here, I planned to come here, *hoping* to see him on business, on the chance of getting a few papers signed. Then this thing happens, he gets his picture in the paper and it's a whole different ball game that I don't know anything about. I think the man's hiding and I don't blame him, do you? He's not a dummy. If he knows people are looking for him he's gonna stay out of sight.

Or he might've already left the country. I don't know. Unless I hear from him—which I admit is a possibility—there's no way I can contact him. So the chances are I'm gonna go home with my papers unsigned."

"Well, it sounds like you're giving me some shit," Valenzuela said. "Except you know the position you're in, so I don't think you'd lie to me."

"Listen, I've always been realistic," Mel said. "I'm not gonna hit my head against a wall if I know a situation is beyond my control."

"Or hit it on the pavement down there, eight floors," Valenzuela said. "You hear from him, Mel, give me the papers. I'll get them signed for you."

When Mr. Bandy poured another scotch Tali thought he might get drunk now because he was afraid and didn't know what to do. But he didn't get drunk. He sat in a chair sipping the drink, the cold glass dripping on his stomach, and smoked a cigar. After looking so helpless, almost pathetic, he was composed now and didn't seem worried. She wanted to ask him all the questions that were jumping in her mind.

But they were interrupted. The men came with the furniture and Mr. Bandy went into 824 to tell them where to place the couch and refrigerator and extra chair. When the men left, Mr. Bandy told her what he wanted stocked in the refrigerator: different kinds of cheeses, olives, soda, smoked oysters. She was to make sure there was always ice.

"Mr. Bandy please," Tali said. "Would you tell me what they want?"

"What do you think?" He went over to the couch and sat very low and relaxed, his head against the cushion, looking up at her.

"I don't *know*. I'm asking you."

"They want to kill him," Mel said. "You understand that much?"

She didn't understand that or anything. Why? Who are they? What is Mr. Rosen, or Mr. Ross? After doing things for him for three years—being paid one thousand pounds a week as his "assistant," as he called her—she realized that she knew nothing about the man. He wasn't a retired American businessman. He was hiding. And these people wanted to kill him. Why?

But Mr. Bandy avoided questions. He said, "You did all right. I liked that about the scotch being a present. See, they've been watching, we know that now, and they're going to keep watching. So what do we do about it?"

"You told them he might have left Israel," Tali said.

"It's possible. But I don't think he'd go right away, knowing his money was due on the twenty-sixth."

"But why do they want to kill him? Who are they?"

"I'm gonna give him five days. If I don't hear from him by then I'm gonna pack up and go home."

"Why are they watching us?"

"But if he does call, then we're gonna have to be ready with a pretty cute idea. You hungry?"

"What?"

"Call room service and get me . . . I think some roast chicken, baked potato, something they can't fuck up. Bottle of chilled wine. Ask them what kind of pastries they've got. Torte or a Napoleon, you know, something like that."

She didn't understand Mr. Bandy at all. He should be afraid or worried, or at least show some anxiety. But he wasn't worried. He was hungry.

7

The man seemed to disappear. He was walking along, up ahead on the wide sidewalk between the buildings and the trees that were spaced along the street, and then he was gone.

It was Dizengoff Street, but ten blocks from the Dizengoff that was the heart of Tel Aviv—a carnival midway of cafés with sidewalk tables, pizza joints, ice-cream stands, and the movie theaters on the Circle. Up at this end, Dizengoff had a few cafés and small stores, but it was quiet and apartment-house residential, without the stream of people on the sidewalk. That's why Rashad couldn't figure out how he'd lost the man. There were only a few other people on the street; it was 5:30 in the afternoon.

He came to about where the man had been: a storefront, a place that looked like it had gone out of business, boarded up and the boards painted red. Except the metal street numbers looked new: 275.

Rashad heard the music before he opened the door. Something familiar—yeah, Barry Manilow trying to get that feeling. Rashad knew he was going to be surprised. But stepping from a near-empty street into a crowded pub, into a hum of voices and music, also brought him a good feeling, a feeling of pleasure. All the people sitting in booths and at a long row of tables and two deep at the bar—where the guy he'd been following was reaching over a shoulder to take a drink from the barmaid—Rashad liked it right away. A place where everybody was friendly and talked and where the new guy in town could ask dumb questions. A sign over the bar—tacked up over some of the snapshots that were on display and notes that had been pinned there—said HAPPY HOUR—DRINKS ½ PRICE. A neighborhood saloon in a city where you could count the no-shit beer-and-whiskey establishments on one hand without using the thumb. But no name outside.

He'd save asking it. He made his way through the happy hour crowd toward the bar. Mostly Americans, it looked like. Young dudes in sport shirts or work clothes. American-looking girls, too, dressed for the office, and a few Israeli groupies in tank tops and jeans. There was an English accent, a friendly Limey sound coming from a gutty-looking little guy wearing a hardhat. He seemed popular, everybody saying things to him. There was a black guy at the corner where the tight little bar made a turn. Rashad kept moving—he didn't need a brother today—finally getting next to the guy he'd been following and saying, "How's a man supposed to get a drink in here?"

Davis glanced at him. "What do you want?"

"Scotch'd be fine."

Davis raised his voice a couple of levels. "Chris, a scotch here."

The girl behind the bar said, "You changing, Dave?"

"For this gentleman here."

"Oh, right."

Another Limey accent, Rashad thought. Man, a real barmaid, showing her goodies in the blouse as she bent over to pop the tops off some beers.

But talking to the guy named Dave he found out Chris was Australian. The other barmaid, Lillian—who was also very friendly and knew everybody's name—was Israeli. The gutty little guy in the hardhat was Norman, who was from London and owned the place that had no name outside but inside was NORMAN'S BAR, THE TAVERN. Dave was Sergeant Dave Davis, on Marine security guard duty at the U.S. embassy. There were a dart board and a slot machine in the next room, where the cases of Maccabee and Gold Star were stacked up. During happy hour there were free hors d'oeuvres and new potatoes baked in their skins. The barmaids also fixed beans and franks and pizza in a closet kitchen off the bar. And in the toilet, after his third scotch, Rashad stared at an inscription scrawled on the wall that said, "Fuck Kilroy. The cobrahookie's been here." Yes sir, it was a serviceman's–working man's bar. Loud but very friendly.

"Kamal Rashad," Davis said. "Like Kareem Abdul-Jabbar, huh?"

"Yeah, you hear of the famous ones," Rashad said. "Maybe Elijah Muhammad, the Messenger. But how about Wallace Muhammad? I belong to the Wali Muhammad Mosque Number One in Detroit."

"I guess I don't know anything about the Moslem religion," Davis said. He wasn't sure he wanted to stand here talking about it, either.

"What I believe, mainly, is one thing," Rashad said. "If you take one step toward Allah, he'll take two steps toward you." He sipped his scotch. "It's a good arrangement and can keep you from fucking up on your way to heaven. How long you say you been in, sixteen years?"

"April twentieth," Davis said.

"And now you don't know whether to stay in or get out."

"I'm getting out," Davis said. "What I don't know is what I'm gonna do."

Rashad tried an approach; see if the redneck United States Marine sipping his glass of Jim Beam would follow along. "I don't imagine you able to put much money aside, being in the service."

"Not at two bucks a drink most places."

"Or have a chance to moonlight at some job, make a little extra."

"I guess I never looked at money as a problem," Davis said.

"Some guys, I understand, they get into deals where they take stuff out of a country with them to make some bread. You understand what I'm saying?"

"What've you got," Davis said, "hash? You want me to put a few kilos in my footlocker?"

"Yeah, I understand they get next to a man going home, pack it in with his personal shit. Man going home from the U.S. embassy look even better."

"What've you got?" Davis said.

"Excuse me, my man, but have I said I was dealing anything?"

Davis waited, leaning against the bar, the two girls behind him busy, chattering away with customers.

"But say a person did want to ship something," Rashad said. "How would he know if this United States Marine could handle it? Tell if he had the experience or not?"

"He wouldn't. Excuse me a minute, my man," Davis said. He moved off in the direction of the toilet, talking to people on the way.

Rashad fooled around Norman's for seven and a half hours drinking scotch, trying to get close to the Marine: getting into it again with him—trying to get the Marine to say if he was dealing with somebody or had something going on delivering goods that made him some money—learning one thing interesting, that the Marine was going on a trip tomorrow—but people kept coming up to the Marine or the Marine would see somebody and say excuse me a minute and be gone for a while.

The place was like a club, everybody friendly and knowing one another. Rashad talked to a heavy blond girl from the British embassy who undid a couple of buttons on his shirt and moved her hand over his chest while they talked. People would leave, the place would nearly clear out; then they'd come back and it would be crowded again.

Norman took off his hardhat and showed him the nineteen stitches in the crown of his head where he'd been hit by the drunken Israeli whom he'd asked to leave and who had come back in with a piece of lumber from the construction site on the corner. Norman had the piece of lumber over the bar. He said the Israeli had sobered up but was still in Assuta Hospital. They talked about how come Irish people drank and Jews didn't—except for the guy in Assuta. Scotches kept appearing in front of Rashad. Chris would say it's on Norman or it's on Dave or somebody else. Rashad promised a man he couldn't understand he'd visit him in Wales, in a town he couldn't pronounce. Rashad wasn't even sure where Wales was.

The Marine introduced him to another Marine, a skinny dark-haired sergeant from the U.S. consulate in Jerusalem, Raymond something, a Mexican name, and he watched them standing shoulder to shoulder at the bar, their Adam's apples going up and down as they drank their pints of dark. Davis would switch from whiskey to beer. Listening to him and the Marine from Jerusalem it sounded like they were arguing, the way they talked to each other. The Marine from Jerusalem handed Davis a set of car keys. He said no, he hadn't brought his shotgun along. Was he supposed to? How was he supposed to know Davis wanted it? Davis said because he'd told him. How was he supposed to shoot any birds without a shotgun? The Marine from Jerusalem said bullshit he'd told him. He hadn't told him nothing about a shotgun. Norman came along. He said, "All you want's a shotgun? What else you need? Shells?" Norman had a Krieghoff over-and-under Davis could use, a three-thousand-dollar German beauty you barely had to aim. Norman motioned to Chris to set up a round, took his Campari and soda, and moved off again, adjusting his hardhat.

Rashad got next to Davis again. "You say you going on a trip tomorrow?"

"About ten days."

"Where you going?"

"I don't know. South, I guess."

"What you need the shotgun for?"

"Birds. Do some bird shooting."

And maybe it was for something else he *called* "bird shooting." Maybe he needed a shotgun along for protection. Rashad said, "I wouldn't mind seeing the countryside down there. Whereabouts south?"

But the Marine was bullshitting with the Mexican Marine again. Rashad hit his arm and said, "Hey, you want to get something to eat?" Davis said they were going to get some Chinese later on.

Rashad lost twenty pounds (three dollars) in the slot machine. He lost a hundred pounds throwing darts to one of the Canadian U.N. soldiers he'd met in the Hilton bar the night before—the asshole slapping him on the back and grinning as if they were a couple of old, old friends.

Rashad sat down in a booth. Young Israeli chicks with long hair would look over at him, the way he was lounging against the wall with one leg up on the bench. The goddamn guy from Wales he couldn't understand, speaking English as if it were a foreign language, came over with two drinks and started talking to him again while Davis and the Marine from Jerusalem kept yelling at each other and laughing.

A skinny young guy—looked like a street hustler—came in. Israeli, or maybe Arab. Rashad wasn't sure which, but the skinny guy looked familiar. Big high-heeled funny-shoes and a cheap fake-leather jacket. He went over to Davis—everybody went over to him at one time or another—and had a Coca-Cola while he told Davis something, a long story, Davis listening and finally nodding and saying something. One minute laughing, clowning around with the Marine from Jerusalem. The next minute quiet, serious, not showing any of the Jim Beam in him while he listened to the skinny Arab-looking kid. Rashad couldn't remember where he had seen him before. It didn't matter. The skinny kid left and Davis went on drinking.

Rashad closed his eyes. He'd rest a few minutes.

When he opened them Norman was saying to him, "You gonna spend the night here, are you?"

"Where's that Marine?"

"Dave? I don't know. He left."

The place was empty except for Chris and Lillian, and the Welshman hanging on the bar.

Leaving the place, Rashad tried to think of what had been going on just before he'd fallen asleep. The Marine talking to the skinny kid. Yeah. It was cool outside, the street deserted. No taxis, shit, not even any cars. About six blocks to the hotel. He could see the skinny kid—bony face, long hair—drinking his Coca-Cola in the bar. He could see him inside another place then. Yeah, waiting for luggage. The skinny kid and the Israeli girl with the nice ass, meeting the man at the airport. The same girl talking to the Marine in the lobby.

The Marine was gone, but he was still mixed up in it, wasn't he?

8

Rosen decided there was one employee at the King David who did nothing but watch for him. The guy would say, "Quick, here he comes," and they'd get the basket of fruit up to 732 with the note from Mr. Fink, the manager. "With compliments and sincere good wishes for an enjoyable visit." Rosen had been living in the King David for three years. He'd go to Tel Aviv or Haifa for a couple of days, come back, and find Mr. Fink's note in the fruit.

Usually Rosen ate the banana, apples, and oranges within a couple of days. This time the fruit remained beneath its cellophane wrapper while Rosen paced the floor of his suite and stared out the window. It was a nice view: the lawn and gardens, the cyprus trees around the swimming pool, and, beyond the hotel property, the walls of the Old City at the Jaffa Gate. Directly beneath his window, seven stories down, was the terrace where Paul Newman and Eva Marie Saint had sipped martinis in *Exodus.*

He felt protected within the familiar rooms of his hotel suite. The King David was home; they'd guard his privacy at the desk and the switchboard. But outside, on the road from Netanya to Jerusalem, setting a new personal elapsed-time record of fifty-five minutes, he'd felt vulnerable. The country was too small to hide in for any length of time. He'd have to leave soon, fly to Athens or Paris. But to leave he needed his passport, and to get it he had to find Edie Broder. He pictured her lying in bed looking at him. Yes, at least ten years younger in the dim light. Mature, a grown-up lady, but no excess flesh or fat. Nice tits. He pictured her back home in Columbus, his passport in the pocket of his safari jacket hanging in her closet.

Come on, he had to think.

All right, first try to locate Edie. Check.

Then fly out. Leave the car at Ben Gurion . . .

No, they'd be watching the airport. The colored guy in the *kaffiyeh* would have help by now. Or he might have been replaced. Rosen couldn't get over it: their sending a colored guy to do the job, as if they'd thought it was going to be easy—with only about a hundred and ten colored guys in the whole country—not somebody who'd blend in with the crowd. Christ, they could've gotten a real Arab for twenty bucks.

Instead of Ben Gurion, drive down to Eilat and get an SAS flight to Copenhagen.

No, first call Tali and get the money. Tomorrow was the twenty-sixth. Convert it to pounds on the black market at ten and a half or eleven to one. . . .

Then what? Put it in the bank? What if he didn't come back to Israel? But how was he going to take it with him? Get a hundred thousand U.S. dollars through the security checks—plus the fifty-something grand he had in a Bank Leumi safe-deposit box? There was too much to think about. Too many loose ends. All right, but arrange to get the money tomorrow or the next day. Call Tali and work something out. Thinking of Tali, he thought of Mel Bandy.

Mel was supposed to be here, when? Today.

Something else to think about. He was coming—they'd said

on the phone—to review the business and discuss future plans, which had sounded a little funny to Rosen. They didn't need his approval on anything. Why, after three years out of the business, would they give a shit what he thought about future plans? His business partners seldom contacted him. They sent the money and a Christmas card. Why, all of a sudden, were they sending a lawyer? It hadn't bothered him before, but now it did.

The lawyer arrives the same time a payment is due.

The lawyer arrives the same time somebody is trying to kill me.

Was there a connection?

He was getting off on something else now. He didn't need to imagine problems, he had enough real ones. First, find Edie Broder.

He phoned the Four Seasons in Netanya. There were no messages. He called the Goldar Hotel. The Columbus, Ohio, group had checked out, gone home. The ones at the Pal in Tel Aviv had also checked out. How about Mr. Fine, the tour leader with lawsuits in his eyes? Mr. Fine was at the Samuel. No, he wasn't, the Hotel Samuel said, Mr. Fine had checked out. Voices at the U.S. embassy knew nothing about a Mr. Fine or the Columbus group.

What Rosen finally did—which would have saved him hours hunched over the phone staring at the wall if he'd thought of it earlier—he called Columbus, Ohio, directory assistance. They didn't have an Edie or an Edith Broder. The closest they could come was E. Broder. Rosen got a teen-aged Broder girl out of bed at four in the morning, eleven o'clock Jerusalem time, and asked for her mother. The sleepy, irritated voice said her mother was in Israel. "Ahhhh," Rosen said. "Where in Israel?" On a tour. "Where on a tour?" With some group. "But the group went home." No, her mother had called; she was with another group. "*What* other group?" The girl couldn't remember. "Think!" Well, it sounded like egghead. "Egged Tours," Rosen said. "Where? Where did she call you from and when?" Tuesday night, from Tel Aviv. "You're a sweet girl," Rosen told her. "I'm going to send you a present." Big deal, the sweet girl said.

Rosen called Egged Tours in Tel Aviv. Yes, a Ms. Edie Broder had joined one of their tours, "Hadassah Holiday," and was staying at the Dan Hotel. Closing in, Rosen called the Dan. The Hadassah group, just a minute . . . had gone to Hadera, to the kibbutz Shemu'el, for the day; returning this evening. Eight hours later: the Hadassah group was back, but Ms. Broder was not in her room. Was there a message? Rosen hesitated, then said yes, ask her to please call Mr. Rosen at the King David, Jerusalem.

He felt better. He felt good enough, in fact, to shower and dress and leave the room for the first time in two days.

Silva, the barman, placed a cocktail napkin in front of him and said, "Mr. Rosen, sir. We haven't been seeing you lately." He poured scotch over ice, adding a splash of water and a twist. Then put out dishes of nuts and ripe olives.

"Netanya doesn't have it," Rosen said. "There's only one city in Israel."

"Of course, sir." Silva was Portuguese, born in Hong Kong, and spoke with a British-Israeli accent. To Rosen, Silva *was* the King David. Silva, the oriental carpets, the bellboy who actually rang a bell as he paged and carried the guest's name on a square of blackboard.

Rosen eyed a tourist lady having her lonely cocktail and was tempted. Not bad, though a little too elaborate, with a fixed blond hairdo you could not muss up, though you might chip it with a hammer. More the Hilton type, lost here in the quiet of the King David's lounge. No, he had enough going on and phone calls to make. Three sundowners and quiet conversation with Silva would do this evening. He dined alone, three tables from the blond tourist lady, went up to his suite, left it semidark, and phoned Tali's apartment.

There was no answer.

He'd been afraid of that. Assuming she had picked Mel up at the airport—this had been arranged more than a week before—she might still be with him, knowing Mel. He'd either be dictating letters, eating, or trying to get into her pants. Rosen wasn't worried about Tali. She was a stand-up little girl. If Mel got obnoxious she'd belt him or else politely walk out. What did worry Rosen was the unknown, what might be going on out there in the near world. Tali was alert, she sensed things, and he wanted to talk to her before he talked to Mel.

Well, he would or he wouldn't. Rosen called the Pal Hotel, asked for Mr. Bandy, and Tali's voice said, "*Ken?*"

"Be cool," Rosen said. "Don't say my name yet. I'm your boyfriend calling or your mother, okay?"

"Where are you?" Her voice low.

"Home. Are you with Mel? Mr. Bandy?"

"He's in the bathroom." Her voice rushed at him then. "There were two men here to see him. They threatened him. I didn't know who they were, the way they were talking, saying things about you, asking questions—"

"It's okay," Rosen said quietly. "Take it easy, okay? What were their names?"

"I don't know. Mr. Bandy said . . . first he was afraid, when they were here and threatened him. Then he wasn't afraid anymore, when they were gone. He was a like a different person. He said . . . a terrible thing."

"What did he say?"

"He said they wanted to kill you." Her voice dropped. "He's coming out."

Rosen could hear the toilet flushing. "Did the money come?"

"Yes, but it was more this time."

He could barely hear her. "What? How much more?"

"Two—"

"Listen, okay, tell him it's me. Tali? Don't worry." He heard her saying, away from the phone, "It's Mr. Rosen."

Rosen sat back in his chair in the semidark room, the Jaffa Gate illuminated outside beyond the garden. He looked at his watch. Ten-fifteen. He lit a cigarette and felt ready, a leg up on Mel, ready for Mel's openers. He began to think, If you never liked him much, why did you hire him? . . .

"Rosie, Jesus Christ, man, I been worried sick. I thought you were gonna call this afternoon."

"I didn't know I was supposed to," Rosen said.

"They told you. My flight was due in at one thirty-five. I've been sitting here, Jesus, worried sick."

"How was the flight, Mel? You're feeling a little jet lag, I suppose."

"Rosie—"

"Mel, just a minute. Ross ... Rosen ... even Al. But no Rosie, okay?"

"Sorry. Christ, you're worried about that—Gene Valenzuela was here."

"Yeah, go on," Rosen said.

"I mean right *here* in this room. He's looking for you."

"Mel, a guy tries to run over me with a car and takes five shots at me. You think it's some guy off the street?"

"I mean he walked right in here, he says, 'Where's Ross?' He's not keeping it any secret."

"If *I* already know the guy's after me—" Rosen said. No, forget it. "Mel, tell me what he said."

"He asked me, he wants to know where you are. I told him I had no idea. I said I was here to see you on business, but now I wasn't sure if you'd contact me or not."

"What business?"

"I tried to explain that the reason I was here had nothing to do with what was going on."

"What business, Mel? You said you wanted to see me on business."

"It's not something we can handle over the phone, I mean in any detail," Mel said. "I want to see you—as I told them, it's the reason I'm here—but under the circumstances I think we're gonna have to wait. They'll be watching me like a fucking hawk, every move I make."

"Tomorrow's payday," Rosen said. "I was wondering if it had arrived."

"Yes, the guy brought it, the Marine."

"Did you look, it's all there?"

"Everything's in order." Mel paused. "As a matter of fact there's more this time. Considerably more."

"Why?" Rosen said.

"Jesus Christ, I never heard anybody questioning money coming in."

"Mel, why'm I getting more?"

"I want to sit down and talk to you, Rosie, as I mentioned. But we can't do it over the phone. Right now, the thing to decide is how to get the money to you."

"Why don't you bring it?" Rosen said. "Then we can talk."

"That's exactly what I can't do at the present time," Mel said. "They're on my ass. I go down to the lobby, Valenzuela's sitting there reading the paper."

"What do you want to do, send Tali?"

"Rosie, where are you? You in Tel Aviv?"

"I don't want Tali to deliver it," Rosen said. "You understand? She's not in this."

"Christ, I'm not either," Mel said. "I'm trying to help you on something that doesn't concern me at all, but it's entirely up to you. You tell me where you are or where you're gonna be and I'll get the money to you, somehow, without sending Tali."

"I'll call you back," Rosen said.

"Wait a minute—when?"

"Sometime tomorrow." Rosen hung up.

He lit another cigarette and sat in the evening quiet by the window that faced the Old City. He could still picture in detail the hall in the Detroit Federal Building, could still see Gene Valenzuela and Harry Manza coming along with their attorneys. Valenzuela with his heavy, no-shit look, from the time he had been with the Teamsters and the time he was Harry Manza's construction supervisor: showing the T-shirt beneath the open collar, hair skinned close like a cap over the hard muscle in his head that narrowed his thinking. No style, no imagination. He remembered the time the Teamsters had walked out and the independent hauler had been trying to talk to Valenzuela, explain things, and Valenzuela listening before beating the shit out of the guy and burning his rig. That was business, his job. The situation now was personal.

All right, how did you get through to somebody like that? Rosen smoked cigarettes and thought about it quietly, trying to keep fear out of it. How did you go about stopping somebody like that?

You didn't; you stayed out of his way. There were no alternatives. Get the money and the passport and run.

9

Leaving the Black Muslim asleep at Norman's hadn't been a bad thing to do. He was a big boy, and if he wanted to drink that much it was up to him.

Waking up with the hangover and the Israeli girl who snored wasn't so bad either. Hangovers were made to be cured with cold beer and hot lamb and peppers stuffed inside pita bread. The girl would still be sleeping when he left. At times, though, he wished he could wake up and remember everything from start to finish. The details came gradually and sometimes, long after, unexpectedly.

He had gone to the Singing Bamboo with Raymond Garcia to meet Raymond's girlfriend Rivka, who was the receptionist at the Australian embassy. Rivka was depressed. She had fixed up her good friend Sadrin with a date, an American, and the son of a bitch had stood her up. Like it was Davis's or Raymond's fault because the guy was American. Poor Sadrin was sitting home, dressed, alone, playing her piano. David said why didn't she go to bed; it was eleven o'clock. Rivka made pouting sounds in Hebrew and Davis said okay, call her.

He went to pick the girl up in Raymond's Z-28, which he'd have for the next two weeks, rumbling along the dark street, feeling the car under him: '72 Z-28 Camaro, the hot setup from here to Jerusalem, a screamer with its 302 V-8, Pirelli radials on American racing mags, lime green with a white stripe that came up over the hood and down the trunk lid to the spoiler.

The next part was weird.

The Israeli girl, Sadrin, wore a yellow dress and pearls and played Chopin on the piano softly. He remembered that. He remembered drinking brandy with lemon and soda. She drank more than he had ever seen an Israeli girl drink as they talked, and she started to laugh at things Davis said. They finished the brandy and got into a bottle of white wine that was starting to turn, the girl laughing and telling him how funny he was. He felt good, he felt attractive to her. She said to him, "You give pleasure to my eyes." She put him in the mood with her crisp yellow dress and pearls—that was one of the strange parts— and her round full lips that he told her looked like a basket of fruit. He didn't know where he'd gotten that, but she liked it and laughed some more and when they started kissing it felt like she was sucking his mouth, trying to get him all in. It was good, but it was hard work and she wore him out in bed, working away, her mouth clamped to his, Davis thinking she was never going to come, thinking what the fuck am I doing here? But he saw her in her yellow dress and pearls sitting alone. He remembered how glad she had been to see him, to see somebody, anybody, and he let her work at it as long as she wanted, finally getting his mouth free and telling her she was pretty— she wasn't bad—and that he loved her mouth and her eyes and her body—much bigger and heavier out of the yellow dress— telling her nice things as he held on and she bucked against him. She went into the bathroom after and got sick in the washbasin. She moaned and told him she didn't feel good and

67

wanted to die and didn't have an aspirin. She went to sleep, that big girl, calling for her mother in Hebrew.

Out at the Marine House—he didn't see anyone around—Davis got cleaned up: put on a shirt and jeans and a white snap-peak civilian cap he liked that was broken in, well shaped. He liked to wear it low over his eyes when he was hung over ... taking time now to eat a couple of egg-and-onion sandwiches with two ice-cold Maccabees. Jesus, he was reborn.

He threw extra clothes into a valpac and gathered up a pile of *Louisville Courier-Journals* his aunt had sent him. What else? Stop by Norman's apartment in Ramat Aviv for the shotgun. What else? See Tali and pick up his travel bag full of dirty clothes. Something else. Shit yes, first he was supposed to meet her friend, Mati Harari. At eleven o'clock.

It was twenty to eleven when he drove away from the Marine House and passed gungy Willard Mims jogging back from Afeka in his flak jacket and combat boots. A beer with Norman, in his underwear, took a few minutes. Still, it was only eleven-fifteen when he pulled up in front of the M&A Club on Hayarkon, half a block from the Pal.

He remembered something else he hadn't thought of in the past twelve hours or more and it gave him a sinking feeling. Twenty-six days to go and he'd be on his own.

The M&A—Miguel and Ali's, where Argentina met the Middle East—was a place with a courtyard in front, hidden from the street; it had white stucco walls with dark beams, and impressionist paintings. Not a drinking bar like Norman's, a conversation bar where young Israelis who were making it came in to talk and play backgammon and sip coffee or one glass of wine for an hour. Each time Davis came to the M&A he liked it, the atmosphere, and promised himself to come back and learn how to play backgammon. But he usually ended up at Norman's.

He asked Mati if he wanted something to drink. Mati shook his head. There was no one in the place except Mati Harari, Tali's friend, and Miguel's wife, Orah, behind the small bar. Davis got himself an ice-cold Gold Star from her before he sat

down with Mati and saw his Marine travel bag on the bench.
"You brought it. Good."

"Man, she's anxious to see you. But you got to not go in
through the front."

"I've got to not go in through the front, huh?"

"I'm suppose to show you a way, how you take the lift from
the lower level."

"What're you nervous for?"

"You talking about? I'm not nervous. Listen, they watching
them, man. Tali don't know what's going on."

"I don't either," Davis said. "I don't even know what you're
telling me."

"I'm not going to tell you nothing, so don't ask me." Like,
try and make me. The street kid, the dark Sephardim with his
bandit moustache and his bushy Israeli 'fro. He could look
mean, all right, and Tali had said he'd served time in Haifa.
Davis accepted that. The guy was still about a Grade C hotshot. He'd last about two minutes on the line.

"I don't think we're getting anywhere," Davis said. "Is there
anything else?"

"Follow me," Mati said. "That's all you got to do."

Rashad was across the street from the Pal at Kopel "Drive
Your Self" Ltd., seeing the man about getting a Mercedes before he dumped the BMW. Rashad wasn't watching for anything. He had moved away from the counter and was standing
in the open doorway while the Kopel agent shuffled through
his papers. Rashad was in the right place to see them coming
along Hayarkon, walking in the street. When the Kopel man
said, "Here it is," and began to quote rates, Rashad turned to
him and said, "Hold it, my man. Before we get into that, let me
use your phone. Got to call my father."

Valenzuela answered. Rashad said, "He's back, coming
down the street this way . . . the Marine, man. I'm across the
street at the car rental. The Marine's with the Arab kid again.
Same one as last night. . . . Wait a minute. No, they're going
down the side street next to the hotel. The Marine's got his
overnight bag again . . . going down there like they heading for

the beach. . . . I don't know, maybe he's got something going with the cute Arab kid." Rashad listened, nodding— "Yeah, all right"—and he hung up.

He said to the Kopel agent, "Sorry. My father say I got to come right home."

Through a gray basement hallway and up a service elevator to eight. Tali was waiting for them, the door to 824 open.

"You're very good to come, David. I hope this isn't bothering your trip."

"No bother," Davis said. Entering, he picked up his travel bag from the bed. "I thought you just wanted to give me my dirty laundry."

"Mr. Bandy would like to speak to you," Tali said. "Sit down, please."

The room was like a living room now. Davis glanced around as he walked over to the windows. Now wait for the important lawyer. He looked out at Tel Aviv, at the scattering of high-rises that rose out of the tan five-story skyline, the eastern Mediterranean going to glass walls. Somebody had said to him, "Tel Aviv used to be an ugly town. Now they're building all these Hiltons and Sheratons to hide the view of the sea and it's uglier than it was before." Davis liked Tel Aviv. He wasn't sure why. He liked the people, the younger ones. He'd like to get to know some of their troopers, talk to them. He wouldn't have minded having some of them along in Vietnam. Shit yes, pros; hard fuckers.

"There he is. How you doing, Sergeant? What can I get you?"

Davis turned to see Mel Bandy coming through the connecting doors. He looked different, his face pink, flushed—the guy coming all the way over to shake hands this time, trying to give Davis a good firm one with his fat hand, smelling good of something, all slicked up in a light blue outfit—light blue print shirt with a movie-star collar, light blue slacks, white belt, white loafers with little gold chains on them.

"We're set up, finally," Mel said. "What would you like?"

"Beer'd be fine," Davis said.

"Shit. You name the one thing—Tali, call room service. Get the sergeant some beer."

"No, I don't care. Anything'll be fine."

Mel went to the bar that was set up on the desk and began fooling with bottles, bending over, showing his big can as he got ice and mix from the refrigerator wedged into the desk opening.

"Where you from, Sergeant? I detect an accent."

Davis said, well, he'd been born in Harlan County, Kentucky, but had moved from there when he was six years old. His dad had been killed in a coal-mine accident. They'd moved—he and his mom and sister—they'd gone to live with his aunt, who had a farm in Shelby County. That was about halfway between Lexington and Louisville—Tali and the street kid, Mati, watching him, not having any idea what he was talking about. He'd gone to school one year in Cincinnati, but it was in Louisville that he'd enlisted in the Marines. Boring, Christ, hearing himself. He felt like a straight man when Mel came over and handed him a frosty drink.

"Hundred-proof pure Kentucky bourbon. How about that."

Like it was a treat and all Davis drank was some kind of piss-poor shine. The guy wanted to do more than talk. He wanted something. The drink was all right, something like a bourbon collins. The guy didn't offer Tali or the street kid a drink. He made a scotch for himself and sank down on the couch with one short leg stretched out. He wore light blue socks, too. Davis sat in a chair by the windows. He wasn't in a hurry, but if the guy farted around too long he'd tell him he was. Eleven-thirty Friday morning sitting around having a two-man party. Tali sat quietly, a little expectantly; the street kid hunched over in a straight chair, his dark-skinned left hand holding his right fist.

Davis looked over at Mati. He said, "Don't you want something to drink?"

"No ... nothing." Straightening awkwardly, shaking his head.

Okay, he had tried. Davis looked at the light blue lawyer. "Are we waiting for something?"

"As a matter of fact, we're waiting for a phone call," Mel said. "But I want to take a little time, fill you in first."

The guy was ahead of him, assuming things.

"I'm on leave," Davis said.

"So you got time. Good."

It wasn't what he'd meant. "My car's packed. I'm ready to go." Shit, it still didn't sound right. "I mean I've made plans," Davis said. "I'm taking a trip."

"I understand that," Mel said. "All I want you to do is drop something off for me."

"Where?"

"That's what we're waiting to find out. How's your drink?"

"I'll have another one."

Mel pushed himself up and went over to the bar with their glasses.

"You recall the package, the money. You give it to Tali, right? She's the one set it up, she delivers it. That's the way it's been. This time I want *you* to deliver it. You saw it yesterday? Two hundred grand? *That* money." Mixing drinks, Mel spoke with his back to Davis. "We get a phone call from an individual, a client of mine. He tells us where to make the delivery. You go there and give him the money. He calls again, tells me he's got it. That's all you have to do."

Mel opened the desk drawer and took out a packet of bills. He walked over to Davis and dropped the packet in his lap as he handed him a fresh frosty bourbon.

"A thousand U.S. bucks. That look about right?"

Davis picked it up, fingering the packet of crisp hundred-dollar bills. He watched Mel get his scotch and shuffle back to the couch, the big dealer.

"If it's such a pissy little job, how come a thousand?" Davis said.

"Looking for the catch, huh?" Mel grinned at him. "Well, I'm not gonna lie to you. There could be—there's a very slight chance of a complication. But not if we do it right. Okay, you want the whole story?"

"I wouldn't mind knowing a little bit more," Davis said.

"I'm not gonna give you details, it's a long story," Mel said, "*but*. There's a man by the name of Al Rosen living here who used to live in Detroit. Three years ago he testified for the Justice Department before a federal grand jury. The Justice Department wanted to indict two individuals for murder and they persuaded my client, Mr. Rosen, against my advisement, to testify as a key witness. Okay, the two individuals were never brought to trial and my client was left standing there in his underwear. You follow me?"

"You say his name's Al Rosen?" Davis said.

"Right, Albert Rosen," Mel said. "One of the individuals he testified against had a stroke. He's still alive but he's fucked up, paralyzed on one side, doesn't talk right. The other one served nine months in Lewisburg on a separate, minor indictment— conspiring to defraud. One day my client's car blows up, killing a gas station attendant who had come on a service call. It was a cold morning, the car wouldn't start. Otherwise it would've been my client. You understand? So my client, with the help—if you want to call it help—of the Justice Department, which got him into this, changed his identity and came here to live."

"Who sends the money?" Davis said.

"That's another story. Well, let's just say the company he used to be with," Mel said. "In the mortgage loan business. The company's been carrying him the past three years and we're the only ones who know where he is. Everything's fine . . . relatively. So what happens? Rosen gets his picture in the paper."

"Here?"

"No, it wasn't even in the papers here. The story was about the hotel that burned down last week in Netanya. No, Rosen shows up in the Detroit papers and some others, picture of him standing out in front of the hotel."

Davis was nodding.

"You got it now?" Mel said. "Three days later, not wasting any time, somebody makes an attempt on his life. Yesterday two guys came to see me. They want to know where he is. If I'm here in Tel Aviv then it must be to see Rosen. So they're watching me. They're watching Tali. They're watching the kid here, maybe. Rosen wants to get the hell out and hide someplace else. Change his identity again. But he has to pick up his money first, and we can't deliver it because these guys are watching. They know who we are."

"Okay," Davis said.

"Just like that?" Mel seemed a little surprised. "Great."

"You haven't told him," Tali said. "They also know who David is."

"No, they don't know him," Tali said. "Maybe they saw him talking to you in the lobby."

"It's the same thing," Tali said.

Mel was staring at her, giving her a look. "They don't know his name or what he does, where he lives. That's quite a difference." He turned to look at Davis. "Of course it's up to you, Sergeant. If you'd just as soon pass up a quick thou."

"I'll do it," Davis said. "Where's the money?"

Mel gave him his grin. "You're not getting any ideas, are you, Sergeant?"

Davis didn't say anything. He grinned back.

He listened to the plan Mel described. There wasn't much to it.

They had the metal box that the money had been mailed in wrapped up again with paper and string.

When Rosen called, Mati Harari would take the package, walk through the lobby, get in the Mercedes, and drive off.

A few minutes later, Davis, with the money in Mel's brief-case and the briefcase in Davis's travel bag, would leave by the service entrance. He'd cut through the beach parking area next to the hotel and come out on Hayarkon, where his car was parked in front of the M&A Club. Some plan.

If anyone tried to stop him—well, Davis was not expected to resist. "Unless you want to," Mel said, and then asked him if he'd been in Vietnam. Davis nodded. Mel said, "Well, as I say, it's up to you, considering the remote possibility anything happens. But I can't imagine a Marine taking any shit from anybody."

Davis said, "It's about all a Marine takes."

They sat around waiting. Mel would go into the adjoining room for a while and come out looking at his watch, showing Davis he was as anxious as anybody. He'd walk around with his hands in his pockets, his shoulders hunched. Once he went over to the window and looked down at Independence Park, where the brides had their pictures taken and people walked their dogs, and said he bet fags hung out down there, it looked like a fag park. He didn't offer any more frosty drinks.

At about 1:30 Mel decided it was time to eat and asked Davis what he wanted. Davis said, I guess *shwarma*. Mel said, What the fuck's *shwarma?* And Davis told him—lamb and stuff inside pita. Mel told Tali he'd have a cheese and mushroom omelette and fries. He didn't ask Mati what he wanted. Tali did, and then got on the phone to room service and began speaking Hebrew.

After a few moments she placed her hand over the speaker and said to Mel, "They can't put the dairy and meat dishes on the same table."

"What dairy dishes?"

"The omelette."

"Tell them eggs are from chickens, for Christ sake."

"The cheese in it," Tali said.

"Jesus Christ," Mel said to Davis. "You believe it? Then tell them to put it on two tables," he said to Tali. "I don't give a shit how many tables they use."

That was as interesting as it got, sitting around waiting. Davis talked to Tali a little, asking her about her year in the Israeli Army, and found out where she lived. But he couldn't relax and say funny things to her with Mel in the room.

Finally, going on four, the phone rang and Tali answered it. He knew it was Rosen from the way she turned and looked at him before she looked at Mr. Bandy and held out the phone, nodding.

Davis didn't hear much from where he was sitting. Mel stood with one hand in his pocket looking up at the wall, saying, "Yes . . . of course . . . we've been waiting, we're ready to go," his tone much different, being efficient and a little kissy-ass. He waved the phone at Tali and said, "Here, you get the directions from him. Make sure it's clear." Then he said into the phone, "Rosie, don't worry about a thing. It's as good as done."

Tali spoke to him again. When she hung up she seemed sad. "The address where he is is Rehov Bilu 30 in Herzliya."

"I know about where it is," Davis said.

"Write it down for him," Mel said. "What is it, a house, what?"

"An apartment. Number 23 on the fifth floor. It belongs to a friend of his," Tali said. "There's a lift you take."

Mati picked up the package and left, not looking back when Tali said something to him in Hebrew.

A few minutes later it was Davis's turn, carrying the alligator attaché case inside the Marine travel bag and the thousand bucks in his back pocket. At the door, Tali said, "If you come back this way on your trip, please stop and tell me how Mr. Rosen is, how he looks."

Davis left, wondering if Tali was sleeping with the guy. He was anxious to see this Mr. Rosen.

Mati got no more than three strides out of the elevator before Teddy Cass hit him with a stand-up body block, forearms into Mati's chest, and pushed him back inside. Valenzuela came in after them. The doors closed and the elevator went up. Teddy Cass held Mati against the wall, his forearm now against the skinny kid's throat, staring at the kid's wide-open eyes while Valenzuela ripped open the package.

"Bullshit time," Valenzuela said. "Paper in a tin box." The elevator stopped. Valenzuela jabbed the button for the lobby. "We'll bring him along."

Rashad was over by the taxi stand to the left of the hotel entrance, where a cement stairway led down to the side street that sloped toward the beach. Rashad waited for them as they came out with the Arab-looking kid between them, the kid looking very frightened or sick.

"The decoy," Teddy Cass said.

"Car down the street's got a Marine thing on the windshield. They like to tell you what they do, don't they?" Rashad said.

Next to him, on the cement wall at the top of the stairway, was a plaid overnight bag. "Looks like he should be along any time now. It's one way, so he's got to come toward the hotel before he turns to go anyplace else." Rashad picked up the overnight bag. "I'll see you gentlemen."

He walked down the hotel drive toward Hayarkon and gave a little wave without looking back.

Valenzuela and Teddy Cass walked Mati over to the white BMW parked in the shade of the hotel.

10

He'd go west on Nordau to Ibn Gvirol, then cut over to the Haifa Road. He could keep going north after the stop in Herzliya, drive up to the Golan or Metulla, see if maybe there was some action along the border—terrorists sneaking in. Maybe talk to the troops up there on border watch. He could still make the Sinai in a day.

Davis put the Camaro in gear and got almost to the end of the block. The crazy Black Muslim came running out into the street right in front of him, grinning and holding up his hand. Davis recognized him, couldn't miss him, as he braked to a stop. Next thing, the guy had the door open and was getting in.

"What way we going?"

Davis pushed the gear into neutral. He didn't like it, but he didn't have time to think.

"I'm going north."

"That's fine with me," Rashad said. "I'm ready to see some country." Davis didn't move and Rashad eased up a little. "I don't want to fuck up your plans, my man. You don't want me along, say it. But I would appreciate a lift out of Tel Aviv. Place is beginning to press down on me. . . ."

Davis started up, creeping, and made the turn at Nordau.

". . . All the nightlife, places like Norman's. Man, it's warm and friendly, but it gets to you. Hey, I thought we were gonna have some Chinese."

That was the way it went. Rashad talking, Davis holding onto the steering wheel. Rashad admiring the gutty sound of the Z-28, saying shit, this machine ought to blow the mothers off the road, put a Mercedes on the trailer. Davis began to relax. An insistent Israeli car horn would sound behind them at a light and Davis would give it some revs with the clutch in, letting the horn-blower have some heavy varooms, then release the clutch and sling-shoot the Camaro away from the light. Kid stuff, with gas a buck sixty a gallon. But he enjoyed it once in a while and the black guy ate it up. The guy didn't seem so bad when he wasn't trying to come on, when he relaxed. He asked Davis was that all he had, the one bag? It was on the back seat. Davis said, no, he had stuff in the trunk. Some newpapers his aunt had sent him. Rashad said he liked to travel light. He unzipped his plaid bag and pulled out a white and black *kaffiyeh* and draped it over his natural, saying, man, it made sense. It was cool, and he meant *cool* cool. The guy tried to be entertaining, trying to be friendly. He was tiresome.

On the highway, the Haifa Road, Davis said, "I got to make a stop in Herzliya. It's a suburb up here."

"You going to be long?" Rashad laughed then, taking off the *kaffiyeh*. "Shit, like it makes any difference. Man, I don't even know where I'm going. But if you want me to get out up here, say it. It won't hurt my feelings any. You've been very kind and I appreciate it. I suppose after talking to you last night and all, meeting your friends," Rashad said, "I feel like I'm one of them."

"Well, I don't think I'll be too long," Davis said. Dumb.

Backing down because he felt sorry for the guy. He didn't say anything else until they were in Herzliya, passing streets lined with new apartment buildings.

"I'm looking for Bilu. That's the name of the street."

"You never been here before?"

"Well, it's not a friend," Davis said. "I just have to stop and see a guy for a minute."

Rosen heard the car, the rumbling engine sound. He stepped out onto the balcony to see it roll into the blacktop parking area facing the building: a lime-green American car among the European minis. That would be the Marine.

Except there were two people in the car. Rosen watched the driver, in a white cap, get out and reach in again to get the canvas bag, then slam the door and start toward the building.

Rosen stepped back, a reflex action. He could still see the car and make out the figure sitting in the front seat. He didn't see the man's face, though, until the side window came down and the face inside leaned over to look up at the building. Rosen jumped back again.

The guy in the car was black.

He told himself it couldn't be the same one. Probably another Marine or a guy who worked at the embassy. When he heard the elevator coming up—one door away in the hall—he stepped out to the balcony again. The black guy was still in the car. If it was the one from Netanya he wouldn't be sitting there doing nothing. Rosen went to the door of the apartment and opened it about an inch, then moved to a table facing the door where his attaché case was lying open, the top half of it standing up. The small automatic pistol he brought out of the attaché case was wrapped in tissue paper.

He didn't know for sure that the guy in the cap was the Marine named Davis. Or if the guy was coming here. He was thinking now he should have waited, given it more thought and picked another place. This seemed too close to Tel Aviv. They'd gotten here in twenty minutes. Maybe it should have been out somewhere in the desert, in the Negev. They drop the money and leave and he picked it up later. He should have taken more time. The guy, somebody, was knocking at the door. . . .

"It's open."

"My name's Davis. I've got something for Mr. Rosen."

"Show me your name's Davis," Rosen said. He closed the attaché case, bringing the top part down.

Davis saw the automatic pointing at him. Little .32-caliber Beretta, seven shots. Not a bad weapon if the man knew how to use it.

"Are you Mr. Rosen?"

"Let's see something with your name on it."

Davis dropped the canvas travel bag on the table. He dug his wallet out of his pocket, opened it, and held it out for Rosen to see his Marine Corps I.D. The man was too old for Tali. He couldn't see the two of them making it together. The man would be like her father. Davis wondered if he should take the Beretta away from him. No—leave him alone. The man was nervous and had a right to be.

"Who's the one in the car?"

Davis put his wallet back in his pocket. "Some guy thinks he's a friend of mine."

Rosen looked at him, stared for a moment. He didn't understand, but it wasn't something he was going to get into a discussion about. He said, "You know what it is you're bringing me?"

"Yes, sir. Money."

Davis got the alligator case out of the travel bag and reached over to lay it on top of Rosen's attaché case. He watched the man snap it open.

"You mind my asking, sir—your name's *Al* Rosen?"

"That's right."

"You weren't by any chance a third baseman?"

Rosen looked up at him, his hands on the case.

"You're about the right age," Davis said. "The one played for the Indians, made Most Valuable Player in, I think, '53. Hit forty-three home runs, led the league with a three thirty-six average."

"You want to know something? You're the first person over here's asked me that," Rosen said. "How old you think I was then?"

"I don't know. In your twenties?"

"He hit three thirty-six," Rosen said, "but Mickey Vernon led the league that year. Beat him out by oh-oh-one percentage point with a three thirty-seven."

"Yeah?" Davis was interested and more at ease. "I don't remember what happened to him after that. I was only about eleven."

"Rosen? He retired, thirty-one years of age. Greenberg, the son of a bitch, wouldn't give him any more than twenty-seven five to come back, and Rosen said fuck it. He was already in the brokerage business."

"Greenberg from the Tigers?"

"Yeah, he was general manager of the Indians then."

"I guess I don't recall that," Davis said.

"Yeah, well, I'm about ten years older than you are." Opening the alligator case, Rosen said, "So you remember Al Rosen, huh?"

He picked up a sheet of paper that was inside and his expression changed as he began reading it, squinting or frowning, Davis wasn't sure which. Something wasn't right. Davis stepped around to look in the case. There wasn't anywhere near two hundred thousand inside. Just a bunch of loose hundred-dollar bills.

"You know about this?" Rosen was staring at him again. "He sent five grand. That's all."

"You think I took it?"

"I'm asking if he said anything about it, if he told you what he was doing."

"No, sir. He put two hundred thousand in there yesterday. I watched him."

"You counted it?"

"He said how much it was. There were twenty packs of hundred-dollar bills."

"How long have you been working with Tali, getting the packages?"

"This was the third one," Davis said. "There were some letters other times."

Rosen held up the sheet of paper. "My lawyer says, 'I'm not sure we can trust the Marine.' "

Davis was used to standing on the front side of a desk, at ease or at attention. He made no comment. It was all right, because he felt much different with Mr. Rosen than he did with Mr. Bandy. He respected Mr. Rosen.

"My lawyer says we can't trust *anyone* under the circumstances. 'Anyone' underlined. He says, my lawyer who's been here two days, 'Let's consider this a test run. If you receive the five thousand intact we will know we have established a reliable liaison'—Jesus Christ—'and I will feel more confident in carrying out the responsibility of seeing that you receive the entire amount.' "

"He writes different than he talks," Davis said.

"Fucking lawyer," Rosen said. "His responsibility! It's not his responsibility, he's got nothing to do with the money!"

"Why don't you fire him?" Davis said.

"He says *if* I receive this and so on. He doesn't say anything about if I *don't* receive it. You notice that?" Rosen said. "All right, why wouldn't I receive it? One, you ran off with it. Two, I didn't show up here for some reason. But if I knew it was coming, what's the only reason I wouldn't be here?" Rosen waited.

Davis shook his head.

"Because I'd be fucking dead is what I'd be," Rosen said. "The son of a bitch, he's waiting to see if I stay alive before he delivers the two hundred. I've got to save my ass and he's concerned, he's worrying, he says he wants to feel confident about his responsibility!"

"Why don't I go back and get it?" Davis said.

Rosen looked at him and seemed surprised. "You mean right now? You'd do that for me?"

"He says he wants to establish a liaison. Well, let's show him it's established." He watched Rosen reach into the case and pick up some hundred-dollar bills. "No, I don't need any more. The thousand Mr. Bandy gave me'll cover it."

Rosen paused. "How long you think it'll take you?"

"Forty minutes. If Mr. Bandy's there and he's got it ready."

"He'll be ready," Rosen said. He went over to the phone that was on the counter separating the kitchen from the living-room area. He dialed a number and asked for the room.

Now the lawyer would get chewed out. Davis felt good about that and was anxious to hear it. He didn't want to appear to be listening, though. It wasn't any of his business. Walking out on the balcony, he heard Rosen say, "Tali, let me speak to Mel. . . . Yeah, he's here. Everything's fine." His voice sounded calm; he was in control, knew what he was going to say. The man was all right. People trying to kill him, he still seemed to have it pretty well together.

"Mel . . . I got your note. . . ." Rosen was listening, then: "Mel . . ." not able to get a word in. Davis could picture the lawyer with his hand in his light blue pants, talking, looking up at the wall.

Davis was looking down five stories at the lime green Camaro, the racing stripe—he hadn't realized the white stripe didn't extend over the roof of the car. Just on the hood and the trunk. The car looked empty. The black guy, his new buddy, wasn't inside.

"Mel, you're a wonderful person, I appreciate your concern. . . . Of course not, I understand. . . ."

It surprised Davis, Mr. Rosen's tone, his patience.

There he was. The black guy was over toward the far end of the parking lot standing by a car, leaning against the side, bending down a little now, talking to somebody in the car. One in front, behind the wheel, one or two in the back seat.

". . . I understand, Mel, you don't want to delay this any more than I do. . . . Mel, would you just do one thing for me? *Put the fucking money in a box and have it ready . . . right now!*"

Davis heard the phone slammed down.

"There," Rosen said, quietly again.

"You better come out here," Davis said.

"What is it?"

"You know anybody owns a white BMW?"

* * *

Teddy Cass was the driver. Valenzuela was in back with the worried- or sick-looking street kid, Mati Harari, who sat with his hands folded tight.

"He says he thinks it's the top floor," Valenzuela said. "Number 23?"

Mati nodded.

"No name of Rosen on the mailboxes," Rashad said. " 'Less it's in Jewish. There's a little elevator, one set of stairs, very dark. I think it looks good. You want to hand me something out of the trunk?"

"When the hot-rodder leaves," Valenzuela said.

"What do I do, he comes out?" Rashad said. "I'm standing there."

"No, you better get around the back of the building some-place, till he comes out," Valenzuela said. "He'll think you got tired and left."

"What about him?" Teddy Cass said, half turned on the seat, nodding at Mati.

"He's going with us," Valenzuela said. "He's gonna knock on the door for us."

"It's the same car," Rosen said. "You can almost see the dents in the front end. Son of a bitch with an Arab thing over his head."

"He showed it to me," Davis said. "Jesus, I never had any idea. Guy trying to get you to like him."

"I'm not blaming you," Rosen said. He was standing away from the balcony railing so that he could just see the BMW past the flat cement surface. "You wouldn't have any way of knowing. Maybe—could they have seen you with Tali?"

"I guess that was it, in the lobby. We weren't together more than a minute."

"Then the colored guy sucks up, gets in your car," Rosen said. "The one in front, I think that's the young guy with the hair. I don't know his name. Val's probably in back. You see a guy looks like an off-duty cop, that's Val. Or a fucking line-backer, something like that."

"The colored guy said his name was Kamal Rashad."

"Yeah, they're getting these cute names now," Rosen said. "Alabama Arabians. Well, shit, I don't know—" He turned to go into the room and came around again and stood there.

Davis watched the black guy, Rashad, coming away from the BMW, past empty parking spaces, then go behind some other cars, walking toward the Camaro.

"Which one's your car?" Davis said.

"The black one, right near the walk." It was a Mercedes four-door sedan.

"They know it's yours?"

"I don't see how they could."

It was next to the Camaro. They could run, get to the cars—then what?

All the BMW had to do was back up and it would block the drive. There were shrubs along the street; you couldn't run over the lawn to get out. Well, maybe, but you could get hung up on a bush.

If they sat here long enough the guys in the BMW would come up looking, assuming they wanted to kill Rosen and they knew he was upstairs.

Davis realized he was getting excited. It was a good feeling. Not being aware of it as a feeling, but thinking, figuring out a way to gain control and either neutralize the situation or kick ass.

One option—call the police.

There's a suspicious-looking white car down in the parking lot. Then what? An Israeli cop comes in his white car. But if they were serious and it was their business—the guys in the BMW—they were liable to shoot the cop. Davis tried to imagine calling the police and explaining it in English over the phone, telling a long story.

Or call the embassy. Get somebody there, after he explained it, to call the cops and explain it again, secondhand, in Hebrew. How long would it take? The black guy was opening the door of the Camaro now, getting his bag out, looking up at the building.

They'd be armed. They could be impatient—

"What'd he shoot at you with?" Davis said. "The colored guy."

"I don't know. Some kind of a pistol."

Davis went into the room and picked up the Beretta. "This fully loaded?"

"I checked it," Rosen said.

"You got more cartridges?"

"In the briefcase. With an extra clip."

The Beretta had a three-and-five-eighths-inch barrel that barely extended past Davis's knuckle when his finger was wrapped around the trigger guard. "Are you any good with it?"

"I've had it since I came here," Rosen said.

"Can you put the rounds where you want is what I'm asking," Davis said.

"I've fired a few times, in the desert."

He probably couldn't hit the wall but would never admit it. "Makes a noise for a little thing, doesn't it? Well," Davis said, "I think, instead of us standing around scratching our asses, we might as well be doing something."

"Like what?" Rosen said.

He was nervous but controlling it. That was good. "You want to get out of here," Davis said. "How about if we get the police?"

"The police? What do I say, these guys are annoying me? We're standing there looking at each other? Listen, these people, you put them in a position, they'd shoot the cops cold, no fucking around. I don't think you understand who these people are."

"I said get the cops. I didn't say call them and get into something we can't explain," Davis said. "No, we give your friends a little time to get out. Work it so you don't get mixed up in it and have to answer questions."

"How?"

"Take your money, whatever you're gonna take, go downstairs by the door, and wait. You see their car leave, watch which way it turns going out. You take off and head the other way."

"Where will you be?"

"Don't worry about it. Then, once you're clear, where do you think you'll go?"

"Jesus Christ, I'm standing here—I don't see how I'm going anywhere, for Christ's sake, three, four of them waiting down there—"

"Mr. Rosen, come on. You got it pretty much together," Davis said. "You don't want to lose it now. Tell me where you're likely to go."

"I guess Jerusalem"—calm again—"the King David."

"Okay, later on I'll give you a call, see how you made it."

Rosen was frowning at him again, trying to figure something out. "Whatever you're doing, this is still part of the grand Mel gave you?"

"You worry too much about money," Davis said.

He waited on the balcony with the Beretta, the extra clip, and the box of cartridges, giving Rosen two minutes to get downstairs—seeing the black guy with his bag over the BMW again; the driver with long hair out of the car on the other side; the black guy moving away then, starting across the lawn toward the side of the apartment building.

Davis planned his shots and when he began firing the Beretta—the sound coming suddenly, echoing in the afternoon, in the shadow of the building—he knew where he wanted to place the rounds and fired methodically, steadily, running the black guy back to the car first, then creasing one off the roof of the car and seeing the guy with long hair duck out of sight. Four, three, two, one more. He pulled out the clip and pushed the spare one into the grip with the flat of his hand and began firing at the open space of blacktop close to the car—hoping someone was phoning the police by now—putting a couple of rounds into the doors, but being careful to keep away from the engine and windows. He didn't want to disable the car and he didn't want to hit any of them on purpose. He had fired on and killed people he didn't know before, but it wasn't his purpose now to kill. He was throwing rocks at crows in a planted field, getting them out of there; he wasn't at Khe

San or Da Nang or Hill 881. He reloaded a clip and fired three rounds, then reloaded the second clip before he emptied the first one and reloaded it again. He heard the sirens, the irritating wail becoming gradually louder. He waited, giving the guys in the car time to hear it and think about it, then poured five rounds hard into the flank of the white car. The car was backing out. He was tempted to glance one off the windshield, but it could fuck things up, delay them. The siren wail was doing the job, the sounds coming from different directions now. He fired two more shots, changed clips, fired three times as the BMW backed up, cutting hard, and emptied the clip at the taillight as the car shot out the drive and turned right.

Rosen was outside . . . getting in his car.

Come on, get the fucker out of there! Quick!

Rosen made it. He was out the drive and on the street, then taking his time—good—as three Israeli police cars, sirens flashing, came screaming up Bilu toward the apartment building.

Davis used his shirt tail to wipe the grip of the Beretta. He dropped the gun and the extra clip and the box of cartridges over the side, down five floors into thick bushes.

A squad car sealed him off before he got the door of the Camaro open. He asked them what the hell was going on, man. They patted him down and looked inside the Marine bag and asked to see his I.D. while squad cars came wailing in and police began swarming around the building. Davis gave them an anxious, bewildered look. They asked him if he lived here. He said no, he'd been visiting somebody. The shooting had started and he hadn't known if it was another war or her husband coming in the fucking door. Either way he was getting out of here.

He'd have told them more if they'd wanted to wait and listen.

11

The man seemed to spend half his life in the bathroom. When Tali came back with his cigarettes—after looking around the lobby and then looking outside for Mati or the car, not knowing where he had parked it yesterday—Mr. Bandy was still in the bathroom, the one in 823. The only time he'd used the one in 824 was when he'd say to her, "Hold it, I got to piss," or, "I got to take a leak," telling her what he was going to do.

She thought about the Marine. Mr. Rosen had said yes, he was there, everything was fine. But she knew it wasn't fine, at least not everything, because Mati hadn't come back.

She thought of a friend of hers named Omri who worked for El Al as a flight security officer. He had shot a terrorist and arrested another during an attempted skyjack. It had been more than three years ago. She didn't know what Omri was doing now or why she thought of him. Maybe she wanted to see him again. Maybe the Marine reminded her of him, though they looked nothing alike.

Mr. Bandy confused her a little when he came into the room with the towel wrapped around his middle and carrying a magazine, which he threw on the couch. She could not understand why a man with his body would like to walk around half naked. Even people at the beach would look at him; he was so white. She had to pretend not to notice his nakedness.

"Your cigarettes are there on the table."

"I see them." He was making another drink, which he always did after bathing, before he got dressed.

"Those men weren't in the lobby," Tali said.

"They're probably still following what's his name." Now, as he always did, he sprawled on the couch and raised one of his legs to rest it on the cushion. She could see the fleshy insides of his thighs.

"It wouldn't take him that long to go to Jaffa and return," Tali said. "Even if he walk there." Mati was to go to the archeological excavation in the center of the tourist area and, when it appeared that no one was watching, drop the package into the dig.

"He's cruising Dizengoff in the Mercedes," Mel said. "Lining up some ass."

"He was suppose to come right back." Tali walked to the windows and watched the cars on Hayarkon. "Maybe they didn't follow him."

"Or maybe he took off," Mel said. "Rosie actually trusts him with a Mercedes?"

"Mr. Rosen bought a new one," Tali said. "He's going to sell the one we're using, when he tells me to advertise it in the *Post*." From the window, all the cars on the street looked the same. "Mati should be back," Tali said.

"You sleeping with Mati?"

"No, I don't sleep with him. He's a friend."

"Don't you sleep with friends?"

"I know Mati a long time, when I am teaching at the *ulpan*

in Jerusalem, the language school for immigrants. Do you know the *ulpan?* Like an absorption center."

"I hope you weren't teaching him English."

"No, I taught Hebrew. Mati is Yemenite, but he was living with his family in Bayt Lahm—Bethlehem. Well, one day when Mati was much younger . . . the people there, this day they are Jordanian, the next day they are Israeli. In the '67 War." Tali gave her little shrug. "So we have a place, the *ulpan,* where we teach them Hebrew. Also people from Europe, from all over they come there. I did that when I moved from Beersheba and going to the university."

"You teach Rosie Hebrew?"

"No"—she shook her head in a relaxed sweep, with an innocent expression, thinking of what she was going to say—"after my army service I went to work for El Al as an air hostess. That was where I met Mr. Rosen." She smiled. "He talk to me all the time from New York to Athens. Then I was with him again in a few days here at the Pal where he was staying. We talk some more." She was smiling again. "I laugh very much at the things he say. Then, no, it was weeks later I saw him at Mandy's Drugstore having dinner. He came over by us and asked me if I would work for him."

"To do what?"

"Be his secretary."

"You sleep with him?"

"No, I don't sleep with him." Irritated. "Why do you ask if I sleep with somebody? I sleep with who I want to."

"That's good," Mel said. "That's exactly the way it's supposed to be. You want to go to bed?"

"*No,* I don't want to go to bed."

"Don't you like to fuck?"

She said, "I enjoy to make love, but I do not like to simply, what you said, fuck. What is that? It should be a natural thing."

"What's the difference?" Mel said. "You're with somebody who doesn't turn you on all the way, close your eyes, pretend it's somebody else. You ever do that?" When she didn't answer he said, "Listen, I'm not talking about anything kinky. I don't mind it straight once in a while."

"I'm here to do work," Tali said. "Different things, if you
want me to call on the telephone or write letters, or show you
places in Tel Aviv. Mati or I would be very happy to drive
you." She wanted to be honest without offending him. "But
what is personal to me is not part of the work."

"Let's give it a little time," Mel said.

She didn't know what that meant. She wanted to tell him the
man who came here yesterday was right. Mr. Bandy was like
white dog shit. What did he say. A pile of it. If white dog shit
could be selfish and never consider the feelings of others.

She wanted to be away from him and the sound of the air
conditioning and the room-service trays of dirty dishes sitting
in the hall. She remained because of Mr. Rosen. In case he
needed her. Or to learn something Mr. Rosen would want to
know. She would do anything for Mr. Rosen.

"Well," Mel said. He got up and started across the room.
"What's the Marine's name?"

"David."

"David. When David comes back tell him to wait."

"He's coming back here?"

"I may go downstairs for a while." He went into 823, un-
wrapping the towel.

The BMW looked like it had come over the border from
Lebanon without stopping: bullet punctures all over the body,
lights shot out front and rear. Only the glass had not been hit.
In Valenzuela's mind, that made it the Marine who had been
doing the shooting. Ross would have broken windows trying to
hit somebody. But why the Marine?

They were somewhere in the Tel Aviv area—Ramat Gan,
Rashad said—the BMW parked within the shell of a new
building under construction, in semidarkness, hidden from the
street. Teddy Cass had gone to the railway station, about half a
mile west—they had passed it—to see about renting a car. Rashad was in the back seat of the BMW with the Arab-looking
kid, talking to him. Valenzuela was out of the car looking at the
cement forms and footings, like a building codes inspector.

When Teddy came with the car, they'd switch the guns and
explosives from the trunk of the BMW to the new one. It

would be a temporary car, something to drive until they could pick up another car without numbers or a rental license plate. The man in the Hatikva Quarter who sold guns had said he could get them a good car. Maybe even an American model. He had looked at the BMW early this morning when they'd gone to pick up the Uzis and handguns and the C4. He had run his hand over the front-end dents and red paint on the grille—before the bullet holes were added—and said, "But it would cost you seven thousand lira a week." A grand. Deal, Rashad had said.

They'd leave the BMW here. Rashad might call the man he'd gotten it from and was paying five hundred a week to and tell him where to pick it up. Or he might not.

Rashad, talking to the Arab-looking kid now, said, "For true? They called the Black Panthers?"

Mati nodded solemnly. "They not the same as your Black Panthers are, but they called that name. There was a place, on King George Street in Jerusalem, we used to meet, go there and drink something and talk. Everyone knew it was the place of the Black Panthers."

"You ain't shitting me now, are you?" Rashad said.

"No, I'm not shitting you. We call ourselves that, the Sephardim, the dark-skin ones."

"Things the same all over," Rashad said.

"Giving you the shit," Mati said. "Throwing you in jail."

"Come on," Rashad said, "you done time?"

"Yes, in Jerusalem it was demonstrating. Last May."

"Just trying to make yourself heard, huh? Explain your beef?"

"We were in front of the Knesset to speak to Sapir, the minister of finance. The police come and beat us with clubs. In jail they treat us like animals, don't give us to eat any good food. Also Haifa, I went there before. They arrest me for robbing a rich tourist, stealing his camera and watch. Nine months, man, I was in Haifa."

Rashad said, "Hey, it's a kick, you know it? Meet somebody waaay over here deep in the same shit. Same everywhere you go, have to take the man's shit, huh? How about the man you work for? Keep pushing your head in it?"

"Mr. Rosen?" Mati shrugged. "He don't give me trouble."

"I was thinking of the one at the hotel," Rashad said. "Don't you work for him?"

"That one, he's a fat pig. He sits on your face."

"Yeah—I wonder why this Mr. Rosen would work for a man like that."

"No, the other way," Mati said. "The fat one work for Mr. Rosen."

"Unh-unh." Rashad shook his head. "The fat one was paying this Rosen some money, wasn't he?"

"Yes."

"So this Rosen works for the fat one. We can't understand it. See that gentleman out there? He was a friend of Mr. Rosen in the States, see. Hasn't seen him in a while. He wants to talk to Mr. Rosen, but the fat one don't want him to. You understand what I'm saying?"

"He wants to kill Mr. Rosen," Mati said.

"*No*. Who told you that? No, the fat one is con*trol*ling Mr. Rosen. Got him by the nuts, as we say. And that gentleman, he wants to talk to Mr. Rosen and tell him hey, nobody's mad at you, man. Come on home. See, the fat one's been giving Mr. Rosen some shit, messing up his head. This gentleman, Mr. Valenzuela, just wants to get it straightened out. But *shit*, now Mr. Rosen's got some crazy motherfucker wants to shoot and kill us."

"That Marine," Mati said.

"Yeah, you see any of us shoot back? No, we don't want to shoot Mr. Rosen. We want to talk to the man. But we don't know where he is."

He watched the Arab-looking kid chew on his lip, the kid sitting there covered with snow.

Valenzuela came over to the car, looking out toward the street.

"Here comes Teddy. Get Ali Baba out, we'll have a talk with him."

"We already talked," Rashad said. "Mati here's my buddy."

12

A chimney made of oil drums extended from the top floor of the Park Hotel to the ground: a chute for debris as they cleared out the gutted structure. Davis had read about the fire and forgotten it. He looked at the place now—it was strange—with a personal interest. He knew someone who had been in the hotel that night. A friend of his.

At 6:15 Davis called the King David from a café on the square. They said they were sorry, there was no Mr. Rosen registered at the hotel. Davis said how about if he left his name and a phone number, in case Mr. Rosen checked in?

He sat at a sidewalk table with a Maccabee, watching the people who came out into the evening dusk, beginning to relax as he drank the beer, debriefing himself. The waiter came over and said there was a telephone call that must be for him.

"Hello."

"I couldn't believe it," Rosen said. "Jesus, how many shots did you fire?"

"Twenty-eight," Davis said. "Four clips. You made it all right, huh?"

"Looking back all the way," Rosen said. "Jesus, you don't fool around, do you? Where are you?"

"Netanya. I thought I'd stay here tonight and head north in the morning. What're you going to do now?"

"I just got here a few minutes ago. I'm gonna call Mel first and get a few things straightened out."

"I could go back to Tel Aviv, if you want," Davis said. "Pick up the money for you."

"No, I appreciate it, I really do—everything you've done," Rosen said. "But I'll work something out. It's my problem, something I've been living with. I appreciate it, though."

"I was wondering, driving here," Davis said. "You think your lawyer—you said he was waiting to see if you stay alive before he delivers the money. You think he could be helping them in any way? So he wouldn't have to pay you?"

"Well, it's not like he's paying," Rosen said. "It's my money, out of my company."

"Except it's cash, it doesn't have your name on it." Davis said. "I was wondering, what if he's trying to keep it for himself?"

"He's got to account to people in the company," Rosen said. "He can't just walk off with it. No, I don't think so."

"But what if it looks like he delivered it to you and you were killed after?" Davis said. "Nobody knows what happened to the money. Your lawyer says, 'I don't know, I paid him,' or, 'I sent it to him.' Only he still has it."

There was a silence.

"I can't see him sticking his neck out," Rosen said. "I don't think he's got the balls to pull something like that. What does he do with it? He'd have to get it out of the country. . . ."

"You've been getting it in," Davis said.

A silence again.

"No, I don't think so."

"Well, you know him better than I do," Davis said. "It was just something entered my mind." That was about all he had to say. He waited a moment. Rosen didn't say anything. "Well, let me wish you luck. I hope you make it okay." He listened to Rosen again telling him how much he sincerely appreciated everything, and that was it.

Davis got several copies of the *Courier-Journal* out of the car and brought them to the table. He'd have another beer, check the Kentucky high school basketball tournament scores—"Tourney Trail"—look at the menu and decide if he wanted to eat there. Before too long he'd have to see about a hotel room.

Shelby County 74, Apollo 68
Paducah Tilghman 75, McCreary County 60
Edmonson County 77, Betsy Layne 72
Henry Clay 77, Ballard 74

Blue Devils over the Ballard Bruins, last year's state champions. . . .

Harrison County 75, Green County 54

If they were on Rosen's ass and he was scared they were going to take him out, why didn't he run?

Christian County 67, Ashland 63
Shawnee 85, Clay County 57

What would you do if you were Rosen?

He sat for several minutes staring at the cars moving past in the dusk, circling the parkway, before he got up from the table, dug out a couple of ten-pound notes for the waiter, and walked away. He'd get something to eat in Jerusalem.

The desk man at the King David came back and said he was sorry, but there was no Mr. Rosen registered.

Davis gave the desk man his name and said, "I'll be right over there. See those chairs by the window?"

Fifteen minutes passed. Rosen walked up to him in the

dimly lighted corner of the lobby, Davis sitting low in the easy chair, his legs stretched out, his white cap low on his eyes. Rosen pulled a chair in closer and sat down, looking out the window toward the illuminated walls of Jerusalem's Old City.

"I thought I was just talking to you on the phone."

"The last time I was in this hotel," Davis said, "Kissinger was here to visit Rabin. Some of us were brought over to help with security."

"It was in August," Rosen said. "I remember, they had this place, the whole block, roped off—you couldn't even use the pool in case his wife wanted to take a swim. They moved everybody out of the top two floors, I mean people with reservations—kicked them out. The manager says to me, 'I'm sorry for this inconvenience, Mr. Rosen. We've arranged for you to move to a room on the third floor.' I said, 'Mr. Fink, come on. Are you serious? I've been living here two and a half years, spending something like twenty thousand lira a month, this guy comes once or twice a year, you want to give my suite to some State Department flunkies? Fucking freeloaders?' I said, 'Mr. Fink, is this the world-renowned King David Hotel or a Howard Johnson's Motor Lodge?' I had a Secret Service man in the room all the time Kissinger was here, but I stayed."

"I was in the lobby, over there by the desk," Davis said. "Everybody's standing at attention, all the officials and dignitaries. Kissinger came in with Rabin's military adjutant and some of his aides. He stood there looking around. Just for a moment it was very quiet. And right then, in the silence, somebody let a fart."

"Come on—"

"That's my King David Hotel story."

"I bet I know who it was," Rosen said. "You come all the way to Jerusalem to tell me your King David Hotel story?"

"No, I wanted to ask you something," Davis said. "How come you haven't run? Left the country?"

"I would, but I don't have my passport," Rosen said.

"You lost it?"

"In a way. I know where it is, who's got it, but I'm having a little trouble locating the person."

"Go to the embassy, tell them you lost it."

"If I have to. I'll wait and see."

Davis was silent.

"You came all the way here to ask me that? You could've phoned."

"I came to make a suggestion," Davis said. "Something you might consider."

"Well, I'm certainly open to suggestions," Rosen said. "About all I can see to do right now is get in bed and pull the covers over my head."

"Did you call your lawyer?"

"We had a nice talk. I told him what happened and he said, 'See?' He said now they'd be coming back and hitting on him for not letting them know I called. I said, Mel, tell them who you work for, maybe they'll understand. Mel was very upset. I said shit, Mel, leave the money in the hotel safe and go home. Tell Shapira, the manager of the Pal, that I'll pick it up sometime. But he said no, he was gonna stick it out till I got the money. He said, but I wouldn't be able to come near the hotel without them seeing me." Rosen nodded, looking at Davis. "I know what you're gonna say and I couldn't help thinking the same thing. He doesn't want it out of his hands. He finds out I'm dead, the money's his. He goes home and tells them he paid me the day before I was shot. Christ. I don't know—you want a drink?"

"Not right now, unless you want one," Davis said.

"No, I don't care."

"You say your lawyer's nervous. What if they go see him again?" Davis said. "Rashad and . . . whoever they are."

"He's going to tell them what he comes all the way to Israel to tell me in person and ends up telling me over the phone," Rosen said. "I'm no longer president of my fucking company. That's what he tells me. They voted me out, these clucks on the board, guys I brought in. Let 'em buy a piece of the business. Mel says after three years of *carrying* me, they voted me a final payment, the two hundred grand and that's it, for my stock, everything. I can't bring suit because I'm not there. Two hundred grand, the fucking company's writing a hundred million dollars worth of home mortgages a year. . . ."

"That's what you're in, the mortgage business?"

"Mortgage broker," Rosen said. "We secure government-approved mortgages, usually on low-cost housing around Detroit, and sell them to out-of-state banks at one, one and a quarter percent."

"I don't understand anything about that," Davis said. "I never owned a home."

"It's paper work. You hire bookkeepers and lawyers like Mel, the son of a bitch. He's gonna tell them—the guys you were shooting at—that he contacted me, yes, to tell me I'm out of the business, that's all. So he doesn't have anything more to do with me."

"He explained a little to me about you testifying against somebody in court," Davis said. "But I didn't understand much of that either."

"Well, I was doing some business with a guy named Harry Manza. He was developing land, putting up these twenty-nine nine condominiums, you ever read American papers you've seen the ads, places with names like Apple Creek. There isn't a fucking apple tree in ten miles. Harry was also into a lot of other things, the federal government trying to nail him for a long time—years."

"This guy," Davis said, "he was in the Mafia?"

"I don't know, that's a word. You remember Al Rosen, you might've seen Harry Manza on TV about the same time, the Kefauver Committee, investigating organized crime."

"I think so, but I don't recall the name Harry Manza."

"Well, I knew something about Harry and about a guy that worked for him, Gene Valenzuela, who was one of the guys you were shooting at."

"You saw him in the car?"

"No, but Mel said it was Val came to see him. He's here to do the job on account of I did a job on him. At that time, it was three and a half years ago, the Justice Department wanted to get me on a very minor fraud technicality, but it was the kind of thing could ruin me, put me out of business. They'd drop the indictment, they said, if I'd let them wire me with a bug so they could listen to my luncheon conversations with Harry. You know what that's like, fucking wires taped on you, battery in your pocket? You're waiting for him to say, 'What's that sticking out of your shirt?' You say, 'Oh, it's my new hearing aid.' We'd have lunch, I couldn't even finish a plate of cottage cheese. Also, they wanted me to tell a grand jury what I knew about Harry and Val. They swore, the Justice Department, that the two guys would be put away practically forever." Rosen shrugged. "They never even came to trial."

"You were taking a chance," Davis said.

"Sure, I was taking a chance," Rosen said, "but I was highly motivated, I'll tell you. This guy, Harry Manza, had been wanting to buy a piece of my company. My associates said fine, because Harry scared the shit out of them. I said no fucking way I'm letting him in, I'll go out of business first. It was only a matter of time, I'm convinced, he would've had me killed."

"How do you know?"

"Because I saw it happen. There was a moving-and-storage company Harry wanted to buy into where the owner was killed in an explosion, in his warehouse. Harry played golf with the guy. He'd say to me, 'See, a man tried to do it all himself instead of cutting the pie. It can kill him.' Things like that. But never any reference to it when I was wearing the bug."

"That's what the police wanted him for?"

"The Justice Department, yes, first-degree murder, no fooling around, man, and I was gonna be their star witness. But as I said, after talking to the grand jury and all—Harry and Val *knowing* about it—they were never indicted. The only good thing that came out of it, Harry had a stroke and is practically bedridden. Val, a little later, served a few months for bribery, getting an FHA appraiser laid, some very minor rap, and now Val's in Israel for the shooting season."

"Gene Valenzuela, Kamal Rashad," Davis said. "How many others?"

"One I'm sure of," Rosen said. "Val had somebody with him when he saw Mel, but it wasn't the colored guy."

"Your lawyer said your car was blown up."

"That's right. Killed a guy from the gas station."

"And you say this other one, in the warehouse, was killed in an explosion."

"Yeah, it could be Val's got a dynamite man with him," Rosen said. "Mel said he was a young guy."

"They learn young in the war," Davis said.

"I keep forgetting to ask you," Rosen said, "if you hit anybody."

Davis shook his head. "It wasn't what I had in mind. One thing surprised me a little. Nobody returned fire."

"They wouldn't have come without guns," Rosen said, "if that's what you're thinking."

"No, I guess by the time they figured out where I was, they had to get out," Davis said. "Now they've got to start looking for you again. I imagine they'll go see your lawyer and ask him about it first. There's Tali—maybe Tali should stay out of sight for a while. What I'm saying is, they've got to talk to somebody to find out your habits, where you've been living. . . ."

"Go on," Rosen said.

". . . Where you're likely to be. Say they hire somebody to watch the airport. Or pay somebody at TWA and El Al to let them know if you're leaving. They don't know you lost your passport."

"No."

"They might know about the money, though. Your lawyer could tell them. So they could figure to use it as bait."

"Maybe. Shit, I don't know." Rosen paused. "You said you had a suggestion."

"How about if you called up this guy Val something and told him to get fucked?" Davis said.

"That's your suggestion?"

"Call him up, see if you can reason with him."

"Reason with him about what? Talk him out of it? This isn't an emotional thing with him, it's a score. And scores you settle."

"Well, this idea I've been thinking about," Davis said, "you may not feel comfortable with it, but I believe it could work."

Rosen hesitated, running a few options through his head,

trying to anticipate the idea. "You're thinking, I can't reason with Val but maybe I could make a deal with him."

"Unh-unh."

"Pay him off."

"No, I was thinking you could kill him," Davis said. "Turn it around, hit him before he hits you."

13

The woman from Allentown, Pennsylvania, about sixty, said, "Christ, don't Jews drink? I walked all the way down Ben Yehuda to Frishman and back Dizengoff. If it was New York there'd have been two hundred bars."

She told Mel, sitting next to him in the Pal Hotel bar, that she was on the "We Are Here!" tour with a seventy-three-year-old woman named Dorothy who didn't drink or smoke and was always bitching and sniffing and fanning the air to rid it of cigarette fumes. The woman from Allentown told Mel she had eight grandchildren, that her husband was a steelworker at Bethlehem, and that she found out recently her grandmother was illegitimate—honest to Christ—and her grandmother's father had been a Jew. It had shaken her up to find out she had Jewish blood, she said, and she was over here to learn something about the Jewish faith and see if she could buy any of it.

It was a change from sitting in the room. The bartender, Itzak, would say, "Yes, please, Mr. Bandy," pouring scotch, and serve up plates of olives, peanuts, and soft potato chips. The woman from Allentown, on her third VO and Coke, said if Dorothy didn't quit complaining about her smoking in the room, she was going to tell her to go fuck herself. Mel said to her, "You know who the piano player looks like? Sadat." He got a kick out of that, imagining Sadat moonlighting, flying over from Cairo each evening to play cocktail piano in Tel Aviv. The woman from Allentown said, "Who's Sadat?"

When he got upstairs, Mel let himself into 823. The adjoining room was dark, Tali asleep in the single bed next to the phone. She straightened as he reached the bed. He could see her face and a bare arm in the light from 823.

"I thought you were asleep."

"I was for a little while."

"You want me to get in with you?"

"No, I don't."

"I could've had a winner I was talking to at the bar, gorgeous broad. I came back to you." No response. "The Marine didn't come?" No. "Nobody called?" No one. "You want to just, uh, fool around a little? . . . Well, if you change your mind."

Mel went into 823, undressed, and got into bed. Maybe they had whores available. He should've checked at the bar. He was pretty sure Tali was sleeping naked; or maybe she had just her panties on, skimpy little briefs. He imagined the door creaking and seeing her naked body in the light from the window, Tali saying softly, with her cute accent, "Can I come in with you please, Mr. Bondy?"

The lamp was on when he opened his eyes. It wasn't Tali. It was the Marine, wearing a white cap, looking down at him.

"What the hell do you want?"

"Mr. Rosen's money. He sent me."

Mel squirmed up against the headboard, pulling the cover with him.

"You come in here, I'm sound alseep—where is he?"

"He said he'd just as soon I didn't tell anybody."

"Well listen, I told *him*, he wants the money he'd have to

come get it," Mel said. "I'm not gonna get caught in the middle—those crazy nuts start shooting at each other. What is this, you work for him now? I thought you were on leave."

"I'm helping him out," Davis said.

"Yeah, well, have fun. You must be out of your mind."

"Instead of talking," Davis said, "why don't you give me the money and you can go back to sleep."

"I told him if he wants it, he can come get it. Until I hand it to him personally, it still belongs to the company. And if he doesn't pick it up, I take it back."

"When's that?"

"I haven't decided." Mel was settled again, in control. "Let me ask you something. You seem to be for hire. What if the guys who want Rosen paid you more?"

"More than what?"

"More than Rosen's paying you."

"Where are they? I'll talk to them."

Mel was studying him, realizing something for the first time. The Marine could put you on. He was low key and seemed to know what he was doing.

"Have they been back to see you?" Davis said.

Mel shook his head. "I don't have any idea where they are, but they're around. You realize," Mel said then, "you've got a very good chance of losing everything in this, and I mean your life. These guys don't fuck around, man. They don't go by any rules of war. They're close now, and they're going to stay on him, and I don't see how Rosie's got one fucking chance of making it." Mel paused. "Which leaves me with sort of a problem. A hundred and ninety-five thousand dollars. How do I get it home? I can find a way if I work on it, I'm sure. But you're leaving in a couple of weeks, I think you said. And you're allowed to ship all your personal gear?"

"Seventy-five hundred pounds," Davis said.

"Jesus Christ, what've you guys got?"

"In case you have a car, furniture, things like that," Davis said. "You're asking, if something happens to Mr. Rosen will I get the money home for you? Since I've been handling it, you might say?"

"It's an idea," Mel said.

"Deliver it in Detroit to Mr. Rosen's company?"

"Since he's not with the company anymore," Mel said, "you'd deliver it to my office."

"That's what I thought," Davis said.

"If there was about ten grand in it for you," Mel said, "what difference would it make where you delivered it?"

"Why don't I take it now?"

"Why don't you think about it?" Mel said, "and let me know. I'll be here. I'll be very interested to see how it works out."

As he spoke, Tali appeared in the connecting doorway sticking her shirttail in her jeans, zipping up. Davis glanced at her.

"Ready?"

She nodded and Mel said, "What is this? Where are you going?"

"If you're only gonna sit around and wait to see who wins," Davis said, "you don't need Tali, do you?"

They came out of the hotel from the lighted entrance to early morning darkness and walked along the aisles of parked cars looking for the gray Mercedes. She was worried about Mati again.

He had returned about eight o'clock and had acted strange, Tali said, keeping inside himself and saying very little about his trip to Jaff with the package. Yes, they had followed him. Yes, it had gone all right. Well, where have you been? Oh, with friends. She couldn't stand that air of indifference.

Then she had forgotten about Mati because Mr. Rosen had called again, from Jerusalem, and spoken to Mr. Bandy for at least half an hour.

"He told you he was in Jerusalem?" Davis said.

"No, he didn't tell Mr. Bandy that," Tali said. "I assume it. What he told Mr. Bandy was that he had lost his passport and that you were coming to pick up the money. Then Mr. Bandy spoke for a long time."

"Why did he tell him about his passport?"

"I don't know," Tali said. "It was only one of the things. I could hear Mr. Rosen's voice speaking loud at Mr. Bandy and

Mr. Bandy would speak loud back at him. Then, after that, Mr. Bandy asked me questions about Mr. Rosen, about where he lived and spent his time. Then I look for Mati and he was gone."

Mati was gone and so was the gray Mercedes.

She was tense, asking him about Mr. Rosen as they drove in Raymond Garcia's Camaro to her apartment on Hamedina Square—to pack a few clothes—and didn't begin to relax until they had fixed coffee and were talking quietly on the terrace, David telling her Mr. Rosen was fine, giving her details about his meeting with Rosen and what had happened, where he was now, but not telling her what they planned to do. Davis wasn't sure himself about that part. He had the beginning of an idea. He could picture a controlled situation, a showdown, and could hope to steer them toward it. But he wasn't sure yet of Rosen, to what extent he could count on him. It was strange, getting excited about another man's problem as if it were his own.

He was aware of the darkness beyond the fifth-floor terrace, the dark sky and the dark shapes of buildings. The only lights were the streetlights, below, outlining Hamedina Square. He was aware of the girl also, and of another strange feeling— wanting to hold her and touch her face. He wasn't sure the feeling was sympathy.

"You and Mr. Rosen seem to get along pretty well."

"Yes, I like very much working for him," Tali said. "He's not here, I feel short. Is that what you say? I miss him. He's a very nice person."

"Like a father?"

"Yes, in a way. But the relation is different. He's more fun than a father is."

"Fun in what way?" He felt as if he were prying now.

"Fun because he says funny things. He doesn't laugh, but you know he's being funny. Do you understand?"

He understood. He had caught glimpses of it, but hadn't met the all-out funny Rosen yet. Maybe he never would.

Davis made a swing north out of Tel Aviv, through the empty, early-morning streets, to the Marine House. Tali waited in the Camaro, engine rumbling, while he ran inside and up to his room. Davis didn't bother with the lights. He reached into a drawer and dug out the shoulder holster with the straps wrapped around it and the Colt .38 automatic wedged snugly inside. Also a box of ammo. He then crept across the hall to the room of Willard Mims, the 1st Force Recon Marine—over to the footlocker in the walk-in closet—and was almost out again when Willard opened his eyes and caught him at the door.

"Who's that?"

"It's just me, Willard. I didn't want to wake you up."

"What've you got there?"

"I just want to borrow a couple of claymores. I'll pay you back."

"You'll pay me *back*—how? I brought them all the way from Da Nang."

"Willard, you don't happen to have any grenades, do you?"

"Jesus Christ—" Willard yanked at the sheet to throw it aside.

"Hey, never mind. Trust me, buddy. Okay?"

He was down the stairs, out of there, taking off in the Camaro before Willard got his feet on the floor.

Tali looked to see what he had thrown on the back seat: the holstered gun and the dull, heavy-looking metal objects that were about an inch thick and the size and shape of curved license plates. She thought she recognized them, but wasn't sure.

"Are those explosives?" Surprised.

"Claymore mines. All wired and ready to go."

"You have them at your house?"

"Not officially," Davis said. "This one boy, Willard, keeps some in his closet. I think he's a little crazy." They were silent and he didn't add until some moments later, "But I'm glad he's on our side."

14

They came to Jerusalem in Rosen's gray Mercedes: Rashad in front with his buddy Mati, who was driving; Valenzuela and Teddy Cass in the back seat; Valenzuela with his map open; the Uzis, Berettas, and plastic C4 explosives in the trunk. Rashad's idea: what'd they need to spend a grand a week on a car for when Mati had the man's? Bring Mati into the club along with the Mercedes. They all had to smile at the idea of using Rosen's own car. They hoped Rosen would have time to realize it.

At 7:00 A.M. they topped the rise, coming up out of the switchbacks of the mountain road, and coasted down into the city, the street narrowing and curving, buildings of tan-rose Jerusalem stone rising on both sides, through an old section of the city, catching glimpses of modern high-rises in the distance—clean in morning sunlight—Valenzuela looking from the blue street signs on buildings to his map; then taking a curve off Yafo, the Jaffa Road, past the Hebrew Union College to the King David.

"There," Mati said, slowing down, creeping past the plain, stone, squared-off structure that rose six stories and was topped off by two additional, newer floors.

"That's it, huh?" Valenzuela said. "It looks like a YMCA."

"The YMCA is across the street," Mati said, a little surprised.

"The YMCA looks like what the King David should look like," Rashad said. "Where they keep the cars?"

Mati pointed. "There."

"Turn in."

The Mercedes turned left into a side street and left again through the open gate of a chain-link fence, past a booth where the parking attendant sat. There were no more than a dozen cars in the lot, in two irregular rows, most of them at the fence toward the front, facing the street.

"You see his car?" Rashad said.

"That one," Mati said.

"Yeah, I remember it now," Rashad said. "It was out in front of the apartment. Pull in next to it." When they came to a stop parallel with the black Mercedes, he said, "Who's going in?"

"I am," Valenzuela said. "And you and your friend. Teddy'll wait here."

Mati said, "It would be good, I go talk to him first."

"It would be bad," Valenzuela said. "Teddy, open the trunk."

From the porte cochere of the main entrance they passed single file through the revolving door and went past rows of tour-group luggage being assembled opposite the registration desk, Valenzuela carrying a black vinyl briefcase, followed by Mati and Rashad.

"What way?"

"To, that way." Mati pointed.

They turned right, went past the desk to the elevator.

On the seventh floor they turned right again and walked down the hall to 732. Next to it, on the floor, was a tray on which sat two glasses, an empty champagne bottle, and an ashtray heaped with cigarette butts. Valenzuela nodded. Mati approached the door, cleared his throat, and knocked lightly, twice.

"Hit it harder," Valenzuela said.

Mati knocked again, rapping quickly with his knuckles. They waited.

"Once more," Valenzuela said.

Mati knocked several more times. Cautiously, Rashad leaned in, pressing his head against the door. He came away, looked at Valenzuela, and shrugged.

"Okay," Valenzuela said. Moving away, he looked down at the tray. "He was always neat, I remember that. Couple of times we visited him at his office, he was always getting up and emptying the ashtrays."

In the elevator, Rashad said, "What do you think?"

"I think somebody's in there with him," Valenzuela said. "I don't want to do it that way if I can avoid it. If I can't, if it's a broad, somebody like that who's gonna be with him, then it's too bad, there isn't anything I can do about it."

"Maybe it's the Marine," Rashad said.

"I hope so," Valenzuela said.

"Didn't you hear it?" Edie said.

"It's the maid," Rosen said. He opened the door to the sitting room and listened a moment. "They like to come in and make the bed while you're still in it."

"You're sure it's the maid?"

"Well, it isn't the guy I'm meeting, the one I mentioned to you. We've got a signal."

"Something's going on," Edie said. "I don't understand at all. Who are you trying to avoid?"

She looked cute frowning, pouting a little. Forty-something years old, but she could put on a cute pose and get away with it. She was tanner than before, very tan with the white sheet pulled up around her.

ELMORE LEONARD

"I told you," Rosen said, "somebody I don't want to do business with's been pestering me ... an insurance salesman." That was it. "You know the type I mean? Won't take no?"

Rosen was in his light blue nylon Jockeys this morning. He hadn't eaten lunch or dinner yesterday and he felt very thin, with no need to hold himself in. He had jumped up at the sound of the first knock on the door, calmed himself, gone into the bathroom, and brushed his teeth. Now he got back in bed, and, very gently, pushed Edie down next to him. She looked good first thing in the morning.

"You ever wear curlers in your hair?"

"Not when it's short like this. When it's longer I have it done."

"I like it. My wife used to wear pink curlers and a hairnet."

"You're *mar*ried?" She started to sit up and he had to hold her down.

"No, *when* we were married she wore the curlers. She got a divorce right after I came here. No-fault, no argument, cash settlement. She wouldn't have lasted here a week."

"I love it here," Edie said. "I feel so ... different. I'm in your bed and I didn't even know if you were married or single."

"Swinging singles, that's us. So ... we'll get to know each other. Let it all hang out."

"After you finish your business." With just a slight edge to her tone.

"I'm sincerely, really sorry," Rosen said. "If I could put it off, I would. But I've *got* to spend some time with this guy. He's gone out of his way, doing me a considerable favor. I can't very well tell him hey, wait till I get back from a trip I want to take. You understand?"

"No, I don't understand. You haven't told me anything," Edie said, with the little-girl pout again. It was cute now and he wondered if it would always be cute. Like things his wife had used to do. Dumb little things that finally began to irritate him. The way she used to sit perched on a chair with her back arched and her legs tucked under her, trying to look cute. Or the way she used to put on a little scatterbrained act being cute and saying oh, well, she guessed she was just a little kooky. She

114

wasn't kooky. She was purebred suburban Detroit and didn't know what kooky was. After a while he couldn't stand any overweight woman who tried to act like a little girl. Edie was thin and firm. There was no reason now, at her age, she would ever put on weight. She was nice; she was just trying a few things on him, a few leftover poses. Maybe they were all still little girls in there. How old was *he?* Shit, about nineteen.

"If I'd wanted to avoid you," Rosen said, "would I have called the hotels, the embassy, your home . . . talked to your daughter?"

"You just wanted your passport."

"That reminds me. . . ."

"It's at the hotel. God, what time is it?"

"A little after seven. You've got plenty of time."

"They said to be ready by nine. The bus leaves promptly at nine-fifteen for the airport."

"Don't worry, I'll get you to the hotel," Rosen said. "I promise." Softly then, "Edie? Let's not talk for a while." He began to nibble at her shoulder.

She turned, moving her body against his. She said, "You only wanted your passport," but it was a nice tone now, subdued.

"If that was all I wanted," Rosen said, "when I called the Dan I would've left a message, leave it at the desk, I'll pick it up. No, I asked that you call me, didn't I?"

"I never wanted to see you again," Edie said. "I rushed back to Netanya, took a cab. . . ."

"I know, I should've left word," soothing her. "I thought I'd be right back, but . . . things developed." They had been all through this. Rosen was patient, though; he wasn't going anywhere in the next hour and a half.

"You don't know how I looked forward to it," Edie said, "traveling together, seeing Israel with you."

"I know," Rosen said. "So did I. And we will, I promise."

Last night, after the Marine had left, Rosen had gone into the bar for a nightcap with Silva, turned on the stool to leave, and there she was—sitting right beyond the electric keyboard with three women—staring at him.

The first part wasn't easy, even with his enthusiasm, being glad to see her, rushing over and kissing her, smiling as he was introduced to the "Hadassah Holiday" ladies, then practically forcing her, with her clenched expression, to go with him to the garden . . . to talk, to get a few things straightened out. It was hard work. Women could be stubborn and have to be persuaded nicely to do things they wanted to do. Usually it was a pain in the ass, but last night it had been worth the effort. His passport was in her room at the Hilton. He had her with him and knew he'd get his passport. Then showing her his suite, his home away from home, and ordering the champagne and two packs of Winstons. He liked very much making love to her. He was himself and it was a lot of fun. He told her that and she said she felt the same thing; she felt free and, for some reason, not at all self-conscious or inhibited. "See?" Rosen said. They were meant for each other and nothing was going to keep them apart. Except for the few days he'd have to spend on business. Her tour was flying south to Eilat, to visit Solomon's Pillars and the Red Sea. Okay, he'd meet her there at the Laromme. If for any reason he couldn't make it, he'd call. But they would definitely meet somewhere before the end of her tour and make plans from there.

"The ladies in the group," Edie said, "they're going to give me funny looks when I show up."

"Tell them you're in love," Rosen said.

"I'll tell them I spent the night with you because it was God's will," Edie said. "How have you and God been getting along?"

"My God," Rosen said. "Tell you the truth, I haven't been thinking about it lately."

As a matter of fact, he hadn't thought about his Will of God theory since the night of the hotel fire. It went through his mind: What would God think of him shooting Gene Valenzuela if he got the chance?

The answer was there immediately: He'd probably love it.

Mati came away from the hotel parking attendant to the spot where they were standing behind the gray Mercedes.

116

"He said Mr. Rosen always come and get his car himself."

Valenzuela said, "Did he ask you anything? Why you wanted to know?"

"No, I told him, as you said, you hire me to drive you, to see Mr. Rosen. You want to know is his car here or did he call to have it brought."

Valenzuela looked at Teddy Cass. "How long will it take you?"

"Few minutes, that's all. But it should look like we're doing something."

"We'll jack this one up." Valenzuela put his hand on the trunk lid of the gray Mercedes. "Look like we're changing the right rear. Mati can do that for us."

Mati didn't understand. "You want the tire change?"

"Jack it up, we'll do the rest," Valenzuela said. He turned to Rashad. "Then you and Mati go get a cup of coffee, have a talk. Right?" He pulled the map out of his coat pocket, unfolded it, looked at arrows and circles drawn in ink, and said, "We'll meet you around on Argon Street. Corner of Agron and . . . Ben Shimon."

Mati didn't say anything until they came out of the parking lot and started up the street past the hotel.

"They going to blow him up."

Rashad said, "They do that in Jerusalem, man, not in the civilized world of business."

"Yes, they do it in Jerusalem," Mati said. "So another bomb, they think, oh, the terrorists again, trying to kill Jews. They look for Arabs, they don't look for Americans."

"We're gonna have another talk over a cup of sweet Turkish," Rashad said. "Man, I think I get through to you, explain how the situation is, you still worrying."

"Mr. Rosen never done nothing to me," Mati said.

"He never done nothing to me either," Rashad said, "but he done things to other people—with his money, sending people to jail. With his money, frightening an old man till he had a heart attack and almost died. Man, come on, you see a pile of shit, you don't have to be sitting in it to know it's shit, do you?"

Mati was shaking his head. "I don't know. . . ."

"I know you don't," Rashad said, "that's why I'm explaining it to you. You want to change things, clean up the shit put there by people who like to stick you in it. It's the same thing, man, what we're doing. You got to scare them a little, don't you? Get their attention? Sure, he sees his fine automobile blow up, he says, 'Hey, maybe I better have a talk with them. They serious.' "

"You not going to kill him?"

"Noooo, man, I been telling you, we gonna talk to him, get his reactions. What we want you to do is go back to Tel Aviv and keep an eye on the fatty. You think you can get a bus or something?"

"I have Mr. Rosen's car."

"No, we're gonna use it, buddy. Case we have to be some place in a hurry. What you do, tell Mr. Bandy you gave Mr. Rosen back his car, he wanted it for something. Then you try and stay close to Mr. Bandy if you can. See, Mr. Rosen may not be here. We don't know for sure. And he may call Mr. Bandy and let him know where he is. You understand?"

"Yes." Mati nodded.

"Mr. Rosen wants his money, don't he?"

Mati nodded again. "And his passport."

"Say what?" Rashad said.

"I hear Tali talk to Mr. Bandy about the money and about he lost his passport. When I went back last night."

"You don't mean to tell me," Rashad said. "You keeping that a secret?"

"I didn't think of it before."

"Okay. So you stay with Mr. Bandy," Rashad said. "Tell him you'll rent a car for him if he wants to go someplace. See, then if we want to get in touch with you, find out anything, we call the hotel. So you got to stay close, like in the lobby."

"What if he don't need me? The fat one," Mati said.

"No, my man, *we* the ones need you," Rashad said, putting an arm around Mati's thin shoulders as they walked along David Ha-Melekh Street past the hotel. "You on the team now."

15

In the Camaro, in the hills west of Jerusalem, Tali said, "Do you miss war? Is that it? You miss the screechy, the excitement?"

Davis kept his eyes on the road. "No, I don't miss war."

"Then what are you doing this for? You don't want to protect him. You want to have war with *them*."

"I don't think he has a choice," Davis said. "If you look at it."

"He can wait for them to go. Hide some place they never find him."

"He's tired of hiding," Davis said. "He's been hiding for three years. He thinks he wants to go home, but he's afraid to stick his head out. He's tired of looking over his shoulder and now he sees a chance to end it."

"Why are you helping him?"

"Because he doesn't know how to do it himself."

"That's the only reason? Not for yourself?"

"What do you mean, for money?"

"No, it's why I ask you," Tali said, "do you miss war? Why else do you want to kill someone?"

"Why do you fight wars? Your country," Davis said.

"Because they attack us."

"It's the same thing."

"No, it isn't," Tali said.

Following the switchbacks, in morning shade, he tried to think of things to say and told her about an Israeli friend of his named Zohar who lived near the Marine House and would see them "making gymnastics in the morning"—jogging. Zohar had lived in Eilat for six years, and when he'd moved north with his family, coming from the Sinai desert, he'd said, "We had starvation in our eyes for the green." So they'd bought a house in the trees near Herzliya Pituah.

He told her about visiting Jerusalem the first time, with Zohar, and Zohar showing him where his tank—and the tank of his good friend who was now the Hertz manager in Jerusalem—had been surrounded by Jordanians during the Six Days' War . . . showing him an archway that was like a stone tunnel in a gate and asking Davis if he thought a tank would fit through it—with the Jordanians firing rockets at them—because if the tank became stuck in there . . . but they had to try it and they did get through, barely, scraping the walls. Zohar showed him, in the side of a stucco house, an S-curve of bullet marks he had put there with his Uzi, firing out of the turret of his tank. He had brought his wife and three children here several times on outings. Davis said if he were married and had a family it would be like taking them to Da Nang and Lon Thien. He couldn't imagine it.

Tali said, "You're not married?"

"I almost was a couple of times," Davis said. "I was sort of engaged. But I'd get sent somewhere and by the time I'd get back I wouldn't be engaged anymore."

"When I was eighteen I was in love with an American who was going to dentist school," Tali said. "Do you know Atlanta? That's where he live. I visit him there, but"—she shrugged—"we write to each other for a while, but then we don't write anymore."

"I don't think you have to worry," Davis said.

"About what?"

"About meeting somebody and getting married."

"I don't know—I think I like to be an air hostess again and travel places."

"Maybe, while I'm still here," Davis said, "you could show me Israel. I haven't seen too much."

"Maybe. I don't know."

He wondered if she understood what he meant: traveling with him, staying at hotels with him.

They were on Yafo, in the middle of the morning traffic, when Tali saw Mati and told Davis to stop quick. He couldn't, though, for another half block. When he was able to pull to the curb, Tali jumped out, ran across the street through the traffic, and was gone. Davis waited, looking around. About ten minutes passed before he saw her again, recrossing the street with Mati now, scowling, yelling at him—that thin, nice-looking little girl—giving him hell in Hebrew as they approached the car and Davis leaned over to open the door.

"Mati and I have to have a talk," Tali said.

"Well, get in."

She pushed Mati into the back seat, got in front, and sat half turned, staring at him. "He says he drove them to the King David," Tali said, "but Mr. Rosen wasn't in his room. He says he was with them yesterday, they took him, when you were shooting at them."

"How many, three? Three men?"

Mati nodded.

"Where are they?"

"He says he doesn't know. They told him to go back to Tel Aviv. They kept Mr. Rosen's car." She began railing at Mati again in Hebrew, Mati sitting quietly with the holstered automatic and the claymore mines on the seat next to him, not aware of them, staring back at Tali. He ducked aside then as she tried to hit him with her fist. Davis caught her arm.

"Take it easy. Let's find out what happened."

"He's an idiot!" Tali said. "He thinks they only want to talk to Mr. Rosen." She lashed out at him again in Hebrew and this time Mati yelled back at her.

"Where did they go when they left him?" Davis said. "Where were they?"

They spoke again in Hebrew before Tali said, "At the hotel. He went with the black one to a café, then the black one left."

"The other two," Davis said, "they waited at the hotel?"

"They were in the parking lot by the car," Tali said. She spoke to Mati again in Hebrew. Mati said something to her. "He says they wanted to change a tire. He raised the car for them. . . ."

"Which car?"

"The one he drove," Tali said. "But he says there was nothing wrong with the tire."

Davis had the Camaro in gear, cranking the wheel away from the curb.

"Parked next to Mr. Rosen's new car, the black one," Tali said.

Davis knew that before she told him.

"The Laromme's the best hotel in Eilat," Rosen said. "It's big and flashy and you can get lost looking for the discotheque, but it's a lot of fun—if you don't get taken. A lot of good-looking young Israeli guys prey on tourist ladies, you know. It's like Rome."

"It's like anywhere," Edie said. "There was one at the Dan, I told him I was old enough to be his mother. Do you know what he said?"

"Just a second." Rosen stepped over to the desk, handed the clerk his key, and spoke to him for a moment. The clerk laughed. Rosen came back smiling at Edie and put his hand out to let her go first through the revolving door.

"What'd he say? The Israeli kid."

"He said . . ."

By now Rosen was talking to the doorman, handing him a lira, and the doorman was laughing.

"I'm sorry, go on."

Walking from the porte cochere down the circular drive to the street, Edie said the young Israeli's reply wasn't that much really. He'd only said he was in love with her and it didn't matter how old she was. Rosen said he didn't care how old she was either. What was age? What did it have to do with how you felt? Edie said, "Careful. I have your passport, you know. With your date of birth on it." Rosen said, "Oh . . . that's right."

Eight-thirty-five. They'd get to the Hilton and have time for a cup of coffee.

"I have to change," Edie said.

"Then we'll have it while you change. I'll help you dress," Rosen said. "I'll help you undress first."

"You know, you're very sexy for a man your age," Edie said.

"Tourist ladies who stay at the Hilton like that kind of talk," Rosen said. "It excites them and their thing gets moist and tingles. You're not really a Hilton lady, though. Did I explain that to you? The difference between the Hilton ladies the King David ladies?"

"No, but I can imagine what you're going to say."

She waited again as he stopped to talk to the parking lot attendant and press something into his hand. When he joined her again, taking her arm and squeezing it, she said, "I'll bet you overtip."

"Of course," Rosen said.

They could hear boys playing basketball in the yard of the YMCA—voices in Hebrew, the sound of the ball hitting the backboard—beyond a wall of bushes and a high chain-link fence. The gray Mercedes was parked next to the fence, on Lincoln Street.

They'd hear it all right, Teddy Cass said. Shit, it would break windows in the Y.

But they wouldn't hear it if it didn't go off, Valenzuela said.

They had picked up Rashad on Agron Street and crept through the area in the Mercedes, studying side streets and through routes that Valenzuela had marked on his maps. They had been here now a little more than forty minutes ... almost forty-five minutes when they saw Rashad coming toward them from the front of the YMCA.

"Just leaving the hotel," Rashad said. "Going to the parking lot."

"Alone?" Valenzuela said.

"Has a woman with him."

"Well, there's nothing I can do about that," Valenzuela said.

The King David parking lot attendant was always glad to see Mr. Rosen. Especially with a woman. When Mr. Rosen was alone, he gave him five lira. But when he was with a woman, he gave him ten lira. It couldn't be to impress the woman; she couldn't see the notes. So it must be because Mr. Rosen felt good and was happy. Why shouldn't he be happy? With money and two cars. One of the cars was gone now, taken by the Americans; but the new black one should be enough for him. He watched Mr. Rosen open the door for the woman and come around to this side to get in.

The sound the parking lot attendant heard at that moment was like a racing car streaking down David Ha-Melekh past the hotel, a roar of power, a screeching sound that made him grit his teeth waiting for the crash. But the sound that came was the engine roar again, higher, much louder, *here*, a green car power-sliding through the gate into the yard, raising a wave of dust and throwing gravel at him as the car swerved and came to a stop broadside. A man wearing a cap was out of the car almost as it stopped sliding.

"Rosen!"

Rosen took his hand from the ignition, looking out the side window at the Marine coming toward him and now Tali, behind him, getting out of the Camaro, and someone else. He didn't recognize Mati right away.

"That's the guy I was telling you about," Rosen said.

"My God," Edie said, "he makes an entrance."

Rosen grinned at the Marine. "What're you, out hot-rodding?"

Davis said, "Don't touch the ignition. You better get out of the car. Both of you."

"Jesus Christ," Rosen said. Rosen knew. He didn't have to ask questions. "Edie, come on."

"What is it?"

"We have to get out of here."

"Take the parking guy with you," Davis said. He waved to Tali and Mati to move back.

"You know what to do?" Rosen asked him. He was out of the car now.

"If I recognize it," Davis said. "Go all the way out to the street."

He didn't wait for them to leave. Getting down on his back, inching under the car, he heard the lady with Rosen asking him what was going on. The lady would have found out if Rosen had turned the key and the car had exploded beneath them. There were two fist-size packs of C4 plastic wedged between the undercarriage and one of the frame cross members—one pack would have done the job—like hunks of white modeling clay, with wires and blasting caps attached. Davis pulled the caps out of the plastic material and put them in his pocket before he cut the wires with his clasp knife and pulled the hunks of plastic free.

They were outside the gate on the side street, watching him as he came out from under the car.

He tossed the hunks of plastic in the back seat of the Camaro, got behind the wheel, and drove toward them, seeing them walking into the lot again, stepping out of the way. Rosen hurried toward him.

"Get in," Davis said. "We've got to move."

"Wait a minute—what was it?" Rosen was frowning. It was happening too fast for him. He wasn't used to reacting, not asking questions.

"We don't have time to talk. Get in," Davis said.

"I don't have anything with me. . . ."

The good-looking lady with Rosen was saying, "Will somebody tell me what's going on? What was under the car?"

"Wait a minute," Rosen said, his hands hitting the pockets of the light jacket he was wearing. "I don't have any money with me . . . my sunglasses. . . ." With his beard and hair and blue choker beads, his indecision seemed out of character, weakness showing through.

Tali knew what was going on, her eyes on Davis, staring at him. Mati was a little behind her, alert or asleep, it was hard to tell.

"—Or my clothes. I've got to pack something."

"Mr. Rosen," Davis said, "forget about your clothes. Just get in the car."

Tali said, "What way are you going?"

"South. Stay here till we call you."

"To Beersheba?"

"At least. If we ever get out of here."

Rosen was in the car now, slamming the door. The lady, through the window, looked bewildered. Tali was calm.

"Or Eilat," Davis said. "Maybe you can drive down tomorrow, bring him some clothes."

"Where?"

"I don't know. The Laromme, I guess. We gotta go."

Rosen was leaning close to Davis to look out his side window. "Edie—talk to the girl, Tali. Listen, I'm gonna meet you, so be there. Okay?" And his parting words: "Edie—don't forget my passport!"

Tali watched the Camaro turn out of the lot, the lime-green screamer revving with a howl, and turn again, with a sound of squealing rubber, south onto David Ha-Melekh. She could still hear the car going through its gears, winding up, when it was out of sight . . . and then the gray Mercedes shot past the lot, streaking in the same direction.

16

Three hours south of Jerusalem, somewhere in the Negev, they were keeping the green Camaro in sight: four hundred yards, whatever it was, ahead of them, a speck, a dot on the road. Sooner or later the Camaro would falter or run out of gas or try to hide and they would have them. Rosen and the Marine. It had to be the Marine driving.

Valenzuela would stare at the road—past Rashad and Teddy Cass in the front seat—at the two-lane highway that could have been drawn with a ruler and seemed to extend into infinity, through flat desert landscape, colorless or dry brown and tinted in washed-out, dusty green. Dead land, with the Dead Sea somewhere to the east, left behind. Valenzuela would look from the road to the map that lay open on his legs.

They'd have them pretty soon.

There were only two roads south. One that followed the Jordanian border, and this one that linked the cities of the Negev. Eighty-five kilometers lined with young eucalyptus trees to Beersheba, where they had twice almost overtaken the Camaro scrambling through traffic, running red lights on the boulevard and out past the Arab market. Another twenty-seven miles to Dimona, the gray Mercedes continuing east past the mills and potassium works to follow the highway; then not seeing the Camaro and turning abruptly, realizing the Camaro had taken a secondary road due south out of Dimona, and finally seeing its dust hanging in the air on the way to Mizpeh Ramon.

They were now 237 kilometers south of Jerusalem, about 145 miles. According to Valenzuela's map, there were no through roads, nothing, no destination south of Mizpeh Ramon except Eilat, the Israeli port on the Gulf of Aqaba. Valenzuela liked the way it was working out, but he was getting anxious.

He said, "This would be a good place, along here."

Rashad raised his face to the side. "On the pavement this thing don't have it. Now it's hard to steer around the holes."

"Needs a tune," Valenzuela said. "The cheap fuck, all the money he's got."

"No, the way it was with medals," Davis said, "it was something you thought about *after*. You didn't go out to earn one, get decorated, unless you were pretty gungy, or crazy. In Vietnam, for instance, some guys were grabbing all the medals they could get. But, see, there was an inflation of medals there. NCOs and field-grade officers were writing them up for each other and you couldn't really tell the value, you know, unless a guy dove on a grenade, something like that. You see a lance corporal with a Silver Star, a major might've done the same thing and gotten the Congressional Medal of Honor. It's the way it was."

Rosen was half turned, looking back over the seat rest to the rear window. He was nervous and excited and had been talkative.

"I think they're gaining a little."

"I see them," Davis said. "We're all right." He was staying

approximately five hundred meters ahead of the Mercedes, bringing them along, making sure they didn't get lost.

The road was no more than four meters wide, narrow strips of patched and broken pavement that would end abruptly and continue as rutted tracks of gravel for miles before the pavement would suddenly reappear, a roadway, some poured concrete and telephone lines, the only sign anyone had ever been here. The rest was desert scrub and bleached rock.

Davis held the Camaro between sixty-five and seventy, both hands controlling the twists and strains transmitted to the steering wheel. It was work, hot and with a high level of wind noise. Still half a tank of gas. He felt good, glancing at the rearview mirror and at the red-brown mountains to the east—they were the color of Mars—asking Rosen if he knew why they called it the Red Sea, keeping him from thinking too much.

Why?

Because, see those mountains, the color? Like dull, dirty copper. They go all the way down into Saudi Arabia and they say their reflection on the water makes the sea look red.

Within a few miles they'd come to a stone marker and a side road—not a road, a trail—that led east, toward the mountains. It wouldn't be long. He remembered something.

"Look in the glove box," Davis said.

He'd forgotten until now Tali putting a handgun in there as they drove away from her apartment: a .22 Beretta Parabellum. Low caliber, but an effective, mean-looking gun. Rosen held it in his hands, studying it.

"It's loaded," Davis said. "Keep it on you."

The claymores were on the back seat, each wrapped in about three hundred feet of wire.

He'd need a few minutes to set the caps and attach the wires to the car battery. The Mercedes would have to hang back, cautious, suspicious, and give him time. They could do it, set up a bushwhack and invite the three guys to walk in. This was the place for it. They fought wars here, and they hadn't seen another car or truck or donkey since Mizpeh Ramon. He didn't want to miss the road marker or forget details talking to Rosen, keeping him occupied. He hoped the marker was still there.

Once there had been a sign, Zohar had said, but now the sign was gone. The sign with the name of the village was gone and the people who had lived in the village were gone. Driven out by the tanks.

Rosen said he had to take a leak. Davis asked if he wanted him to stop. He thought of Raymond Garcia—seeing him in front of the Marine House polishing his Camaro—and told Rosen to go on the floor if he had to. Rosen said no, he'd wait. He kept talking.

He said, "Listen, you know what I was? I was a Storekeeper Third. I counted skivvy shirts, for Christ sake. The war was over before I got overseas."

"We don't have time to put you through Boot," Davis said, "but you've had all the experience you need. How long you been driving?"

"I don't know, thirty years. Longer 'n that."

"Okay, you know how to start a car. That's all you have to do. I'll throw the switch if you want," Davis said, "but then I'm not outside watching if something goes wrong."

"I'll do it," Rosen said.

"Just keep telling yourself those guys back there want to kill you," Davis said. "I'd think you'd be anxious to have it done."

"Anxious? Christ, I'm anxious, I'm scared is what I am."

"Well, I am too," Davis said. "Those guys back there— everybody's a little scared, I imagine, nervous. But what can you do? Right?"

They talked and Rosen asked about combat, what the feeling was like, people shooting at you. Scary. And about guys risking their lives. Were they crazy? You don't think, Davis said, you do it. That's what all the training was about. And medals—Rosen got on medals again. (Is that what he wanted?) What did you have to do to win different medals? Did you think at the time if it was worth it or not?

It was a situation you found yourself in, Davis said. "Over there, a Bronze Star was like a good-conduct medal. Win a Silver Star, maybe you held off twenty gooks coming through the wire with an M-16 and a bayonet. Navy Cross, you held off two hundred gooks coming through the wire with the same thing. And a Medal of Honor, you held off that many without an M-16 or a bayonet."

"Were you decorated?" Rosen asked.

"Silver Star and two Hearts."

"Really? You were wounded?"

"I got shot," Davis said.

"Jesus . . . and you got a Silver Star? What'd you do?"

The road marker was about fifty meters ahead on the left, coming up fast.

"Hang on," Davis said.

Rashad thought it was a gust of wind blowing sand across the desert. But then Teddy Cass saw it and sat up, hunched toward the windshield.

"He turned off. You see him? That's his dust," Teddy said. "Val, is there a road here, going east?"

"Nothing," Valenzuela said.

"Maybe a kibbutz, or some kind of historic site," Teddy said.

"Nothing's supposed to be there." Valenzuela held the map up, squinting at it.

"Well, there's *some*thing," Rashad said. He could see flashes of green leading the column of dust, sun reflections on the Camaro. And beyond—something. It looked like a rock formation at first. Rashad slowed the Mercedes and turned at the stone marker, expecting a road and seeing only faint tracks through the sand and scrub ahead of the car. The dust from the Camaro was thinning, blowing away. They could see the shapes of buildings now. Inside the Mercedes, moving at about twenty-five now to avoid the rocks and depressions, they were aware of the stillness, the silence outside. There was no sign of the Camaro.

"He's making his move," Valenzuela said. His tone was like a sigh.

It had been a village of immigrant Jews from India, a village of stone and cement houses with flat roofs built around a square where there had been a well with a dripping faucet. Ein

Kfar. The village had appeared in the sights of Israeli and Jordanian tank gunners in October 1973, during the Yom Kippur War, and had been shelled out of existence as a place to live. Fragments of the village remained: the outline of the square, the dry faucet, walls pierced by explosives, cisterns blown out of the ground, hollow buildings with open doors, rubble in the desert sun.

A year ago Davis had passed through Ein Kfar with Raymond Garcia and Zohar, and Zohar had told them about the tank battle: how his tank had been hit by a rocket, how he had lost his gunner and loader and had been burned on his hands and face and had lain for a day in the field hospital that was set up in Ein Kfar.

Davis could still picture the village. He remembered a Coca-Cola sign lying in the rubble. He remembered thinking that Coca-Cola in Hebrew looked like Coca-Cola in English upside down.

He remembered the square—it was the same—and the narrow street to the right of the square where the sign had been. The sign was still there. And the cement walls with windows and doors blown out.

They would have to move fast now and hope that the Mercedes would hang back, not seeing the green car, and approach the village cautiously. They would have maybe five minutes.

From the square, halfway down the side street, Davis pulled the Camaro into a space between two buildings. The way ahead was clear if they had to run; they wouldn't have to back out. Okay, open the trunk. Get the shotgun first.

He said to Rosen, "Ready?"

"God," Rosen said, but he was out of the car. He walked out to the street, toward the square.

Davis pulled the Kreighoff out of the trunk, loaded both under-over barrels, and stuffed a handful of shells in the right-hand pocket of his jacket. He leaned the shotgun against the side of the Camaro.

From the back seat he got his Colt automatic first, stuck it into his pants in front; the box of cartridges went into his left-hand pocket. Then the claymore mines.

It took less than two minutes to attach the electrical wires from the claymores to the alternator under the Camaro's hood, then unreel the wires, carrying the curved, green-painted mines one at a time out to the street, several houses down toward the square, where Rosen was piling rubble in the narrow street: old boards, hunks of concrete, pieces of furniture. Davis planted the claymores in the rubble. When he brought the third one out and buried it, he dragged the Coca-Cola sign over it and laid it across the heap of debris that now blocked the street.

Rosen looked at him, tense, his eyes wide open. He took out a pack of cigarettes and got one lit. Davis adjusted his cap, looking toward the square in the sunlight. There was no sound yet, no movement.

"We're about ready," Davis said.

They walked back to the Camaro and Davis picked up the shotgun. "I'll be across the street"—he nodded—"in that window. You stand by the corner of the house. Right here. When they come, they'll see all that shit piled in the road. What're they gonna think? We're trying to delay them. Maybe we've got guns, they don't know. I imagine they'll be careful at first. But when nothing happens—they got to get out of the car to move all that stuff. When they do, when they're bending over the pile, you reach into Raymond Garcia's hot setup and turn the key on."

"You'll be right across the street," Rosen said.

Davis nodded. "I'll be right across the street. Maybe all three won't get out. Whoever's driving maybe. I'll take that one."

"You think the mines'll do it, huh?"

"They got a punch. They'll do it."

"Then what?" Rosen said.

Davis looked at him a moment. "See if they're all dead."

"Jesus," Rosen said.

The Marine touched Rosen's shoulder and walked away with the shotgun. He walked across the street. Rosen watched him. He didn't hunch his shoulders or run, he walked.

Davis looked back when he was on the other side, then stepped through a doorway, into a house with plaster ripped from the walls and only part of a roof, a house he had been in before in Phu Bai and Hue.

Rashad pulled closer to the buildings on the right, still in the square, and stopped. His hand dropped to the Beretta, 9-mm, that was on the seat next to him. Teddy Cass's Uzi submachine gun lay across his lap, the clip sticking down between his legs. Valenzuela had taken his Uzi out of the attaché case and held it so that the barrel stub rested on the back of the front seat.

"Go on a little more," Valenzuela said. "Up to the street."

Rashad put the Mercedes in gear and eased it, creeping forward, past the building on the corner. They saw the pile of rubble halfway down the side street.

"What's going on?" Valenzuela said. "Okay, they went down that way. What're we supposed to think about it? Does the street go somewhere else? You see any dust?"

"Looks like a road way down there," Rashad said. "They could be gone by now."

"Or they could still be here," Valenzuela said.

"Maybe that's what they want us to do," Rashad said. "Waste some time."

"Fucking Marine," Valenzuela said. "He's got no fucking business in this."

Davis watched them advancing: the heavyset guy, Valenzuela, on this side of the street, and the thin guy with the hair on the other side, both with Uzis, banana clips, thirty rounds each, both of them staying close to the walls of the houses, coming to doorways and windows and poking the machine guns in as they took a look. The Mercedes was creeping along, staying even with them. Half a block, they'd get tired of it. They'd be anxious, realize soon they were wasting time. Clear the stuff out of the road and get moving—look for the car, find the car first, that would be the way to do it.

If he had an M-16 all three of them could be dead in the time he thought about it and pictured himself doing it. They thought they were being careful, but they didn't know shit about entering a village.

Across the street, Rosen was watching them, pressed against the wall, inching his bearded face past the corner, then pulling it back. Twice Rosen looked over his shoulder at the Camaro, making sure it was still there.

Davis held the Kreighoff cradled in his arms, his back to the front wall of the house, looking on an angle through the open window. He'd have to shoot left-handed. The shotgun had a nice balance and feel—the checkered walnut stock, the delicate, thin little gold-plated triggers. Twelve gauge: it would hold a shot pattern two fists wide from the window to the pile of rubble. Put both of them through the windshield of the Mercedes as the smoke cleared and go out with the Colt, if it was necessary to finish up.

Rosen was peeking again, holding the Beretta at his side. The rear end of the Camaro was shiny though filmed with dust. Rosen was still watching them.

They were about three houses from the rubble. The heavy-set one, Valenzuela, was coming out into the street, in front of the Mercedes, saying something to the one with the hair. Now the one with the hair was coming over. Then Valenzuela motioned for the car to come on, follow them. They were walking toward the pile of rubble, tired of fooling around.

Walking into it. Davis watched them. Two houses from the rubble. He glanced over at Rosen, across the street. About thirty seconds more.

Rosen was pressed to the corner of the building.

No—he was turning away, moving quickly to the Camaro and getting in . . .

Davis couldn't believe it. Not yet! Wait!

. . . slamming the door.

Actually slamming it. Christ, he could hear it across the street. They heard it too, both of them, down the street past the pile of rubble, looking up, raising the machine guns this way.

The claymores went off as Rosen turned the ignition key— two of them did—with a hard, heavy, ear-splitting BA-WHAM-BA-WHAM, and the Coca-Cola sign and the lumber and concrete exploded in gray smoke and fragments of junk and metal, fanning out in the arc-shape of the oval claymores, blowing the shit out of the pile of rubble but missing—Davis *knew* it—the two guys flat in the street now and the black guy safe in the car. Shit. He brought up the Kreighoff and gave them both loads, knowing it was too far, knowing it was time to get the hell out—and ran across the street with the shotgun, digging the Colt out with his free hand, letting go at them, snapping shots as they got up—one of them still on his knees—firing bursts from the Uzis, trying to catch him, spray him with the dry chattering sound, taking out cement from the corner of the house as he got past it and landed hard against the trunk lid of the Camaro.

When he got around to the side, there was Rosen behind the wheel, looking up at him.

"I get 'em?"

"Shit," Davis said. "You got shit."

They drove out of there, straight out across the desert, bounding over holes and washes, tearing through the scrub, beating the hell out of Raymond Garcia's hot setup in a wide arc that should bring them to the highway.

"Well, for Christ sake," Rosen said. "A noise like that, Jesus, why didn't it kill them?"

Davis hung onto the wheel. He wouldn't say anything to the man for a while. He'd be looking at the rearview mirror again. Shit. He was tired of looking at the mirror, but he'd be looking at it now all the way to the Red Sea.

17

They said Teddy Cass, before he turned freelance, had done beautiful work in the precision application of explosives. He made destruction a work of art.

With Universal Demolition, Inc., Teddy had torn down at least a dozen major structures. He'd torn down, for example, the Broadmoor Hotel in Atlantic City, twelve stories, in less than twelve seconds, not even rattling the windows in a building twenty feet away—using, Teddy had once said, "a little dynamite and a lot of gravity."

The pay had been good, but it hadn't compared to what he could make working contract jobs on his own, and he'd done several for Val and Mr. Manza. (He'd gotten a grand for the first one: letting Val tie up a guy on the top floor of the Huron Hotel in Saginaw before he blew it down.) This one, five grand plus expenses. Good wages. Probably a grand or fifteen hundred more than Clarence "Rashad" Robinson was making. But the contract hadn't said anything about taking on the fucking Marines.

Teddy told Valenzuela—in the Mercedes again going south—that it was time to renegotiate. He didn't mind discussing it in front of Rashad, because he knew Rashad would be on his side and it would be two of them Val would have to keep happy if he wanted a job done.

They were somewhere behind the green Camaro. They knew it hadn't doubled back north, they'd seen enough of its dust trail to be sure of that. But the Camaro wasn't in sight now—even with Rashad hitting ninety on clear stretches of blacktop—and they didn't know what the problems would be locating the Camaro in Eilat or at points south.

Valenzuela was not a man who became excited. He took things one at a time and looked at them.

He said, "I agree, it's different than it was on paper. We told you Ross, Rosen, never packed but was likely to now. Or he might've hired somebody who packed. But, no, we never saw something like this, a guy who carries fucking grenades in his car or whatever it was he used. So all right, you feel you're entitled to combat pay, whatever you want to call it. Let me know what you want. Harry or myself, we're not gonna argue with you. Harry wants it done, so do I."

Rashad, holding his gaze on the road and the sweep of desert, said, "Something you might consider. The man has money. He's living on something. And we know his lawyer come to give him some more. If we was to get our hands on that money and cut it up—" Rashad said. "Hey, sight unseen, I'd go for a share, not even knowing how much we talking about."

"That's a possibility," Valenzuela said. "When you take Ross, I doubt we'll have time to ask him where his money is. But Mel, that's something else. I'm agreeable to, as you say, renegotiating. The thing is, if we keep after him we're gonna get him, I know that. We're too close to blow it now and have to start over. We're gonna agree—whatever you want and think is fair. I just don't want to stop and talk it over. The other thing—"

Valenzuela looked down at his map. "Where they going? How far? Well, they could go to Eilat and try and hide there—it looks like a pretty good-size place, a resort town, the Miami Beach of Israel—or they could keep going south, down to the southern tip of the Sinai. Then what? Go back up the other side? They keep going they'll be in Egypt. So I don't know where the fuck we're going. All I can tell you is, don't worry about the expense. Okay? Shit, we're this far. You got something else you'd rather do?"

They passed army vehicles going north and a road that pointed west, to the Timna Mining Company. About three miles from Eilat, they approached a security checkpoint: a shed at the side of the road with yellow markings and two Israeli men in khaki clothes—though not army uniforms—with submachine guns slung over their shoulders.

Rashad said, "Uh-oh."

Teddy Cass pushed his Uzi under the front seat. Valenzuela's lay across his legs, beneath the open map of Israel. He put his hand on the weapon as the car crept up to the two security men studying them, one with his hand raised. The hand moved then, waving them past. Rashad began to accelerate. Valenzuela said, "No, hold on. Stop."

Rashad braked. One of the security men walked over to the open window on Teddy's side. "Ask him about a green car," Valenzuela said.

"Yeah, say," Teddy said to the security man, who was middle-aged and weathered and had probably been in several wars, "did a green American car go by here a few minutes ago? Some friends of ours, we're supposed to meet them down here."

The security man was nodding, saying yes and waving his arm, yes, it went by.

"Thank him," Valenzuela said.

They came to Eilat feeling better about their prospects—to the desert town on the side of a hill, a boom town of new houses and young trees and children—young people everywhere—the town spreading up the hill from the gulf, down the south coast into the Sinai, with its airport right in the middle. Valenzuela studied his map and made a plan.

They dropped Rashad off at the airport to wait there, which was fine with him, get out of the car for a while. Teddy slid behind the wheel and they circled around the airport to drive through the parking lots of the half dozen hotels lining the curve of the gulf that was called the North Beach. No green Camaro. Rosen and the Marine couldn't have taken the road east, because it didn't go anywhere. The road stopped at the border, at Aqaba, and you couldn't get into Jordan from Israel without a visa. You couldn't sneak in farther north because of the mine fields. There was nothing west but desert and mountains all the way to Suez.

So they drove south, winding along the shore of the gulf, past the port facilities and oil storage tanks, slowing down at a couple of motels, stopping at the Laromme to inspect the parking area, and then going on another five or six miles, between the mountains and the coral beaches on the edge of the sea—to another security checkpoint.

Valenzuela, in the front seat now, said, "You wouldn't happen to've seen a bright green American car go by here, would you? With a white stripe?" "A Z-28 Camaro?" the security man with the M-16 asked. "Yeah, that's the one," Valenzuela said. No, the security man said, he had seen that car one time and heard its engine and liked it very much, the sound, *rrrrrrruuuuum*, but he had not seen it today. He wanted to know if the owner was a friend of theirs and how many liters the engine was and if the owner wanted to sell it. Christ, discussing a hot rod, with the mountains of Jordan and Saudi Arabia over there across the gulf and a Bedouin going by on a camel.

It was worth it. Rosen and the Marine were in Eilat.

"Now what?" Teddy said.

"We'll check with Clarence," Valenzuela said. He was thinking as he spoke. "We got to station ourselves somewhere, different places, but so we can get ahold of each other quick. You know what I mean? Say Clarence stays at the airport. You're in town, or I'm in town. The other one drives around.

You go to the checkpoints a few times a day, shoot the shit with the guy about cars, and find out if a green one happened to go by lately. That's what we do, keep looking, ask around for our friends. Hey, you know a guy who drives a green Camaro? Pretty soon one of them's gonna go to the store for a six-pack. It's a matter of time," Valenzuela said, nodding, thinking about it. "That's all it is. Time."

18

Off the south beach road, a few miles from the Hotel Laromme, there was a place called Wadi Shlomo where pilgrim caravans from North Africa, on their way to Mecca, would come down out of the high desert to the sea.

Now, a trail followed the wadi, the dry wash, twin ruts that twisted through the hardpack for several miles—a mystery trail that offered little hope of leading anywhere—before coming within sight of the doctor's residence.

There. A whitewashed adobe, a desert home with a low, flat roof. Not bad in Tucumcari, New Mexico; a dazzler in the Sinai, sitting there with its patio and carport, a bird feeder on a pole, windmill and stock tank in back, the house edged with scrub trees and coarse grass, a low stone fence across the front of the property with a wooden gate that was open.

"They're not home," Rosen said. "Both cars are gone."

Coming through the gate, they could see that the carport was empty. Davis drove slowly, looking around, staying in the ruts that curved up to the house.

"Well, I guess it doesn't matter," Rosen said. "There's supposed to be a key in the birdhouse. He's something; he goes off into the desert to take care of the Bedouins, he locks the house and tells everybody where the key is. Says in case he and Fay are gone, go in and have a drink, make yourself at home. Reginald drinks some kind of Arab piss, raki or arak or something. It's awful. But I know Fay keeps a bottle of Johnny Walker Red in the cupboard over the sink."

Rosen was talkative again, the nervous excitement gone out of him, high now on a feeling of relief. From Ein Kfar to Eilat he had kept shaking his head and saying shit no, hey, that kind of business was way way out of his line. He didn't have the background to stand there and watch them and wait for just the right moment. Christ, those guys had ma*chine* guns. He could still hear it, the gunfire. He hadn't thought it would be that loud or affect him the way it had. He was sorry, he wasn't making any excuses, it just wasn't his line. Christ, all the time in the Navy during the Great War, Storekeeper Third, he hadn't fired a gun in anger, shit, he'd hardly even fired one at all except in boot camp, and then the noise, the racket inside the place on the firing range from the oh-threes going off, drove him nuts. Shit, he didn't even qualify with the oh-three.

Now he felt safe and could relax and tell Davis about the Bedouin doctor who lived in Eilat and devoted his practice to the Sinai desert Arabs, going out in his Land Rover to visit the trailer clinics he had established during the past twenty years. Reginald Morris and his wife, Fay. Reginald very British and proper in his blazer and rep tie, with a sense of humor as dry as his desert, a leftover colonial from the time of the raj, his own man, who grumbled about ineffective governments and saved lives. Fay, Rosen said, was sort of a nutty lady. He loved her English accent. She chattered, and she could carry an evening all by herself and keep you smiling. She was comfortable while Reginald pretended to be gruff. She accepted the desert in the fashion of a colonial wife, and when she felt a little down or bored or lonely, she could always take a pull on the Johnny Walker Red above the sink. Rosen had felt good here, in their company. It was another reason he felt safe now—once they'd found a ladder to get the key out of the birdhouse and covered the Camaro, in the carport, with a canvas tarp.

There was anything they wanted to drink, except bourbon; even cold beer in the humming refrigerator. No phone; but electricity, hot water, and a bathtub.

Davis said he'd have a beer and walked through the rooms looking out the windows at the stone fence and at the scrub growth and desert on four sides.

The patio, with its umbrella table and old-fashioned striped canvas beach chairs, was on the left side of the house looking out. Coming in through the sliding glass doors, the change was abrupt: from desert living to country English, a room full of heavy pieces—deep chairs and a sofa slipcovered in floral designs, dark wood tables, and secretary with china figurines on the shelves.

There was a low roof or ramada that ran along the front of the house to the carport on the other side. The two bedrooms and bath were on that side of the house. The kitchen extended across the back, with a heavy oak table separating it from the living room.

The living room wasn't the place to be if they came from the patio side. The glass doors offered no protection. Windows filled the front wall. They opened out and gave a view of the yard and the stone fence about fifty meters away. One of them would have to be here, to watch the front and the patio side of the house. The other one would have to be in the back bedroom, to watch the side, past the carport, and the whole backyard area. It wasn't a good place to defend.

If they came, he'd have to get Rosen out of here and go up into the rocks, find some high ground. He'd have to take a look after a while. Rosen, sipping his scotch now, saying, "Ahhhh," would argue and not want to go. They needed more guns.

"Here are some pictures of them"—Rosen standing by a wall of photographs in the living room—"a good one of Fay.

Here's Reginald in a Bedouin outfit. He's always Reginald, never Reg or Reggie. Very formal guy on the surface."

"Does he hunt?" Davis said.

"You mean go hunting?"

"Does he have any guns?"

"Well, I don't know if we should nose around in their personal things. Having a drink, well, he said to."

"Let's look," Davis said.

He found a Mauser safari rifle, 30-06, five-shot, in the front closet, oiled, in perfect condition.

Rosen came out of the back bedroom with a heavy revolver that had "Enfield Mark VI" stamped on the side plate. It was at least seventy-five years old, but it was loaded. He made another drink and watched Davis assembling the guns on the oak table—three handguns now, the shotgun and a good rifle, with boxes of ammo—and then slipping on his shoulder rig and putting the Colt automatic in the holster.

Rosen said, "Come on, sit down and rest a while. They're not gonna find us."

"Maybe not today," Davis said.

"Fine, then we'll worry about it tomorrow," Rosen said. "I'll tell you, the worst thing in any situation is not knowing what you're gonna do. But once you make the decision, the hard part's over. All you have to do then is do it. I'm not gonna fight those guys. I've got no business even thinking about it. So I'm getting out. Fuck the money. I'll call Mel, have him deliver it some other time. I'm not gonna worry about that now. All I want to do is get my passport and get out of the country."

Davis said, "That's all, huh?"

"I know, it's gonna take some juking around," Rosen said. "But look, Edie's at the Laromme—they flew in, she got there even before we got here. The hotel's right down the beach. Cut across the desert, you could probably walk it in a couple of hours."

"If you don't get lost," Davis said.

"I'm saying it's a possibility. And Tali'll be here tomorrow with the car."

"Probably tomorrow."

"A day or two doesn't matter now. I fly out of here or drive up to Ben Gurion and get the first plane to Athens, either way. I mean when we see it's clear, and that's where we—or I should say *I*—will have to do some finessing around first, I know that. But I'm going. You guys with the firearms, man, that's way out of my line. I'm not saying I haven't *seen* any of it before, don't get me wrong." Rosen paused and took a drink of scotch.

"I understand what you mean," Davis said. "We tried something and it didn't work. Only it isn't a question now of you saying okay, fine, let's forget about it and go home."

Rosen wasn't listening to him.

"I'll tell you something," Rosen said. "The way I started out, I could've easily been on the other side of the fence, I mean working for somebody like Harry Manza. Shit, I could've *been* Harry Manza. Years ago, the things I was into—but on the fringe, not all the way. I worked for a guy in the loan-shark business. I was his bookkeeper. I worked for a guy in the pro- tective insurance business—listen, that hotel fire that got my picture in the paper. You think it *caught* fire? That was the protection business. Even said it in the papers. That's the kind of shit they pull if you don't want to sign up and make your payments. They burn down the whole fucking hotel. I worked in a guy's office who was in that business. I was just twenty- three years old. I was with the Teamsters—that's a long story, I won't go into it, but I was in Jimmy Hoffa's Local 299 in De- troit, back in the fifties, and you didn't have to go to the movies if you wanted to see some action. I've had some situations since that time where you're dealing with people . . . well, you know, I told you about some of that. You get the Justice Department on you, get squeezed between the bad guys and the fucking good guys, the government lawyers, who don't give a rat's ass what happens to you, leave you standing there with your yang hanging out. I know about dealing with all kinds of people. I know what those guys eat for breakfast, and I also know when to pull my head in to keep it from getting shot off. If it was a deal, we were talking to those guys, shit, I could sell them any- thing. How about some development land out in a fucking mine field between Israel and Jordan? They'd buy it. But if I can't get close enough to talk and know they're gonna listen, then, man, I walk away."

"I'm not arguing with you," Davis said.

"What I am, what you see, is a retired businessman," Rosen said. "I'm getting a little too old for this kind of bullshit. Listen, I'll admit it."

"I don't see that age has anything to do with it," Davis said, "if they come to kill you."

Rosen hesitated a moment. "You believe in God?"

Then Davis hesitated. "Yeah, I guess so."

"Well, I'll have to tell you what I think about the Will of God," Rosen said. "You might be interested. Mainly it's accepting things that happen to you. But it doesn't mean standing there when you can move out of the way. I'm too old to be playing guns," Rosen said. "But I'm not too old to run like a son of a bitch."

19

At dusk, Davis took the Kreighoff and went on a recon, down the road that followed the wadi, for almost a mile, then came back and circled the perimeter of Dr. Morris's house in the gray desert silence. He couldn't imagine people walking across this land, coming all the way from Egypt and the Suez. He couldn't imagine the Bedouins living out there. The first Bedouin he had ever seen—on the trip with Zohar and Raymond Garcia, west of here at Um Sidra, the Wadi of Inscriptions— was a boy of about fourteen; he'd worn a yellow sport shirt and black pointed shoes with thin soles and had seemed to appear out of nowhere with a guest register under his arm, asking for their signatures. Visitors, centuries before, had carved their names in the rocks of Um Sidra; now they signed a guest book. Zohar had asked the boy in Arabic where he lived. He'd pointed off somewhere at the empty desert. Zohar had asked him where he got water and he'd pointed in another direction. Davis thought of the tourists who came to the desert in their hiking boots and safari outfits, and the guidebook warnings to keep your head covered in the sun; and then he thought of the Bedouin boy in his yellow shirt and pointy shoes and no hat.

Maybe, as Rosen said, you could walk to the Laromme from here, approach the hotel from the desert. That would be the way to do it. They couldn't drive the Camaro. It would be better, too, if he went alone and Rosen stayed at the house. He'd wait for Tali and bring her back here with Rosen's clothes and passport. Maybe drive him down to Sharm el Sheikh. Fly out from there.

He didn't see any high ground or good protection within a mile of the house. But if they came during the night it would be all right. He could slip out of the house at night and if he located them he could do some mean and dirty things.

"On that kind of patrol," Davis said, "we'd be dropped in, all camied up, no helmets, equipment taped. We didn't even talk out loud. At night we'd sleep, everybody holding hands, with two guys awake, and if they heard something we'd give each other hand signals. We never dug in or left any sign we'd been there. The time I got the Star we were in there watching traffic on a supply trail and it seemed like a whole battalion of NVA got on us the first night."

"What's NVA?" Rosen said.

"North Vietnamese Army. The regulars, not the VCs."

There were shadows outside on the patio, in a haze of moonlight; the living room was dark where they sat in flowered easy chairs: Rosen with a scotch, Davis with a can of beer and the Kreighoff next to his chair.

"See, sometimes we'd go in, we'd put up posters that said, 'The First Recon Marines are in your area. Drop your fucking weapons and surrender.' But this one was a sneak-and-peek mission and I was the patrol leader."

"How many men?"

"Twelve that time. We lost four. What we'd do, we'd radio our position before we settled in for the night, give the artillery four coordinates—what was called a killing cross—with us in the middle. We'd key the hand set. Then later on, when the NVA got on us, we'd give our signal, like"—almost whispering then—" 'Magic Pie Two, this is Swift Scout,' then click twice and they'd know we needed artillery cover."

"What happens if they're off a little? The artillery," Rosen said.

"Yeah, some fuck-ups smoking dope lay it on you by mistake," Davis said. "You get fucking killed is what happens. That time on the supply trail the cover was fine, but there were too many of them. They kept trying to run over us, and our heavy stuff, our M-60 and our grenade launchers, were out, so we called back to let up on one coordinate and we slipped out that way and met our extract. That's the helicopter that pulls you out. I mean it *yanks* you out. They drop a cable and you're wearing like a parachute harness with a ring you snap on the cable and it jerks you out of there with everybody on the line banging into each other. But you're so glad to get out you don't care."

"What'd you get the Silver Star for?" Rosen said.

"For that. I was the patrol leader," Davis said. "We killed a bunch of the NVA, held them off, and I picked up an NVA field officer, brought him along. The guy was hanging onto me, he had a death grip around my neck all the time during the extract, flying out of there. But you know what the worst part of it was?"

"What?" Rosen said.

"The guy's breath. All the time he's hanging on me, strangling me to death, he's breathing in my face with a breath like he'd been eating fucking garbage and hadn't brushed his teeth in five months."

"I can't imagine living like that," Rosen said, "doing it every day."

"That time we did a job, I guess," Davis said. "We brought the NVA officer out and we brought out our dead. That was something you could count on. We always brought out our dead."

"You said you were wounded, got a couple of Purple Hearts," Rosen said. "Was one of them on that patrol?"

"No, it was another time, an emergency extract," Davis said. "This Medevac landed to pick up our wounded and I ran out with a guy over my shoulder. I got him inside all right, I looked down, there was all this blood pouring out of my leg. I didn't feel anything at the time or hear anything because of the rotors, all the fucking noise they were making. As the Medevac was rising up, I banged on the door and yelled at him, 'Hey, shit, I'm wounded too! Open up!' Davis shook his head, thinking about it, and had a sip of beer.

"What was the other time?" Rosen said.

"It was practically the same time. We got up in the air and the fucking helicopter was shot down. I had my feet caught in something and when we hit I tore the tendons in the backs of my legs. That was my second Heart in about five minutes."

"But you got out."

"I'm here," Davis said.

"And you're worried about what you're gonna do. I mean when you're discharged," Rosen said. "I don't understand that. All you've been through, situations you've handled, what're you worried about?"

"I told you. I don't have a trade. My military occupational specialty is infantry, and I don't think there's much call for infantrymen in civilian life."

"Learning a trade, doing one thing the rest of your life, that's for clucks without imagination," Rosen said. "You don't, in the business world, you don't prepare yourself for a certain job and that's it, like a bookkeeper, a tax accountant. You hire those people. What you do, you keep your eyes open, you use a little imagination seeing how you can fit into a situation, or how you can bend the situation around so it fits you. What did I know about real estate and the mortgage business? Nothing. But I saw an opportunity, a chance to get in, talk to the right people and convince them they should be doing business with me."

"Okay," Davis said. "But I'm not worth a shit at talking to people. They'd see right away I didn't know what I was talking about. I mean if I tried to fake it, tell them I'm some kind of an expert."

"No, they wouldn't," Rosen said. "It's how you do it, your

tone. They're busy thinking about themselves, what hotshots they are. They're thinking what they're gonna say to impress you. If you start right off, they see you've got confidence, you look right at them, you compliment them, bullshit them a little, they think ah, he's got good judgment, he must know what he's doing. That's all. Don't be afraid of people—Christ, I'm telling you not to be afraid. I mean in a business situation. Don't let people scare you; because nine times out of ten they don't know any more than you do. Or even less. They got there pushing and shoving, acting, conning, bullshitting. If they had to get by on basic intelligence alone—most of the people I've done business with—they'd be on the street selling Good Humors and probably fucking up the change. . . . How old are you?"

"Thirty-four," Davis said.

"I didn't get into the mortgage business till I was thirty-eight. No, thirty-nine. I didn't even know there was such a thing—lining up a shitload of mortgages and selling them to banks. A hundred million dollars worth of paper at one percent. What's that?"

"A million dollars," Davis said.

"You bet it is. A year," Rosen said. "With not an awful lot of overhead, either. Don't worry about the type of business, it's all pretty much the same. Take your time, talk to people, decide what you'd like to do, then start doing it. What I always say is, making the decision's the hard part. All this time, I mean for three years, I've been thinking I want to go home, back to the States. Then something like this happens, I have to look at my life closely again and make a decision. Why do I want to go home? Or, do I really want to go home? No, it turns out, after I analyze it, I'm happier here than I've ever been in my life. What do I want to go home for? . . . You like it here, don't you?"

"Yeah, it's all right. I guess I've had a pretty good time," Davis said.

"Palling around with Kissinger at the King David Hotel, I guess you have," Rosen said. "That reminds me, you never said who it was let the fart that time. Do you know?"

"It was me," Davis said.

"People look at you?"

"A few. There wasn't anything I could do about it, so I didn't do anything. I stood there and looked back at them."

Rosen liked that. He sat up in his chair and turned back to Davis. "See? What do you mean you can't handle a situation with people? That's the whole idea, be natural, be yourself, you can't miss. Your only problem, as I see it, is making the initial decision. That's why you're here. You know that?"

"That's why I'm where? You mean sitting here?"

"Right. You're afraid to make the decision to go home."

"I'm going home," Davis said. "I just don't know what I'm gonna do."

"Yeah, but this is like delaying it. Also it's a confidence builder, it's something you know how to handle. I couldn't figure it out at first. Why you'd want to risk your neck. What're you getting out of it? You haven't said anything about money. Now I see why you got involved. You're putting off making a decision. You're sticking to what you know as long as you can."

"That's what I'm doing, huh?"

"Take my word," Rosen said. "Also believe me when I say you've got nothing to worry about dealing with people. Forget what I said about bullshitting anybody. In your case, look right at them and play it straight and you'll win. You've got a nice natural style."

The security man with the green baseball cap and the submachine gun came up to Rashad the next morning at about 8:30—after he'd spent the night in the airport—and asked him what he was doing here.

Rashad said yeah, he was supposed to meet a friend coming in from Ben Gurion, was supposed to be yesterday, but shit, he didn't know when his friend was gonna get here now. He just had to wait.

He also had to show another security man—downstairs in one of the private security booths—his passport and empty his pockets and explain again no, he wasn't an Arab, man, he was a Muslim, born in Dalton, Georgia, lived in Detroit, and had never been to any Arab country in his life.

They still watched him. He'd walk over to the Arkia counter and look at the TV screen of arrivals and departures—almost every hour of the day between here and Ben Gurion—and then walk over to the lunch counter and have a cup of coffee and go look out the window or stand by the stairs going down to the lower level and look in the big mirror mounted on the landing that showed the security booths and the departure waiting area.

The arrivals didn't come in through the terminal. They'd get off the plane, pick up their luggage from the train of baggage carts, and walk through the gate to the street. At ten o'clock, outside for some fresh air, watching a group of passengers that had just gotten off a plane, Rashad saw a familiar face.

A woman. A nicely dressed woman with a group of women laughing and carrying on, acting like little girls. Americans. Maybe from the Hilton. Or the Pal. He might've seen her in the lobby one time.

Staring at the woman he made himself remember. It wasn't in Tel Aviv, it was Jerusalem. And not *in* a hotel, but coming out. With the man, Mr. Rosen. Walking to his car.

All the women were crowded around the entrance of a red-and-white Egged Tour bus while their luggage was being loaded on. Rashad waited. He was the last one to step aboard, jumping in just as the door was about to snap closed. When the driver looked at him funny, Rashad handed him a ten-pound note.

"You going the hotel, aren't you?"

The driver nodded.

"I just want a lift, man. I'll stand right here out of the way."

That was how Rashad got to the Laromme on the south beach road and how he came to be hanging around the lobby, watching the woman friend of Mr. Rosen's, when another friend of Mr. Rosen's, the Israeli chick with the nice ass, Tali, walked up to the woman and started talking to her.

On the phone a few minutes later, when he heard Valenzuela's voice, Rashad said, "You gonna like what I got to tell you."

20

What Gene Valenzuela liked was the view of all the cement work going on.

At half past ten, when the phone rang in the café, Valenzuela was on an upper-level terrace not more than a half mile from Rashad. The terrace, which ran along in front of the café in a clean new complex of minimall shops and fast-food places, got the sun directly and was hot at midmorning, but it gave Valenzuela a treeless view of everything. Directly below him, the road came curving in from the south beach and fingered out in three directions: across open, undeveloped land to the North Beach hotels; to the airport; and up the hill to town.

The cement work was done in a hurry; it didn't have a nice finished look. But it was new and clean. He'd think about the old, gray-peeling cement at Lewisburg (with the highest homicide rate of any federal prison), hard motherfuckers fighting over the queens. He'd watch the Israeli girls walk by in their jeans with their Jewish asses. There was a crowd of young stuff here and enough cement work—a guy with a half a dozen transit-mixers could make enough to retire in three years.

When the phone rang in the café he thought of his wife and pictured her talking on the phone in her smart-ass voice to her mother—"*I* don't know where he is, the son of a bitch. Who knows? He never tells me where he goes and I personally don't care."

She'd never find him, either. She'd never even heard of Eilat. Shit, who had? He'd bet Harry Manza had never heard of it. But if it was a money-maker, it wouldn't matter to Harry where it was. Get some development capital from him. Cash. Sneak it into the country. Nothing signed with him, no written agreements. Harry had to die sometime. Valenzuela saw himself sitting here with a growing business. Let his wife keep wondering where he was. Let her bitch and never have to listen to her again.

On the phone, talking to Rashad, he said, "Okay, stay there. Teddy's due to call or come by here in about . . . fifteen, twenty minutes. We'll meet you outside the hotel."

"Israeli girls are funny," Davis was saying to Rosen at ten that morning in the kitchen having coffee. "Or maybe all girls are funny, I mean different, and I don't know how to read them."

"It's a knack," Rosen said. "First you've got to never be awed. Though you're polite, of course."

"This girl I picked up one time at the Shalom Tower," Davis said. "We're getting along fine, having a coffee. She says she's meeting her girlfriend from England at the El Al terminal. So we pick her up, a really good-looking girl with the long blond hair and the English accent and all, and we go to the Israeli girl's apartment. She says she's got a bottle of wine there and some hash. So I'm thinking fine, one girl or the other, I can't miss. We get to the apartment, the Israeli girl's *hus*band's there. Listen to this. I end up talking to the husband about the

West Bank situation while the two broads are off in the bedroom making out."

He was never sure Rosen listened, because Rosen seldom
commented. He would start talking right away, saying something that didn't always follow.

"I learned a long time ago," Rosen said, "the most overrated
thing in the world—you know what it is?"

"What?"

"Teenage pussy. That young stuff, you say, oh, man—they
don't even know half the time what to do with it. They're
thinking about their hair. Their minds jump around too much.
From my experience—you don't have to believe this, but it's
true—the best is a younger middle-aged woman recently divorced or widowed. By recently I mean within a couple of
years. I'll qualify that still further. Naturally she's got to be
good-looking and you don't want a real fat one or one that
wears a lot of makeup to hide her age and looks great only in
the Hilton lounge, but after—you know what I mean. It's true.
Good-looking, stylish, middle-aged broads with some background, you know, somebody you can talk to. Otherwise, if all
you want's a jump, get a whore, it's cheaper. No, but you see
stylish tourist ladies—you see them all the time at the King
David, the Hilton, the International. Well, the International,
I'm not so sure. But which ones do you think'd be better in
bed, the tourist ladies that stay at the King David or the ones
that stay at the Hilton? You've been to the Hilton, haven't
you? In Jerusalem?"

"Yeah, I've been there."

"And you know what the King David looks like."

"Sure."

"Okay, which you think would be better?"

"What's the difference?" Davis said.

"I'll tell you," Rosen said, in the kitchen of the desert house,
seated at the table, looking up at Davis standing by the sink.
"The Hilton lady, usually her clothes are more expensive. She
spends a little more on herself, her hair, and she's more likely
to wear designer labels. The King David lady is a little plainer
on the average, though in very good taste. She's quieter and not

as easy to meet. But once you get next to her—you know what I mean—the King David lady is better in bed. You know why?"

"Why?"

"Because usually it's been a longer time since she's had it. She's more grateful and, hence, she gives more of herself."

"That's interesting," Davis said.

"It's a fact, based on research," Rosen said. "Eight out of ten divorced wives of doctors and orthodontists who stay in the King David are better in bed. Make it sound more scientific."

Davis put his cup in the sink. His hand came up and touched the Colt holstered beneath his jacket.

"Well, listen, I'd like to stay and chat with you some more, but I think I better get going."

"You come back," Rosen said, "bring me some Winstons. Hey . . . and my passport."

Rashad had to look for the gray Mercedes; first, standing in the shade of the canopy over the entrance, then seeing he'd have to walk through the aisles of cars. He found it parked down near the end of a row. The engine was running and the air conditioning was on. Rashad stooped at the window on Teddy's side, looking past Teddy at Valenzuela.

"You see him go in? The Marine?"

"He's in there?" Valenzuela straightened.

"It was good I saw him first. I'm standing in the lobby. I turn around, he's walking over to the desk."

"Yeah? What'd he do?"

"He got in a elevator, went upstairs."

"How long ago was that?"

"Five minutes," Rashad said. "I just seen him. I couldn't believe it, I turn around, there he is with his cap on."

"But no sign of Rosen, huh?"

"No, I looked around some."

"How about the girl, Tali?"

"She went up before, with the woman."

Valenzuela nodded. "Then the Marine comes and he goes up. Like they have it arranged." Valenzuela was silent a moment. "You didn't see the girl at the airport. Just the woman."

"That's right," Rashad said.

"So she got a ride or she drove his car. We'll look around for it." Valenzuela was silent again. He shrugged. "Then see what happens."

Edie, sitting on the bed, told them the story of how the charter flight had been canceled yesterday after they'd waited around the airport for hours, of then going back to the Hilton on the tour bus, another hour, and of waiting again while the baggage was unloaded and carried up to the room, of then not having anything to do yesterday afternoon. . . .

Tali sat there patiently. Davis sat there thinking, Come on, get to the end!

. . . Then this morning doing it all over again, going out to the airport at seven, two hours earlier, waiting some more, going through security, and the charter finally leaving at ten.

Why is it so important to her? Davis was thinking.

Why didn't she ask about Rosen? She had asked, yes, how he was. But why wouldn't he be the only thing on her mind? Tali must have talked to her yesterday and explained a little of the situation. Why wasn't she concerned about him? No, people had their own concerns—canceled flights—that were just as important.

He said, "You have his passport?"

"I thought I was going to see him," Edie said, surprised now after all that.

"In case he doesn't get by this way," Davis said. "I don't know what his plans are."

"Well, if that's the way he wants to be," Edie said. "If he wants to keep on being the mystery man . . ."

Davis looked at Tali as the woman went over to her suitcase and pulled out Rosen's safari jacket. Tali glanced at him, but her expression told him nothing.

"Tell him we're leaving here tomorrow afternoon at five-thirty," Edie said. "If he wants to call me, I think it would be nice."

"There's no phone where he is," Davis said. "Maybe you don't understand. He's in a lot of trouble."

Edie came over to hand him the jacket. "Maybe I don't understand," she said. "According to Tali, some crazy people are trying to kill him. But I know he tends to be a little dramatic. The mysterious American living in the Middle East. Am I supposed to believe he's a spy, something like that? I'll say one thing, he's entertaining. But I'm afraid I don't have enough motivation or incentive to wait around while Al Rosen plays his games, or whatever he's doing. If he wants to see me today or tomorrow, fine. If he doesn't, well . . . his passport and sunglasses are in the pocket."

"I'll tell him," Davis said.

Tali brought the black Mercedes up to the front entrance and when Davis got in and they drove off, turning south, she continued to tell him about the woman, saying she thought the woman had no feeling or the woman had something else on her mind.

"She was very nervous yesterday," Tali said, "when I drove her to her hotel. Then I didn't see her again until this morning."

"How about Mati?" Davis said. Find that out first.

"He went back to Tel Aviv."

"You're sure?"

"Yes, I drove him to the highway to hitchhike. The woman . . . I thought she was worried about Mr. Rosen, but now I think she believes I was telling her a story. Something Mr. Rosen thought of to kid her with."

"That's something he can worry about," Davis said, "if he wants to." Davis was half turned on the seat, watching the road through the rear window.

"Yes, if he wants to," Tali said. "But I think she's too old for him."

"He's older than she is."

"He's not. Mr. Rosen is forty. He told me. That woman is at least forty-five. He'll still be young when she's old."

Davis had the jacket on his lap, Rosen's passport in the pocket.

Forget it. People lived in their own world and believed what they wanted to believe. They worried about the wrong things.

Little pissy things with big problems staring at them. Tali was doing it. She believed in Rosen. She honored him. She was probably in love with the old bullshitter and didn't even know it.

"Have you been to the doctor's house?"

"Yes, once with Mr. Rosen."

"You travel with him?"

"Sometimes I do."

"His idea is to leave Israel for a while and then come back."

"Not go to the States?"

"No."

"He talked about that when I saw him last time in Netanya," Tali said. "About going home, if he could do it."

"He's decided he likes it here," Davis said.

"Good. I know, the time I'm with him, he can be very happy."

"He thinks they'll get tired of looking for him after a while."

"Yes, why not? If they see it's so very hard to catch him, then they stop and say oh, well, never mind."

"You and Rosen," Davis said, "you live in a dream world. He's got a friend, or somebody he knows, guy left home, ran out on his wife and kids and owed people a lot of money. He said for ten years this guy hid out, changed his name, moved around. And you know what?—this is what Rosen says—nobody was looking for him. They were glad he was gone. That's the way Rosen thinks it'll be with him."

"I believe it," Tali said.

"Well, if nobody's interested in him, how come they're here?"

"Because of his picture. But that was an accident," Tali said. "He can be careful; it won't happen to him again."

"We've got to get him out of here first," Davis said. "I was thinking, drive him down to Sharm el Sheikh and fly Arkia out of there. Maybe go to Tiberias, someplace like that."

"Of course, all the places he can go, he would never be catched." She shrugged, cocking her head to one side. "Then they get tired and go home. I'm not worry about that part. If he agrees it would be easy."

"What part are you worrying about?" Davis said.

"You." Tali glanced at him and brought her gaze back to the road. "I'm afraid you'll talk to him about fighting a war with them."

"He can do what he wants," Davis said. "I'm not in this anymore. . . . Here's where you turn."

The security man at the south beach checkpoint came over to the car smiling, shaking his head at his friend Teddy Cass. "No, he wasn't by here this morning. I know that car. It's a very good car, the green one, but I still don't see it."

When they had turned around and were heading north again, Teddy said, "Between here and the hotel. That's only about a five-mile stretch. What'd we pass?"

"There was one road," Valenzuela said. "The only one I saw."

"Where?"

"You'll see it."

There was no sign at Wadi Shlomo, only the indication of a road: the two ruts in the hardpack that followed the dry creek bed up into the desert. Rashad got out with an Uzi and ran ahead of the car, scouting each bend and rise, then waving the gray Mercedes to come on. It was slow. Rashad was cautious, but he was also eager and knew it wouldn't be long.

Teddy Cass and Valenzuela held on through the creeping, jolting ride, staring at the windshield. They were eager, too, but also patient, waiting for the sign from Rashad. When he was out of sight, beyond a bend and a stand of scrub trees, and was gone this time for ten going on fifteen minutes, they sat listening to the hum of the air-conditioning unit, the sun glaring hot on the windshield, and neither of them spoke.

Then Rashad was coming back, approaching from the sandy creek bed, slipping, skinning his knee as he came up the bank, but smiling.

21

Tali smiled, happy and relieved, as Rosen hugged her and kissed her on the cheek. He took the short-sleeved safari jacket from the Marine, put it on, buttoning one button, set his shoulders and patted the pockets as they walked past the front of the house to the patio.

"I'm home," Rosen said. "I put this on I can do anything. Tali, you're the cutest little broad in Israel and I love you. What'd you do with Edie? You talk to her?"

Davis saw Tali's expression change, the light go out of her eyes.

"She's waiting for you at the Laromme."

"She's not exactly waiting," the Marine said. "She told us you could call her if you wanted." He saw Rosen's frown. "She thinks you're pulling her chain and she's getting tired of waiting for you."

"*Waiting* for me. She's running all over Israel with my passport. All she had to do was leave it somewhere. She said that? She's tired of waiting?"

"I don't think she understands it," Tali said.

A blue plastic pitcher and four glasses were on the patio table, beneath the umbrella. Rosen put his hand in the pitcher and stirred with one finger. They could hear the ice tinkle, the sound of something cold in the desert sun. The Marine stopped at the edge of the patio and looked back across the yard to the Mercedes in the drive and, past it, to the opening in the stone fence. In a few minutes he'd bring the car up closer to the house. Pull up behind the Camaro and maybe turn it around, pointing at the road.

"Some broads, I'm telling you," Rosen said. "They don't go one step out of their way if it's inconvenient. Okay, if I don't see her—it looks like I won't have time anyway, if we're going to Sharm el Sheikh."

Davis came over. "Why don't you take Tali with you? Have somebody to keep you company." Glancing at her. "I don't think Tali'd mind resting a while, after all the running around she's been doing for you. But let's go inside and talk about it."

When Rosen looked at her, Tali gave her little shrug and said, "It would be fine. Whatever you want me to do."

"I *was* thinking about it," Rosen said. "I'm gonna need a cover, and I'm gonna need somebody to make contact, call my company, tell them to mail a certified check—quit screwing around with the cash idea, take the bank exchange. Listen." He turned to Davis then. "I'm gonna take care of you, too, and I don't want to hear anything about what Mel gave you. Okay?"

"I thought we were friends," Davis said.

"Of course we're friends."

"I mean I didn't sign on for pay."

"I know you didn't. But you've got a funny idea about accepting money I want to help you change. It's nice to stand up and be independent, but you can't be selfish about it. You've got to give me a chance to show off, too, and I do it with money. Okay, we're gonna make some plans. First, though"— he raised the pitcher and began pouring—"we'll have a vodka and orange juice in honor, in recognition, of my two best friends saving my ass."

He was saying, okay? Handing a glass to Tali. Saying, if you need another excuse, think of one, but we're gonna have a drink. Coming over to hand a glass to Davis . . .

Davis saw the blood coming through the breast pocket of the safari jacket, the red popping out and sounds, a grunt from Rosen, the wind knocked out of him, dropping the plastic glass. He heard the grunt and the sound of automatic weapons in the desert and the sound of the glass patio doors shattering with the continuing hard, thin chattering sound of the automatic weapons and Tali's scream, Tali holding Rosen on his feet. Davis thought she had been hit as he grabbed Rosen around the body, tight to his own body, and got him inside, into the near corner against the stucco wall, and eased him down gently. Tali was next to him, on her knees, moaning something in Hebrew, staring at Rosen.

Davis brought the Colt automatic out of its holster and began firing past the ragged edge of the glass door into the desert, making out the figures now lying in the scrub, two of them, as they continued to fire into the room, riddling the figurines in the secretary and the glass in the framed photographs of the Bedouin doctor and his wife, wiping them from the wall. There was a pause, silence.

Waiting for it, Davis ran across the opening and got to the oak table as a burst from the Uzis took fragments from the glass door shattered a lamp. He got to the kitchen window with the Mauser 30-06, jacking a shell into the chamber. He got there in time and squeezed off two rounds at the figure running through the scrub toward the stock tank. The figure stopped dead, hesitated, and ran back, throwing himself behind a low rise. Davis stepped aside. A burst came through the kitchen window, blowing out the panes of glass.

He picked up dish towels from the sink and moved back to the table to stuff 30-06 cartridges in his jacket, then picked up Tali's Beretta and skidded it across the floor, past the oriental rug to where she was kneeling over Rosen. With the rifle, the shotgun, and the old Enfield revolver, he ran back across the wide-open doorway, bringing a quick burst from the desert.

Rosen was propped against the wall, his chin on his chest, looking down at the blood soaking his jacket. The exit wound was just below the right breast.

"It went through you," Davis said.

Rosen looked up at him, glassy-eyed, his mouth open, as Davis opened his jacket and shirt and pressed a folded dish towel against the wound. A bad one, a sucking chest wound, percolating air and blood. With splintered pieces of his ribs in the wound. Rosen's expression said he couldn't believe it. He was perspiring. A cold, clammy sweat. He was in shock.

"Turn over a little."

He helped Rosen roll his body so he could press a dish towel against the entrance wound, which was small and showed very little blood, and then brought him back gently to lie on his back.

"We'll get you fixed up in a minute," Davis said. He took Rosen's right hand and laid it on the towel covering the air-sucking hole in his chest. "Here, keep your hand on it and press, just a little."

"I've been shot," Rosen said.

"You'll be okay. Try not to move."

"I *can't* move. Christ."

That was good, his tone. But he had to calm him down. "Don't fight to breathe. Try and relax."

"I brought them," Tali said. "I made this happen."

Davis glanced at her. "Take your gun, it's on the floor there. Go in the back bedroom and watch the other side of the house."

"They shoot him, it's my fault. . . ." She was looking at Rosen with an awful expression: pain, anguish, wanting to cry, wanting to lie down with Rosen and give up.

"Jesus Christ!" Davis said. "Will you get out in the goddamn bedroom? Go *on*." He picked up the Beretta and forced her to take it.

As she finally moved, he rose with the shotgun and fired both barrels past the edge of the doorway—for noise rather than in a hope of hitting them. There was no return fire, and when he looked he didn't see the figures in the scrub. He reloaded the shotgun and brought the Mauser with him, crawling a few steps to the nearest of the front windows. He had to rise up to push it open. Then he squatted again and laid the Mauser on the window sill. There was no sign of their car. Nothing moved beyond the stone fence. No sounds from the other side of the house. He hoped she had qualified with a handgun. He hoped she wouldn't choke and freeze. Jesus Christ, he thought. What are you doing here? He let his gaze move back along the stone fence, then moved his position to the edge of the doorway and looked out. Nothing. He'd try them.

When he ducked past the opening to the other side, there was no gunfire. There was no movement. No sign of anything from the kitchen window. He moved through the hallway to the bedroom.

Tali stood between the side and back windows, holding the Beretta at her shoulder, the barrel pointing up. She looked over at him and seemed calm now.

"Anything?"

She shook her head. "Is he going to die?"

"I don't know."

"We have to get him to the hospital."

She said it so simply he stared at her and didn't know what to say.

"How're we gonna do that?"

"Tell them he's been shot. Tell them he's dying and they'll go away."

Was she that dumb? No, she was hoping. Or imagining a truce, a cease-fire to collect the wounded. Maybe they did that in the desert. "They won't take our word," Davis said. "And if they come in to look, they'll finish him."

"Then what can we do?"

"See what the doctor's got. There's a medicine chest in the bathroom closet and some pills and stuff."

"He's going to be all right, isn't he?" Wanting him to say yes.

"I've seen a lot worse. You stay here, okay? But don't show yourself in the window."

She nodded and he turned away, going into the bathroom. He hoped there was morphine, though he didn't think the doctor would leave it in the house. The rib fragments would be like knife blades in him. Morphine would help. A goddamn sucking chest wound. He could tell by the sound, the wound trying to breathe, that Rosen had been shot through the lung.

The jacket was ruined, the front of it dyed red in funny designs. The towel beneath his hand felt dry. With his fingers he had probed carefully beneath the towel and pulled his hand away when he felt something wet, something sharp and hard sticking out. Jesus. Something that was part of him. He didn't want to think about it, his body ripped open by a machine-gun bullet, blood pouring out. But it was good that he could think about it. He was here and able to think. He tasted blood in his mouth. He didn't know where the Marine was, or Tali. He had heard their voices before, the Marine yelling something. Not yelling, but his voice hard. It was easier to breathe when he relaxed. Before, he had thought he was suffocating, or drowning. Now it was easier and he felt less afraid of not being able to breathe, though he was nauseated and afraid he might throw up. The sound was still there when he breathed, like bubbles in a straw, but not that loud. It was difficult to move. It felt as if a spike had been driven through him, holding him to the floor. He felt the floor moving, someone walking. The Marine was close, kneeling now, looking at him.

"How you doing?"

"Christ, I got shot. You know it?"

The Marine had white towels and some other things in his arms, setting them on the floor.

"Let's get you fixed up," Davis said. "You're gonna have to roll over again, on your left side."

He felt the coat pulling and heard the scissors then.

"You cutting my jacket off?" Somewhat alarmed.

"You can get a new one," Davis said. He raised Rosen's arm to pull the right side of the jacket from Rosen's body. "Look at these. See if you know what they are." He put several bottles of pills, without labels, on the floor by Rosen's face. "You picked the right house. We've got compress bandages, sulfa powder—what do you see there?"

"Aspirin, tranquilizers . . . halizone tablets," Rosen said.

"Dramamine, in case we get seasick. Where's Tali?" Again alarmed, remembering she was here.

"She's all right, she's in the bedroom. Hold still."

He got Rosen's wounds dressed, front and back, and brought him blankets and pillows—a pillow for his head and one to elevate his feet—deciding this corner of the front room might be the safest place in the house.

Rosen felt the Marine walking across the floor again. Then felt more vibrations with sounds that went through him. He turned his head to look. The Marine was moving furniture around. Christ, rearranging the room. No, he was pushing the heavy couch and easy chairs into the open doorway of the patio, turning them over to form a flowery barricade of cushions.

"I'm thirsty," Rosen said.

He heard someone calling then, from outside.

"The goddamn Marine," Valenzuela said. "He's in there, he's got no business being there. How much's he paying him? He could've left—you know what I mean? He sees how it is, shit, he knows. But he comes back here."

"He's paying him *some*thing," Rashad said. "Man ain't doing it for the love of his country. Say he shoots for money. We say to him how much does he want to quit shooting, walk away and mind his business."

"I don't know," Valenzuela said. "If it's like that, if he's got a price, then maybe we ought to find out."

Teddy came in a crouch along the stone fence to the spot where they were sitting on the ground, near the open gate. Teddy had stayed out there, looking for a shot.

He said, "Well, what do you think?"

Valenzuela looked at him. "What do I think? What do *you* think, for Christ sake?"

"I'm pretty sure we got him," Teddy said. "Didn't you see him? He stumbled, the Marine and the girl, it looked like both of them grabbed him."

"I didn't see him stumble," Valenzuela said. "I saw the Marine pull 'em into the house. Fucking Marine, I'll tell you."

"Listen, I know we hit him," Teddy said, "and I think it was me. I had it right on his back. You said go, I pinned him, I know it."

"If he was dead," Rashad said, "it would be over. They wouldn't have no reason to stay in the house."

"I didn't say he was dead," Teddy said. "No, but I'm pretty sure I hit him. You know, it looks like a setup. They're in the hole, nothing they can do. Trapped. But they got a place. They got food, water, whatever, and we're out here in the fucking rocks. What if somebody comes along? I mean we don't have time to sit around. If he's still alive, then we've got to finish it."

"Why don't you rush the house?" Rashad said. "All he's got is a rifle, a shotgun, and some other shit. He could even have the place mined. You know it?"

"We got to get him out of there," Valenzuela said.

"Or keep him busy," Teddy said. "Say if I could get up there close enough to plant a charge. One of you—how about this? One of you go up and talk to him. See if he'd just as soon go home alive. I'll take some stuff, see what I can do. Put a hole in the place and we drive in."

"Let's do it," Valenzuela said. He looked at Rashad. "Call him. Tell him you want to talk."

"You want me to do it?"

"You're his buddy," Valenzuela said. "Go on."

Rashad moved to the stone fence on his knees and gradually began to pull himself up.

"Hey, Marine!"

The rifle shot sang off the rim of stone and ricocheted into the desert. Rashad was on the ground again. He looked up at the top of the fence and at the sky.

"Hey, my man! . . . We not mad at you! We want to talk!"

Rashad was waving something white, a handkerchief. Standing in the open gate now, testing him. Or testing himself.

Davis put the front sight of the Mauser on Rashad's chest.

Now the skinny one with the hair was coming out, starting up the drive with Rashad, both of them holding their hands out from their sides.

"No guns!" Rashad called.

170

Shoot them. It was in Davis's mind.

The third one appeared then, Valenzuela, standing up behind the stone fence that was waist-high on him. Valenzuela held his arms out.

Davis moved the rifle sight to the left a few inches, held in on Valenzuela, then moved it back to the two figures coming up the drive.

"Come on out and talk," Rashad said. He began to angle across the coarse grass toward the house, still holding the white handkerchief. The one with the hair continued up the drive, looking toward the house, the three of them becoming more spread out as they approached. Maybe armed, but not with Uzis. Not Rashad or the one with the hair. Maybe pulling something, but not, apparently, coming to shoot.

Rashad said, "How's Mr. Rosen?" He waited. "If you ain't gonna talk, my man, how we gonna have a talk?"

Valenzuela was still moving along the fence. The one with the hair was approaching the rear of the black Mercedes, still looking toward the house.

Davis glanced over his shoulder. "Tali! Come here!" He looked at Rosen and saw his eyes open with a startled expression, the glassiness gone.

"What is it?" Rosen said. His eyes began to roll back again.

Rashad, in front of the house now, thirty meters away, said, "Hey, David, we got nothing against you, man. We got no reason to hurt you."

Tali, coming into the front room, said, "What? Is he all right?" Looking at Rosen, then seeing Davis at the window with the rifle.

"Watch the one in the driveway," Davis said. "Take the shotgun." The Kreighoff was next to him, leaning against the sill. "Can you shoot it?"

"I think so."

He watched her as she pushed a window open and raised the Kreighoff, extending it through the opening.

"Who's that," Rashad said, "Mr. Rosen? No, hey, that ain't Mr. Rosen, is it? Where's he at?"

"Get down," Davis said to Tali.

"Look," Rashad said then, "we got nothing against you or

her either. The two of you can get in the car, man, and leave. But if you stay here ... shit, you gonna die. You know that. For what? Some money? How much he paying you?"

Valenzuela had stopped. Now he was moving along the fence again, almost even with the patio. Fifty meters to Valenzuela.

Thirty to Rashad.

"David!" Tali's voice. "He's behind the car!"

Davis swung the Mauser. He could see the one with the hair through the side windows of the Mercedes. She should have fired and kept him back, but it was expecting too much. It would have happened too quickly for her.

Davis aimed at the rear-door window and fired and saw the window and the window on the other side fragment in a web of lines, drilled cleanly by the high velocity 30-06, the figure back there suddenly gone. Rashad was running. Davis swung the Mauser on him, then went down as the windows exploded with the hard clatter of Valenzuela's weapon and pressed against the wall below the sill, seeing Tali on the floor with the shotgun, embracing it, holding on tight, her eyes squeezed closed. The sound stopped.

Davis rose up. He saw Rashad running for the gate. He saw Valenzuela behind the fence with the Uzi. He fired at Valenzuela, squeezing off two rounds, seeing him drop behind the fence, swung the Mauser and tried to nail Rashad with the two rounds he had left, but not in time. Rashad was through the gate. There was no sign of the third one. He had run off into the scrub, beyond the car.

"I took a pretty good look," Valenzuela said. "I didn't see the hole we're supposed to drive a car through in the wall. In fact, I didn't hear any explosion at all."

"I changed my mind," Teddy said. "I think when I saw the rifle sticking out the window, fucking elephant gun. I started picturing what this guy must look like in his uniform with the ribbons and medals and I figured one of them said 'expert.' Not somebody throwing wild shots, *expert.* Fucking Marines, they got all that shit on them, all the medals. But wait." Teddy had a cigarette in his hand and paused before lighting it, looking from Valenzuela to Rashad. "Did I come back empty-handed? You bet I did."

"What'd you do with it?" Valenzuela said.

"I stuck a wad under the left rear fender. The wire goes out into the bushes over there."

"What's that do for us?" Valenzuela said.

"Blow the car. Show 'em they're not going anywhere."

"Or wait and see if they try and *use* the car," Rashad said. "Thinking they can sneak out across the desert after it gets dark. Man, if we gonna be here that long—and I don't see why we won't."

It was a good possibility. Teddy left in the gray Mercedes— parked down the wadi from the stone fence—to run into Eilat and get some supplies, some food and something to drink, like ice-cold beer. They'd never felt the sun press so hot. Got them cornered, Rashad said, and we the ones dying of thirst.

He said to Valenzuela, after Teddy had left, "They can stay in there a week, but we can't stay out here. We can cut the electric wire, it wouldn't hurt them none. We can mess up their water pump, they probably got something else to drink. You understand what I'm saying?"

"We got to get to the Marine," Valenzuela said. "Christ, I know that."

"Yeah, but with something he can see," Rashad said. "We tell him we don't want to kill him. What does he think about that? It's not something he can see and say yeah, I want that. It's only driving away from here, having in his head he left Rosen. You understand? But we offer him something good— hey, look at this—then he's got something else in his head when he drives off. Or when he thinks he's gonna drive off."

"Offer him money," Valenzuela said. "What else?"

"No, that's it, money. But how much we got? You gonna write him a check? But see, we offer him a whole *pile* of money, then his head starts working and he can give himself excuses for leaving, like, we gonna get Rosen anyway ... he can't stay with Rosen the rest of his life ... he's not responsible for the man. Things like that. He can take something from us and say why not, the man's gonna die anyway."

"Where's the pile of money?" Valenzuela said.

"I believe the lawyer's got it," Rashad said. "How big a pile, I don't know, but the Arab kid said he had money, my buddy. See, after the money was supposed to've been delivered the lawyer's still here. Least he was yesterday. So I don't believe he delivered it. I believe the lawyer's still got Rosen's money, waiting for Rosen to come get it."

"We don't know that," Valenzuela said.

"No, but there's a way we can find out," Rashad said. "How long's it take to drive to Tel Aviv, four hours?"

Valenzuela pulled the highway map out of his coat pocket and, sitting with his back to the stone fence, opened it to the mileage chart.

"Three hundred and forty-two kilometers." Valenzuela began to nod, estimating time and distance. "Yeah, you could be back here in eight, nine hours. It's an idea. Maybe bring Mel with you."

"I was thinking that," Rashad said. "Use him to talk, so we won't be exposing our bodies. Standing out there, man, playing the friendly nigger, that ain't my style."

Holding the Mauser on the stone fence fifty yards away, knowing they were there, behind the fence or maybe in the shade of some scrub, he imagined telling Master Sergeant T. C. Cox about it.

"See, they came up the drive with their hands held out from their sides, showing they were unarmed. The other one was over behind the wall."

T. C. Cox: The ones trying to kill you.

DAVIS: Yeah, trying to kill this Rosen.

T. C. Cox: Trying to kill you too, as I understand it.

DAVIS: Well, at this point it looked like they wanted to talk.

T. C. Cox: What was there to talk about? They wanted to kill you.

DAVIS: See, the girl was covering the one with the hair, but he got behind the car.

T. C. Cox: He got behind the car. What'd you let him do that for?

DAVIS: Well, the girl was watching him.

T. C. Cox: I thought you watched the both of them come up the drive.

Davis: I did.

T. C. Cox: Then why didn't you kill them?

Davis didn't hear himself say anything.

T. C. Cox: What were you waiting for?

Davis: All that sitting around the embassy like a bank guard . . .

T. C. Cox: You had the chance. Why didn't you kill them?

It scared hell out of him. How fast you could forget how to react.

22

During the afternoon he changed Rosen's dressing. There was very little blood now, but the wound bubbled and sucked air when he uncovered it and put on another compress. He knew Rosen heard the sound.

"I'm breathing out of both ends," Rosen said. He rinsed his mouth with water and spit it in the pan Davis had placed next to him. There was a milk bottle for when he had to take a leak, but he hadn't used it yet.

"I'm not supposed to drink, how about if I smoke?"

"Your lung's got enough trouble," Davis said.

"I won't inhale. No, it'd be a good time to quit. You know how many times I've quit in the last year? That goddamn fire—you know, I started smoking again right after that. Pack and a half a day . . . hey . . . what's gonna happen?"

"I'm going out when it gets dark," Davis said.

"Get help? The police?"

"It'd take too long, a couple hours or more. I just want to look around. I've got some plastic in my car, but not much wire and no way to fire it, unless we hook it to a light switch. But that would be if we were pretty desperate. Get them coming in. Your car's sitting out there. Tali says she left the key in it. Maybe that's a way, if we can get you to the car. Shoot out through the back. But I don't know—shit, there isn't any road back there. It's all rocks and gullies. The other thing, one of them was by your car and he might've rigged it with a charge. I don't know, but I better find out."

"Or tell them okay, you'll leave," Rosen said. "Take Tali and get out of here. I appreciate it—listen, you don't know, but this doesn't have anything to do with you."

"You want them to shoot Tali?"

"That's what I'm talking about, if she stays here. If *you* stay," Rosen said.

"You think we walk out there they won't shoot us? Alive, we're witnesses. Dead, we go in the same hole you do."

"We're gonna get out," Rosen said. "Right?"

Davis nodded.

"I mean what I said—I'm gonna give you something," Rosen said. "In fact you can name it. Anything I've got, you can have." Rosen was silent a moment. "Listen, if I die . . ."

"If you want to live, then live," Davis said. "That's what you do. You don't think about anything else."

"It's funny the things you do think about." Rosen smiled. "Dr. Morris comes home—holy shit, what happened to my house? I keep seeing his face. Thinking about the expenses I'm gonna have, then it isn't so funny."

"You need a couple of windows in your car," Davis said.

"And the other one, the gray one—Christ, how about those guys using my car?—I imagine it's all shot up." Rosen shook his head. "It's funny what you think about. It's funny I'm not more scared. But I think, well, whatever happens—it's interesting because something like this, you can imagine, has never happened to me before. Like watching it and not being in it. Is that how you look at it? I was thinking how it might be in combat. It's always the other guy who's gonna get hit, isn't it? Well, okay, whatever happens. It's interesting . . . I know a guy had a lung collapse on him. He said it hurt like a son of a bitch, something about the lining—I didn't understand that part—but he said they pumped it back up. I guess I got some broken ribs, too. Well, I had that before in a car accident. Rear-end collision, I went into the fucking steering wheel. But they're all broken off, aren't they?"

"The wound's clean," Davis said. "We keep it clean, everything else can be fixed."

"I'm glad you know what you're doing," Rosen said. "You may not feel the same way, but I'm glad you're here. As I told you once before—Christ, just last night, it seems like a week ago—you'll make it. You've got a nice natural style."

"How do you spell it?" Mel said to the girl sitting next to him at the Pal Hotel bar. She was fairly good-looking—dark skin, rosy makeup, and black black hair. Mel figured she would have a very heavy black bush. He liked that.

When she had spelled her name for him he said, "That's Guela. Ga-way-la."

"No, no," the girl said. "Geh-oo-lah. Say it."

"Gay-woo-la," Mel said. "That's Jewish, huh?"

"Yes, Hebrew."

"I never heard it before. Isaac?"

Itzak, the barman, came over. "Yes, please, Mr. Bondy."

"Same way. Campari and soda. Give her one."

The girl smiled and thanked him and moved a little closer, hanging her hip off the stool to touch his thigh.

"Save it," Mel said. "I'm buying a drink. We haven't agreed I'm buying anything else. How much?"

"Four hundred lira." Quietly, close to him.

"Your ass."

"Yes?"

"That means you're high. It's too much."

"Too much? The same as fifty dollar."

"The same as fifty dollar is three hundred lira," Mel said.

"Today's rate of exchange at the Bank of Israel, determined by the devaluation of the common-market dollar discount. And if you believe that, we can go upstairs and fall in love."

"All right," the girl said. "Three hundred lira."

"How many times?"

"How many times? One time. How many times you good to do it for?"

That's how it happened that Rashad found Mel with his white ass up in the air, his face buried in a pillow, and Guelah doing her routine, moaning and gasping with her eyes open.

Rashad pressed the barrel of the Beretta into Mel's left buttock and said, "Now, if you can keep going, my man, *that's* savoir faire."

Rosen said to Tali, who was sitting close to him in the darkness, "I'm gonna tell you something I never told anybody before."

"Yes?"

"I'm part Jewish." He waited.

Tali said again, "Yes?"

"Well, are you surprised?"

"I always think you are a Jew," Tali said. "What does it mean *part?* Part of what?"

"You thought I was? Why?"

"I don't know." Tali shrugged. "I always think it. Your appearance . . ."

"Come on."

"Your name . . ."

"My name, I made up the name. You know who I really am? Baptized? James C. Ross. Jimmy Ross. But most people, even my wife, called me Ross."

"It's a nice name, Ross. It's not Hebrew?"

"I don't know, I guess some people named Ross are Jewish, but I didn't know that, because my mother was Irish, her name was Connelly, and she was always talking about the Irish, like there was something special about them, a gift, or talking about her people coming from Cork. So I thought Ross was Irish almost all my life. Then when my dad died—I was nineteen, I came home from the service for the funeral—I found out our name originally was Rosen. My dad's grandfather changed it when he came over from England. But see, nobody on my dad's side ever practiced the Jewish faith, so I didn't know anything about it till I came here. And you know what? It's interesting. I don't buy all the kosher business, Christ, the diet laws. What does almighty God care if you eat butter with steak? He's got enough to think about, all the fuck-ups in the world. But the history and all, it's interesting."

"My name, Atalia, is from the history time."

"Is that right? I thought it meant from Italy."

"No, it's from very far back, but I don't read about it in a long time."

"See, you're the new breed," Rosen said. "You can't be bothered with religion, all the ceremony."

"We have our meal together, the family, on Friday evening," Tali said. "I still want you to meet my mother sometime."

"What do I want to meet your mother for? She fool around?"

"No, of course not."

"What do you mean, of course not. You probably don't even know her. You ever talk to her about what she feels and thinks, what you feel? Kids don't know their parents. They grow up and start thinking about them as real people after they're dead. People waste time, years, playing games with each other—who am I?—and never get to know anybody."

"Is this true?" Tali said.

"Yes, it's true," Rosen said. "I think I'm getting close to something, a truth about how to live life and not waste it or mess up. I'll get it clear in my mind and tell you about it."

"I would like to hear that," Tali said. "Learn what to do with my life before I get old."

"It's simple," Rosen said. "It's not easy, but it's simple."

When Tali rose and moved away he could hear the Marine talking to her. Then the Marine came over—feeling his steps on the floor—and crouched down next to him. He could see the Marine's face in the light from the window as the Marine stared outside. Looking down at him, the Marine's features vanished in the dark.

"You want to know something?"

"What?" the Marine said.

"I never told anybody this before and you may not believe it, but I'm part Jewish."

"Yeah?"

The Marine didn't seem impressed.

"I don't mean I'm a convert. I mean I was born part Jewish, on my father's side."

"Is that right?"

"You don't believe me."

"I never thought you weren't Jewish," the Marine said. "Listen, I'm going out again. I looked around back, there's nobody there, like they don't think we'd try to leave that way. I don't know if it does us any good, I've got to see if we might use your car first. Or see if I can catch them asleep or looking the other way. I don't think they're much for watch-standing. You hang in there and we'll get this thing done soon as we can."

"Why'd you think I was Jewish?" Rosen said.

It was not the same darkness as Indochina. The sky seemed wider and closer here because of the desert. The shadows seemed different, or there were fewer shadows because there was less vegetation. He would have to get used to the shadows. Then he hoped he wouldn't be here long enough to learn a new set of shadows.

Going out of the doctor's house was not the same as going out of a helicopter after sitting with his eyes closed during the fifteen- or twenty-minute flight, opening his eyes and going out black-faced with a recon patrol. It was different. But he was not afraid of being alone in dark places. The difference here was that he knew what the enemy looked like. They had faces. And they knew what he looked like and could be expecting him, even dressed in Dr. Morris's black coat sweater and dark gray trousers. He had taken his cap off for the first time in two days.

It was 3:20 A.M. when he left the house.

He moved around back, past the dry stock tank that might have been used at one time for goats or sheep. Or maybe the doctor had kept horses. The blades at the top of the windmill structure stood motionless. The desert was empty, its shadows motionless. People were close, but there were no sounds and nothing moved. He had said to Tali, "Don't shoot me when I go by a window or when I come back."

From the side of the house he moved into the carport, working his way along between the tarp-covered Camaro and the cement wall. He thought about going under the tarp to get the C4 on the back seat. But what would he do with it if he couldn't run out a line and explode it? Shooting the plastic with a bullet wouldn't set it off. It took an electrical charge. Or what would he do if he got under the tarp and they knew he was there? They'd wrap him up in it. So leave the C4.

The black Mercedes was down the drive about twenty meters, almost halfway to the gate in the stone fence. (He remembered Tali stopping there when they arrived, wondering why she hadn't driven up to the house. But then he remembered she had seen Rosen coming from the patio and had stopped abruptly and jumped out to run to meet him.) From the carport he studied the black Mercedes gleaming in the darkness, about forty thousand dollars' worth of car in Israel. Rosen had a pretty good life. It wouldn't be hard to get to the car. Davis slipped his hand into the unbuttoned top of the coat sweater and drew his Colt.

On his belly now, using elbows and knees, he moved from the carport to the front bumper of the Mercedes. He listened. He rolled to his back and inched under the car, using his heels now, moving close to the wheels on one side because the spine of the driveway was high between the wheel ruts. His hand moved over the underbody and frame. He didn't think he would find anything. The one with the hair hadn't had time to get underneath. The guy hadn't opened a door, Davis was pretty sure of that. He pulled himself out on the desert side of the Mercedes, remained low, and felt along the rocker panel to the rear-wheel housing, feeling inside the fender above the left rear wheel and there it was, a hunk of plastic with the wire coming down and trailing out to the side. The guy hadn't tried to hide the wire; he hadn't had time. The wire was wedged beneath the tire and led off across the gravel to the edge of the property, where the detonator would be. Or else the wire made a turn there, around the base of a tree, and continued down toward the front of the property, to the stone fence. That was more likely, so the guy would be there with his buddies and not have to sit off in the scrub. They'd be nervous and want to be together. They were from a city. They'd sit out here in the bush and see things and have to be cool in front of one another.

They were somewhere behind the stone fence. Davis had to assume that. The fence was protection. They weren't spread out the way they should be—the way he would have positioned them—so they were back there. He hoped they were close behind the fence, near the gate. If they were, there was a good chance of finishing it.

He holstered the Colt, then pried the C4 from beneath the curve of the wheel housing and pulled out the blasting cap attached to the wire. Belly-down again, with the end of the wire in one hand and the hunk of plastic in the other, he began inching along the driveway toward the stone fence. He hoped there was enough wire. He wouldn't have to go all the way. . . .

Get close enough. Stick the cap in the plastic again and throw it against the stone fence.

They might hear it, they might not.

He'd be moving then, back to the Mercedes. Reach in and turn the key.

They'd hear the engine start.

The one with the hair would run to his detonator.

The other two would come to the stone fence.

Davis got to within ten meters of the fence. He waited, listening, pulled the wire toward him, slowly, bringing it across the gravel and coarse grass, then planted the blasting cap in the ball of plastic. Rising to his knees, he again drew the Colt out of the sweater. He threw the ball of plastic underhand and watched it arc toward the fence. It disappeared in darkness against the stones.

He was moving back toward the Mercedes when he heard

the sound, a faraway groaning sound—a car laboring in low gear—coming from somewhere in the desert. He looked back. Beyond the fence and past a stand of trees, a beam of light was reflecting off the rocks.

23

All that time being Jimmy Ross had been a long time. It seemed longer than the twenty-five years or more he was just Ross. He had been Rosen hardly any time at all.

Growing up, it was a matter of always looking into the future for something, always hoping or planning for something, never knowing when you would get there and not knowing it when you did. Jimmy Ross to Ross to Rosen. He wondered what the real Al Rosen was doing, if he was still in Cleveland.

All right, this Rosen was here. He had finally made it. It had taken him fifty years to learn that *being* was the important thing. Not being something. Just being. Looking around you and knowing you were being, not preparing for anything. That was a long time to learn something. He should have known about it when he was seven, but nobody had told him. The

185

only thing they'd told him was that he had to be *some*thing. See, if he'd known it then, he'd have had all that time to enjoy being. *Except it doesn't have anything to do with time,* he thought. Being is an hour or a minute or even a moment. Being is being, no matter where you are. In a house in the Sinai desert at night. But if you have to be somewhere, why not be somewhere good?

Sitting by the pool at the Laromme. In another few weeks it would be too hot, unbearable, in Eilat.

Netanya, on the Mediterranean.

Or go over to one of the Greek islands. See if there was a difference between Hydra tourist ladies and Mykonos tourist ladies.

No, he had done that, the tourist-lady comparing. Do something else.

Or don't do anything. Sit. You don't have to do anything, he told himself. You don't have to prove anything.

"Avoid running at all times. And never look back. Something might be gaining on you." Rules for success and happiness courtesy of Satchel Paige, who had missed playing with the Original Al Rosen by a couple of years.

Make sense?

Yes, of course. Tali said that. Yes, of course. Tali was nice and it would be nice to tell her things and watch her nod seriously and then laugh when she saw he was kidding. But that was planning and he wasn't going to plan. He was going to do nothing. He began to think that it would be better to do nothing in the sunlight than in the dark. Thinking was doing something. He wished he could stop thinking. He wished it wasn't dark. He wished he wasn't nailed to the floor and could move. He wished he could swallow some water. He wished he wasn't cold. He wished he didn't feel as if he were drowning. He wished he hadn't talked to the government lawyers. No, he thought then, you had to have done all that to be where you are and know what you know. Unless he could have learned the same thing serving a one-to-five at Lewisburg for conspiring to defraud the United States government. With time off for good behavior. Yes, he was pretty sure he could have learned it at

Lewisburg. The point being that learning required a change of attitude and sometimes, usually, pain. He knew that but wasn't sure how he knew it. He wondered if it would do any good if he called out for his mother. Shit, Rosen thought. Just when he was getting there.

24

(Two things were happening at the same time.)

The wheels of the gray Mercedes, Mati driving, had skidded off the wadi trail into deep sand. The left rear wheel was spinning as Mati gunned it and as Rashad and Valenzuela grunted, trying to push the car out with their hands. Valenzuela was asking Rashad why he had let the Arab kid drive, for Christ's sake, and Rashad said because he was a driver, it's what he did, ar.d had driven fine all the way from Tel Aviv. Then Valenzuela blew up, realizing Mel was sitting on his fat ass in the front seat with Mati while he and Rashad were doing the work. He yelled at Mel to get his ass out here, then said to Mati okay, hold it, turn it off for a minute. They were down the wadi trail a short distance. Around the next bend and past the stand of trees was the stone fence. Valenzuela looked up to see Teddy, his submachine gun slung over his shoulder, standing in the low headlight beams.

(The other thing that was happening, in the yard of the desert house, was that Davis was reaching into the black Mercedes to turn on the ignition.)

Valenzuela said, "Hey, would you like to come help us?"

"I thought I heard something," Teddy said.

They all heard it then: the sound of a car engine starting.

Teddy turned and was gone.

Valenzuela had to stop and look around for his Uzi lying on the ground and pick it up. And Rashad hesitated a moment, looking at Mel standing there and thinking about Mel's attaché case in the back seat of the car. So the two of them started off well behind Teddy.

They got to the bend in the road and saw Teddy reach the gate and cut left, over into the scrub where he had hidden his detonator box. They saw the black car up in the yard and could hear the engine rumbling and in that moment Rashad saw something else, a figure, something, moving across the yard toward the patio. He paused to pull his Beretta and began firing as Valenzuela saw the movement and opened up with the Uzi, spraying bursts at the front of the house. The pause saved their lives.

Teddy, looking at the black Mercedes, turned the switch on his detonator box.

A twelve-foot section of the stone fence exploded in a black shower of sand and smoke and rock fragments.

Valenzuela was hit by bits of rock and took Rashad with him over the edge of the cutbank into the wadi. They tried to cover their heads as the hard fragments pelted down on them.

Rashad was up first. He found Teddy in the bushes with blood coming out of his dusty hair, streaming down his face, still holding the detonator box. Now Valenzuela was partway out of the wadi, firing over the bank at the front of the house, raking the windows until the clip was empty.

Rashad said to Teddy, "Say you the explosives expert, huh? Say shit."

* * *

Davis waited on the patio until the machine-gun fire stopped. He rose by the tipped-over couch and reached into the darkness of the room.

"Tali, hand me the rifle." She sat looking down at Rosen and began to turn only when he said, "Come on, give me it!" and reached for the Mauser leaning against the front windowsill.

Handing it to him, she said, "David—"

"Stick the shotgun out and keep watching. I'm gonna try and scare something up, see if we got any of them."

"David—" Her voice low, subdued.

But he was gone, across the patio and moving in a low crouch into the desert, still hearing her voice, the sound of it— no excited questions about the explosion—and then she was gone from his mind as he reached patches of scrub growth and made his way down to the stone fence, to the place where it ended and wire strung between posts continued out into the desert.

He went over the wall crouched, looking down the length of wedged, fitted stones to the rubble of broken stones he could see as an outline, a mound in the darkness. There were shapes he did not wait to study, something moving. Davis opened fire, squeezing off five solid rounds, hearing them sing off the rocks, and went over the wall into the yard and crouched low again as he reloaded the Mauser. He waited, but there were no sounds, only what was left of a ringing sensation close to his head. He waited a quarter of an hour for some sign from them, but heard nothing.

Davis returned to the house the way he had come, crossed the cement patio, and stepped over the sofa barricading the doorway.

Tali rose from the corner, coming to him out of deep shadow.

"I try to tell you about Mr. Rosen," Tali said.

Davis looked down, seeing only Rosen's legs in the faint light from the window.

"How is he?"

"He died," Tali said.

25

Maybe they'd used to wail and pull their hair. The Marine thought of that. The girl was making herself feel responsible, punishing herself, not crying much but making sounds as though she were in pain. It wasn't a reasonable laying of blame, it was more like a rite: working herself up to feel guilt and anguish.

The Marine held her and stroked her gently, feeling a little self-conscious, staring out the window and across the yard to the stone line, the boundary.

Finally he sat her on the floor by the window and looked at Rosen, his hands one over the other holding the clean compress bandage. He felt Rosen's throat for a pulse, then closed his eyelids, listening to the girl string *ifs* together: if she had realized ... if she had gone to the police instead of the hotel ... if she had been alert and not led them here . . . The Marine was patient for a while; he gave her time. He sat with her and put his arm around her, bringing her close to him, as he would comfort a child, occasionally making his own sounds—"I'm sorry . . . I know how you feel, but . . . no, don't say that . . ." —trying to ease her sounds of pain. She would say things to him in Hebrew in the mournful tone and it would sound even more ceremonial to him, from a time thousands of years ago when a man had died in the desert and the women huddled by a fire. He tried to think of things to say to her that would help. Her eyes were closed, squeezed closed. He wondered how long she would keep it up, if she would stop abruptly or just wind down from exhaustion and fall asleep. He didn't know what to say that would help or what to do other than hold her. She told him she wanted to die. She told him Mr. Rosen would be alive if it weren't for her. She told him Mr. Rosen had trusted her and she had failed him and now she couldn't live with herself anymore.

He said to her, "He's dead. What you do to yourself doesn't change it."

She wasn't listening to him. She said, "He was going to be safe. Go to Sharm el Sheikh or Santa Katarina and stay there and be safe with me to help him. He said to me, he called me to come and said, 'Atalia, I want you to have something.' He said in his billfold was the key to the safe box of his bank. He said he wanted me to have it, to sign his name the way he signed it, with the initials, and take out the money. I said, 'Why? It's your money.' He said, 'No, now it's yours.' I said, 'But why?' He didn't say anything more. I went away to look out the windows—"

"Then he knew it," Davis said.

"I came back . . . I felt him, I breathe in his mouth. . . ."

He took her face in his hand and raised it to look at him and waited until her eyes opened.

"He's dead," Davis said. "They killed him." Her eyes closed and she tried to turn her head. "Look at me. *They* killed him."

"But it wouldn't have happen . . ."

"Look at me!"

Her eyes opened—her face close enough to see into her eyes and what she was feeling, the little girl experiencing something beyond her imagination, in a place she had never been before.

"They killed him," Davis said. "But they don't know it."

She was listening now, beginning to come back into the world. "We tell them?"

Davis shook his head. "No, we don't tell them."

"But if we say we want to take his body with us for burial, they would understand. Everyone respects that."

Davis's hand relaxed and brushed her cheek as he let it drop to her shoulder.

"I think if they knew he was dead they'd leave and wouldn't bother about us. Mr. Rosen said it was like a business with them. They don't have personal feelings about it. If it's done, then they're not gonna sit out there in the heat just to get at us. See, I don't think they care. I don't think they're afraid of what would happen if we told them. They'd already be gone."

"I don't understand," the girl said. "We don't do anything?"

"I don't want them to leave yet," Davis said.

"Why?"

"I'd like to talk to them again."

"But why?"

He was staring out the window at the first trace of morning, pale strips of light rising beyond the desert and the sea and the Arabian mountains.

"I've got something to say to them," Davis said.

"Call to them to come out."

"I don't know yet how I want to say it," Davis said. "But I will."

Tali made coffee and sat with her cup, staring at Mr. Rosen, remembering him saying funny things to her. At times she would smile. She didn't bother the Marine now, who sat with his legs folded and his back sloping, staring out the window at the yard and at the opening in the stone fence that was wider now with part of it blown away. She let him be with himself.

Valenzuela's shoulder hurt where he had fallen on it going into the wadi. His head hurt, too, but not as much as Teddy's.

Teddy needed stitches. He had tied a patterned scarf around his head and with his hair and bodyshirt he looked like an art deco pirate.

Rashad was the only one who sat on the cutbank of the wash and seemed to enjoy the lukewarm beer and dry-roasted peanuts they had for breakfast. He was very patient. He had let Valenzuela sleep and wake up stiffly to see the morning before showing Val and Teddy all the money in the alligator briefcase. Courtesy of Mel, the little lawyer, sitting over there inside the gray Mercedes that would be like an expensive oven pretty soon. Mel inside and his keeper, the Arab kid, sitting in the sand outside the car, playing with the sand, picking up a handful and letting it sift through a fist like time running out. Rashad liked the picture.

He said, "What's a little temporary discomfort when it's almost done? This is the number gonna bring him out, a hundred and ninety-five." And he tapped the alligator skin of the briefcase, doing a drum roll with his fingers. "Then, I assume, we gonna cut it? Otherwise, I'll tell you I thought about it seriously, I'd never have brought it."

"We cut it," Valenzuela said. "Comes to what? Sixty-something."

"Sixty-five each," Rashad said, "a day's wage." He looked over at Teddy. "Make your head feel better?"

"You want to know something?" Teddy said. "That fence blew, I got fucking stoned. With real stones, man." Yeah, he was feeling better, grinning, thinking sixty-five and five for the job was seventy and he wouldn't have to blow anybody up for two years. He said to Valenzuela, "We don't have to renegotiate, Val, I think this'll be fine."

"You like the picture?" Rashad said. "We use the man's car, now we using the man's bread to take the man out. It's like he's committing suicide, huh? Killing himself with his own bread. Lawyer says to me, 'What money? I don't have no money.' Standing there bare-ass pleading no, I don't have no money, and the whore, she's like this on the bed, leaning on her elbow?"—Rashad placed his open palm against the side of his face—"and with the other hand she's scratching her cooz, listening to us, don't even know she's doing it."

"That lawyer," Teddy said, "I think he likes to go around naked. Time we went to see him he was bare-ass."

"Cuz of his beautiful body," Rashad said. "He like to show it to people. He saying, 'What money, man?' It's under the bed with his airplane ticket. He say, 'Oh, the *comp*'ny money.' He was taking that back to the *comp*'ny today."

Valenzuela wasn't joining in or smiling. He was thinking about the money, yes—sixty-five each, that was all right, he'd split with them and it wouldn't matter to Harry, he'd get a kick out of it, using Rosen's money—but he was also thinking about the Marine.

"How much do we offer him?"

Rashad looked over. "All of it. The whole thing."

"He's gonna smell something," Valenzuela said.

"Sure he is, he's gonna smell money," Rashad said. "We let him look at it and feel it. There it is, sitting on the ground. Pick it up, man. Walk over to your car and drive away."

"Why would we offer him that much?" Valenzuela said. "Don't we want any? I'm talking about what he's thinking."

"Tell him the truth, it's Rosen's money," Rashad said. "We not out anything. See, he knows how much there is. What Mel say, he delivered five of the two hundred grand was sent here. So, we tell him the truth. Here's the rest of it. It ain't our money, he can have it if he walks away. Enough to retire on for life."

"What if he can't be bought?" Valenzuela said.

Rashad shook his head. "Who can't be bought? Name somebody. Shit, we got enough here to buy the whole United States Marines."

"He's gonna see it," Valenzuela said. "It isn't, you know, realistic, handing him that much money."

"That's the whole idea," Rashad said. "Make his eyes big and fuck up his head. When we talking about that much—look, it's sitting right there—the man knows he's taking a chance. See, it's got to be enough to take a chance *for*."

"No." Valenzuela was shaking his head now. "It's too much. There's a limit. You go over it and it isn't real or even possible anymore. Something in his head right away'd say no, don't touch it."

"All right, then don't offer him the whole thing," Rashad said. "Offer him what?"

"Half," Valenzuela said. "A hundred grand. It's a big number, but it sounds real, you know? Also it sounds like we're letting him in on something. We've talked it over and decided to split with him, like we're partners. We're all in it together. You see what I mean?"

"Yeah." Rashad was nodding. "I think maybe you're right. Like we're bringing him in. Uh-huh, so he can feel he's in it enough and can trust us, but not far enough he's helping to kill the man. Yeah, let his head work out that part of it."

"Gene—"

It was Mel's voice, Mel inside the gray Mercedes looking out at them.

"Hey, can I talk to you?"

"Probably has to go pee-pee," Rashad said. "Two times we had to stop so he could go in the ditch."

"You want to use him, huh?" Valenzuela said.

"You want to walk up to the house?" Rashad said. "The Marine gets nervous—that's fine, me and Teddy'll split the money. The lawyer can do it fine. Tell the Marine whatever we want to say."

Valenzuela waved to Mel to come over. They watched him get out of the car squinting, mopping his face with a handkerchief, adjusting the crotch of his light blue trousers, very busy as he approached them.

Rashad said, "Hot enough for you?"

"Man, this is a vacation spot, huh? Eilat?"

"Down closer to the water," Rashad said.

"I know dis ain't de place." Mel was being one of the boys. He said, "You know, I'm supposed to be on a TWA flight out of here—out of Tel Aviv, I mean—at nine o'clock. But doesn't look like I'm gonna make it, does it? I gave up trying to see Rosie. I decided stay out of it; it isn't any of my business."

"You might see him anyway," Valenzuela said, "but the man we want you to talk to is the Marine."

Mel opened his hands to show his innocence. "Look, I got nothing to do with this. What do you want to get me involved for?"

"He doesn't ever know nothing. One of those guys who doesn't know anything," Valenzuela said.

"Have I interfered with you in any way?" Mel said. "Have I given you any trouble? No, I've stayed out of it. You've got the money, okay, I can be very realistic about that. It's company funds. I gave the money to Rosie and something happened to it. It's too bad, I tell the company, but it's their problem or Rosie's. I mean I'm not out anything personally."

"He doesn't want to get involved," Valenzuela said.

"I'm *not* involved. You know that as well as I do."

"He gonna tell the comp'ny we took it from him and the comp'ny tell the FBI or somebody," Rashad said, playing with Mel.

"For what? What good's that do anybody?" Mel said, standing in the hot sun in the Sinai desert with two guys who killed people and didn't believe him. "Look, the company gave it to me to give to Rosen. Okay, as far as anybody knows, I gave it to him. That's the only thing I tell. Otherwise, shit, they might think I kept the money and put it somewhere for a rainy day."

"Which was your original idea," Rashad said.

"Okay, you're gonna think what you want," Mel said. "But believe this, because it's true. There's no way in the world I could finger you or testify against you. I mean even if I wanted to. Because there's no way in the world a complaint could be filed against you in court. What court? Here? Who's the complainant? Not me. In the U.S.? No way. Where are the witnesses? The proof? It would be strictly hearsay, my word against yours. But you think I'd ever be irritated enough to make a statement? What do I get out of that? As I said, I'm not out anything personally and I've kept my nose out of it because it's none of my business. So what more can I say?"

Mel raised his hands in a helpless gesture, looking from Rashad to Valenzuela to Teddy Cass and back to Valenzuela.

"Gene . . . how can I help you?"

"You can quit talking," Valenzuela said. "Clarence'll tell you what you're gonna do."

There had been a car down by the wadi. Davis was sure he had heard a car, and headlight beams reflected on the rocks.

Probably the gray car. One of them had gone to get something, a case of Maccabee and three pizzas to go. One of them could've been sleeping by the wall. Or back somewhere. One of them had triggered the detonator and that one could have also been by the wall. So he might have gotten one, maybe two of them. But he couldn't count on it. There was no way to find out except go down there.

It was eight o'clock, a bright, still morning, the sky filled with glare, cloudless.

Tali, sitting by Rosen's body, looked up as the Marine rose from the window and walked away. He came back unfolding a blanket and draped it over Rosen's body, beginning at his feet, bringing it up, then stopping as he reached Rosen's hands folded on his chest. He knelt down across from her. She watched him turn Rosen's body, reach beneath him, and draw a billfold from the back pocket.

What he was doing gave her a terrible feeling. She couldn't believe it, the Marine looking in Mr. Rosen's wallet and bringing out money. When he tried to hand her the money she drew back and said "No!" surprised at the loudness of her voice.

"Take it. Five thousand dollars and a little more," Davis said. "Here's the key to his bank deposit box."

"I can't."

"You want to bury it with him? Would that make sense?"

"I can't take his money."

"He's giving it to you," Davis said. "You have to take it."

"But in the safe box he had very much money," Tali said. "And this, it's too much for me."

"He told me himself," Davis said, "you have to learn to accept money without your pride getting in the way. He's giving it to you because he liked you, he loved you, so don't insult him and try to change things when he's not here. Do whatever you want with the money. Buy clothes, take tap-dancing lessons if you want. But take it and thank God you knew the man."

He handed her the money and the key, then pulled the blanket up over Rosen, covering his face.

"I didn't know him very long, but I think he taught me a few things." Davis paused, thought for a moment, and said, "The wake's over."

Tali was looking at the money, holding it in front of her. "Will you take some of it?"

She didn't get an answer.

The voice came to them from outside; it was the black one, Rashad, calling out, "Hey, Marine! Here's somebody want to see you!"

26

"No shooting, man! Time's out!"

Rashad stood up at the wall, testing the Marine, giving him a moment.

"You hear? Man's lawyer wants to come out! Have a talk with you!"

He dropped behind the smooth stones again and waited. There was no answer from the house. He didn't expect one. All he wanted to do was get the Marine's attention. He didn't particularly care if the Marine shot Mel thinking it was somebody else, except then they'd have to talk to the Marine some other way, directly, and standing out there wasn't any fun. Now he crawled back to the thicket of dusty trees before rising and moving around the bend in the road to where they were waiting: Valenzuela and Teddy with their machine guns slung over their shoulders, the scared-looking lawyer with his resort outfit on standing between them, holding the alligator case. Mati, the Arab-looking kid, was hunkered down over the cutbank, watching.

Rashad waved for Mel to come on. "Okay, go on up there and give your speech. But stay in the yard. You understand? He invites you in the house, you say, 'No thank you.' "

"I tell him and I come right back," Mel said. "That's all."

"You show him the money," Valenzuela said, "and wait and hear what he says."

Mel nodded quickly. "Okay. And then I come right back."

"Open the briefcase, leave it in the yard," Valenzuela said.

"Right. Leave the case in the yard. I won't forget."

Rashad looked over at Mati. "The kid'll go with you, keep you comp'ny."

Teddy turned, unslinging his Uzi and waving the stubby barrel. Mati got up, wiping his hands on his pants, and came toward them. It didn't seem to matter to him one way or the other.

They held back at the bend in the road, waiting, letting Mel and Mati continue on toward the opening in the stone fence.

"Might as well get everybody in the yard," Rashad said. "Do 'em all at one time."

"It's Mati," Tali said, surprised. "And Mr. Bandy?"

Davis watched them come through the gate and start up the drive, Mel carrying his expensive alligator case. The light blue lawyer and the skinny Yemenite in his fake leather jacket. They didn't go together, wouldn't have anything to say to each other. They had both been pushed into this, brought here—the sound of the car last night, the headlights reflecting in the darkness.

"Did they come here by themselves?" Tali was still speculating. There was no sign of the three gunmen.

But Davis wasn't going to get into a conversation about it. He said, "Take the shotgun. Watch the car and see if anybody tries to circle around the other side. If they do, shoot them. Don't tell me about it, shoot them."

Picking up the shotgun, she looked over at him. His tone was quiet, but he was concentrating now, not wasting words, raising the Mauser and extending the barrel out the window.

"They don't want to come out," Davis said. "They send Mel ... no, there they are." He brought the Mauser to his shoulder but waited. They were beyond the stone fence, near the gate and the section that had been blown apart. He could see little more of them than heads and shoulders and realized that the ground sloped away toward the wadi.

"I see them," Tali said.

He told her to concentrate on the one nearest the gate opening, the one with the long hair and a scarf or bandanna covering his head. Mel and Mati, who was dragging behind, were coming over from the drive now, crossing the grass toward the middle of the yard.

Mel moved carefully, his gaze holding on the front windows. Mati's hands were in his pockets. He seemed to have no purpose other than to watch what was going on.

"Sergeant, you in there?"

"Right here," Davis said.

"I can't see you. . . . Where's Rosen?"

"You want to come in?"

"No, I'm supposed to stay here. Is that Rosen—hey, Rosie, is that you?"

"He's in the can," Davis said.

Mel thought that was funny. "Listen, you mind if I use it after? I've got kind of a nervous bladder. I don't know what the fuck I'm doing here at all." He glanced over his shoulder, then looked back at the windows. "I'm sure you understand this isn't my idea. I'm supposed to be on a plane in half an hour."

"You're not coming in," Davis said, "what do you want?"

"I'm speaking for them, you understand. None of this is my idea."

Davis waited.

"They want to offer you something. A hundred thousand dollars."

The three gunmen were at the stone fence now, not more than a few yards separating them. He would have to squeeze and fire and snap the next two shots, though he would be sure

of getting the first one. Davis placed the front sight on Valenzuela, then raised his head to look at Mel again.

"You hear what I said? A hundred thousand. It's in here."
Mel raised the attaché case.

"For what?"

"If you leave. Get out of here."

"Alone?"

"You can take the girl."

"But leave Rosen, huh? Just a minute." Davis turned to look
at Tali. She was staring at him and seemed more tense than a
few moments before.

"They don't know," Davis said to her.

"But if he's already dead? They'll come in to see him, won't
they?"

Davis looked out at Mel.

"Rosen says he doesn't like the idea."

"Jesus—" Mel was shaking his head. "Look, tell him I'm
sorry, but there's nothing I can do about this. You can stay
here and see what happens or you can accept the hundred
grand and leave. That's it."

"Mr. Rosen's money, huh?"

"What difference does it make?" Mel said. "You want to see
it?" He went down to one knee, placed the attaché case on the
grass, snapped it open, and turned the lid toward him to show
Davis the open case. "Can you see it? That's a hundred grand,
man."

"Where's the rest?" Davis said.

"What rest?"

"We started with two hundred thousand," Davis said. "You
sent him five. Where's the rest?"

"Well, see, what they're doing, they're splitting it with you,
giving you the bigger half. What do you say?"

Davis was silent. He watched some of the hundred-dollar
bills blow out of the case as a wind stirred in from the desert.
Mel said, "Jesus Christ—" and almost fell making a grab for
them.

"All right? Come on, before it blows away."

Davis waited. He said then, "Tell them, they want to give
me the whole thing, it's a deal."

"Christ, this is a hundred grand here!" Mel said. "What do you want?"

"I just told you, I want it all," Davis said. "Or I stay here and they sit out in the sun till the police or an Israeli Army patrol comes along."

"I'll have to ask them," Mel said. He rose, turning, as more bills blew out of the briefcase, and yelled toward the fence, "He says he wants the whole thing!" Mel waited. "What?"

Davis held the sight on Valenzuela. He watched him wave for Mel to come back.

Mel turned to the windows again. "I guess they want to talk it over." Mel stooped to close the briefcase, but Valenzuela called something to him and Mel straightened and walked off, glancing back at the money blowing, swirling across the yard, then motioned to Mati to come with him.

"Watch them," Davis said.

Tali glanced at him, saw him move to Mr. Rosen's body and pull back the blanket. She looked out the window and then at the Marine again. He was lifting Mr. Rosen's hands now—the bent arms rising stiffly with the hands—then drawing the Colt automatic from its holster and placing it on the compress bandage covering Mr. Rosen's wound, making sure the safety was off. It shocked her and made no sense.

"Why are you doing that?"

"Watch outside."

Davis took another compress from the pack of bandages on the floor, placed it over the automatic, and brought Rosen's hands down to cover the compress. The grip of the Colt, part of it, was all that showed.

"Please, what are you *doing*?"

Davis glanced out the window, seeing the five of them at the opening of the fence. He picked up Dr. Morris's heavy Enfield revolver from the floor and tried it in the shoulder holster. It rested too high beneath his left arm. He pulled the gun out and stuck it into the waist of his trousers.

He said to Tali then, "I've thought of what I want to tell them."

* * *

"Say, fine, he can have the whole thing," Rashad said. "What's the difference?"

"Watch them," Valenzuela said to Teddy. He motioned Rashad away from Mel and the Arab-looking kid and they moved down the road toward the gray car.

"He won't believe it," Valenzuela said. "We're agreeing too quick. Why would we do it?"

"You want to sit here," Rashad said, "wait till tomorrow to make it look real? What's the difference? A hundred, a hundred ninety-five, if he smells something he'll smell it either way. No, I believe what he's doing, he's putting it all on one roll. Got nothing to lose. He knows we're playing with the man's money. He sees a chance to take it all. But tell me, how's he gonna get out with it? Man, we're standing there."

"He's pulling something," Valenzuela said.

"Pulling what? He hasn't had time to think about it. He's seeing how much he can get, that's all. He's got nothing to lose, we got nothing to lose giving it to him."

"Mel said there's no sign of Rosen."

"I agree with Teddy, the man's probably been hit," Rashad said. "But he's in there, isn't he? No place else he could be."

Valenzuela thought about it a little more. Finally he said, "All right. We'll say we'll give him the whole thing. The other half when he comes out."

Mel returned to the middle of the yard, Mati trailing.

"Sergeant!"

He stopped, looking around, and began picking up the bills that were scattered about the grass.

Davis waited, watching from the window. He saw Mati pick up several of the bills and slip one in his pocket as he walked over to the lawyer with the rest. Davis glanced at Tali. He was very tense now and it was a moment of relief.

"You see that?"

"Mati takes care of himself," Tali said. "I hope nothing happens to him."

The lawyer was squinting, looking this way again.

"Sergeant? . . . They said okay. You can have the whole thing."

Just like that, Davis thought. They give away money.

"They said, you come out, get the briefcase here. One of them will come over and give you the rest."

"Tell them I want to see all three of them," Davis said. "If I come out, I don't want anybody staying back there behind the wall. All three of them have to come out."

Mel shrugged. It didn't make any difference to him. He looked at Mati and said something and Mati started back toward the fence. They had given Mati something to do.

"You understand? All three of them," Davis said.

Mel was nodding. "He'll tell them."

"They give me the money and I'll give them Rosen." Davis waited, making sure the lawyer heard him. "I'll even bring him out."

Mel was alert again, studying the windows. "You mean when you leave, they won't have to go in and get him?"

"I said I'll bring him out."

"Well—what does he have to say about that?"

"Nothing," Davis said.

Mel hesitated. "I don't quite understand."

"You don't have to. Go tell them."

"Just a minute," Mel said. He hurried back toward the stone fence.

Davis looked over at Tali. "You ready?"

The girl nodded, holding on tight to the shotgun resting on the window ledge.

"There are some other ways," Davis said, "but none that I like. Is it all right with you?"

The girl nodded again, afraid to speak.

"Then let's do it," Davis said.

He lowered the Mauser, resting it against the windowsill next to the girl, and walked over to where Rosen's body lay on the floor.

They came with the lawyer and Mati walking in front of them: Valenzuela and Teddy carrying the submachine guns at their sides; Rashad in the middle with a canvas athletic bag. The rest of the money would be in the bag, if Davis wanted to see it.

And a gun, Davis thought, watching them. He was holding
Rosen in his arms, the body bent enough to appear natural
from a distance, the head stiffly erect against Davis's shoulder.
He tried not to look at Rosen's face. He stepped over the couch
blocking the doorway and crossed the patio to the yard.

They saw him now. They were looking at him, the five of
them coming across the grass from the fence, Davis approaching them from the desert house to meet where the money was.
The five men arrived first. Mati walked aside. The lawyer was
more subtle. He began picking up hundred-dollar bills as he
moved away from them.

Valenzuela, at about thirty feet, said, "What's the matter
with him?"

Davis didn't answer. He approached to within ten feet, almost to the open briefcase, before sinking to one knee and
lowering Rosen's body to the ground. He remained there,
looking up at them. He wished the two with the machine guns
were standing together and not separated by Rashad. Their
clothes were dusty and stained with sweat marks. They were
dark figures with the sun behind them. The sun was all right, it
didn't bother him. It outlined them cleanly. They had not
taken their eyes off Rosen. Davis remained on one knee, his left
hand resting on Rosen's hands.

"Well," Rashad said, "here we are." He was holding the
canvas bag in front of him now, his hand inside the opening.
Looking at Rosen's face, the closed eyes, he said, "What'd you
bother for?"

In the moment before it happened, Davis could see it happening.

He said, "We bring out our dead."

He lifted Rosen's hands, drew the Colt .38 from beneath the
compress bandage, and shot Rashad in the chest as the man's
hand was coming out of the bag. Davis saw him punched sideways, but couldn't wait to see if he was going down.

He shot Valenzuela in the stomach and in the chest as the
Uzi was pointing at him, the Uzi going up in the air as Valenzuela was socked hard and Davis knew he was out of it.

Somebody was yelling something, the one with the scarf tied
over his hair like a pirate.

He shot Teddy in the face as Teddy was crouching to fire and saw his arms go up with the Uzi, his chest exposed, and shot him again, in the chest.

He had to get to Rashad because he wasn't sure of Rashad, and by the time he put the Colt on him, shit, he was a moment too late, the Colt pointing at a Beretta. The Beretta fired first and Davis felt it this time—not like the time getting in the Medevac with the blood pouring out of his leg—he felt the bullet tear into his thigh, the same leg, three times now, leg wounds, three times and out of it, home, as he held the Colt on Rashad with Rashad looking at it and shot him four times in the chest. There. One round left in the Colt and he didn't need Dr. Morris's revolver stuck in his pants. It was uncomfortable. He pulled it out and dropped it on the ground. He was aware of the silence. He looked at Valenzuela and the other one, knowing they were dead, and shoved the Colt into the shoulder holster and tried to stand up, then had to try again before he made it. His leg didn't hurt yet, it was a reaction, seeing the blood and afraid to touch the leg, afraid it might shatter if he stood on it; but he was all right now, he was up. He was sweating a lot.

Mati came over to him first and tried to help him, offering to hold him up; but he was okay he told Mati. He heard Mel's voice and heard Tali. She was saying, "David . . ." coming out to them. It always surprised him when he heard her say his name.

Mel was picking up the rest of the loose bills, putting them in the briefcase. He took the canvas bag from Rashad, trying to do it without touching him.

Mel said, "Wow," reverently, then said it a few more times. "I don't believe it. Christ, I was standing right there—you know how long that took? About eight seconds, no more than ten." He walked over toward Davis, looking down at Rosen. "I'm very sorry about Rosie, but—well, what can you say, huh?" Now he was looking at Davis.

"Are you all right?"

"I will be."

Davis looked at Tali and smiled at her worried expression. He was stooped slightly, holding his thigh, pressing his hand against it. In a minute he'd go in the house and take a look and get it cleaned up. The bullet was still in his leg and he'd have to go to the hospital in Eilat, but it didn't hurt at all right now. He'd worry about the hospital later.

"When I say the company is gonna be most grateful to you, that's an understatement," Mel said. "And I know they won't question my giving you this. In fact, we spoke before about getting these funds back home, which we can discuss again later on. Sergeant, with my deepest gratitude." He extended a pack of hundred-dollar bills to Davis.

"What's that?"

"Ten thousand dollars," Mel said. "You earned it."

Davis said, "All this, it's the money that was sent to Rosen, right?"

Tali stepped in. "You brought it to the hotel yourself. You saw it."

He said to Mel, "So it isn't company money anymore, is it?"

"Well, insofar as it's recovered money," Mel said.

"Recovered from what?" Davis said. "They took Rosen's money from you and gave it to me. What I want to know is, how come you're offering me some of my own money?"

"Now wait a minute," Mel said. "All we're really talking about is a reward. And I mean ten big ones, not a few bucks."

Davis reached over and took the briefcase from him, brought his hand up bloody from the wound, and took the canvas bag.

"I don't think I need a reward," Davis said. "Why don't I just settle for what's mine?"

Mel wasn't sure if he was serious and tried to smile. He said, "Hey, come on. You can't just walk off with a hundred and ninety-five thousand dollars, for Christ sake."

"Why not?" Davis said.

It seemed that simple. Why not?

209

SWAG

1

There was a photograph of Frank in an ad that ran in the *Detroit Free Press* and showed all the friendly salesmen at Red Bowers Chevrolet. Under his photo it said *Frank J. Ryan*. He had on a nice smile, a styled moustache, and a summer-weight suit made out of that material that's shiny and looks like it has snags in it.

There was a photograph of Stick on file at 1300 Beaubien, Detroit Police Headquarters. Under the photo it said *Ernest Stickley, Jr.*, 89037. He had on a sport shirt that had sailboats and palm trees on it. He'd bought it in Pompano Beach, Florida.

The first time they ever saw each other was the night at Red Bowers Chevrolet on Telegraph when Stick was pulling out of the used-car lot in the maroon '73 Camaro. Frank walked up to the side window as the car stopped before turning out on the street. He said, "You mind if I ask where you're going?"

The window was down. Stick looked at the guy who was stooped over a little, staring at him: nice-looking guy about thirty-five or so, long hair carefully combed, all dressed up with his suit and tie on. A car salesman. Stick could smell the guy's aftershave lotion.

Stick said, "I could be going home, I could be going to Florida." Which was his intention, the reason he was taking the car. He said, "What do you care where I'm going?"

Frank's first impression of Stick was a guy off the farm who'd come to town and somebody had sold him a genuine Hawaiian sport shirt, he wore with the collar spread open, showing a little bit of white T-shirt. Frank said, "Since you didn't buy the car, I mean pay for it yet, I wondered."

"Uh-unh," Stick said. "I come here to price a new one."

Frank kept staring at him. "You always shop for a car after the place's closed?"

"Yeah, that's what I found out. The showroom's all lit up but it's closed. Hey," Stick said, "maybe you think this is one of yours because you got one like it."

"Maybe that's it," Frank said. "Even down to the Indiana plates. It was parked over there where there's an empty space now." He said, "You say it's yours, you want to show me the registration?"

"Fuck no," Stick said, and took off, leaving Frank standing there in the drive.

Frank went into the used-car office, called the Detroit police, and gave them a description of the car. He didn't do it right away. He took his time, thinking the guy must be a real farmer to try and steal a car off a lot that was all lit up. The guy had been very cool about it, though. Slow-talking, relaxed, with the trace of a southern accent. But he might have been putting it on, acting sincere. Frank himself would give customers a little down-home sound every once in a while and grin a lot. It wasn't hard.

He didn't give a personal shit if the guy got away with it or not. The car belonged to the Red Bowers Chevrolet. He wasn't out anything. But there was something personal about it if the guy was driving down Telegraph grinning, thinking he'd aced him. That's why Frank called the police. Also he called to see how the police would handle it. To see if they were any good.

They weren't bad. A squad car turned on its flashers as soon as the Camaro was spotted on the Lodge Freeway. It took another twenty minutes, though, and three sideswiped cars on Grand River, before they got him. They found the wrinkled Camaro in a parking lot and Stick sitting in the bar next door with a bottle of Stroh's beer.

The next time Frank saw Stick was at Detroit Police Headquarters on Beaubien, looking through the one-way glass at him standing in line with the five plainclothes cops who stood patiently staring into the light glare. It was funny. Frank hesitated again before saying, "Second one on the left."

"You're sure he's the one?"

"I'm sure it isn't one of those cops," Frank said.

Out in the office he asked the detective sergeant about the guy, who he was and if he'd been arrested before, and learned the following:

Ernest Stickley, Jr. No aliases. Address: Zanzibar Motel, Southfield, Michigan. Born in Norman, Oklahoma, October 11, 1940. Occupation: truck driver, transit-mix operator. Marital status: divorced; ex-wife and seven-year-old daughter residing in Pompano Beach, Florida.

The sheet also listed previous arrests. The first time for joyriding; sentence suspended. Arrested two years later on a UDAA charge—unlawfully driving away an automobile—and received one-year probation. The final one, arrested for grand theft, auto—transporting a stolen motor vehicle across a state line—and convicted. Served ten months in the Federal Correctional Institution at Milan, Michigan.

Frank said to himself, Well well well well. An auto thief named Ernest, with a record. Maybe a hick but a fairly nice-looking guy. Mid-thirties. Had nerve. Didn't seem to get excited. Obviously knew how to steal cars. In fact, Frank was pretty sure, the guy had stolen a lot more cars than were listed on this sheet. Four arrests now and most likely another conviction.

The third time Frank saw Stick was at the pretrial examination on the fourth floor of the Frank Murphy Hall of Justice. It was an air-conditioned, wood-paneled courtroom with indirect lighting and enough microphones placed around so the people in the audience could hear the proceedings. There were a few cops in off-duty clothes, some cute young black ladies and skinny guys in modified pimp outfits who were either pimps or pushers or might be felony suspects—B and E, robbery or assault—out on bond. There were a few spectators, too: mostly retirees who came up to watch felony exams and murder trials because they were more fun than movies and they were free.

Frank was surprised when he saw the assistant prosecutor: a young black guy in a tight sport coat. Young and short and fat. He had thought all young black guys in Detroit were at least six-seven and went about a hundred and a half. Frank decided the black guy was very smart and had passed the bar in the top ten. He looked like he was enjoying himself, shuffling papers, moving around a lot to talk to the judge and the court clerk and the defense lawyers; then turning away from them, smiling at some inside remark, having fun being a prosecuting attorney.

Frank had a feeling the people watching the guy were probably thinking, Look at that little mother. Little kiss-ass with the big horn-rim glasses on to show how smart he is. Everybody in the courtroom was black except Frank, a couple of Jewish lawyers in their sixties, and the off-duty cops waiting to be called as witnesses.

Stick hadn't been able to make bond. They brought him in through a side door and sat him at the end of a table facing the witness stand as the judge, a black guy with graying hair and a neat gray moustache, called a number and read Stick's name from a big file folder he was holding. Then the prosecutor called Mr. Frank Ryan, and he went through the gate and over to the court clerk, who swore him in and told him to sit down in the witness chair, take the mike off its stand, and hold it in front of him. They didn't waste any time. The little prosecutor asked him if he would please tell what happened the night of May twenty-second in the used-car lot at Red Bowers Chevrolet.

Frank told it. Most of it.

Then he was asked if he had, the next day, identified the same man in a show-up at Detroit Police Headquarters.

Frank said yes, he had.

The little prosecutor said, "And do you see that same man in this courtroom?"

Frank said, "No, I don't."

"And would you point—" The little prosecutor stopped. "What'd you say?"

"I said no, I don't see him."

"You *iden*tified him. Didn't you point him out at a show-up?"

"I thought he was the one," Frank said. "But now I see him again, I'm not sure."

Ernest Stickley, sitting about fifteen feet away, was staring at him. Frank met his gaze and held it a moment before looking at the prosecutor again.

"I mean maybe it's the same person, but I have to tell you I've got a reasonable doubt it isn't. I can't *swear* it's the same person."

"You're sure one day," the little prosecutor said, "now today you're not?"

"I didn't say I was sure. The police officer asked me if he was the one and I said, I think so. I said, He's certainly not any of those other ones."

The little prosecutor didn't seem to be having fun anymore. He began trying to put words in Frank's mouth until Stick's lawyer, appointed by the court, felt he had better object to that and the judge sustained it. Then Stick's lawyer put a few words of his own in Frank's mouth the way he slanted his question and Frank repeated no, he could not positively identify anyone in the courtroom as the person who'd driven off in the '73 Camaro. The prosecutor wouldn't let go. He went at Frank again until the judge told him to please introduce a new line of questioning or else call another witness.

The prosecutor thanked the judge—Frank wasn't sure why—and the judge thanked Frank as he stepped down. The judge was quiet, very polite.

Watching all this, especially watching the guy from the

used-car lot, Frank Ryan, Stick kept thinking, What the hell is going on? He couldn't believe it. He sat very still in the chair, almost with the feeling that if he moved, this Frank Ryan would look at him again and squint and say, Wait a minute, yeah, that's the one.

The guy from the used-car lot went out through the gate. Stick didn't turn around, but he had a feeling the guy was still in the courtroom.

He watched the officer who had arrested him take the stand, wearing slacks and a black leather jacket that was open, his holstered police special on a direct line with Stick's gaze.

The patrolman recited in Official Police how he and his partner had noted the Indiana license plate on the alleged stolen vehicle and had pursued the suspect, witnessing how he had apparently lost control taking a corner upon entering Grand River Avenue and proceeded to sideswipe three cars parked along the west side of the street. Because of the traffic they were not able to keep the suspect in sight, but did locate the vehicle in a parking lot adjacent to the Happy Times Bar located at 2921 Grand River. Upon entering the premises the patrolman asked the bartender who, if anyone, had come in during the past few minutes. The bartender pointed to the person later identified as the suspect. When approached, the suspect said, "What seems to be the trouble, Officer?" The suspect was placed under arrest and informed of his rights.

"And is that person now in this courtroom?"

"Yes sir," the patrolman said to the smart little prosecutor. "He's sitting right there in front of me."

Stick didn't move; he stared back at the policeman. Finally his lawyer leaned toward him with his cigar breath and asked in a hoarse whisper if he would be willing to take the stand, tell what he was doing in the bar and how he got there, show them he had nothing to hide.

Stick whispered back to him, "You out of your fucking mind?"

He didn't have to go up there and testify to anything if he didn't want to. They'd have to prove he had gotten out of the '73 Camaro and walked into the Happy Times Bar, and there wasn't any way in the world they could do it.

The prosecutor tried for another few minutes, until the judge called both attorneys up to the bench and politely told the prosecutor to please quit mind-fucking the court, produce some evidence that would stand up in trial or else everybody was going to miss lunch today. That was how Stick got off.

2

After he was released he didn't see the guy from the used-car lot in the courtroom or in the hall. He saw him on the steps outside the building, lighting a cigarette, and knew the guy was waiting for him to come over.

"You want one?"

"I'm trying to quit," Stick said. He hesitated. "Yeah, I guess I will," he said then and took a Marlboro from a pack the guy offered.

Holding a lighted match, the guy said, "I'm Frank Ryan. I wasn't sure if you heard my name up there."

Stick looked at him. "I heard it." Neither of them offered to shake hands.

Frank said, "You're lucky. That judge seemed like a nice guy. No bullshit."

"I guess I was lucky, all right," Stick said, looking at the guy's neatly combed hair. He was an inch or so taller than Stick, about six feet even, slim build in his green, lightweight, shiny-looking summer suit, with the coat open. Stick had on the same yellow, green, and blue sport shirt he'd worn for almost a week. He said, "It's funny how sometimes you get lucky and other times everything goes against you."

"It is funny," Frank Ryan said. "You want to get a drink or something?"

"I wouldn't mind it. I was in that Wayne County jail six days and six nights and they didn't serve us any cocktails or anything. I guess that's when you were deciding I wasn't the guy after all."

"You were the guy," Frank said.

Looking at each other, squinting a little in the sunlight, they were both aware of the people passing them on the steps and could feel the Frank Murphy Hall of Justice rising above them with its big plate-glass windows. Stick said, "You got a place in mind?"

They walked down St. Antoine toward the river and over a side street through Greektown to the Club Bouzouki. Stick had never heard of the place or the drink Frank ordered once they were sitting at the bar. Ouzo. Frank said why didn't he try one; but Stick said he'd just as soon go with bourbon, it seemed to do the job. He looked around the place, a big, flashy bar, mirrors and paintings, a dance floor and bandstand, bartenders in red vests, but only a few customers in here at 11:30 in the morning. It was dim and relaxing. Stick wasn't in a hurry. It was up to Frank; it was his party. He didn't seem to be in a hurry either. He sipped his milky-looking drink and said to Stick he ought to try it sometime. It tasted like paregoric, so it ought to be good for the stomach. Here he was, after six days in jail, sitting in a bar shooting the shit with the guy who'd put him in then gotten him out. Even though it didn't make sense, Stick wasn't going to rush it.

"You know, the whole thing was," Frank said, "I had a feeling you thought I was a cluck. I catch you dead nuts in the middle of the act, you don't even act nervous or anything."

"What was I supposed to do?" Stick said. "You walk up to me—you think I'm going to get out and run? I got the thing in drive."

"I know, but it was what I felt. Like you're thinking I'm too dumb to do anything about it."

"I wasn't thinking so much of you as just getting out of there."

"See, I go to the show-up," Frank said, "and I'm still a little pissed off. So I identify you. As far as I know, the cops have you nailed down, so it doesn't make any difference. Then I find out I'm the only eyeball witness they got. Also I find out your name's Ernest."

"That's it," Stick said, "Ernest. But I didn't pick it."

"I started thinking about that old saying about being frank and earnest," Frank said. "You be frank and I'll be earnest."

Stick waited. "Yeah?"

"It seemed to fit."

"It seemed to fit what?"

"Also I learned a few things about your record, about doing time at Milan. You want a cigarette?"

"I got to buy some, I guess, if I'm going to keep smoking," Stick said.

Frank struck a match and held it for him. "Something I was wondering," he said. "If you got a gun. If you ever carried one."

"A gun?" Stick looked at him. "You don't need a gun to pick up a car. You don't *want* a gun."

"Well, I didn't know if that was all you did."

"I'll tell you something," Stick said, "since you'll probably ask me anyway. The other night—I hadn't picked up a car in over five years. That's a fact."

"But you picked up plenty before that, huh?"

"You could be a cop and I could give you places and dates, but it wouldn't do you any good. Time's run out."

"Well, you know I'm not a cop."

"That's about all I know," Stick said, "so I'll ask you a question if it's okay. What're you besides a used-car salesman and a sport that drinks a white Greek drink that looks like medicine?"

222

"I don't drink it all the time," Frank said. "Only when I come here."

"Is that your answer?"

"I'm not ducking the question. It's not so much what I am," Frank said, "as what I want to be."

"Yeah, and what's that?"

Frank hesitated, drawing on his cigarette, then took a sip of the milky-looking ouzo. "What do they call you? Ernie?"

"You call me that, I won't answer," Stick said. "No, I used to be Ernie, a long time ago. Still once in a while people call me Ernest. It's my name, I can't do anything about that. But usually they call me Stick. Friends, guys I work with."

"Because you stick up places?"

"Because of my name, Stickley, and I was skinny, like a stick in high school, when I was playing basketball."

"Yeah? I did, too," Frank said. "Was that down in Oklahoma you played?"

"Up here. I was born in Norman," Stick said, "but I guess you know that, huh?"

Frank nodded. "I don't detect much of an accent, though."

"I guess I lost most of what I had," Stick said, "moving around different places. We come up here, our family, my dad worked out at Rouge twenty-three years."

Frank seemed interested. "We got a lot in common. My old man worked at Ford Highland Park. I was born in Memphis, Tennessee, came to Detroit when I was four, and lived here, I guess, most of my life, except for three years I spent in L.A."

"You married?" Stick asked him.

"Twice. And I got no intention right now of going for thirds. Let's get back," Frank said. "I want to ask you, you never stuck up a place? Used a gun?"

Stick waited a moment, like he was trying to see beyond the question, then shook his head. "Not my style. But since we're opening our souls, how about you?"

"Uh-unh, me neither," Frank said. "Well, years ago I was into a little burglary, B and E. Me and another guy, we didn't do too bad. But then he went into numbers or something—he was a black guy—so I quit before I got in too deep. In and out, you might say."

"You never used a gun during that time?"

"We didn't have to. We only went into places there wasn't anybody home."

"But now you got a sudden interest in guns, it seems."

"Not a sudden interest." Frank came around on his stool, giving it a quarter turn. "I've been studying the situation for some time now, ever since I got back from L.A., reading up on all the different ways people break the law to make money. You know why most people get caught?"

"Because they're dumb."

"Right. Or they're desperate. Like a junkie."

"Stay away from junkies," Stick said. "Don't have any part of them."

Frank raised his eyebrows, impressed. "You believe that, huh?"

"It's the first rule of life," Stick said. He finished his drink, making sure he got it all, shaking the ice in the empty glass. "I'd buy a round," he said, "but I got eight bucks on me and it's got to last till I find out where I'm at."

Frank looked over at the bartender and made a circular motion for a couple of more. He said to Stick, "Don't worry about it. Listen, I was going to ask you what you had in mind. The cop I talked to said you were unemployed."

"Not in Florida. I can get all the work I want in Florida. Cement work. I was going back there to see my little girl."

"I understand you're divorced, too."

"Finally. Listen to this, you want to hear something? We're living in Florida, my wife starts bitching about the hot weather, how she doesn't see her old friends anymore, how her mom's driving her crazy? Her mom lives down there. Wonderful woman, old lady's never smiled in her life. She's watching television, that commercial used to be on a couple years ago about brotherhood, working together and all? It shows all these people standing in a field singing that song—I can't think of how it goes now. All these people singing, and in there you start to recognize some celebrities, Johnny Carson . . . lot of different ones. Her mom squints at the TV set and says, 'Is that niggers?' I'm taking her to the eye doctor's, the car radio's on. Every Friday I'd take her to the eye doctor's. She listens to this group playing some rock thing and says, 'Is that niggers?' We come back up here, sell this house we got that's right off the Intercoastal—come back, my wife's still bitching. Now it's the cold weather, busing, the colored situation, shit, you name it. We're arguing all the time, so finally we separate. Not legally, but we separate. Now what does she do? She goes back to Florida and moves in with her mom. Divorce was final last month."

"Listen, I believe it," Frank said. "Man, every word."

"I don't know what's going to happen there," Stick said, "but I like to see my little girl once in a while."

"Fortunately," Frank said, "neither of my wives had any children. Or any of my acquaintances, I mean that I know of."

Their drinks came and Frank stirred his, watching the clear liquid turn milky as it mixed with the ice cubes. Stick waited for whatever was next and Frank said, "It's funny you mentioned staying away from junkies as a *rule*. That's one of my rules. Don't have anything to do with them. Don't even go to a place where they're liable to hang out."

"You never get in trouble doing that," Stick said.

"I got some other rules, too," Frank said. "In fact, I've got ten rules. I mean, written down."

"What? How to live a happy life?"

"Sort of. How to be a success in a particular undertaking. Which could certainly lead to a happy life."

"You going to tell me," Stick said, "or I got to ask you what they are?"

The bartender rang up their tab and put it on the bar. Frank waited until he moved away.

"I told you I've been studying, well, different ways of making money. I'm not talking about anything tricky like embezzlement, you know, or checks. I've hung a little paper, not much, there's no excitement in it. Christ, it's like work. No, I'm talking about going out and picking up some dough. You know how many ways you can do that?"

"I don't know—auto theft, B and E, burglary, strong-arm—" Stick paused. "There's probably a hundred ways. Some that haven't even been thought up yet."

"What you mentioned, you're talking about things you can

take," Frank said. "Yes, cars, TVs, silverware, fur coats, household shit. But you got to convert it into money, right? You've got to sell it to somebody, and he knows you didn't get the stuff laying around your basement or out in the garage."

"It's unavoidable if you got to fence it."

"That's what I'm talking about," Frank said. "The thing you do first, you eliminate the secondary party. You only take money. And money you can get rid of anywhere. Man, you spend it."

"So then you're into mugging, strong-arm, I mentioned that." Stick paused. "Bank robbery—is that what you want to do, rob a bank?"

Frank looked around and then at Stick again. "I'll tell you something. Nobody's going to rob banks as a career and get rich *and* stay out of jail. Not both. Not with the time locks, the alarm systems. The teller doesn't even have to press a button. You lift the money out of the drawer and a bell rings at the Holmes Protection Agency. They got the TV cameras. You pull a gun, you're on instant replay. The odds are lousy, less than fifty-fifty. Like the average take on a bank job in New York City last year was eleven thousand two. Not bad. But those are the guys that got away. Half the clowns didn't make it."

Frank paused to draw on his cigarette and take a drink. "Let me ask you something. What do you think pays the most? Wait a minute, let me rephrase it. What do you think is the fastest and, percentagewise, safest way to make the most money?"

"Not the horses," Stick said. "I used to spend weekends I wasn't working at Gulfstream or Hialeah."

"No, not the horses," Frank said patiently. "Think about it. What's the fastest and relatively safest way to do it?"

Stick was thoughtful. "Big payoff? Maybe kidnapping."

Frank was losing some of his patience. "Christ no, not kidnapping. FBI, you don't have a fucking chance kidnapping."

"Are we talking about something I never heard of?"

"You heard of it."

"All right," Stick said, "you tell me. What's the best way to make a lot of money fast? Without working, that is."

Frank held up the palm of his hand, his elbow on the edge of the bar. "You ready for this?"

"I'm ready."

"Armed robbery."

"Big fucking deal."

"Say it again," Frank said, "and put it in capital letters and underline it. Say it backward, robbery comma armed. Yes, it can be a *very* big deal. Listen, last year there were twenty-three thousand and thirty-eight reported robberies in the city of Detroit. Reported. That's everything. B and E, muggings, banks, everything. Most of them pulled by dummies, junkies, and still a high percentage got away with it."

"Going in with a gun," Stick said, "is something else."

"You bet it is." Frank leaned in a little closer. "Ernie . . . Ernest—"

"Stick."

"Stick . . . I'm talking about simple everyday armed robbery. Supermarkets, bars, liquor stores, gas stations, that kind of place. Statistics show—man, I'm not just saying it, the *statistics* show—armed robbery pays the most for the least amount of risk. Now, you ready for this? I see how two guys who know what they're doing and're businesslike about it"—he paused, grinning a little—"who're frank with each other and earnest about their work, can pull down three to five grand a week."

"You can also pull ten to a quarter in Jackson," Stick said.

"Listen," Frank said, his voice low and very serious, "I read a true story about two guys who actually did it. Two, three hits a week, they had to keep getting a bigger safe-deposit box. Lived well, I mean *well*, had all the clothes, broads they wanted, everything. It was written by this psychologist or sociologist, you know? who actually interviewed them."

"They told him anything he wanted to know?"

"They trusted him."

"Where was this, where he talked to them?"

"Well, at the time they were in Lucasville, Southern Ohio Correctional, but they went three and a half, four years straight, without ever being arrested. Oh, they were picked up a couple of times, on suspicion, but not for anything nailed down. See, any business will fail if you fuck up. I agree the end result is slightly different here. You don't just go broke, you're liable to give up a few years of your life, confined, you might say. But I don't see any reason to get caught. And that's where my ten rules for success and happiness come in. I see this strictly as a business venture. What I'm wondering now, if you're the business partner I'm looking for."

3

Frank Ryan's ten rules for success and happiness were written in blue ink on ten different cocktail napkins from the Club Bouzouki, the Lafayette Bar, Edjo's, and a place called the Lindell AC. Some of the rules, especially the last few, were on torn napkins with crossed-out words and were hard to read. The napkins said:

1. ALWAYS BE POLITE ON THE JOB. SAY PLEASE AND THANK YOU.
2. NEVER SAY MORE THAN IS NECESSARY.
3. NEVER CALL YOUR PARTNER BY NAME—UNLESS YOU USE A MADE-UP NAME.
4. DRESS WELL. NEVER LOOK SUSPICIOUS OR LIKE A BUM.
5. NEVER USE YOUR OWN CAR. (DETAILS TO COME.)

6. NEVER COUNT THE TAKE IN THE CAR.
7. NEVER FLASH MONEY IN A BAR OR WITH WOMEN.
8. NEVER GO BACK TO AN OLD BAR OR HANGOUT ONCE YOU HAVE MOVED UP.
9. NEVER TELL ANYONE YOUR BUSINESS. NEVER TELL A JUNKIE EVEN YOUR NAME.
10. NEVER ASSOCIATE WITH PEOPLE KNOWN TO BE IN CRIME.

The angle of the venetian blinds gave Stick enough outside light. He sat by the window in his striped undershorts, placing the cocktail napkins on his bare leg as he read them again, one by one, concentrating on making out some of the blotted words. He was smoking a Marlboro and taking sips from a can of Busch Bavarian that sat on the metal radiator cover beneath the window. He didn't look up until the groaning sound came from the bed and he knew Frank was awake.

"What's that noise?"

"Air conditioning," Stick said. "You want a beer?"

"Jesus Christ." Frank got up on an elbow, looking at the window, squinting. "What time is it?"

"About nine-thirty. My watch's over on the TV." Stick took a swallow of beer as Frank got to his feet on the floor and finally stood up. He was wearing jockey shorts and black socks.

"Where'd you sleep?"

"Right there in bed with you," Stick said, "but I swear I never touched you."

He waited until Frank went into the bathroom, then reached over and pulled the cord on the venetian blinds, raising them and flooding part of the room in morning sunlight. He wanted to get Frank's reaction when he came out and saw the bright pink walls.

He didn't notice them right away. When he came out, he said, "There's four cans of beer in the washbasin."

"Three for you and one for me," Stick said. "I've already had a couple."

Frank was looking at the pink walls now. "Jesus, where in the hell are we?"

"Zanzibar Motel. You're about a mile and a half from where you work. You can walk it if you want."

Frank stooped over a little, squinting, looking across the room at the sunlight filling the window. There wasn't much to see: empty asphalt pavement, and beyond that, a four-lane highway with a grass median, Telegraph Road. A few cars and a semi went past. They could hear them above the humming sound of the air conditioning.

"Where's my car?"

"You couldn't remember where you parked it."

Frank went into the bathroom and came out with a Busch.

"Then how'd we get here?"

"You remember looking for your car?"

" 'Course I do." Frank took a drink of beer and let his breath out, feeling a little better.

"You lost your parking ticket," Stick said.

"I know, that's why I couldn't find the car. All those streets over there look alike. At night, shit, you can't tell."

"You remember trying to get that waitress to take her clothes off?"

Frank hesitated, then drank some more of the beer. "We had a pretty good time, didn't we?"

Stick said, "You remember standing in front of the J. L. Hudson Company, in the middle of Woodward Avenue, taking a leak?"

"I really had to go, didn't I?"

"Eileen sure got a kick out of that."

Frank looked at him. "Eileen, huh?"

"The one you picked up at the Lafayette Bar. Wasn't she a size?"

Frank managed to grin and shake his head. "Yeah, she sure was."

"I was surprised she didn't get sore, you started calling her Fatty."

"Just kidding around," Frank said. He went over to the dresser, opened his wallet, and fingered the bills inside. "Yeah, I guess we had a pretty good time." Looking at Stick he said, "I must have paid for the cab, huh?"

"Taxicab? We didn't take any cab anywhere."

"All right, you win," Frank said. "How'd we get here?"

"In a 1975 Mercury Montego." Stick watched Frank look toward the window again. "You remember we're standing in front of the Sheraton-Cadillac?"

Frank's expression began to open and show signs of life. "Yeah, they wouldn't let us in the bar because you didn't have a coat on."

"We're standing out in front," Stick said, "when the Merc pulls up and the guy gets out, looking around. You remember?"

Frank seemed happier as he began to recall it and could see the Mercury—dark brown, shiny—in front of the hotel and Stick walking over to the guy who got out, and now Frank was grinning. "Yeah, you went up to the guy and said something—"

"I said, 'Good evening, sir. Are you a guest at the hotel?' "

"Right. And he said he'd only be about an hour and handed you the keys."

"And a dollar tip," Stick said.

Frank was still grinning. "Sure, I remember it. Where's the car?"

"Up the street, in the Burger Chef parking lot. You go out, don't look at it. Don't even walk past it." Stick held up the ten cocktail napkins. "You remember these?"

"Sure I remember them. What do you keep asking me that for? I remember everything that happened." Frank took the napkins over to the dresser, spread them out, and stood there idly scratching his jockey shorts as he looked at them.

Stick watched him. After a moment he said, "I been reading your rules for success and happiness. And you know what?"

Frank kept scratching. "What?"

"I think you got an idea."

Frank looked over now. "Yeah? You think so, huh?"

"I think it might be worth looking into. It's a wild-ass idea—two guys who don't know shit going into the armed-robbery business. But you never know, do you?" He watched Frank go into the bathroom again and raised his voice. "I'm thinking maybe it's the way to make a stake. Be able to put a down payment on something that'll carry you. Instead of working all your life. That's what I been doing, working. What have I got? Eight bucks in my pants, nothing, not a cent in the bank."

"Working is for workingmen," Frank said, coming out with two cans of Busch. He walked over to Stick and handed him one, raising his own. "To our new business, huh? What do you say?"

"To the new business." Stick raised his beer and took a sip. "I'll tell you a secret, buddy, put your mind at rest."

Frank seemed interested. "What's that?"

"Last night, you didn't take a leak in the middle of Woodward Avenue."

"I didn't?"

"Uh-unh. I did."

First they had to find Frank's car, which wasn't actually his, it was a demo.

Frank called a friend of his at Red Bowers Chevrolet, a salesman, and got him to drive them downtown to look for it. On the freeway the friend kept asking, "But how can you lose a car? Not have it stolen, *lose* it. A car." Frank told him it could happen to anybody. Get turned around, forget exactly where you parked it. "See, this guy here had the ticket, with the address on it and everything, and he lost it." Stick didn't say anything. They found the car, paid six and a half to get it out, and Frank bought them a couple of drinks at the Greek place.

After the friend left, Frank said, while they were downtown, they might as well look up Sportree and see about the guns. Right?

Stick hesitated. This was the part he wasn't sure of.

"Look," Frank said, "you got to have a gun or it isn't armed robbery, is it? You don't have a gun, the guy says go fuck yourself and you're standing there, your hand in your pocket, pointing your finger at him."

"I'm not talking about the guns," Stick said. "I'm talking about the source." He'd been thinking about it and his idea was maybe they ought to run down to South Carolina or someplace.

"Buy them?" Frank said. "Fill out the papers? Registered in

whose name, yours or mine?" No, Frank said, the only way to do it was to talk to Sportree, his old B and E associate.

Stick said how did they know they could trust this guy Sportree? Where was he getting the guns? Were they used before? Get caught with the goddamn piece and they check it and find it killed some colored guy the week before. "I never dealt with a colored guy," Stick said, "on anything important, and I don't know if I want to."

Frank told him to quit thinking about it. Sportree wasn't going to sell them the guns. All he'd do was set it up so they could put their hands on a couple of clean pieces. Once they found him.

Frank hadn't seen Sportree in a few years. When he tried to call, he got an operator who told him the number was no longer in service. Stick said why didn't he look in the phone book. Frank said, Jesus, that'd be like looking up Gracie's Whorehouse. Stick said why didn't he try it anyway.

That was how they found the listing for Sportree's Royal Lounge on West Eight Mile.

In the late afternoon and early evening Sportree's offered semidarkness and a sophisticated cocktail piano and was a spot for Southfield secretaries who worked in the new modern glass office buildings for companies that had moved out of downtown Detroit. They'd stop in after five and let guys buy them drinks. Or a secretary might come in with her boss, or with a salesman who called on her boss. A good-looking black girl with red hair and horn-rimmed glasses played cocktail Cole Porter from five to eight, getting the secretaries and the executives in the mood. Then she'd cover the piano keys and take her sheet music upstairs to the apartment over the Lounge.

Also at eight the two white bartenders, who had come on at noon, went off, and two black bartenders took over. By nine, the executives and the secretaries were out of there. By ten, the clientele was solid black and the cute redheaded piano player came down without her sheet music and played soul on and off until 2:00 A.M.

When Frank and Stick got there a little before seven, it was cocktail time and the secretaries were sitting around in the moody dimness with bosses or salesmen or waiting for live ones to come in. Walking in, Frank liked the place right away. He said, "Hey, yeah." A few of the girls looked up and gave them a quick reading, without showing any interest. Nothing. A guy who slept in his clothes and a garage mechanic off duty—probably what they thought. It bothered Frank. He felt seedy and needed a shave and imagined he had rotten breath. He wanted to go home and change, come back later. He wasn't disappointed at all when the bartender told them Sportree wouldn't be in till around ten.

They drove out to Stick's motel, the Zanzibar, picked up the ten cocktail napkins, the can of Busch Bavarian left over, and Stick's suitcase that looked like it had been through a lot of Greyhound bus stations and held nearly everything he owned. After that they went to Frank's apartment on Thirteen Mile in Royal Oak.

Frank told Stick to unpack and make himself comfortable while he took a shower. Stick looked around; it was a small place, one bedroom, not much. He didn't unpack but took a pale-green sport coat out of the suitcase and draped it over the back of a chair. He wondered if Frank had an iron. Probably not, the place was pretty bare, a few magazines lying around and ashtrays that hadn't been emptied. The place didn't look lived in; it looked like a waiting room in a hospital.

Frank put on a clean shirt, a dark-blue shiny suit, and asked Stick if he was going to change.

"I already did," Stick said, "this morning." He had on a faded blue work shirt.

Frank looked at the sport coat on the chair. "I guess you couldn't wear it anyway till you had it cleaned."

"I haven't worn it in a month," Stick said. "What do I need to get it cleaned for?"

"I mean pressed," Frank said. "Let's get out of here."

They stopped for something to eat and got back to Sportree's a little after ten.

As soon as they were inside the door, Stick said, "What's going on?" He kept his voice low. "What the fuck is going *on?*"

He followed Frank over to an open space at the bar, seeing the young black guys with their hats and hairdos turning to look at them.

Frank said to the bartender, "Bourbon and a scotch, please. Splash of water."

He looked over his shoulder at the tables. There wasn't another white person in the place. The light was off where the redheaded black girl had been playing the piano. The heavy chugging beat of West Indian reggae was coming from a hi-fi. The place seemed darker.

Frank waited for the bartender to put their drinks down. He said, "Where's Sportree? Tell him Frank Ryan. He knows me."

The bartender looked at him, didn't say a word, and moved away.

Stick said, "What's going *on?*"

"I got an idea," Frank said. "I don't know, but I got an idea."

When Sportree approached a few minutes later, Frank saw him coming in the mirror behind the bar. He looked over his shoulder at Sportree, at his open body shirt and double string of Ashanti trading beads, and said, "Where you going, to a drag party?"

Frank could feel the people near them watching, and felt good seeing the warm, amused expression in the man's eyes. He hadn't changed; he still knew who he was, in control. A good-looking, no-age black man with straightened long hair glistening across his forehead, a full, curled-down moustache, a little bebop growth beneath his lower lip, and liquid, slow-moving eyes.

Sportree said, very quietly, "Frank, how you doing? It's been a while."

Frank said, "I'd like you to meet my business associate, Ernest Stickley, Jr., man, if you can dig the name. Stick Stickley. And this is Sportree in the Zulu outfit, in case anybody doesn't know he's a jig."

Sportree didn't change his expression. He said, "You come down to learn some new words? Don't know whether you're Elvis Presley or a downtown white nigger, do you?"

"Well, you know," Frank said, "it's hard to keep up with all that jive shit living with honkies. Actually what we're looking for is a cleaning lady."

Sportree's expression held, then began to relax more, and he almost smiled. "A cleaning lady. Yeah, why don't we go upstairs, be comfortable? Talk about it."

They went outside to the entrance and up a flight of stairs to the apartment over the Lounge. The good-looking young black girl with red hair was sitting on the couch smoking a homemade cigarette. Sportree said, "A bourbon and a scotch, little water." Stick could smell the cigarette. He watched the girl get up without a word and go into the kitchen: little ninety-six-pounder in a white halter top and white pants.

As they sat down Sportree said, "You all want to smoke?"

Frank said, "Hey, don't start my partner on any bad habits. He's straight and I want to keep him that way."

Stick didn't say anything. He listened to Frank ask the black guy how the numbers business was, and the black said numbers, numbers was for little children. He was in the saloon business now. You mean in front, Frank said, with a pharmacy in the rear. The black guy said well, maybe a little coke and hash, some African speed, but no skag, uh-unh, he wouldn't deal shit to a man he found in bed with his lady.

The redheaded black girl brought the drinks in and left the room again, still without a word or change of expression.

Stick listened to Frank talking about the car business, L.A., smog, traffic on the Hollywood Freeway, how he'd worked in a bar in North Hollywood, screwed a starlet once, and finally, after thinking a while, remembering the name of the picture she was murdered in, which Stick and the black guy had never heard of. Stick went out to the kitchen and made himself another drink. The red-headed black girl sitting at the table reading *Cosmopolitan* didn't look up. He went back into the living room, which reminded him of a Miami Beach hotel, waited until Frank got through saying no, he wasn't in jail out there, and said, "You having a nice visit?"

Frank gave him a deadpan look. "Why, you in a hurry?"

"I thought we were looking for a cleaning lady."

Sportree was watching them both with his lazy, amused expression. He said, "Yeah, I believe somebody mentioned that." His eyes held on Frank. "Your business associate know what he's doing?"

"Cars," Frank said. "He's very good with cars. Many, many years at it, one conviction."

"If that's your pleasure, what you need with a cleaning lady?"

"That's his credentials. I'm saying we're all friends," Frank said. "Kindred spirits. Birds of a feather."

"Man," Sportree said, "you do need some new words."

"I'll take a side order," Frank said, "but for the entree how about a nice cleaning lady with big brown eyes?"

"You going back in the business? It's hard work, man. For young, strong boys with a habit."

Frank shook his head. "No, we got something else in mind. But first we got to locate a couple of items."

"Like what items we talking about?"

"Well, what this cleaning lady should look for are, you know, color TVs—"

"Yeah."

"Fur coats."

"Yeah."

"Watches. Jewelry."

"Go on."

"Silverware maybe, you know, silver stuff. And firearms."

Sportree grinned. "You almost forgot to mention that. Any particular firearms you got in mind?"

"Well, like the kind you might find in the guy's top drawer," Frank said. "Underneath his jockeys."

"No hunting rifles, anything like that."

"No, I had more in mind the smaller models you can hold in one hand."

"Put in your pocket, or in your belt."

"Yeah, that kind."

"You remember my cousin LaGreta?"

"That's right, your cousin."

"She used to have big eyes. I can talk to her," Sportree said. "Seems to me the rate was twenty bucks a house. I mean a house, you know, there's goods in it. She give you the plan, where everything is, twenty bucks."

"That's fine," Frank said. "Twenty bucks, if that's the going rate, fine."

"She's with this Rent-A-Maid and also a catering service," Sportree said. "Work parties, weddings, you understand? And does some cleaning jobs, too. She don't do floors, though. I remember her saying she don't do floors."

"Long as she gets in the house," Frank said, "I don't care what the fuck she does in there."

"Nice thing," Sportree said, "she gets around. You know, doesn't work for the same people all the time. That wouldn't be so good."

"Listen, that sounds fine," Frank said. "In fact it's exactly what we're looking for. If LaGreta's got the eyes you say she has."

"Nice big eyes," Sportree said.

"Can I ask you if she's on anything?"

"She smoke a little, that's all. Vacuum that big house, clean the oven, polish the furniture, she like to visit friends and have a little something. But what she make you know, she ain't on any hard shit."

"You think you can set it up?"

"I'll talk to her. You give me your telephone number."

Frank hesitated. "I better call you. We're in and out a lot. Maybe we're not there when you call."

Sportree said, "Frank, I hope you still the same person I used to be associated with." His gaze moved to Stick. "Just as I hope your friend here is pure."

"I'll tell you something," Stick said to him. "I enjoyed the drinks, but I don't know a rat's ass about you either, do I?"

It was the quiet way he said it that jolted Frank. He couldn't believe it—the first time Stick even opened his mouth. Frank said, "Hey, let's not have any misunderstandings," and looked over at Sportree.

"It's all right," Sportree said, his tone a little cooler than before. "You call me in a couple of days. Maybe I'll have something for you, maybe I won't."

When they were outside Frank said, "What're you trying to

prove? The guy's doing us a favor, you come on like you're some dangerous character."

"All I said was I didn't know him very well."

"But I do." Frank was tense. "I've known him a hell of a lot longer'n I've known you. You don't like the way I'm handling it, go back working cement, maybe I'll see you around."

"You're handling it," Stick said. "You made up the rules. It seems to me one of them, it says don't even tell a junkie your name. The first guy we talk to, it happens, runs a dope store."

"You don't know anything about him."

They got in the car and drove off and didn't say anything for a while, each feeling the other's presence. Finally Frank said, "Listen, this is kind of dumb. We got something going or we haven't. We don't blow it over a few words."

"I'll tell you the truth," Stick said. "I thought the guy was all right. I probably wasn't talking so much to him as I was to you."

Frank looked over. "I don't follow you."

"There you are," Stick said. "And I don't follow you around either, you say go pee-pee, I do it. You don't say to the guy I don't want a smoke. If I don't want it, I'll tell him."

Frank glanced away from the windshield again. "Is that all that's bothering you?"

"That's all," Stick said. "I thought I might as well mention it."

4

They spent the weekend on a slow tour of some of Detroit's industrial suburbs on the northeast side—Clawson, Madison Heights, Warren, Roseville—Stick driving, Frank taking notes, writing down the names and locations of bars, supermarkets, liquor stores, with a few words to describe the traffic and the fastest way out of each area. There was a liquor store in Warren that Frank especially liked and said maybe ought to be the first one. The liquor store was on a four-lane industrial street that was lined with machine and sheet-metal shops, automotive supply houses. Hit the place on a Friday, payday. How'd that sound? Stick said if they were going to start, the liquor store was probably as good a place as any.

Monday, Frank went back to Red Bowers Chevrolet and told the sales manager he was leaving the end of the week. The sales manager didn't seem too upset about it. Frank looked around the used-car lot and gave himself a good deal on a tan '72 Plymouth Duster that needed a ring job and some transmission work. If they had any luck at all, they wouldn't have the car very long.

After he got home he drove Stick around downtown Royal Oak until Stick spotted Al's Plumbing & Heating on South Main and said, "There. I think I like that one." He liked the way they parked the panel trucks behind the building with no fence or spotlight to worry about.

Tuesday, Stick took his green sport coat to the cleaner's, then stopped at an auto parts store and had some clips made for shorting and hooking up electric wires. The guy at the place didn't ask him any questions. He bowled and drank beer most of the afternoon, rolling a 186 he felt pretty good about.

Wednesday, Frank called Sportree, who told him to come down, he had something they might like.

What it was: a sheet of Ace tablet paper, lined, with the addresses of two homes in Bloomfield Hills and a list of the goods they'd find in each place. The words looked like they'd been written by a child, in pencil, but that was all right. They could read the words without any trouble. Especially the one that said *guns*.

"This one place, LaGreta say the man's got a gun collection in his recreation room, down in the basement," Sportree explained. "The whole family's out to the lake for the summer. Sometime the man stop off home, but usually he drive out there from his work. How's that sound to you for forty dollars? Whole mother collection to pick from."

Thursday night, they went to a ten o'clock show in Royal Oak, watched Clint Eastwood kill some people, and at twelve walked out of the movie theater, across the street, and down two blocks to Al's Plumbing & Heating. Frank waited on the corner while Stick went around the back. A few minutes later a panel truck with Al's name on the side stopped at the corner and Frank got in.

"That was pretty quick."

"It used to take me less than a minute," Stick said, "but with these newer models, I got to figure things out."

"You jump the wires?"

"Not under the hood." Stick patted the dashboard. "All the work's done underneath here. You look, you see some clips I had made."

Driving out to the gun collector's house in Bloomfield Hills, he told Frank what he used to do when he spotted a certain car he liked that had the dealer's name on it. Get the serial number off the car, then go to the dealer and tell them you lost the key and have one made. Simple.

They found the address and Stick pulled into the side drive of the big Colonial.

It was Frank's turn now. "They all do the same thing," he said, "leave two lights on downstairs and one up, and you're supposed to think somebody's home."

Stick sat in the truck while Frank rang the bell at the side door and waited. He rang it again and waited almost a minute before he broke a pane of glass in the door, reached in, and unlocked it. Stick got out of the truck and went inside, down a hallway past the kitchen to the family room, where a lamp was on. Frank was looking at the TV set, a big Motorola that was like a piece of furniture.

"What do you think?" Frank said. "Use the top for a bar, get rid of that little black-and-white I got. Except it's a big mother, isn't it?" He looked at Stick. "You think we can handle it?"

"If I remember right," Stick said, "we come here for guns."

There was a locked cabinet full of them down in the recreation room. Three rifles, three shotguns, and an assortment of handguns: several new-looking revolvers, a couple of Lugers, a Japanese automatic, and a Frontier model Colt .44, the kind Clint Eastwood had carried in the movie.

Stick had a feeling Frank would pick it up first. He did—pulled the hammer back and sighted and clicked the trigger, then hefted it in his hand, feeling the weight and looking at it from different angles. Frank held the Colt .44 against his hip, then threw it out in front of him and did it again.

"Fastest gun in Royal Oak," Stick said. "You know how to shoot?"

"Pull the trigger," Frank said. "Isn't that what you do?"

Stick considered a P-38 Walther, it looked pretty good, but

chose a Smith & Wesson .38 chief's special with a two-inch barrel. After Frank finished fooling around, he picked a big Colt Python 357 with a ventilated rib over its six-inch barrel. They found boxes of cartridges for both revolvers and got out of there.

The next day, Friday, Frank bought the Deluxe Anniversary Edition of *Gun Digest* and read off the vital statistics of his two revolvers, his forty-seven-ounce number and Stick's stubby little fourteen-ouncer. The Colt Python listed for a hundred and ninety-nine dollars and ninety-five cents new. Stick's little Smith only cost ninety-six. Stick said, "But I don't have to carry four pounds of metal around in my pants, do I?"

At noon Frank reported in at Red Bowers Chevrolet for the last time, sold two late-model used cars and made eighty-six bucks in commission. A good sign, everything was working. Stick got his sport coat from the cleaner's and had it on with a starched white shirt and a green-and-yellow-print tie when Frank got home. Frank didn't say anything about the coat or the tie. He changed and they each had a couple of drinks. At 6:30 they couldn't think of anything else they had to do, so they went out to hold up the liquor store.

Stick got a car from a movie theater parking lot in Warren, a '74 Olds Cutlass Supreme, drove it up the street to where Frank was waiting in the Duster, and picked him up. Frank asked if he had any trouble and Stick said, "What'd it take me, two minutes?"

Frank felt pretty good, anxious and a little excited, until they were approaching the liquor store. Then he wasn't sure. They came even with the building that was in a block of storefronts. There was plenty of parking space. Stick slowed down but kept going, his eyes on the rearview mirror.

"I wanted to look at it again," Stick said.

They went around the block, past vacant lots and plant-equipment yards.

"What we have to consider," Frank said, "what if we don't get much? Like fifty, sixty bucks, something like that. The guy could have most of his dough locked up somewhere, hidden. Then what do you do, he refuses to tell you where it is, shoot him?"

Stick was looking around. His eyes kept going to the rear-view mirror. "Or try another place," he said. "There's plenty around."

"What I mean is," Frank said, "maybe it's more trouble than it's worth. Nobody's forcing us. We go in a place because we want to. We try it or we don't. What're we out? Nothing. We could sell the guns. Maybe even the car, dump it off on somebody."

They were on the four-lane street again, with very little traffic going either way. A quiet, daylight-saving-time early evening in the summer. A car pulled away from the liquor store, leaving the curb empty for at least sixty feet.

"Well," Frank said, "what do you think?"

Stick swung the Olds in to the curb. "What do I think about what?" he said. "Let's do it."

He pulled up a little past the store entrance and put the lever in park, then accelerated to make sure the engine was idling.

As Stick opened his door, Frank said, "What's Rule Number One?"

Stick paused. "Always be polite. Say please and thank you."

Frank said, "You know, when I worked at the dealership a man came in to teach us how to sell cars over the phone. Call up people, find out if they're in the market. He says to me, 'What's your name?' I tell him Frank Ryan. He says, 'No, it's not.' He says, 'Not over the phone. You call a prospect, you say, "Hi, I'm Frank Duffy of Red Bowers Chevrolet." Duff-ee. You always use a name that ends in y or i-e. Because when you say it you got a smile on your face.' "

Stick waited, staring at Frank for a moment before he got out of the car.

The counter and shelves of liquor ran along the left wall. Down the middle of the store were wine bins and displays of party supplies. Along the right-hand wall the beer and soft drinks were in coolers with sliding glass doors. Two guys were standing over there.

245

Frank and Stick walked up to the liquor counter. The guy behind it was about sixty but big, over two hundred, with tight curly gray hair. He laid his cigarette in a chrome ashtray and said, "Can I help you?"

Frank wanted to look around, but he didn't. He hesitated and said, "Yes sir, you can," unbuttoned his suit coat, took out the Colt Python, and rested the butt on the counter so that the gun was pointing directly at the man's wide expanse of stomach. The man closed and opened his eyes and seemed tired.

"You can empty your cash register," Frank said. "But sir? I see anything in your hand's not green and made of paper, I'll blow you right through the fucking wall."

It was happening. Frank watched the guy punch open the cash register without a word. Maybe it had happened to him before. He held the gun on him and his hand was steady. He motioned with his head then.

Stick walked around the rack of potato chips and Fritos to the two guys standing by the beer cooler. They were hunched over, trying to decide, one of them reaching in then for a six-pack of Stroh's.

Opening his sport coat, Stick said, "Excuse me, gents." When they looked at him he said, "You see what I got here?" They didn't right away, until they saw he was holding his coat open.

The one with the six-pack said, "Jesus," and dropped it on the floor. Stick kept himself from jumping back.

The other one didn't say a word, his eyes on the butt of the .38 special sticking out of the waistband.

"You don't want to get hurt," Stick said, "and I certainly don't want to hurt you. So let's march to the rear, see what's in back."

Past the potato-chip rack he could see Frank holding open a paper bag and the man behind the counter dropping bills into it.

There was a young clerk in the storeroom, sitting on a stack of beer cases holding a sandwich and eating from a half-pint container of coleslaw. He looked surprised to see three men coming in, but he was also polite. He said, "Can I help you?"

Stick spotted the big walk-in reefer and said, "No thanks, I guess I can handle it myself."

He walked over, opened the door to the refrigerator, and nodded for the two customers to go inside.

The clerk said, "Hey, you can't go in there. What do you want?"

"You, too," Stick said. He held open his coat again. "Okay?"

When he came out into the store he thought the place was empty and got an awful feeling in his stomach for a moment. Then, near the cash register, Frank rose up from behind the counter with the paper bag.

As he came over the counter, the bag in one hand—the top of it rolled tightly closed—and the Python in the other, Stick said, "Where's the guy?"

"On the floor." Frank looked over the counter and said, "Stay down there, if you will please. Because if you raise up too soon, if you see me again, then I'll see you, won't I? And if I see you again, I won't hesitate to shoot and probably kill you."

Stick said, "Tell him the other people're in the icebox."

"You hear that, sir?" Frank looked over the counter again. "In the icebox."

"Tell him much obliged," Stick said.

"Yeah, much obliged. Maybe we'll see you again sometime."

Neither one of them wanted to look anxious. They walked out, taking their time.

In the car Stick put the gear into drive and waited, looking at the rearview mirror, until he saw the big guy with the gray curly hair appear suddenly in the doorway and stop dead. Stick got out of there then, tires squealing as he peeled away from the curb.

Frank turned around to look straight ahead again. "He saw the car, I'm sure. Maybe even the license."

"You bet he did," Stick said. "Now I drop you off at your car, head back to the picture show, and you pick me up there."

"It seems like a lot of trouble," Frank said.

"Yes, it does," Stick said. "But it sure keeps the police busy, looking for a '74 Cutlass Supreme, doesn't it? How much we get?"

Frank held the bag on his lap, the top tightly folded. "Rule Number Six," he said.

As soon as they were in the apartment Stick took off his sport coat. He was sweating. The Duster didn't have air conditioning. He looked at Frank, who was sitting on the couch lighting a cigarette like he had his lunch in the bag and there wasn't any hurry getting to it.

Stick said, "You going to count it or you want me to?"

"Why don't you make us a couple of drinks?" Frank said.

Stick went out to the kitchen. He poured scotch in one glass and bourbon in another, then got a tray out of the refrigerator and began filling the glasses with ice. It was all right that Frank counted it, but he wanted to watch, at least. He put a splash of water on the drinks and went back out to the living room.

"I don't believe it," Frank said.

He was hunched over the coffee table, looking down at the neatly stacked piles of bills, like a guy playing solitaire. He laid a twenty on one pile, a fifty on another. As Stick approached he was peeling off tens from the wad he held in his hand.

"Jesus," Stick said. "How much?"

"Don't talk, I'll have to start over."

Stick put the drinks down carefully, got a cigarette and lit it, and walked over to the window that looked out on the parking area behind the building. It was quiet back there, sunlight on the cars and long shadows, the end of the day. The cars looked hot. The tan Duster without air conditioning was parked there. A VW and a Pinto wagon and a Chevy pickup and a bike, a big Harley that made a racket every morning at seven fifteen—

"All right, how much you think?"

Stick turned from the window. "Why don't you tell me?"

Frank was sitting back with the scotch in his hand, all the bills stacked in front of him, now in five neat piles.

"How about six grand?" Frank said. "How about six thousand two hundred and forty-eight fucking dollars, man? Tax free?"

Stick came over to the table and stared at the money.

"Six, comma, two four eight," Frank said. "Most of it was in a box under the counter."

"Jesus, what a business," Stick said. "One day he makes that much?"

"You mean one day *we* make that much. No, what it is," Frank said, "the guy cashes paychecks."

"Yeah?"

"See, to get the hourly guys to come in, working in the shops. So he's got to have a lot of cash on hand payday. Keeps it in the box with the checks he cashes, from all different companies around there."

Stick looked up at him. "Endorsed? I mean the checks were signed?"

"I thought of that," Frank said, "but I figure it's not worth all the trouble, unless you know somebody likes to buy checks."

"Yeah, I guess so," Stick said. "Then you're dealing with somebody else."

"I figure we hit him earlier, we could've gotten even more. You know? Around three thirty or so, before the first-shift guys start coming in."

"You complaining?" Stick said. "First time, Christ. I don't believe it."

Frank started to grin. "Guy took one look at the Python— you see him?—I thought he was going to shit. I say to him, very polite, 'You can empty the cash register, sir. But I see anything in your hand isn't green or made of paper, I'm going to blow you right through the fucking wall.' "

Stick was grinning, too, shaking his head. He said, "I gave the two guys over by the beer cooler a flash of the Smith. I didn't take it out, I just showed it to them. I said, 'Hey, fellas, you see what I got here?' Just the grip sticking out. The guy drops his six-pack. The fella out in back's eating his lunch. He says, 'Can I help you?' "

"We're home counting our wages," Frank said, "they're still looking for the car. Or they got it staked out. The guy comes out of the show and they bust him."

"It's the only way to do it," Stick said. "Takes a little longer, but you keep your car clean, off the sheet. Yeah, it's a very good rule. In fact, that told me right away you had it pretty well thought out."

"You think it's worth it then, huh, all the trouble?"

"What trouble?"

"That's the way I see it," Frank said. "If they're all this easy, I believe we found our calling."

5

Frank would stand at the bar in the living room with one leg over a bamboo stool, pick up his scotch, and say, "Well, here we are."

Stick would say, "You sure?"

And Frank would say, "You look out and see if the broads are still there. I'll go count the suits."

It was a ritual after three months in the business and twenty-five armed robberies—after they'd bought the clothes and the new car and moved into the apartment building where nearly half the occupants were single young ladies. Frank liked to strike his pose at the bar and say, "Well, here we are."

During the first few weeks, when they were still in the small, one-bedroom place, he'd say, "You believe it?" He'd finish laying out the stacks of bills on the coffee table, look up at

Stick, and say, "You believe it? They're sitting out there waiting for us. Like they want to get held up, dying for it." Going
in, Frank had told himself over and over it would be easy—if
they observed the rules and didn't take chances—but he never
thought it would be this easy.

After the first few weeks he began to take it in stride. They
were pros, that's why it was easy. They knew exactly what
they were doing. Look at the record: twenty-five armed robberies, twenty-five stolen cars, more money coming in than
they could spend, and they had yet to get on a police sheet,
even as suspects.

Frank would say, "Partner, what do you want? Come on,
anything. You want it, buy it."

Frank didn't waste any time getting five new suits, a couple
of sport outfits, slacks, shirts, and a safari jacket. Stick bought a
suit, a sport coat, and three pairs of off-the-shelf pants for sixteen dollars each, studied the pants in the mirror—clown
pants, they looked like—and had the store cut off the big bell-
bottom cuffs before he'd buy them. They traded the Duster in
on a white '75 Thunderbird with white velour upholstery, air,
power everything, and went looking for a bigger apartment.

The third place they looked at was the Villa Monterey, out
in Troy: a cream-colored stucco building with dark wood trim,
a dark wood railing along the second-floor walk, a Spanish tile
roof, and a balcony with each apartment overlooking the backyard where shrubbery and a stockade fence enclosed the patio
and swimming pool. There was also an ice machine back there,
a good sign.

Stick said he thought it looked like a motel. Frank said no, it
was authentic California. He told the manager, the lady who
showed them the apartment, okay, gave her the deposit and
three months in advance to get out of signing a lease, and that
was it. They got two bedrooms, bath, bar in the living room
with bamboo stools, orange-and-yellow draperies, off-white
shag carpeting, off-white walls with chrome-framed graphics,
chrome gooseneck lamps, chrome-and-canvas chairs, an off-
white Naugahyde sectional sofa, and three dying plants for
four and a half a month, furnished. Stick didn't tell Frank but
he thought the place looked like a beauty parlor.

The first Saturday they were in, Frank went out on the balcony. He looked down at the swimming pool and said, "Holy shit." He said it again, reverently, "Holy shit. Come here and look."

There were five of them lying around the pool in their skimpy little two-piece outfits. Nice-looking girls, none of them likely to be offered a screen test—except one, who turned out to be a photographer's model—but all of them better than average, and they were right there, handy. Frank and Stick went to the pool just about every afternoon they weren't working—Frank in a tank suit with his stomach sucked in, and Stick in a new pair of bright blue trunks—and got to know the regulars pretty well. Frank called them the career ladies.

There was a nurse, Mary Kay something, an RN who worked nights on the psychiatric floor at Beaumont Hospital. Dark hair, very clean-looking. Also very skinny, but with wide hips. A generous pelvic region, Frank said. Mary Kay was a possible. Stick said, Maybe, if you looked sincere and told her you loved her.

There was a redheaded girl, frizzy red hair and bright brown eyes, who wore beads and seven rings with her bikini. Arlene. She was a little wacky and laughed at almost everything they said, whether it was supposed to be funny or not. Somebody was paying Arlene's rent, a guy in a silver Mark IV who came twice a week, Tuesday and Thursday, at six, and was usually out by 10:30. Arlene said he was a good friend.

There were several Jewish career ladies. Frank was glad to see that. He told Stick he liked good-looking Jewish girls because they had a lot of hair, big tits, and usually pretty nice noses once they had them fixed. He told Stick he'd been out with plenty of Jewish girls, including the little starlet in L.A. Stick said he wasn't sure if he ever had. He asked Frank if it was all right to mention the word *Jew* in front of them or refer to them as being Jewish in any way. Frank said, "You dumb shit, that's what they *are*. Don't you think they know it?"

There was a schoolteacher named Karen who didn't talk or look like a schoolteacher. Stick didn't think she looked Jewish either. Karen said some funny things about her sixth-graders being sex-crazed and how the little girls stuck out their training bras for the horny little boys. Frank started taking Karen out and sometimes he spent the night at her apartment. Stick didn't think she seemed too impressed with Frank, though. She was off all summer with nothing to do.

There was a dental hygienist by the name of Donna who had a boyfriend but wasn't going to marry him until he made as much as she did. She told them how much a dentist with a good practice could make and referred to net and gross a lot. Donna was way down at the bottom of Frank's list of things to do.

Sonny, the photographer's model, was the winner of the group. But she was unresponsive to drink offers. She seldom came up to their apartment with the others. She'd lie there behind her big sunglasses and hardly ever laugh when they said something funny. Frank said she was battery-operated. You pressed a little button on her can and she'd say, "Hi, I'm Sonny. I'm a model. So fuck off."

Stick noticed that Frank watched her, studied her, more than he did the others. Sonny was the only one Frank had trouble talking to.

There was a girl in the next apartment—a career lady but not one of the group—who they found out was a pro. Stick called her Mona because sometimes, through the wall, he'd hear her in there with a guy, saying things to him and moaning like she was about to die it was so good. Frank called her what's-her-name. He was polite to her but not interested. He said a guy would be out of his mind to pay for it at the Villa Monterey. Stick never mentioned it to Frank, but he liked her. He liked her straight dark hair parted in the middle. He liked the calm expression in her eyes and the quiet way she talked, though she never said very much. She was fragile-looking, a thin little thing with bony shoulders sticking out of her sleeveless blouse. When he'd see her outside he couldn't believe she was the same girl he'd hear moaning and carrying on through the wall. Maybe sometime, when Frank wasn't around, he'd get talking to her in private and find out which one was the real Mona.

They both liked the cocktail waitress, Jackie, who worked at a place called the Ball Joint and wore a kitty outfit with little ears and a tail. Jackie wasn't the smartest girl there, but she was very friendly. Also she had the biggest pair at the Villa Monterey, even when they weren't pushed up by her kitty outfit. She showed the group one time, in her bikini, how she placed drinks on a table, bending her knees and keeping her body straight so they wouldn't fall out. Frank said if they ever did and hit somebody, they'd kill him. Jackie worked nights and usually didn't drink in the afternoon, but was liable to bang on their door when she got home, 2:30 in the morning, if she saw a light on and heard the hi-fi playing. It wasn't unusual.

Their apartment had become a little social center, with the best-stocked bar in the building. Frank started it, inviting people up, especially on weekends. After a while they could count on people dropping in whenever there was a sign of something going on.

There'd be a good selection of career ladies.

There might even be some of the young married set. Frank would lure them away from their cookouts with Chivas Regal and talk about car prices and inflation with the husbands while he appraised the cute little housewives.

There might be two or three young single guys, somebody's date, and Barry Kleiman for sure. The career ladies called Barry the Prince. Stick thought because he looked like Prince Valiant with his hair, but that wasn't the reason. Barry was successful, owned a McDonald's franchise, wore bright-colored sport outfits with a white plastic belt and white patent-leather loafers, and was only about twenty pounds overweight. Barry would stand with his elbows tucked in close and his wrists limp and say, "Listen, when I was a kid, the neighborhood I grew up in? It was so dirty I'd sit out in the sun for two hours and get a nice stain." Then he'd wait for their reaction with an innocent, wide-eyed expression. Karen said he used to do Jerry Lewis imitations.

"Not a bad guy," Frank said. "He could be a pain in the ass, you know? But he's not a bad guy."

"You go for Barry, you must really like the place," Stick said.

Frank seemed surprised. "Yeah, I like it. You don't?"

"It's all right, I guess."

"All *right?* You ever had it like this, pouring cement?"

No, he'd never lived in a place with a swimming pool and had a party going most of the week with two guns in the closet and fifteen hundred bucks in an Oxydol box under the sink. It was funny, he never had.

When Frank recited his line—"Well, here we are"—instead of saying, "Are you sure?" he should say, "Where, Frank? Where exactly are we? And for how long?"

It was like getting excited and moving to Florida and having the Atlantic Ocean down the stret and palm trees and a nice tan all year and wondering, Now what? Sitting in a marina bar, watching gulls diving at the waves and seeing the charter boats out by the horizon, it didn't make the beer taste better. He'd tell himself this was the life and go home and have to take a nap before supper.

He wondered if he missed working, putting in a nine-, ten-hour day driving the big transit mix and pouring the footings for the condominiums that would someday wall out the ocean from Key West to Jacksonville Beach. There was plenty of work down there. It was on his mind a lot and he wasn't sure why, because the thought of going back to hauling cement bored the shit out of him.

He'd say to himself, What do you want to do more than anything?

Go see his little girl.

All right, but what do you want to do with your *life?*

He'd think about it a while and picture things.

He didn't see himself owning a cement company or a chicken farm or a restaurant. He never thought much about owning things, having a big house and a powerboat. He didn't care one way or the other about clothes. He'd never been much of a tourist. The travel brochures made it look good and he could see himself under a thatched roof with a big rum drink and some colored guys banging on oil drums, but he'd end up thinking, Then what do you do? Go in and get dressed up and eat the American Plan dinner and listen to the fag with the hairpiece play his cocktail piano and get bombed for no reason and go to bed and get up and do it over again the next day. He could picture a girl with him, on the beach, under the thatched roof. A nice-looking, quiet girl. Not his ex-wife. He never pictured his ex-wife with him and he never pictured the girl as his wife.

Maybe, Stick told himself, this was the kind of life he always wanted but never realized it before. Hold up one or two places a week, make more money than he could spend, and live in a thirty-unit L-shaped authentic California apartment building that had a private swimming pool and patio in the crotch of the L and was full of career ladies laying around waiting for it.

It sounded good.

Didn't it?

Yeah, Stick guessed it did.

6

They liked supermarkets. Get a polite manager who was scared
shitless and not more than a few people in the store, that was
the ideal situation, worth three or four gas stations even on a
bad day. The only trouble with supermarkets, they were big.
You never knew who might be down an aisle somewhere.

They hit the Kroger store in West Bloomfield early Saturday morning.

It looked good. No customers yet. The checkout counters
were empty. The only person they saw was a stockboy stamp-
ing prices on canned goods. Stick asked him for the manager,
saying he'd been called about a check that'd bounced and he
wanted to cover it. He followed the boy to the back and waited,
holding the swinging door open, seeing the manager back there
talking to a Budweiser deliveryman and a few of the checkout
girls drinking coffee. When the manager and the stockboy

came out, Stick let the door swing closed. And when the manager said, "May I have your name, please?" Stick said, "No sir," taking the Smith from inside his jacket, "but you can give me your money."

The manager said, "Oh, my God," and the three of them paraded up to the front where Frank was waiting. Frank got the cash register key from the manager and headed for the checkout counters. Stick and the manager and the stockboy went into the cashier's enclosure, Stick bringing a Kroger bag with him.

The manager kept saying, "Oh, my God." He told Stick he'd only been manager here one week. Stick said well, he was getting good experience, wasn't he? The stockboy was a heavy-boned, rangy kid who kept staring at him, making him nervous, until Stick told him to lay on the floor, face-down. He told the manager to clean out the cash drawer and open the safe. The manager had to get a piece of paper out of his wallet with the combination written on it, then kept missing numbers as he turned the dial and would have to start over again; but finally he got it open and pulled out a trayful of bills and personal checks. When he started to count the bills, Stick told him never mind, he'd do it later. The manager thanked him.

"What about these?" the manager said, picking up the checks.

"Keep 'em," Stick said.

"I appreciate that very much," the manager said. "I really do."

"Just the bills," Stick said, "no change. You can keep that, too."

"Thank you," the manager said. "Thank you very much."

Frank was at the third checkout counter, digging the bills out of the cash register and stuffing them in a Kroger bag. He looked up to see a woman with hair curlers pushing a cart toward him. He was taken by surprise and his hand went into his jacket for the Python. He'd looked down the aisles and hadn't seen anyone in the store. The woman began unloading her cart—coffee, milk, bread, and a few other items—not paying any attention to him. Frank brought his hand out of the jacket. The best thing to do was get rid of her, fast. He said, "How're you this morning?" and began ringing up the groceries, not looking at her. She was a pale, puffy woman with a permanent scowl etched in her face. And the hair curlers—in case anyone thought she wasn't ugly enough she had light-blue plastic curlers wrapped in her light-blue hair.

The woman squinted at him. "You're new."

"Yes, ma'am, new assistant manager."

"Where's your white coat?"

He was going to say that a jacket and sunglasses was the new thing for assistant managers, you cluck, you dumb, ugly broad, but he played it straight and told her they were getting him a white coat with his name on it. He punched the total and said, "Four sixty-eight, please."

The woman was digging in her purse, looking for something. She took almost a minute to bring out a piece of newspaper, unfold it, and hand it to him.

"Coupon for the coffee," the woman said. "Twenty cents off."

Frank took the coupon and looked at it. "Okay, then that's four forty-eight. No, wait a minute." He noticed the date on the coupon. "This offer's expired. It's not, you know . . . redeemable anymore, it's no good."

"I couldn't come in yesterday," the woman said. "It's not my fault. I cut the coupon out and there it is."

"I'm sorry," Frank said. "It says, see? Thursday and Friday only. Big letters."

"I've been coming here fifteen years, using the coupons," the woman said. "My husband and I. We buy all our groceries, our dog food, everything here. I'm one day late and you're going to tell me this is no good?"

"I'm sorry, I wish there was something I could do about it."

"Yesterday Earl took the car, had Timmie with him. All day he's gone, didn't even feed Timmie the whole while, and I had to sit home alone."

"All right—" Frank said.

"After all the money this store's made off us," the woman said. "I could've been going to Farmer Jack, Safeway. No, I come here and then get treated like I'm somebody with food stamps."

Frank was about to give in, but he changed his mind. He looked right at the lady now and said, "I got an idea. Why don't you take the coupon—okay?—and the one-pound can of Maxwell House coffee and shove 'em up your ass."

When they were in the stolen car, the Kroger bags on the floor, turning out of the parking lot, Frank said, "That fucking Earl. He stays out with their car all day, their dog, his old lady gets pissed off and makes life miserable for everybody. Jesus."

Stick wasn't listening. He was anxious. He waited for Frank to finish and said, "The manager, you know what he says when I'm leaving? Honest to God, he says, 'Thank you very much, sir, and come back again.' "

"That poor fucking Earl," Frank said. "I sure wouldn't want to be him."

They got a little over seventeen hundred at Kroger's. The story in the paper said, "about three thousand." Typical. Four days later, to show you how it could go, they hit a place and didn't get anything. The guy wouldn't give them the money.

It was a good thing it didn't happen on their first job. They would have quit. The guy was Armenian, a little bald-headed, excitable Armenian who ran a party store. No liquor, but imported beer and wine and expensive gourmet items, and the store was in a good location, out North Woodward near Bloomfield Hills. They went in on a Saturday night at ten. Frank took out his Python and Stick turned the OPEN sign around to CLOSED and pulled the shade down on the glass door.

Right away the little Armenian said, "What do you want to do this to me for? I never done nothing to you. I never saw you before." He stood there with his hands raised in the air.

Frank said, "Sir, put your hands down, will you?"

"I don't want this happening to me," the Armenian said in his high, excitable voice. "Since I move out here it never happen before. Never. Good people live out here. Why aren't you good people? You don't have to do this to me."

"It won't hurt at all, you do what I tell you," Frank said. "You understand? Now put your fucking hands down!"

Stick found the guy's wife in the back room, a little dark-

haired lady with a moustache, clutching her hands in front of
her like she was praying. Stick said, "Everything's going to be
all right, mama. Nothing to worry about." He moved her into
the toilet compartment, closed the door, and poked around the
storage room that was stacked high with beer and soft-drink
cases.

Frank looked up from the cash register when Stick came
back out.

"He's got a safe or he hid it somewhere."

Stick shook his head. "Not out there."

"Thirty-eight bucks and change," Frank said. "For tomorrow. He's cleaned out the drawer."

Stick went over to the Armenian, turned him around to face
the shelves, and felt the pockets of his white store coat.

"Nothing."

"It's somewhere," Frank said.

"All the money I have, in the cash register," the Armenian
said to the shelf of canned smoked oysters and clams. "I don't
have no more than that."

"Hey," Frank said, "come on. All day you make thirty-eight
bucks? Where is it? You hide it someplace?"

"I took it to the bank."

"No, you didn't. You been here all day."

"My wife took it." His voice went higher as he said, "Where
is my wife—what did you do to her!"

"This guy here raped her," Frank said.

Stick made a face like he was going to get sick.

"Now I'm going to rape her, you don't tell us where the
money is."

The Armenian didn't say anything. He was considering
whether he should give up the money or let his wife get raped
again.

"Come on," Frank said to him, touching the back of the Armenian's head with the Colt Python, "where is it! You don't
get it out by the time I count three, I'm going to blow your
bald head apart. . . . One."

"Do it!" the Armenian said in his high voice.

"Two."

"Kill me! You take my money, kill me!"

"Three."

Frank clicked the hammer back with his thumb. The Armenian's shoulders hunched rigid and held like that. Stick waited, feeling his own tension.

After a moment Frank said, "Shit."

There was no point in wasting any more time. They could tear the place apart and not find anything.

Frank said to the Armenian, "You're lucky, you know that? You're dumb fucking lucky, that's all."

After they left and were driving away, Stick said, "Shit, we forgot the thirty-eight bucks."

There weren't any textbooks on armed robbery. The only way to learn was through experience.

They found out gas stations weren't as good as they looked. Hand the kid a twenty and watch him go over to the manager or owner who'd take the wad out of his pocket and peel off change. But it didn't amount to that much: a bunch of singles and fives. There were too many people using credit cards now. Also, the high-volume service stations, where the money would be, always had five or six guys working there, using wrenches and tire irons, some hard-looking guys, maybe not too bright, who might see the gun pointing at them and decide to take a swing anyway. In their three gas station hits they went in and got out fast, the best take seven-eighty, which they figured was about as good as you could do.

They crossed off gas stations and altered a couple of their ten rules for success and happiness, finding it was all right to be polite, but you still had to scare the guy enough so he'd know better than to try and be a hero. It was all right, too, to dress well, look presentable. But they realized they'd better not become typecast or pretty soon the police would be writing a book on the two dudes who always wore business suits and said please and thank you. So they wore jackets sometimes, and raincoats. Stick had a pair of coveralls he liked he'd bought at J. C. Penney. They were comfortable and no one seemed to bother looking at him. Frank liked his pale-tan safari jacket with the epaulets. Very sharp, big in California. He liked the way the Python rested in the deep side pocket and didn't show. Usually, after a job, they kept the guns locked in the glove compartment of the T-bird. Stick thought they should put them away somewhere, hidden. But Frank said it was better to have them handy; they saw a place they liked, they were ready. Keep them in the apartment, some inquisitive broad could be snooping around and find them. Ho ho, what're these two business types doing with loaded firearms? Stick wasn't convinced, but he couldn't think of a better place to keep them.

Speaking of rules, Stick said maybe there was one more they should add. Number Eleven. Never try and hold up an Armenian.

They had taken in, so far, close to twenty-five thousand, spent a lot, but still had ninety-six hundred in a safe-deposit box at the Troy branch of Detroit Bank & Trust and about fifteen hundred or so spending money in the Oxydol box under the sink. They didn't divide the money. Except for major purchases—like the car and an eight-hundred-dollar hi-fi setup Frank picked out for them—the money went from the bank safe deposit to the Oxydol box, usually a thousand at a time, where it was available to both of them for pocket money and personal expenditures. There was no rule as to how much you could take; it was whatever you needed.

Two months ago, when they'd moved in, Stick had questioned the arrangement. He'd see Frank dipping in every day or so for fifty, a hundred, sometimes as much as two hundred. Finally he'd said, "Don't you think it'd be better, after a job, we divvied it up?"

Frank said, "I thought we were partners."

"Equal partners," Stick said. "We divvy it up, then we know it's equal."

"Wait just a minute now. You saying I'm cheating you?"

"I'm saying it might be better to split it each time, that's all. Then we know where we stand, individually."

"You know where the dough is," Frank said, "right? Under the sink, that's where we keep it. And you know you can go in there and take as much as you need, right? So how am I cheating you?"

"I understand the arrangement," Stick said. "I'm only asking, you think it would be better if we each took care of our own dough?"

"What're you, insecure? You want to hide it?"

"If half the dough's mine, why can't I do anything I want with it?"

"Jesus," Frank said, "you sound like a little kid. Nya nya nya, I got my money hidden and I'm not gonna tell you where it is. What is this shit? We partners or not?"

Stick let it drop.

From then on, he took two hundred dollars a week out of the Oxydol box, over and above what he needed, and put it away in his suitcase.

7

Stick was on the balcony, looking down at the empty patio. It was quiet, the pool area in shadows. He turned when he heard Frank come out of his bedroom and watched him walk over to the bar in one of his new suits and finish a drink he'd made and forgotten about.

"You taking the car?"

"No," Frank said, "we're going to walk. Broads love to get taken out to dinner and have to walk. You going out?"

"How?"

"What do you mean, how? You going out?"

"I mean *how*. What am I supposed to do, hitchhike?"

Frank took his time. He said, "It seems to me I remember I said maybe we better get two cars. You said, 'Two cars? Christ, what do we need with two cars?' You remember that?"

"How come you figure it's yours?" Stick said. "Take it any-time you want."

"Jesus Christ," Frank said, "I don't believe it. You want a car, steal one. You want it bad enough, *buy* one, for Christ sake. Take it out of the bank thing."

"Have a nice time," Stick said.

Frank was shaking his head, a little sadly, patiently. "Some-times, you know what? You sound like a broad. A wife. Poor fucking martyr's got to sit home while the guy's out having a good time."

"I'll wait up for you," Stick said. "Case you come in, you fall and hit your head on the toilet when you're throwing up."

"How long you been saving that?"

"It just came to me, you throw up a lot."

"You're quite a conversationalist," Frank said. "I'd like to stay and chat, but I'm running a little late." He went out.

There was a junior executive group at the Villa, a few guys with friends who were always coming over. Sometimes in the evening, after they'd changed from their business outfits to Levi's and Adidas, they'd sit on the patio and drink beer. If Stick was out on the balcony he'd listen to them, see if he could learn anything.

Usually it was about how stoned one of them got the night before. Or the best source of grass in Ann Arbor. Or why this one guy had switched from a Wilson Jack Kramer to a Bancroft Competition. Or how a friend of one of them had brought back eight cases of Coors from Vail. Then he wouldn't hear any-thing for a minute or so—one of them talking low—then loud laughter. The laughter would get louder as they went through the six-packs, and the junior executives would say *shit* a lot more. That was about all Stick learned.

This evening he didn't learn anything. They had two beers and decided to go to the show. Stick wondered what Mona was doing. Frank was gone. It'd be a good time if he was going to do it. He liked her looks and could picture her clearly in his mind, but he couldn't see her making all those sounds.

He wondered how much she charged.

He went out past the Formica table at the end of the living room to the kitchen and got a can of Busch Bavarian, came back in, sat down on one of the canvas chairs, and stared at an orange-and-yellow shape on the wall, a mess of colors, like somebody had spilled a dozen eggs and framed them.

He put the beer on the glass coffee table, went over and got Donna Fargo going on the hi-fi. He listened to her tell how she was the luckiest girl in the U.S.A., how she would wake up and say, "Mornin' Lord, howdy sun," and studied himself in the polished aluminum mirror on the wall. He looked dark and gaunt, a little mean-looking with his serious expression. Howdy there. I'm your next-door neighbor. I was wondering—

Going out the door and along the second-floor walk, he was still wondering.

I was wondering, if you weren't busy—

I was wondering, if you were free—had some free time, I mean.

He said to himself, Shit, let her do it. She knows what you want.

He knocked on her door and waited and knocked a couple more times. Still nothing, not a sound from inside the apartment. Stick went back to his own place, picked up the can of Busch, and walked out on the balcony. It was still quiet, with a dull evening sky clouding over. A lifeless expanse of sky, boring.

But there was somebody down there now. In the swimming pool. A girl doing a sidestroke, trying to keep her head up and barely moving. She was actually in the water, and Stick couldn't recall any of the career ladies every actually swimming before. He thought she had on a reddish bathing cap, then realized it was her hair—the redheaded one with the frizzy hair the guy in the silver Mark IV came to visit a couple of times a week. That one.

Arlene saw him standing there with her purple beach towel as she came out of the pool in her lavender bikini, her beads, and her seven rings. She said, "Hi," and laughed.

Stick handed her the towel, asked her how she was doing, and learned, Just fine.

He said, "Your friend coming over tonight?"

"He's tied up," Arlene said. "Had to go to Lansing." She began drying her wiry hair, rubbing it hard, and Stick couldn't see her face for a while. He watched her little boobs jiggling up and down. They were small but well shaped, perky. She had freckles on her chest. Stick figured she was a redhead all the way.

"What're you supposed to do when he doesn't show," Stick said, "sit around, be a good little girl?"

She answered him, but he couldn't hear what she said under the heavy towel.

"Do what?"

She peeked out at him through the purple folds. "I said he never told me I had to sit and twiddle my thumbs."

Stick gave her a little grin. "Don't you like to twiddle?"

Arlene grinned back and giggled. "I don't know as I ever have, tell you the truth. Is it fun?"

"You're from somewhere, aren't you?" Stick said. "Let me guess. Not Louisville. No, little more this way. Columbus, Ohio."

"Uh-unh, Indianapolis," Arlene said.

"Close," Stick said. "You take Interstate 70 right on over to Indianapolis from Columbus. Used to be old U.S. 40." He wasn't going to let go of Columbus that easy.

"I was Miss NHRA Nationals last year," Arlene said. "You know, the drag races? I was going to go out to California—a friend of mine lives in Bakersfield—but I was asked to come here instead, to do special promotions for Hi-Performance Products Incorporated. You know them?"

"I think I've heard the name."

"They make Hi-Speed Cams. That's their main thing. Also Hi-Performance Shifters. Pretty soon they're going into mag wheels and headers."

"It must be interesting work," Stick said.

"You'd think so. But what it is," Arlene said, "it's a pain in the ass. Those drag strips are so dirty. I mean the dust and grease and all. The noise, God. The first thing I do I get back to the motel is dive in the pool. I love to swim."

"I noticed, I was out on the balcony there," Stick said, glancing up at the apartment. "You're like a fish in the water."

"I love it, the feeling, like I don't even have a body."

"I guarantee you got a body," Stick said.

Arlene laughed, raised closed eyes to the dull sky, and shook her wiry hair. It barely moved.

Stick was looking at her mouth, slightly open, her slender little nose and the trace of something greenish on her eyelids.

"I was thinking," he said, "after all that swimming, how'd you like a nice cool drink now to wet your insides?"

Arlene loved the apartment. She said it was cool, it looked like it would be in California. Stick thought Arlene looked pretty cool, too, on the bamboo barstool in her little swimming suit, bare feet hooked on the rung and her legs sloping apart. He fixed her Salty Dogs, once she told him how, kept the vodka bottle handy, and sipped a bourbon over ice while she told him what it was like to put on a little metallic silver outfit with white boots and pose for camshaft promotion shots, with the hot lights and all. She said it wasn't any picnic and Stick said he bet it wasn't. He watched her rubbing her eyes and blinking, but didn't say anything about it until she'd put away three Salty Dogs and was working on number four.

He said, "It's that chlorine in the pool. What you ought to do is go in and take a shower."

"You mean here?"

"What's the matter with here?"

"But I don't have anything to put on after," Arlene said, "except this wet swimming suit."

If that was all she was worried about, Stick knew he was home. He said, "I'll get you a robe or something. How'll that be?"

That was how he got her in the shower. He put her drink on the top of the toilet tank, adjusted the spray nice and warm, and went out, closing the door.

Stick didn't own a robe. Maybe Frank had one, but he didn't

bother to look. He went into his bedroom and got undressed, put his shoes and socks in the closet, hung up his new pants and shirt, got down to his striped boxer shorts, thinking he could have taken her to dinner, spent twenty bucks. He could have taken her to a movie and then to a bar, hear some music, then coming home ask her if she wanted a nightcap at his place. He could have gone through all that and then have her say thanks anyway, she was tired. Find out first, then take her out after; that was the way to do it. He couldn't figure out why he had hesitated going to Mona's, trying to get the words right. Mona was a pro, whether she looked like one or not. Arlene was a—what? Hot-rod queen. A flake. Part-time camshaft model and kept lady. But he really didn't know her or how she'd react.

She might scream. She might say, Now wait a minute, or, Get the hell out of here, or threaten to call the police, or be so scared she couldn't say anything.

What Arlene did say, when he pulled the curtain back and stepped naked into the shower with her, was, "Hon, get me another Salty Dog first, will you?"

They were in bed, dried off and smelling of Mennen's talcum powder, when Mona started.

That faint sound through the wall, a caressing sound without words.

Stick hadn't heard her come in. Probably while they were in the shower. He was on an elbow right now, half over Arlene with a leg between hers, giving her a little knee, feeling strong with his gut sucked in, giving her nice tender kisses and feeling her hands moving over the muscles in his back.

Arlene opened her eyes.

"What's that?"

"What?" He put his mouth on hers to keep her from talking.

"Like somebody's in pain."

"I doubt if it's pain," Stick said. He got back to it and Arlene began to squirm and press hard against him.

Mona, in another bed in another room, said, "Oh, Jesus. Oh, God. Oh, Jesus."

Arlene's eyes opened again. "Listen."

"Oh please—"

Arlene slid around him and sat up. "Where's it coming from, next door?"

"I guess so."

"Who lives there?"

"The one—I don't know her name."

Arlene frowned. "The mousy one with the straight hair?"

"I don't know as she's mousy. A little plain maybe. Not what you'd expect—"

Arlene stopped him. "Listen."

She got out of bed, carefully climbing over him, and followed the faint murmuring sound to the wall where the dresser stood. Stick watched her crouch there—a naked redhead who looked especially naked to him because her skin was white and didn't show tan lines—her face alert, pressed to the wall, her perky little boobs hanging free.

"You want to learn how it's done. Is that it?"

"Shhhhhhhh."

"I thought you knew. You seemed to be doing all right."

Arlene didn't look over or change her expression. The room was silent. Stick could hear the sound again.

After a moment Arlene said, "Oh ... *now*, please, Oh, please, please, please," keeping her voice low.

"I'd be glad to oblige," Stick said.

Arlene was fascinated, glued to the wall, her eyes alive and mouth slightly open.

"Give it to me. Give me everything, oh, please. Oh, God, Jesus."

"Maybe what she's doing," Stick said, "she's saying her prayers."

"Uh-unh. She just said the word."

"What word?"

"I can't say it out loud. God, now she's saying it over and over."

"Spell it," Stick said.

He got a Marlboro off the night table with the Chinese figurine lamp and sat up in bed to smoke and watch Arlene and tried to imagine what was going on in the bed on the other side of the wall. He could picture Mona's face, her eyes closed; but he couldn't picture her saying anything or picture the guy with her. He didn't want to picture the guy. Arlene's eyes opened a little wider. It wouldn't be long now. Arlene looked good. He wondered if he could like her seriously. Studying her he realized she was very pretty. Delicate features. Slim body. Flat little tummy. Not at all self-conscious about standing there naked. But she couldn't say the word.

Arlene must have been thinking about it, too. When she came back to bed and crawled over him she said, "I could never say that. I can do it, God, no trouble at all. But I can't say it. Isn't that strange?"

Stick said, "I was thinking, why don't you take your rings off? So nobody'll get hurt."

8

The bar in Hazel Park was on Dequindre, only a few blocks from the racetrack. They had been in once before and watched a couple of big winners buy rounds for the house. They weren't sure if bars were worth it and picked this one as a good place to find out.

When they went in at 1:30 A.M., a half hour before closing, it was filled with the sound of voices and country music playing on the jukebox. The bar section was still very much alive, though the tables were empty now and the waitress was standing by the service station counting her tips.

Once they pulled their guns, Stick would cover the people at the bar and put them down on the floor while Frank concentrated on the bartender, a woman, and got her to empty the cash register. Before Frank could get his Python out, Stick touched him on the arm.

"Let's sit down."

They got a table. The waitress brought them a couple of draft beers and left.

"The guy with the hair," Stick said, "at the end of the bar."

The guy was at the curved end nearer the door, facing the length of the bar: thick hair over his ears, big arms and shoulders in a dull yellow-satin athletic jacket. Frank drank some of his beer as the guy's head turned toward them.

"What about him?"

"He eyed us when we came in. Watch him, keeps looking around."

"Maybe he's waiting for somebody."

"Or maybe he's a cop, staking the place out. You read about it? They been doing that."

"A cop," Frank said. "He looks like a bush leaguer never made it."

"Cops put on these outfits now, play dress-up," Stick said. "You never know anymore."

"If you don't feel right about it," Frank said, "let's go. Maybe it's not a good idea anyway. Six, seven, nine with the waitress, that's a lot of people to keep track of."

"Wait," Stick said. "I think he's leaving."

They watched the guy in the yellow-satin jacket slide off the stool and pick up a leather case that must have been leaning against the bar on the other side of him.

"He's got pool cues," Frank said. "I thought he was a jock. He's a pool-hall cowboy."

"Going to the can," Stick said.

There was an inscription on the back of his jacket. They watched it go into the men's room.

"Port Huron Bullets," Stick said. "He's one of the famous Port Huron Bullets. You ever heard of them?"

"We'll wait'll he leaves," Frank said. He finished his beer. When he took a cigarette out Stick did, too, and got a light from him.

Dolly Parton was singing on the jukebox. Stick had been in love with Dolly when he used to watch the "Porter Waggoner Show" and paused to listen before he said, "You want to do it, huh?"

Frank looked at him. "What's the matter, you nervous?"

"No more than usual. You bring a bag?"

"Shit, I forgot," Frank said. "They probably got something behind the bar. Wrap it in the broad's apron or something."

"She doesn't have an apron on."

"We'll put it in *some*thing, okay?"

"I don't know," Stick said. "I don't feel we're a hundred percent this time. You know what I mean?"

"When're we ever a hundred percent sure?"

"I don't mean sure. I mean ready, wanting to do it. We come in, right away we hang back."

Frank was looking past him. "Here he comes."

Stick saw the change in Frank's expression and heard him say, "Jesus Christ," softly, with a sound of awe. He heard that and heard Loretta Lynn now saying they didn't make men like her daddy anymore, as he turned and saw the guy in the yellow-satin jacket and the door of the Men's Room behind him, the guy raising a pump-action shotgun level with his waist.

"Don't nobody move! This is a holdup!"

The guy shouted it, drowning out Loretta Lynn. "I'll shoot the first one moves!"

When he swung the shotgun at their table, Frank and Stick were looking right at him about fifteen feet away. "You two— don't make a move. Don't anybody. I'm warning you. I'll shoot to kill."

"Wants everybody to know he means business," Frank said.

They watched him move hesitantly toward the bar, telling people who were looking over their shoulders at him to turn the fuck around. Loretta Lynn was finished and it was quiet in the place now as he got around behind the bar and moved down to where the woman bartender was standing at the cash register.

"How come he doesn't make 'em lay on the floor?" Stick said. "You believe it?"

"He doesn't know what he's doing," Frank said. "Dumb pool-hall cowboy. Tells everybody on his jacket where he's from."

"That shotgun'd be a pain in the ass," Stick said, "wouldn't it? You imagine carrying a shotgun around?"

"Keep your hands on the bar!" the guy shouted at somebody.

"He's pretty nervous," Frank said. "Maybe it's his first time."

"He's more nervous than I am. Look at him wave that scattergun," Stick said. "Doesn't know where to point it."

"What he ought to do," Frank said, "is put it on the waitress. Tell 'em he'll blow her off if anybody moves, or if the broad doesn't give him the money."

"Yeah, get 'em laying down first, they don't see where he's at." Stick shook his head. "Dumb cowboy, I wouldn't be surprised he had a horse outside."

"Runs out in the street waving his shotgun," Frank said. "Or you suppose he puts it back in the case first?"

"He goes in the toilet," Stick said, "and comes out again pretending he's got pool cues in it. Now he's getting the change off the bar. What'd she put the money in? The broad."

"Looked like her purse."

"Runs out with a shotgun and a purse," Stick said. "That'd be a sight, wouldn't it? How much you think he got?"

Frank was silent for a moment, watching the guy as he moved carefully toward the end of the bar.

"He isn't out of here yet."

Stick looked at Frank, then back to the guy, who was coming around the bar and now backing toward the door.

"It's an idea, isn't it?" Stick said.

"If we see the chance."

"I think when he goes to open the door," Stick said.

The guy seemed more nervous than before. He glanced over at their table but was concentrating on the people at the bar. "Don't nobody move," he said. "I go out, I'm liable to come back in to make sure. Anybody I see moved gets a load of twelve-gauge, and I *mean* it."

"He talks too much," Stick said.

The guy turned to the door, raising the shotgun barrel straight up in front of him, and started to push it open.

"Drop it," Frank said.

The guy hesitated, his back to them and the shotgun upright against the door. He had a moment, but when he finally turned, it was too late. Both Frank and Stick, standing away from the table, ten feet apart, had their revolvers on him, aimed at arm's length.

"Come on," Frank said, "put it down."

When the shotgun was on the floor, Stick walked over to the guy and took the purse from him.

He said, "Much obliged, partner. We appreciate it."

The story in the *Detroit News* the next day described how for six hours the would-be holdup man and the bar patrons were locked up together in a storeroom where all the liquor and bar supplies were kept. When they were found the next morning, the newspaper account stated, the would-be holdup man appeared to have suffered a severe beating, while the bar patrons were in a festive state of intoxication.

"Can you see it?" Stick said. "The Port Huron Bullet comes out, blood all over him, can't open his eyes. Hasn't got any idea what happened to him. Keeps asking himself, over and over, 'What went wrong?' "

"A customer comes out," Frank said, "absolutely fried. Cop says to him, 'Sir, you want to tell us how much you had stolen? Any valuables?' The guy, the customer, looks at him with these bleary eyes and says, 'Who the fuck cares?' "

They got a kick out of the Hazel Park bar robbery, plus a little better than eleven thousand in cash.

They decided they didn't like bars, though: too many people and too unpredictable with booze involved. So they crossed off bars along with gas stations and would concentrate on other types of establishments.

9

Three of the career ladies were at the pool when Frank and Stick came down: two of them lying face up, eyes closed— Mary Kay, the skinny nurse with the wide hips, and Jackie, the cocktail lounge kitty—and one on her stomach, face hidden in an outstretched arm. Frank knew by the short, dark hair and deep tan it was Karen, the schoolteacher. Karen had her bra strap unfastened, out of the way, and there was no line. Her brown skin glistened with oil, smooth and bare all the way down to where the little bikini bottom almost covered her can.

Stick, with his towel and a rolled-up magazine, eased into the first empty lounge he came to, near the edge of the grass.

Frank made a production of it. He stood with his gold beach towel over one shoulder, looked at his watch, checked the angle of the sun, then dragged a lounge chair around—with the sound of aluminum scraping on cement—to catch the direct rays.

Without opening her eyes Jackie said, "Frank's here."

"I'm sorry, honey, the chair wake you up?" He brought a tray table over for his towel, his watch, and for the drinks he'd have later on.

"You're supposed to lift it," Jackie said. "It leaves marks."

"Yeah, I always forget."

Karen's face rose from her arm.

"Frank, while you're up, you want to do my back?"

"I'll force myself," Frank said.

Stick had his magazine, the last issue of *Oui*, folded open. He had looked at the pictures already, the boob and crotch shots. Now he was reading about Alex Karras and what Alex thought about Howard Cosell and doing NFL color on TV. Looking over the top of the magazine, he watched Frank sit down on the edge of Karen's lounge.

The nurse, Mary Kay, was watching them, too. Mary Kay usually didn't say much. She listened; sometimes she laughed.

Stick wondered what she thought of them. Probably nothing. She probably saw so many weird things up in that nut ward nothing down here would shock her.

"Cut it out," Karen said.

"What am I doing?"

Stick looked over there again. As Frank's hands caressed her back, one of them slid into the space between her arm and body.

"*Fra*-ank!"

"What's the matter? I'm not doing anything."

"That's enough."

"Little more right . . . *there.*"

"Frank—"

As he stood up and moved about idly, wiping his hands on his chest and stomach, Stick said, "Sure is full of the devil, isn't he?"

Frank looked up at the sun, raising his arms and stretching.

"Oh, man. Perfect day, isn't it? Sun, the sky's clear, little breeze so it's not too hot . . . Jackie, you got a perfect navel, you know that? Anybody ever tell you?"

She pressed her chin to her chest to look down at it.

"What's so different about it?"

"It's round," Frank said, "like a bullet hole. Pow, right in the navel."

"I don't know, Frank," Jackie said, "sometimes I wonder about you."

"What do you wonder?"

"If you're all there."

"I'm all here. Hey, look at me. Jackie, look. You see anything missing?"

"The exhibitionist," Karen said. "You ever see him go out with his raincoat on? Sunny day, he's wearing a raincoat. We heard about guys like that, Frank. Our moms told us a long time ago."

Frank looked over at Stick, and Stick said mildly, "He's insecure is all. Wears drawers under his pajamas, and socks to bed."

"See, I'm right," Jackie said. "He's a little strange."

Frank liked it there in the center of things, playing around with the career ladies. He looked over at the nurse, to get them all involved.

"Mary Kay, honey, you got room for me in your psycho ward? Maybe I better have some tests."

"We're overcrowded," Mary Kay said. "We don't have enough beds the way it is."

"How about if I stood up?"

Stick felt sorry for her—put on the spot and not having a smart-ass reply ready. Everybody had to be a smart-ass, get a laugh and make it look easy. It wore you out, thinking, just staying in a conversation.

He said to Mary Kay, "How about giving him a shot, then, to quiet him down? Case anybody wanted to take a nap?"

Mary Kay smiled but didn't say anything.

Stick let it go. It looked like too much of a job to bring her out. And if he got her out, then what? There had to be something better to do. He went up to the apartment, poured a half bottle of vodka and a quart of tonic into a plastic pitcher, threw in some limes and ice and carried it down on a tray with a half dozen plastic poolside glasses.

Arlene was in his lounge chair, looking at the magazine. She didn't notice him right away. Frank was talking to Karen.

"It's funny nobody ever asked before. What'd you think we were, retired?"

"Are you kidding?" Karen said. "We thought you were out of work."

Frank looked up at Stick and moved his towel, making room on the table next to him.

"You hear that? She thought we were out of work."

"It just looks like it sometimes," Stick said. He picked up the glasses as Frank poured them. Mary Kay shook her head and said no thanks. Jackie took a sip and made a little sound of appreciation. Karen was snapping her bra and he had to wait for her to take the glass. Arlene smiled at him. She said, "Here, there's room. Come on."

Stick sat down on the edge of the chair, feeling the aluminum tube beneath his thighs. He saw Mary Kay watching and then look away.

"What we are," Frank said, "we're sales motivators. We go in a place, say a car dealership, okay? We motivate the salesmen, get them off their cans, by actually showing them how to cultivate prospects and close deals. I demonstrate what we call the *frank* approach, how to appear open and sincere with customers, sympathetic to their needs. Then Ernest here, better known as Stick, shows them how an *earnest*, confident attitude will close the sale every time."

Arlene gave Stick a little poke. "You must travel a lot. You ever been to California?"

Frank answered her. "Many times. Write us care of the Continental Hyatt House, Sunset Boulevard."

"I'd love to go out there," Arlene said. "I've got a friend in Bakersfield."

She went into the pool after a while and Stick got a chance to stretch out again with his magazine, half listening to Frank bullshitting the ladies. Finally he heard Frank say, "Which reminds me, partner. We got a sales meeting this afternoon." As Stick got up Frank was telling the ladies they hated to leave but would see them again real soon. Stick kept trying to think of something to say, something a little clever.

Walking away from the patio with the pitcher and tray and magazine under his arm, he glanced back and said, "You all be good now."

10

There was a six o'clock wedding at the Shrine of the Little Flower, on Woodward in Royal Oak. Stick took a Chevrolet Impala that was parked in line at the side of the church—washed, key in the ignition, ready to go.

Frank was waiting in the T-bird, in the lot behind the Berkley Theater on Twelve Mile Road. They changed from their suit coats to lightweight jackets, took off their ties, and got their revolvers out of the glove box. Frank put on sunglasses; Stick, a souvenir Detroit Tiger baseball cap. They left their suit coats and ties in the T-bird, got in the Impala, and drove over to the A&P on the corner of Southfield and Twelve. On the way, Stick said he almost took the car with the pink-and-white pompoms all over it. He didn't because he was afraid Frank might feel a little funny riding in it.

It was a good-looking A&P, in a high-income suburban area. But Frank didn't like all the cars in the parking area. Too many.

They drove back to a bowling alley–bar on Twelve in Berkley to kill some time and had a few vodkas and tonic in the dim, chrome-and-Formica lounge. Sitting in a bar in the early evening reminded Stick of Florida. He didn't like the feeling.

"I was thinking," Stick said, "you could tell them the truth and nobody'd believe it. Girl says, 'What do you do for a living?' And you say, 'Oh, we hold up stores, different places.' And Jackie or one of them would say, 'I believe it.' Only she wouldn't. None of them would."

"You think that'd be funny, huh?" Frank said.

"You'd think it was funny if you'd thought of it," Stick said.

"You heard what Karen said about wearing the raincoats?"

"She thinks you're queer, that's all."

"That's what she does," Frank said, "thinks. She's got those big knockers, she's got nothing to do all day, she sits around and thinks."

When they got back to the A&P, there were only about a dozen cars in the lot. Stick pulled up, almost at the front entrance, where there was a NO PARKING—PICKUP ONLY sign.

"I'll see you," Stick said.

Frank slid over behind the wheel when Stick got out. He lit a cigarette and took his time smoking it, five or six minutes, then left the motor running and went into the store.

The manager was inside the cashier's enclosure. Frank could see his head and shoulders through the glass part of the partition. Stick wasn't in there.

Another employee, maybe the assistant, was working the Kwick-Check, eight-items-or-less, counter, where several people were lined up waiting. Only one other checkout counter was open. A woman was unloading a cart with a week's supply of groceries while a checkout girl in a red A&P smock rang them up.

The assistant, or whoever it was at the Kwick-Check counter, looked over at Frank, then down at the counter again.

Frank got a cart and pushed it down to the end of the store, turned left at baked goods, stopped at dairy products for a wedge of Pinconning cheese and some French onion dip, found the potato-chip counter, and was two aisles over before he ran into Stick.

Stick was putting two boxes of Jiffy corn bread mix in his cart. He already had lettuce, cucumbers, tomatoes, a sackful of potatoes, and four cans of Blue Lake mustard greens.

"Hi there," Frank said. "It certainly does save to shop at A&P, doesn't it?"

"It saves your ass if you got your eyes open," Stick said. "You see the guy at the counter?"

"I thought he might be the assistant."

"He might've been," Stick said, "if he hadn't gone into police work instead."

"You sure?"

"There's one just like him over in produce weighing tomatoes. You know the look, their face, when they look at you? Like they see clear through and can tell you what color drawers you got on."

"I don't know," Frank said. "You thought the guy in the bar was a cop."

"I could be wrong," Stick said, "but I got no intention of finding out if I'm right. I think we ought to get out of here."

Frank shrugged. "Well, if you don't have your heart in it, I guess that's it."

"Go over and look at the guy in produce," Stick said. "Big, hardheaded-looking guy. He might just as well have his badge pinned on his apron."

"I'm not doubting your word," Frank said, "you want to go, let's go."

"I'll be right behind you." Stick turned his cart around and started back up the aisle.

"Where you going?"

"Get some salt pork for my mustard greens."

They cruised down Southfield looking for another store and passed two shopping centers, one with a Wrigley, the other with a Farmer Jack, before Frank said anything.

"You didn't like either of those?"

Stick was driving. "I don't know. The parking, all the stores there, it looked congested. I see us trying to get out and some broad in a Cadillac's got everything fucked up."

"How about over there?" Frank said. "Nice neat little post office." It was a red-brick Colonial with white trim. "You ever hear of somebody knocking down a post office?"

"There's a good reason," Stick said. He saw determined-looking, clean-cut guys in narrow suits who never smiled. "It's called the Federal Bureau of Investigation."

Frank looked back as they passed it. "It might be an idea, though. U.S. Post Office. Save it for around Christmastime when business's up."

Stick didn't bite. He realized now what Frank was doing.

Coming to Ten Mile Road, Frank said, "Hey, there we are. What do you say?"

Stick looked at the bank on the southwest corner. Michigan National. He didn't say anything.

"You don't like it?"

"I like it," Stick said. "It's just I don't love it."

"How about the Chinese place? All right, you guys, give me all your fucking egg rolls. You like egg rolls or you love them?"

"The next one," Stick said, "I think I might go for."

It was a Food Lanes supermarket. Stick turned in and pulled to a stop facing the building. He liked the location, the alley running next to the store, the ample parking on two sides. Or they could park across the alley at the Chinese place. That might be better.

"It's up to you," Frank said. "Go in and look it over. I'll wait here."

He was still playing his game. Stick didn't say anything. He went in and took his time walking around the store and bought cigarettes. Frank had a bag of potato chips when he got back in the car and drove out.

"You still like it?"

"Not bad," Stick said. "The only thing, you notice the doors? The cashier's place's in the front, in the corner, and there's doors on both sides. Two doors to watch. Also there's a magazine rack. So from the cashier's place you can't see much of the store."

Frank put a potato chip in his mouth and crunched it between his teeth.

"But no cops in there dressed up like grocery boys?"

"Fuck you," Stick said.

"You want a chip? Lay's. They dare you to try and eat just one."

"You didn't like the looks of the guy any more than I did," Stick said. "I said he looked like a cop, you agreed."

"I said you also thought the guy in the bar looked like a cop, with the fucking shotgun."

"You're trying to make it look like it's my fault we didn't hit the place," Stick said. "Like I'm chicken or something. You want to hit the post office? How about that bank there. All that shit."

"Watch the road," Frank said.

"Watch your ass. You don't like the way I drive, get the fuck out."

"You know, it's funny," Frank said, "you come on as a very easygoing person. Then bang, no reason, you get a hard-on like you want to kill somebody."

"No reason, no, none at all," Stick said.

"I was being funny, for Christ sake, you get pissed off. Like the other day you're pissed off at me using the car. Think about it," Frank said. "You got this down-home, you-all delivery like nothing in the world bothers you, but you know what? I think you could be a pretty mean son of a bitch underneath it all."

Frank was turning it around again, making it all his fault. There was no sense arguing with him when he did that. Stick kept his eyes on the road and didn't say anything. It always irritated him and he would begin to think about how he'd got into this and wonder if he should get out, now, while he still had a choice and walk away.

But he had to admit they were doing better than he'd expected, and maybe it was natural for two guys as different as they were to rub each other the wrong way sometimes. So what, right? He could live with it, as long as they kept the jobs simple and didn't overextend themselves.

Frank offered the potato chips again and he took some.

"You want to do one or go home or what?"

"Well, as long as we're out," Stick said, "we may as well. You got a hundred on you?"

The hundred-dollar bill usually worked. It was something they had thought of after the experience with the Armenian and could save a lot of threatening and gun waving. Make a purchase and hand the guy the bill. He would always hesitate, then look in the cash register, then hesitate again. Then, with Frank standing there looking prosperous and honest in his suit, the guy would fish a roll out of his pocket or say, Just a minute, and step into the back room. Stick would come in and they'd find the guy taking his excess cash out of a safe or wherever he kept it hidden.

They stopped by the T-bird to put their suit coats back on, cruised around for a while and found a drugstore with a liquor department. Frank bought a bottle of J&B and handed the guy the hundred-dollar note. This led them back to the prescription department where the pharmacist was making change out of a drawer. Stick tied up the clerk and pharmacist with Ace wraps and one-inch adhesive—the same tape he had used to do his ankles before a basketball game—while Frank hit the cash registers and the secret drawer for sixteen-fifty, their all-time record drugstore take.

They stayed out, had dinner, and closed the bar at the Kingsley Inn, singing along with the piano player, talking and making friends but not seeing anything worth picking up; all too old. Driving home, going through the business section of Birmingham, they noticed an appliance store holding its Annual Twenty-four-Hour Marathon Sales Spectacular. They looked at each other, full of drinks, and grinned.

The two guys who ran the store were dressed up in flannel nightshirts, still smiling and friendly at 2:30 in the morning. Frank and Stick each got a free-gift yardstick with the store's name on it for coming in. They looked around for a few minutes. Then Frank picked out a couple of ice trays that were sale priced at $2.98 each and handed the hundred-dollar bill to the cluck behind the counter in his nightshirt. The cluck looked at Frank and at the bill and finally shook his head and said gee, he was sorry but he didn't have enough cash in the store to make change.

Walking out, Frank said, "Bullshit."

Stick said, "You cheap bastard, why didn't you pick out a radio or something?"

"Don't worry," Frank said.

A half hour later they met the cluck down the street, at the local bank's night-deposit box. They pressed a free-gift yard-stick into his back, relieved him of a little more than seven hundred in cash, and left the cluck standing there in his nightshirt.

Frank could be a pain in the ass sometimes, but they usually had a good time and it was a pretty interesting way to make a living.

11

The time before he had looked for Mona and found Arlene. Tonight it was the other way around.

Arlene wasn't in her apartment. He went there twice and knocked and waited.

Frank was out for the evening, with the car and probably Karen. Stick didn't bring up the car again. If he wanted a car he'd get his own. He didn't feel like going out, though. He made a drink and went down to sit by the pool for a while.

He liked the darkness and the lights beneath the clear water and the sound of crickets in the shrubs. The bourbon was good, too. It was nice, sitting by himself having a drink and a cigarette.

It could be his own private patio and swimming pool. He wondered if he'd enjoy it any more if it was.

Mona appeared out of the darkness, without a sound, and sank into a lounge chair by the deep end of the pool. He wondered if she had seen him, the glow from his cigarette. She sat with the backrest up, her legs stretched out, staring at the illuminated water. She didn't move. He wondered if her eyes were closed, staring at the water but not seeing it.

Stick said, "How you doing?"

Mona looked over.

"Hi. How're you?" She said in quietly, without putting anything extra into it.

She reminded him of somebody. Her face was pale in the reflection of the underwater lights. Her hair seemed darker. It was her nose and her mouth and the way her hair hung close to her face. She reminded him of somebody in the movies he used to like.

He almost told her that—bringing the aluminum chair over next to her lounge—but it would sound dumb, like he was making it up. It didn't make sense, did it? Trying to think of something to say to a hooker that wouldn't sound dumb. Hooker or call girl or whore, prostitute, whatever she considered herself. That might be something to talk about—if there was a difference between them. Get in a conversation about it, like he was making a study. When did you first consider turning pro? First accept money? What do you think got you doing it? Is it true whores really don't like guys? And all that bullshit.

He had been with whores in Toledo, Findlay, Ohio; Columbus, Fort Wayne, Terre Haute, Rock Island, Illinois; Dubuque, and Minot, North Dakota. Most had been nice, a few had had no personality at all. But he had never met a whore with a nose and mouth like Mona's. And he couldn't look past her nose and mouth and see her as a whore. Also she seemed too small and frail to be a whore—even though he had read that women were better than men at withstanding pain or punishment. He pictured her taking her blouse off, no bra, and asking for the money; then imagined a guy punching her in the mouth, threatening to do it again, and getting it for nothing. It could happen, a guy who didn't have any feeling. It must be a pretty tough life. He wanted to get into it with her, but didn't know how.

What had he said to all those other whores from Toledo to Minot? He'd said, "How much?"

He said to Mona, "You want a drink? I can get you one."

"No, thank you, though."

"How about a sip then? It's bourbon."

She hesitated. "All right."

As she was taking a drink he said, "No trouble to get you one. Salty Dog, anything you want."

"No thanks." She handed the glass back. "I'm going up in a minute."

He wanted to say something so there wouldn't be a silence, but it came. She was staring at the pool again.

"You know, you remind me of somebody. I can't think of who it is."

"Is that so?"

"Somebody in the movies."

He said it and it didn't sound as bad as he thought it would.

"My dad used to say I reminded him of a Labrador retriever we had. His name was Larry. The dog, I mean."

"You sure don't look like a Labrador retriever," Stick said. "Maybe the hair."

"It was when Larry was a puppy. I think the feet had something to do with it," Mona said. "We both had big feet."

Stick looked at her legs, at the white sandals pointing out of her white slacks.

"They don't look very big."

"Seven and a half quad." She looked down at them and wiggled her toes. "I have trouble getting fitted, except sandals, something like that."

There was a silence again.

"You sure you don't want a drink?"

"No, I think I'll go up."

"I still can't think of who it is you look like."

"Somebody in the movies, huh?"

"Dark hair, really pretty."

"Oh, it's a girl?"

"Sure it's a girl. She was in—I know she was in one John Wayne was in."

"I don't know who it could be," Mona said. "I don't go to the movies much."

"It was on television. I think the Monday night movie about a month ago."

"I guess I was out."

Stick hesitated. "Working?"

"Could've been."

"How much you charge?"

"Fifty," Mona said. "How's that sound?"

Mona squeezed her eyes closed and said, "Oh, God. Jesus."

Stick said, "Hey, don't do that, okay? Unless you really mean it."

12

Stick didn't know why he expected her to be different. He realized now the person in there, behind the calm expression, was predictable and he'd met her before, many times. She wasn't a mystery person at all; she was really kind of dumb. She had never heard of Waylon Jennings or his hit record *Midnight Rider*. She hadn't even heard of Billy Crash Craddock or Jerry Reed, the Alabama Wild Man. She liked Roger Williams and Johnny Mathis. She also liked Tab with Jack Daniel's. Stick was disappointed, then relieved. He fixed himself some greens with salt pork and ring baloney and Jiffy corn bread mix, fell asleep watching the late movie, woke up, and went to bed. He didn't know what time Frank got in.

The way he knew he was home was seeing the colored girl in the kitchen the next morning.

He got the paper in and came into the kitchen in his striped undershorts, scratching the hair on his chest, reading a headline about Ford and not sure which Ford they were talking about. A pan of water was boiling on the range. The colored girl was looking in the refrigerator. She had on a bra and panties, that's all, and was barefoot.

She looked over at him and said, "I don't see no tomato juice."

Stick saw her as she spoke and maybe he jumped, he wasn't sure. It was pretty unexpected. Good-looking colored girl standing there in her underwear, he walks in the same way, like they were married or good friends. He felt funny, aware of his bare skin.

"What'd you say?"

"Tomato juice." She was relaxed, like she was in her own kitchen.

"In the cupboard," Stick said, "if we got any."

He watched her open the cupboard, look over the shelves, and reach for the gold can of Sacramento: slim brown body and white panties very low, legs stretched, on her tiptoes. He really felt funny. He didn't know if it was because she was black or because she was in her underwear. He tried to seem at ease and sound casual.

"You the maid?"

"Yeah, the cleaning lady," the girl said. "But I don't do floors or any ironing."

"LaGreta," Stick said. "Are you LaGreta?"

The girl turned and looked at him. "You know somebody that name?"

"I don't know her. I think I heard of her."

"Uh-huh. Where's your opener, love?"

"In the drawer there."

He watched her get it out and pry two holes in the top of the can.

"You and him work together, huh?"

"You left me," Stick said. "I thought we were talking about LaGreta."

"She's my mother."

"Oh." Stick nodded.

"You see it now?"

"Well—not exactly. You might think we're somebody else you heard about, I don't know."

"Yeah, that's it," the girl said. "You're somebody else."

"You and . . . my friend, you meet each other at Sportree's, I bet."

"Hey, baby, don't worry about it. Just tell me where I can find the vodka."

"I'll get it." Stick went out to the bar, still holding the newspaper in front of him, still not at ease talking to the girl. Young little colored girl, and he felt awkward. He came back in with a bottle of vodka. The girl was lacing a glass of ice with Lea & Perrins and Tabasco.

"He like it hot?"

"Probably."

"I hope so. It's the only way I fix it." She took the vodka bottle, poured in a couple of ounces, and filled the glass with tomato juice.

"You work with your mamma?"

"I told you I was a cleaning lady."

"Come on, really. What do you do?"

"I suppose you'll learn sooner or later anyway," the girl said. "I'm a brain surgeon." She moved past him with the Bloody Mary.

Stick watched her tight little can cross the living room and go into the hall, then heard her voice.

"Come on, sport. Time to open those baby blues and face the world."

Stick made bacon and fried some eggs in the grease.

When the girl came out again she was dressed in slacks and a blouse and earrings, a jacket over her arm. She didn't care for fried eggs, asked if they had any real coffee and settled for freeze-dried instant. Stick got up the nerve to ask her a few questions while she drank her coffee and read Shirley Eder and Earl Wilson. Her name was Marlys. She was twenty years old, not a brain surgeon, she worked in the office of a department store as a secretary.

Marlys grabbed her jacket and purse, yelled into the bedroom, "See you, sport," and was gone.

When Frank came out in his jockeys with the empty glass, looking like he'd been through major surgery the night before, Stick said, "What's Rule Number Nine?"

Frank said, "For Christ sake, lemme alone."

He looked terrible first thing in the morning, his hairdo mussed up and needing a shave, sad, wet eyes looking out of a swollen face. Stick could understand why the colored girl was anxious to leave. Frank's bedroom probably smelled like a sour-mash still.

"Don't feel so good, huh?"

"I'm all right. Once I have some breakfast."

"You throw up yet? Get down there and make love to the toilet bowl?"

Frank didn't answer. He turned the fire on under the pan of water.

"Rule Number Eight," Stick said. "Never go back to an old bar or hangout. You go to Sportree's."

"An old hangout. I've been there twice, three times."

"Rule Number Nine. Never tell anyone your business. You pick up a broad, her *mother* knows what you do."

"She doesn't know me," Frank said, "not by name. We never met."

"Never tell a junkie even your name," Stick said. "The place is a dope store, full of heads. Rule Number Ten—you want another one? Never associate with people known to be in crime. Your friend Sportree—into many things, right? beginning with dope—and probably everybody else in the place."

Frank jiggled the pan of water to make it boil faster. "The guy's a friend of mine. I talked to him for a while, then Marlys came in, we been getting to know each other."

"Marlys," Stick said. "I thought you went out with Karen."

"I went out with Sonny, since we're keeping records. I ran into her coming in, waited an hour while she changed into an identical outfit, and we went out, had dinner."

"Yeah?"

"Yeah what?"

"What happened?"

298

Frank looked over from the range. "It's a long, boring story. For your record, Sonny doesn't kiss and hug on the first date. Maybe not on the second or third or fourth, either. Maybe she never does. Maybe not even if you married her."

"What'd you do, try and rape her?"

"I bought her dinner. Forty-eight bucks with the tip. She takes a couple of bites of filet and leaves it. We come back here, it's nighty-night time, that's it."

"What'd you talk about?"

"Her. What do you think? She's in a couple of Chevy ads, you'd think she was a fucking movie star. I told her I'd been there already, used to take out a girl was in the movies. She isn't even listening. You tell her something, she's thinking about what she's going to say next about herself. It's not worth it. Forty-eight bucks—I say, You want to go somewhere else, hear some music? No. How about, I know a place we can see some interesting characters. No."

"So you went alone."

"I couldn't find anybody and it was just as well I didn't," Frank said, "since I ran into Marlys."

"She must be pretty good."

Frank looked over again as he took the water off the fire.

"Buddy, it's all good. Like chili, when you're in the mood. Even when it's bad it's good."

"I guess so," Stick said. "Matter of degree." He waited a moment, then said it. "I never done it with a colored girl."

"Or a Jewish girl, as I recall," Frank said. "Only white Anglo-Saxon Protestants."

"No, my wife was a Catholic at one time, when we first got married. There was another girl I used to go with when I was about eighteen, she was a Catholic, too."

"That's interesting," Frank said. He poured a cup of instant and took it over to the table. "You certainly talk about interesting things." Stirring the coffee, he began looking at the morning paper.

"You want to see something interesting," Stick said, "page three. Another guy shot knocking down a liquor store." He watched Frank turn the page.

"Where?"

"Down near the bottom. Bringing the total to six in the past week. You see it? Six guys shot, four killed, in attempted robberies. What does it tell you?"

Frank was looking at the news story. "The cop, it says Patrolman William Cotter, called out, 'Freeze! Police officer!' The suspect, Haven Owens—a jig," Frank said, "you can tell by the name—pointed his revolver at Patrolman Cotter, then turned and attempted to run from the store. He was shot three times in the back . . . wounds proved fatal . . . pronounced dead on arrival at Wayne County General. I like that wounds proved fatal—hit three times in the back with a fucking thirty-eight."

"What does it tell you?" Stick said. "Doesn't come right out and say, but the cop's waiting there, isn't he?"

"Of course he is. I know that. Christ, a little kid'd know it."

"So you go in a place now, since they're cracking down," Stick said, "how do you know it isn't staked out?"

"Because we don't work in Detroit. These suburban places, Troy, Clawson, for Christ sake, they don't have cops for stakeouts."

"You know that for a fact?"

"Hey, have we seen any? I don't mean feel it, as you say, imagine it, like the A&P. Have we actually seen any stakeouts?"

"All we need is one," Stick said. "We won't see any more for ten to twenty-five years."

13

The bright green repainted Chevy Nova stalled three times before they were out of the shopping center.

"The idle's set too low," Frank said. "I don't want to seem critical but how come, all the cars, you pick this turkey?"

"I think what sold me was the key on the visor," Stick said. "It's just cold."

"*Cold?* It's seventy degrees out."

"It was probably sitting there all day. Belongs to some kid works in one of the stores." When they were stopped at a light and the engine stalled again, Stick said, "Or else the idle's set too low."

It was 8:20 now, almost dark. Stick turned onto Southfield and eased over to the right lane, in no hurry, the store would be waiting.

Frank said, "You go any slower, this thing is going to roll over and die."

Stick didn't say anything. Maybe he was putting off getting there and that's why he didn't mind the car stalling. They were both stalling. He'd watch the approaching headlights, then shift his eyes to the rearview mirror. Police cars were black and white with blue-and-red bubbles. Oklahoma State Police were also black and white. And Texas. Texas Department of Public Safety. Black and white with three flashers on top—count 'em, three—in case anybody didn't know they were cops. He thought of something else, what an old boy from Oklahoma had said. "Do you know why there's a litter barrel every mile going down the highway in Texas?" "No, why?" "To dispose of all the shit they hand you in that state."

In Missouri they were cream-colored.

They drove past the bank, parked on the dark side of the Chinese restaurant, and walked across the alley to the Food Lanes supermarket.

Stick went in the front entrance and took a shopping cart as he moved along the aisle past the checkout counters—only two of them busy with customers. He'd circle through the store before coming back to the checkouts.

Frank went in the side door. Past the magazine rack Stick had mentioned, he looked toward the brightly lighted produce department, then glanced over at the cashier's enclosure and saw two heads, one bald, one a tall blond beehive.

Frank walked through the empty produce department to the back of the store, to the double doors with the little glass windows, and looked into the storage area. A couple of stockboys were loading cases onto hand trucks. By the time Frank got back to the front, Stick was at one of the checkout counters with a few grocery items in his cart, waiting behind a customer. A man in a sport shirt was standing at the magazine rack. He picked out a copy of *Outdoor Life* as Frank walked past him, to the cashier's window.

Frank looked over his shoulder. The guy was leafing through the magazine. He turned to the window again and the blond girl with the beehive, a two-hundred-pounder, was waiting for him.

"Can I help you?"

"Yes, you can," Frank said. He took the Python out of his safari jacket and rested it in the opening. "You can unlock the door if you will, please, and let me in."

Stick watched him go around, wait by the door a moment, then slip into the enclosure. He could see three heads in there now, the blond one higher than Frank's and the bald one. No one else seemed to have noticed Frank. The two checkout girls looked tired and probably wouldn't give a shit if the place caught fire, long as they got out.

Stick's turn came and the checkout girl began ringing up his groceries, a few things they needed anyway.

She said, "You like these buckwheat flakes?" pausing to study the box.

"I sure do," Stick said. "They're honey-flavored."

"I'll have to try them," the checkout girl said. She tore off the tape and gave him the total: $4.09.

Stick opened his poplin jacket and showed her the Smith sticking out of his pants. Like a dirty old man in front of a little kid.

"You see it?"

"Oh, my," the checkout girl said. She was in her forties and seemed like a friendly, easygoing person. "I've never been held up before. Lord, this is the first time."

Stick was pretty sure she wouldn't do anything dumb. "Something to tell your friends about," he said.

"I sure will." She tensed up then. "I mean I won't if you don't want me to."

"No, it's okay. Put the money in a bag. Just the bills." He got his own bag from the end of the counter and put the groceries in it while the checkout girl emptied the cash register. "Then get those other ones down there," Stick said, "the other cash registers."

The checkout girl at the next counter was busy with a Jewish-looking lady who was unloading a cart piled with groceries and telling the girl how a hundred dollars a week used to take care of everything, her hair and her cleaning woman, and now it barely covered food the way prices were, but she wasn't going to cut down or skimp because her husband insisted on

303

only prime sirloin, filets or standing rib and also liked his snacks and that's where the money went, on meat like it was from sacred cows and the snacks, pastries, ice cream, he loved peanut brittle, something sweet to snack on watching TV.

The checkout girl was concentrating on ringing up the items, then would pause and lay on a buzzer for a few seconds to get a carry-out boy who never appeared. She probably didn't hear anything the woman said. That was fine, she was busy and had things on her mind.

"I'll tell you what," Stick said to his checkout girl. "On the other cash registers, take out the tray inside—you can carry four—and take them over to the cashier's place." He picked up his groceries and the shopping bag with the money in it. "I'll be right behind you."

If the Jewish lady ever finished and left, he'd come back for that cash register. He hoped he wouldn't get involved with her and have to tell her to lie down on the floor or something. The woman looked like she'd scream. The last thing he wanted was a screamer. That's why he liked his checkout girl—following her along the front of the counters as she stepped into each one and collected the cash register tray—she was excited and naturally scared, but she was probably already thinking how she was going to tell it after, the biggest thing that ever happened to her.

Stick noticed the guy at the magazine rack, half turned away from it. He wondered if the guy had looked down, just then, at his magazine.

Frank opened the door to the cashier's enclosure. Stick and the checkout girl stepped inside with her trays.

"Come on in," Frank said. "Mr. Miller here's having a little trouble with the safe."

The manager was down on his knees, fooling with the dial of the safe built into the counter. The big girl with the beehive was watching him, biting her lower lip.

Stick handed the checkout girl the bag of currency. "Put everything in here, will you? Except checks and silver." He touched Frank on the arm then and nodded toward the magazine rack.

"I saw him," Frank said.

The big girl glanced over.

"Honey, get down there by Mr. Miller, will you, please? Tell him he doesn't open the safe right now, I'm going to cause him pain and suffering."

"The guy just looked over," Stick said.

Frank's head rose. He studied the guy, not saying anything.

"He knows something's going on," Stick said. "Five people in here having a convention."

"Take it easy," Frank said.

Take it easy? Stick looked at him. He was taking it easy, his voice was calm, what the fuck was he talking about, take it easy.

Frank was stooped over the manager again, touching the big Python gently to the man's head.

"I'm going to count to three, Mr. Miller."

"I can't help it," the manager said, "I'm trying. I can't see the numbers with these glasses, they're my old pair. My regular glasses that I use, the frames broke—"

"Okay," Frank said.

"—and they're in being repaired. I was supposed to have them the next day, but they didn't have the frames—"

"Hey," Frank said, "I believe you, no shit, I really do. Just get out of the way." He glanced at the big girl's name tag. "Let Annette get in there. Give her the numbers."

Stick watched the guy close the magazine and put it under his arm. The guy hesitated but didn't look over. He got himself ready and started for the side entrance.

"Hey—" Stick said.

Frank looked up. The guy was going through the door, hurrying now as he moved through the breezeway to the outer door.

"He saw us," Stick said.

"Mr. Miller," Frank said to the manager, "a guy just walked out with a magazine without paying for it—the cheap son of a bitch."

"We better move," Stick said.

Frank looked at him. "Take it easy, okay?"

It got to him again, hooked him. Stick waited, making sure his voice would be calm, and moved closer to Frank.

"The guy's out, and if he's got a dime in his pocket we're going to be seeing the fucking colored lights in about three minutes."

"Or maybe he didn't notice anything," Frank said. "We're here, man, we're going to get what we came for." Looking down again: "Annette, would you mind, please, opening the fucking safe?" Saying it calmly, for Stick more than for the big blond girl.

Stick knew it. He had to keep himself in control again. It was crowded in here, the checkout girl staring at him then looking away quickly, he wanted to take what they had right now and get out. But the big blond girl was saying something. She had the safe open and Frank was stooped down next to her, holding the grocery bag. Stick looked at the clock on the wall.

Frank told everybody to lie down and not move and if he saw a head raise up he'd blow it off, giving them the farewell address in his cool-gunman voice. Stick took the bag from him. Going out, he glanced at the clock again. The Jewish-looking lady was still there, the checkout girl loading bags and buzzing the buzzer. Stick wasn't sure how much time had passed since the guy left with the magazine. Enough, though. He didn't see the guy outside anywhere. He didn't expect to. He kept a few steps ahead of Frank, who was holding back on purpose walking to the car. Fucking games.

They got in the Nova. Frank slammed his door, it didn't catch and he had to open it and slam it again.

"I hope it starts," Frank said, "and doesn't konk out. You think it's cold?"

Stick didn't say anything. He pushed the accelerator down halfway, held it, and snapped on the ignition. The engine caught at once with a good, heavy roar. Stick gave it a little more gas to be sure and listened to the idle. It was fine. But there was another sound, far away, a shrill, irritating sound that went *who-who, who-who,* and kept it up, getting louder, scaring the shit out of anybody sitting in a stolen car with a grocery bag full of money, scaring them way more than the old standard siren ever did.

Frank said, "Let's get out of here." Not quite as cool as before.

The blue-and-red flashers were coming down Southfield, weaving through the traffic, still a couple of blocks away. They saw the flashers as they came out of the shadow and turned in front of the Chinese place. Stick glanced and saw enough, looked away to figure out where he was going, and saw the man coming out of the restaurant, the man with a magazine running out across the drive, then stopping dead as he saw the green Nova and the two guys inside. He was about five feet away from them when he ran back into the restaurant.

The red-and-blue flashing squad car with its awful *who-who* wail almost lost it taking the corner, got itself straightened out passing the bank and the Chinese place, and swerved into the Food Lanes parking lot as Stick eased the Nova around the far corner of the restaurant, cut through the open blacktop area behind the Michigan National Bank, and hit Southfield already doing thirty, not fast enough to attract attention but enough to get them out of there. Stick could picture the guy running over to the squad car, waving the magazine at them and pointing. *A green car!* Or if he knew anything, *A green '72 Nova! Went that way!* Shit.

Frank was hunched around, looking back. "Nothing yet." He spotted the flashers a half mile back as they were going through an amber past Michigan Bell. "There they are."

Stick edged over to the left and followed the curving ramp that led to the Lodge Expressway. He didn't take it, though. He ducked out on the spur that connected with the Northland service drive, followed it to the first overpass, crossed the expressway, and two minutes later was weaving through the mile-long parking area on the east side of the Northland shopping complex.

Stick felt better.

There was no hurry now, no red-and-blue flashers in sight. They were hidden among rows of shining automobiles, protected by the mass of the department store, Hudson's Northland, rising above the arcades of shops and stores and neon lights that formed a wall against the darkness and the police, wherever they were, over there somewhere.

Stick felt pretty good, in fact, realizing he was in control and had been in control from the time the cop car came fishtailing around the corner. He had used his head and timed it and got out of there without squealing the tires or doing anything dumb. That was a good feeling, once it was over and he could look back at it. Frank, Mr. Cool, was still tense, watching for cops.

Stick glanced at him. "How about a J&B?"

"How about a couple?" Frank said. He paused and got some of his calm back. "Since we got nothing else to do."

14

The dining room was paneled and brightly lighted. Not in there, Frank said. In the cocktail lounge that was marble and velvet and dark wood, with imitation gas lamps and waitresses in French-maid outfits. Stick said, "You think we're dressed all right?"

Frank said, "Relax."

He was getting it all back now.

"It's the same booze in the bottles," Frank said. "The rest of the shit is overhead. But not bad, huh? I used to come here."

He called the waitress with the dark-dyed hairdo and rosy makeup "dear" and ordered doubles, scotch and a bourbon. It was funny, Frank was at ease now and Stick felt awkward, sitting in the booth with his poplin jacket on and the Food Lanes shopping bag next to him—the groceries in with the money, maybe two grand or more in there—afraid the manager or somebody was going to come over and ask them to leave because they weren't dressed right.

"Here's to it," Frank said. He raised his glass and took a drink. "You were right about the guy with the magazine. You see him outside?"

"See him—I almost ran over him."

"You should've. Teach him to mind his fucking business."

"Another half a minute," Stick said, "we wouldn't be here."

Frank sipped his drink. "Adds a little color. Otherwise it'd be routine, like a job. Same thing all the time."

"It was close," Stick said.

"Sure it was close, in a way it was. We're looking in the fucking whites of their eyes. But we did it. Suck in a little, let them go by, then take off. It's called timing. We don't have to put it down as a rule because we've got it, instinctively."

"You telling me you like it?" Stick said. "The flashers, that sound? That's a terrible sound to hear coming at you."

"It's part of it. You don't have to like it, no," Frank said. "You accept it, the possibility, and when it happens you keep it together."

"What're the odds?" Stick said. "One close one out of what, thirty? That's not bad, but maybe we've been lucky and it's starting to catch up."

"No, if you know what you're doing, each one is like the first time only better, because you've been there. Incidentally, it's thirty-one."

"But things can happen," Stick said. "In the grocery, I tell you the guy saw us. No, you're playing some fucking game, you're going to stay there till you get the safe. That's not going by instinct or rules or anything, that's so fucking dumb it's stupid."

"We're here, right? And we got what was in the safe."

"We're here—you want to do it like that every time?"

"All right—" Frank paused and lit a cigarette, then motioned to the waitress to do it again. "You're saying don't take unnecessary chances. I agree, up to a point. But the nature of the business, you play it as you come to it. The rules are basically good, *but* what I'm saying, you can't fit them into each and every situation."

"You're the one made them up," Stick said, "ten rules for success and happiness. Now you want to throw them out."

"Did I say that?"

"It's the same thing."

"Look, we start with the rules, fine. We obey them like the fucking Ten Commandments, nothing wrong with that, we're just starting out. But we also have experience now, instinct. We know as much about it, maybe more than anybody in the business."

"I don't know," Stick said, "thirty in a row—thirty-one in a row—maybe it's time to rest a while. It doesn't seem like much at the time, but it's hard work, it takes it out of you."

"That's right, it's not the kind of work for somebody with a heart condition. Hernia, it doesn't matter. Picking up money never gave anybody a hernia. It's hard work but not hard labor." Frank paused. "Actually, the amount of effort to pick up one or two grand, it doesn't take any more to lift twenty or thirty or, say, fifty grand. You follow me?"

"I'm ahead of you," Stick said. "I can see it coming."

"Don't start shifting around, listen a minute. I'm talking about what if we do the same thing practically we've been doing, only we pick up, say, fifty times more. What's wrong with that? One shot, we take a trip, we don't work for months."

"It seems to me we discussed banks one time, savings and loan," Stick said. "What're the odds, fifty-fifty?"

"I'm not talking about a bank."

"You going to tell me, or I have to guess? I remember this other time we're in a bar you get me into a quiz game. What's the best way to make the most money? The simplest way."

The waitress came with the drinks, giving Frank a chance to sit back and take his time. He waited until she walked away.

"I've been giving this a lot of thought," he said. "I'm not talking about some half-assed stunt like we walk into the downtown branch of the National Bank of Detroit. This one's real."

"Okay, it's not a bank. How many more guesses do I have?"

"I wasn't going to tell you about it till I thought you were ready. I'm still not sure you are." Frank paused, but Stick didn't say anything. "I'm talking about your attitude," Frank said. "I want to lay something on you and be able to discuss it like I'm talking to a pro, man who's been there. But if this thing tonight shook you up, then I don't think you're ready and maybe it's possible you never will be."

"I drove the car," Stick said.

"Yeah, you drove the car." Frank waited.

Stick took a drink. He could see a couple of kids arguing. Unbelievable. You were the one was scared, I wasn't. You were, too. I was not. Were, too. Maybe not in those words, but it would be the same thing.

He said, "All right, when you think I'm ready. Then again, if you don't think I'll ever be ready, you know what you can do with your great idea."

"I'll tell you something else," Frank said, "since you're in a nice open frame of mind. There'd be some other people involved."

Stick shook his head, very slowly, watching Frank, the two of them staring at each other in the gaslit cocktail lounge.

"You're trying different ways—why don't you come right out with it?"

"With what?"

"You want to knock off this twosome shit, split up. All right, that's fine with me, any time you want."

"I say anything about splitting up?"

"You haven't said anything at all yet. Everything is what you *didn't* say, for Christ sake. You want to say something, say it, and quit jerking around."

"I'm considering something," Frank said.

Stick had the urge to punch him out, go over the table and give him one. The son of a bitch, sitting there doing his cool number.

"I've got a proposition," Frank was saying, "but I don't want to spring it on you prematurely. I want to be sure you've got the balls for it before I tell you the whole thing."

"Leak out a little at a time. That's what you're doing, trying to get me to bite."

"Uh-unh, getting reactions."

"Why don't we talk about it again," Stick said, "sometime when a flasher's coming up behind us and you're pissing your pants."

Frank looked up at Stick as he slid out of the booth, the Food Lanes shopping bag in his hand.

"We're a little edgy, huh? I must've said something hit you where you live."

Stick was tired of it and didn't want to play anymore. "You going to stay or what?"

"No, I'm ready. I'll get the bill, you get the car." He looked for the waitress, then at Stick again. "A different one, right? In case they spotted that green turkey out there."

"I had that in mind," Stick said. His voice was calm, he wasn't going to let Frank rattle him anymore, not tonight. "You want any particular make or model?"

"One that doesn't stall'd be nice," Frank said. "See what you can do."

There was valet parking, but no board with keys on it by the entrance. The attendants probably parked the cars in the shopping plaza lot as close to the restaurant as they could and maybe even put the keys under the seat.

Stick rolled the top of the grocery bag a little tighter in his hand and walked out past the people waiting for their cars.

It would be easy to take one. If he didn't have to wait for Frank or swing back and pick him up—and see the owner of the car running out yelling for him to stop. Gee, I'm sorry, sir, is it yours? I guess I got the wrong one. And go through all that.

Frank complicated things. If he'd knock off the shit and stick to the rules, they could do very well in a year, shake hands, and dissolve the partnership.

He had told Frank about where he'd be, down toward the end of the lot, past the light poles and the car bodies shining in the darkness, and maybe over a couple of rows. He'd probably have to use the clips, do some rewiring under the dash. There were enough cars, a good selection, but he was tired and didn't feel like concentrating and getting himself into a calm-alert frame of mind. He shouldn't have let Frank bother him like that. He shouldn't have said he'd get a car, asking him what kind he wanted. That was dumb, playing Frank's game with him, like a little kid. Two kids playing chicken. Frank acting, talking about the big hit, fifty grand and some other people involved, trying to get a rise out of him with the big mystery bit. What he should do maybe, call Frank on it. Say, Come on, sure, I'm ready, let's go. Except the dumb shit might think he had to quit talking about it and do it and they'd walk in someplace for the big hit playing I-dare-you and get their fucking heads blown off.

He looked back, glancing over his shoulder, to see if he was far enough away from the restaurant.

Someone was coming along behind him.

Not Frank or a parking attendant, he was pretty sure. A guy taking his time. About thirty feet back, keeping pace, a thin, elongated figure against the lights of the restaurant. Not anyone he had noticed in front. He had a feeling the guy was black, and it tightened him up a little. The feeling just came, a reaction. There was no reason to be suspicious of the guy. The guy was going to get his car. A car he owned. That was kind of funny, he was out here to steal one, commit a crime, and he was worried about being robbed.

Stick moved through the rows of cars on his left, parked in two rows front end to front end, to the next aisle. He looked back. Nothing. He continued on toward the end of the lot. There were streetlights beyond the darkness and the sound of cars. When he looked back again, the guy was in the aisle, thirty feet behind him.

The second guy stepped into the open directly in front of him and stood waiting. Stick could see he was black. Tall like the one behind him, a couple of basketball players with easy moves. The guy's arms were folded, his hands beneath his biceps. He could be waiting for his friend, the guy following him.

Which was about as likely as waiting for a streetcar.

Stick moved out to walk around the guy, and the guy stepped out with him. He had to stop then or keep going and say excuse me or turn around and run. He stopped.

The black guy unfolded his arms so Stick could see the revolver in his hand. He was pretty sure it was real. The black guy said, "How you this evening?"

"Pretty good," Stick said. "Well, no, I take that back." He grinned to show the guy he was easy to get along with.

"Where your car at?"

"You might not believe this," Stick said, "but I don't have one."

"You don't, huh? You out for a stroll?" His gaze shifted as the tall, skinny one who'd been following came up on Stick's left. "He say he don't have a car."

"Put your arms out," the skinny black guy said.

Stick did it, holding the grocery bag extended in his left hand. He felt the guy pat him down, his jacket pockets and then his hips and back pockets. The guy's hands didn't go around to the front. He lifted Stick's wallet, took out the money, and dropped the wallet on the pavement.

Stick said, "Thank you." It just came out. He thought of the manager at the Kroger store who'd thanked him and told him to come back again.

"Twenty and three singles," the skinny black guy said. "Man, where your keys?"

"He left them in the car," the black guy with the gun said. "Come on, man, show it to us."

"I'm telling you, I don't have a car. I got to get one myself."

"You going to steal it?" the skinny black guy said. He sounded amused.

Stick looked at him, at his sweatshirt with the sleeves cut off, showing his long, stringy muscles. Six-three or four, with a nice outside jump shot and tough under the boards. They could go to some schoolyard with lights and play one-on-one.

"If all you want's a car, shit, help yourself," Stick said. "What one you want?"

"We'll take yours, man, anything you got," the black guy

with the gun said. "What's in the bag? You got some booze?"
"Buckwheat flakes," Stick said. "Cereal, a few other things."
The guy motioned with the gun. "Hand it to him."

Stick turned a little to face the skinny guy, backing away and
bringing the grocery bag up in front of him with both hands on
it. He felt the rear bumper of the car behind him, against his
legs.

He said, "You guys want groceries, why don't you go to the
store, help yourself?"

The black guy with the gun said, "Man, what you got in
there you don't want us to have?" He motioned to his partner.
"See what he's got."

Stick's right hand went under his jacket and closed on the
butt of the .38. That was as far as he got. Before he could pull it
or jerk the grocery bag out of reach, the skinny black guy got a
grip on the bag, pushed him, grunted something, and threw a
quick, hard jab into the side of his face. The grocery bag tore
open between them, ripped apart, as Stick fell against the car,
rolled to keep his balance, and held onto the trunk lid. He was
dazed, his face numb, but he was still gripping the .38 under
his jacket, like he was holding his stomach.

Both of the black guys were looking at the pavement, at the
money scattered in a little pile with the cereal and the bread
and boxes of Jell-O. The skinny black man stooped down and
began to pick it up, saying, "Man, look, man, look at the moth-
erfucking money the motherfucker's got, man, *look at it*"—
scooping it up as fast as he could and stuffing it in the torn re-
mains of the grocery bag.

The black guy with the gun looked from the money to Stick
lying against the trunk of the car. He said, "Man, you robbed
some place, didn't you? Shit." He began to grin, looking at the
money again, and laughed, getting happy-excited about it, like
finding money in the street.

"Man *robbed* a place, put it in a bag—"

He stopped—because if the man was a holdup man, if he
was an armed robber—

Stick had the .38 out, extended, pointed at the guy.

The black guy with the gun said, "Shit," the excitement

gone out of his voice. He had his revolver in front of him but pointed at a down angle and away from Stick.

The skinny black guy hadn't looked up. He was down there, getting it all back into the torn-up bag, saying, "Look at it. Man, will you . . . look . . . at . . . it."

"Turn around," Stick said to the guy with the gun, "and let's see your arm. Throw it down there as far as you can."

The skinny black guy stopped talking and looked up from the pavement.

Stick could see him but kept his attention on the guy with the gun. When the guy didn't move, Stick said, "I don't know what you got, some Mickey Mouse piece. This one's a thirty-eight Smith. It'll go clean through you and break some windows down the street. Now turn the fuck around and throw it away."

The skinny guy crouched on the pavement said, "They two of us, man. How you going to get us both?"

Stick turned toward him a little but kept the .38 on the other one. "You worried about it," he said, "I'll do you first."

"Buuullshit. You ain't going to do nobody." The skinny guy got to his feet, holding the torn sack against his body. His free hand went into his pocket and came out with a clasp knife. Watching Stick, he opened the blade with his teeth.

"Shiiit, come on, man, hand me that thing. Let's cut out the bullshit."

"Do what he say," the black guy with the gun said. He was careful with the gun, not moving it, but he seemed confident again. It was in the tone of his voice.

Neither of them moved. The skinny guy waited, his hand extended with the knife in it—five, six feet away—patient, sure of himself. He said, "Man, you ever shoot that thing? You know how? Come on, give it to me. We let you go home with your buckwheat flakes."

Stick wasn't sure if the safety was off.

He wasn't sure which one of them he should look at.

He wasn't sure if he could fire the gun at either of them. He didn't like the guy's sound, the skinny black guy holding the money, but he didn't know if he could shoot him. He had had them for a moment and now he was losing it. He knew it and could feel it and he couldn't think of anything to say.

If he had had a little more time to make up his mind, maybe he would have said it wasn't worth it, shit no, and handed over the gun and taken his groceries and gone home. Maybe he looked like he was wavering, scared. Or he looked so easy the skinny guy couldn't resist going for him.

That's what the guy did, rushed him, pulling his knife hand back to throw it into him.

Stick shot him, not more than a yard away, and heard his scream with the heavy report of the gun.

The other black guy was caught by surprise, not ready until it was already happening, hurrying to get the revolver on the man, firing once, too soon.

Stick shot him twice, he was pretty sure in the chest. The guy fired again, wildly, a reflex action, and made a gasping sound, like the wind was knocked out of him, as he fell to the pavement.

The skinny black guy was running, holding the grocery bag against his sweatshirt. Stick heard himself yell at the guy to stop, to hold it right there, seeing the guy running and knowing he was going to keep running, and he fired almost as he yelled it, one shot from the .38 that caught him in the middle of the back. The skinny guy bounced off a car and hit the pavement face-down.

Stick didn't roll him over or feel for a pulse. He pulled the torn bag out from under him, in a hurry to get it, knowing he was leaving some bills but not caring about them, not wanting to touch the guy. He remembered that. He remembered the sound of someone running on pavement, coming this way, a dark figure against the restaurant sign, the way the skinny black guy had appeared when he first saw him. That seemed like a long time ago. Some other night. But he had talked to the guy less than a minute ago and now the guy was dead. The black guy with the gun lay on his back with his eyes open, staring at nothing. Maybe he could've talked to them a little more. Said, Look, you know how it is. I went to a lot of trouble for this, man. You want some, go get your own. Talk it over with them, couple of guys in the same business. No, a different type of business, but they'd understand things he did. He felt like he knew them. Couple of guys, shoot some baskets, play a little one-on-one, have a few beers after. The sound of the running steps was close, almost on top of him. He could hear someone breathing, out of breath.

"Jesus Christ," Frank said. He looked at the two black guys on the pavement and at Stick holding the .38 tightly against the grocery bag, and said it again, "Jesus Christ."

15

It was in the *News* the next afternoon. Frank went out for beer and brought back a paper. He read the story through, twice, and had a beer open for Stick when he came out of the shower and sat down in his striped shorts.

Stick lit a cigarette first and drank some of the beer. He was anxious, but at the same time he wasn't sure he wanted to read it. Maybe it would be better not to know anything about the two guys.

"Nobody saw us?"

Frank shook his head. "Uh-unh. I figure we were in the cab before anybody found them."

"It say who they were?"

"Read it."

Stick looked down at the paper.

"Man, you did a job," Frank said.

There was a quiet tone of respect in his voice Stick had never heard before.

The one-column story referred to it as "The Northland Slaying" and related how Andrew Seed and Walter Wheeler, both residents of Detroit, had been found shot to death in the parking lot of the shopping plaza, victims of an unknown assailant. Police were proceeding with an investigation, though there were no witnesses to the shooting or apparent motive other than attempted robbery. Both victims were known to the police.

Seed had been arrested several times on charges of robbery, felonious assault, and rape, and had served time in both the Detroit House of Correction and the Southern Michigan Prison at Jackson. Wheeler had a record of narcotics arrests and a conviction in addition to a list of assault and robbery charges. Both were also described as having been outstanding athletes while in high school, seven years before. Both had won All-City basketball recognition, first team, and All-State honorable mention.

"I knew it," Stick said. "It was a funny feeling, the way they moved or something, I knew they'd played and I wondered, What're they doing out here trying to hustle somebody?"

"You played," Frank said. "What were you doing, trying to steal a fucking car?"

"I wasn't that good, All-City. Those guys made All-City, All-State honorable mention."

"You were good with the Smith," Frank said. "Jesus, I couldn't believe it. Bam, bam—that's it, no fucking around. I wish I could've seen their faces. They're going to pull this easy hustle in a parking lot. Guy comes along with a bag of groceries, going home to mom and the kids. Yeah? That's what you think, motherfuckers. Man, next thing they know, they're fucking dead. That time just before, that few seconds, that's what I'd like to have seen. You should've waited for me. I'd have helped you."

"You could've done the whole thing," Stick said. "Any time. Listen, I think about it, I don't even believe it happened. I see the guy running away, I can still see him—this light-colored sweatshirt on with the sleeves cut off—I yelled at him to stop and I shot him, I mean I killed him."

"Because he wouldn't stop," Frank said. He sounded a little surprised. "What were you supposed to do, let him get away? He's got our twenty-three hundred, forty-eight bucks. Guy's a fucking thief."

"You don't kill somebody because he steals something."

"Bull*shit*, you don't. What do the cops do? They shoot you, man. You don't stop, they shoot you."

"I don't know," Stick said. "This is different."

"He was taking our money. You're supposed to let him take it? Sure, go ahead, any time. Bullshit, you're protecting our property."

"Frank, we stole it."

"Right, and that makes it ours. They weren't taking it from the store, going to all that work and getting their nerves stretched out, no, they think they're taking it from some meek, defenseless asshole who isn't going to do anything about it. Well, they made a mistake. And one's all you get."

Stick drew on his cigarette. He could see the skinny black guy running with his shoulders hunched. He should have gotten in between some cars, but he ran instead, already with one bullet in his side. The guy had nerve. He was holding all that money and he was going to keep it. Stick wondered if the guy was married and had a family. He wondered if he'd be listed in the death notices and if there'd be a funeral and if many people would attend. The two guys must've had friends. They'd gone to school in Detroit. He imagined a lot of black people at a cemetery. He thought about his little girl for some reason and wondered what she was doing.

"Maybe we ought to rest a while," he said to Frank.

"What're we doing?" Frank said. "We're sitting down, we're resting. I was thinking we ought to have a party."

"I mean knock it off for a while," Stick said. "Make sure they don't have something on us."

"The police? How could they?"

"They said there weren't any witnesses, but they wouldn't

say if there were, would they? I mean maybe there's a way we can be traced."

Frank shook his head. "No way. No car, no gun. We got the cab at least, what, a mile away from there. Nobody saw us or even knows it was two guys, right? And if there's no way they can even begin to trace us, we're clear."

"We're clear," Stick said, "but I still killed two guys."

"You sure did," Frank said. "Man. Listen, forget everything I said, we were talking in the bar, I said maybe you weren't ready for this thing I had in mind? I take it all back. You're ready."

"In the bar—you mean just before?"

"I told you I'd been working something out?"

"Yeah, I remember."

"Couple of days we'll know."

Stick wasn't sure he was following. He hadn't slept very well. All night he kept waking up and hearing the .38 going off and seeing the two black guys, not dreaming it but thinking about it, especially seeing the one who'd tried to run.

"Couple of days we'll know what?"

"Whether or not we can set it up. It's going to take a little doing."

"*We*," Stick said. "You mean more than just you and me. You mentioned in the bar, you said, since I was in a nice, open frame of mind—"

"That was a little smart-ass of me," Frank said. "I take it back. Forget it. But yes, there would be a few other people involved, because of the nature of the job. Couple of helpers, guys to watch more than anything else. And one on the inside. She's already there. In fact, it's because of her I got the idea. We've been talking it over."

Stick was listening, paying close attention now. He knew Frank was serious.

He said, "You mean one of the broads lives here?"

"No, no, those broads, Christ," Frank said. "This one's got it together and she likes the idea. You understand, she wouldn't be in on it, involved directly, so to speak, but she'd give us all the inside information we'd need."

"If she doesn't live here—" Stick said. He stopped then. "You mean the colored broad? What's her name? Marlys?"

"That's right, you met her. I forgot," Frank said. "Very smart and grown up for her age."

Stick could see her again, in the white bra and panties. Cute little black girl, yes, very grown up.

"She said, I think she said she worked downtown, in an office."

"She works at Hudson's," Frank said. "Up on the fifteenth floor."

Stick frowned. "That's a department store."

"You bet it is," Frank said. "The biggest one in town."

"You're crazy," Stick said, "Jesus," and shook his head. Frank waited.

"You're out of your fucking mind. Hudson's."

"The J. L. Hudson Company," Frank said. "You know how many cash registers they got in the store?"

"I don't want to know," Stick said. "I don't give a shit if they got a thousand."

"You're close," Frank said.

16

At one point in the evening there were fifteen people in the apartment. Frank found most of them; others dropped in. They'd come and go.

The way it started, Frank went out for a couple of hours in the afternoon—Stick didn't ask where—and when he got back he brought four of the career ladies up from the pool, Karen, Jackie, Mary Kay, and Arlene, and started making them drinks. Stick got out the grapefruit juice for the Salty Dogs and Arlene came over to help him. Even Mary Kay said she'd have one. It was strange to see four girls sitting around the apartment in swimming suits. Frank said they dressed up the place. Stick thought it looked like a Nevada whorehouse, the way he imagined one would look. Frank had had a few—wherever he'd gone—and was already a little high. He told Stick to come on and quit moping around. Stick decided, Why not? He'd have some fun and quit thinking about the two colored guys.

Then Frank told him Marlys was going to try and stop by later, and winked, and Stick thought about the two guys again. He wondered if Marlys knew them.

A little later Stick asked Mary Kay, didn't she have to go to work? And was surprised when she told him she was going to call in and say she was in bed with the curse. It was amazing, one and a half Salty Dogs.

Still a little later Frank went down to the ice machine, ran into Barry Kleiman in his white belt and white loafers talking to Sonny the Model and one of the young married couples, the Kaplans, and got them to come up. Frank went in and put on his safari jacket and wore it with a chain he borrowed from Arlene, no shirt. Barry Kleiman said, "Hey, cool."

They weren't sure when Donna, the dental hygienist, and her boyfriend came in; but they were there and after a while seemed like they'd always been there. Donna's boyfriend, Gordon, was working on his Ph.D. in something that had to do with clinical psychology and he spent a lot of time with Karen.

Every time Stick looked around, Arlene seemed to be watching him. That was the feeling he got. Like he was committed to her. She seemed to want to talk and finally steered him toward the balcony. But when they were out there, he spotted three of the junior executives down on the patio drinking beer and yelled at them to come up and be sociable.

The junior executives came in cautiously, like gunfighters in their tight Levi's, and slouched around a while; but pretty soon they were mixing it up with the others and Stick was glad he had invited them. It didn't hurt to be friendly. He told Arlene to be nice to them. The poor assholes were giving their lives to IBM and the Ford Motor Company and they deserved a little fun.

They were good-looking young guys with families in Bloomfield Hills, two of them named Ron and one named Scott. Ernest Stickley, Jr., could see them jogging through life in their thirty-dollar Adidases, never knowing it was hard. But he didn't hold it against them. He didn't give a shit, one way or the other, what they did.

SWAG

One of the junior executive Rons went down to his apartment and brought back a Baggie of grass and a pack of yellow cigarette paper. He said it was Nicaragua gold, which impressed Karen and Jackie. Karen named a couple of other kinds she had smoked. Ron got a few joints going and pretty soon everybody was taking drags. Stick tried it. It was all right, but he didn't feel anything from the two drags and he didn't like the smell at all. Frank said, "Man, you know what we used to call this, this kind of scene? Reefer madness." Ron, rolling the joints, said you could call it anything you wanted, but why get mad? Stick asked him if they let you smoke grass out at the Ford Motor Company. Ron looked at him and said, "Ford Motor Company? I'm with Merrill fucking Lynch, man. How's your portfolio?"

Frank was cruising on scotch and reefer. He'd poke Stick and say, "Hey, are we having a party or we having a party?" Like he was celebrating something. Stick would say yeah, they were having a party.

Arlene was following Stick's instructions, being nice to the junior executive named Scott. She looked small and frail sitting next to him on the floor. Scott was studying the hammered silver pendant that hung between her breasts. Arlene told him it was a Navajo love symbol or else a sheep spirit, she'd forgotten which, and Scott was nodding, showing his interest in primitive art.

Stick went over to the eight-hundred-dollar hi-fi and put on a Billy Crash Craddock while he picked out a Loretta Lynn, an Olivia Newton-John, and a brand-new LP by Jerry Reed, the Alabama Wild Man.

Mary Kay said, "You like that music?"

He looked up to see her standing close to him with a smudged empty glass in her hand, blue eyes looking at him that he bet were blurry inside. Nice, clean-looking girl letting go. Why did that surprise him? Or what did clean-looking have to do with it?

Stick put the LPs down, took Mary Kay by the arm, and said some of the words along with Billy Crash Craddock, telling her perfect love is milk and honey, Captain Crunch, and you in the morning.

Stick said, "To answer your question, it's not one of my top ten favorites, but I guess I like it pretty well."

Mary Kay said, "I think it's a bunch of shit. Perfect love, milk and honey, and all that. It's a lot of bullshit."

A voice told Stick to get out, quick. If he hesitated, she'd tell him how she was the oldest girl in a family of ten kids and how she had to do all the housework and pay her own way through Blessed Sacrament because her dad drank and sat around the house in his undershirt reading paperbacks, and how she went to mass regularly, prayed for a vocation, worked hard, always did what she was told, and how she was a registered nurse with her own apartment, a savings account, and five doctors who wanted to get her in bed. If he didn't listen to the voice, he'd ask her, What's the problem? and she'd say, What's the *problem?* What good was all the hard work and being good? *This?* Then they'd get in a half-assed discussion about the meaning of life and maybe he'd get her in bed and maybe he wouldn't. Talk about bullshit. Mary Kay was just learning.

Stick said, "Listen, let me get back to you, okay? I think we need some ice."

He got out of that one, for the time being, but missed the scene with Frank and Sonny, which he'd have gotten a kick out of.

Sonny had had a glass of milk all evening; nothing else, no potato chips and dip or Pinconning cheese. She was out on the balcony with Barry Kleiman and one of the junior executives, the quieter of the two Rons. He and Barry were standing with their fingers in their tight pockets, posing with the poser, very cool and serious about it.

Frank had nothing personal against Sonny. He kind of liked her style, the fashion model put-on and all that. He liked it even though it pissed him off. Look at her. She was skinny, no tits to speak of; bony hips; long, thin, dumb-looking hair she liked to get out of her eyes with a lazy little toss of her head. No personality, no real person in there Frank could see. She stood around with her box pushed out like she was daring anybody to make a grab for it. That's what got him the most.

When Frank walked up to them Sonny handed him her empty milk glass.

"How about another one?" he said. "If you think you can handle it."

"No thanks." She didn't look at him. She turned to Barry and said, "I've got to get going," like it was his place and he was the host. "Have to be at the studio by seven tomorrow. I think we're doing some Oldsmobile stuff."

"Listen," Barry said, "what we were talking about. How can I help you? Tell me."

She gave him a little shrug. "I don't know. Talk to your agency."

"I mean it," Barry said, "you'd be terrific. I don't mean behind the counter, one of the broads there in the uniform. I mean a customer . . . high fashion, a very chic chick. You bite into this quarter-pounder. Your eyes are saying mmmmm, great. And here's the part. You get some mustard right here, on the corner of your mouth. Jesus, you'll have every guy watching TV wanting to lick it off."

Sonny was nodding, picturing it. "That's earthy," she said. "Or how about, just the tip of my tongue comes out?" She demonstrated. "In a tight close-up."

"Ter-*rif*ic."

"With kind of a down-under look." Sonny lowered her head slightly and gazed up with a sleepy, bedroom look in her eyes. "What do you think?"

Frank said, "You mind if I ask you a personal question?"

Sonny made it seem an effort to turn and look at him. "I think not, if it's all the same to you."

"What do you mean, all the same?"

"If you don't mind, then."

"But I mind. That's why I want to ask you something."

"All right, what is it?"

"You ever been laid?"

Sonny's composure held. She said, "Have you?"

"A few times."

"Good for you." She looked at Barry again. "You mind walking me down?"

"Do I *mind*? Does a bear—no, strike that." Barry held out his hand to Frank. "Man, it was fun, I mean it."

Frank said, "You going to try your luck?"

Barry frowned, a quick expression of pain. "Hey, come on, let's keep it light, okay?"

"He'll be right back," Sonny said. "Unless he's going home."

Frank looked at the quiet, good-looking Ron with his big shoulders and golf shirt.

"You following this?"

"Am I following it?"

"What's going on. The principle involved. The great truth. You know what it is?"

The quiet, good-looking Ron shook his head. "I guess you lost me."

"It's called," Frank said, "the myth of the pussy."

"Hey, what?" Barry was grinning. "Come *on*. The myth of the—what?"

"The myth of the pussy," Frank said again, solemnly. "It seems like a simple little harmless thing, doesn't it? Something every broad in the world has. But you know what? They sit back on their little myth and watch guys break up homes over it, go in debt, mess up their lives. It can make an intelligent man act like a little kid and do weird things . . . this idea, this myth that's been built up. Girls say, You're bigger and stronger than we are, buddy, but we got something you want, so watch it. They use the myth to get you to open doors and give them things and pick up checks. And some use it more than others." He looked at Sonny. "Some think it's really a big deal, and you know what? They don't even know what it's for."

"That's wild," Barry said, a little awed. "It really is."

"No, what it is," Frank said, "it's a fucking shame."

A little before eleven they drove over to Woodward to find a liquor store open. They needed scotch, vodka, and beer.

"And grapefruit juice," Stick said. Stick had got to the car first and he was driving. "All the broads I think're drinking Salty Dogs. You taste one?"

"They're having a good time," Frank said. "Everybody is. I think there's only one turd in the bunch and she left. No, maybe there's two, I don't know."

"Who do you mean?"

"That Irish broad, the nurse."

"She's all right. She's going through her first change."

"I'll check it out," Frank said. "That cute little housewife, I think she's another sleeper. Her husband's busy with Jackie, looking down her kitty outfit. Or I could steer him over to Karen. Yeah, I could do that. She'd keep him busy. Christ, her appetite, she'd eat him up."

Stick glanced over. "You wouldn't mind that?"

"What do you mean?"

"You wouldn't care if he got her in the sack?"

"Why should I?"

"I just wondered."

"Karen's all right," Frank said. "You know, nice build and all. Maybe a little bigger than she looks. I'd say she goes about one thirty-five. But she's kind of bossy. You see her there? Like she's the hostess, getting Jackie to pass the cheese and crackers. That's the way she is. In the sack she says, 'Okay, that's enough of that, now do this. Yeah, that's it right there. A little more. No, a little up. That's it, good. Okay, the other thing again. All right, let's try this.' It's like doing it by the fucking numbers." Frank put his head back on the seat cushion, relaxed, comfortably high. "It's something," he said. "All that scratch in one place. You believe it?"

"You don't say that anymore," Stick said. "Now you say, 'Well, here we are.'"

"That's right. Well, here we are. And you say, 'You sure?' Say it."

"You sure?"

"You bet your ass I'm sure," Frank said. "That's a quiz show on TV. It isn't really, but those dumb broads, they believe anything you tell them. Hey, am I sure? You better believe it I'm sure, because we got it fucking knocked and it's going to get even better. I don't know what happened to Marlys. I saw her this afternoon, I told her stop by, she wasn't doing anything. What's tomorrow?"

"Sunday."

"All right we'll wait'll Monday, we'll go down there, I'll show you around. It's not worked out yet, you understand, but

I want you, I think you ought to start to get the feel of the place."

"I've been to Hudson's, Frank. Lots of times."

"Upstairs, where the offices are?"

"I think so."

"End of the day," Frank said, "they leave fifty bucks in the cash registers, everything else goes upstairs."

Stick was a little high but alert, moving along in the night traffic on North Woodward, watching for a liquor store that was still open. He didn't want to get in an argument with Frank or even a discussion with him now. It would be pointless. Frank would start yelling and wouldn't remember anything.

Stick said, "You look on your side."

He saw it then, in the next block across the street, the neon sign and the lights inside, and felt himself relax again.

"There's a place, Frank. It's still open."

They parked in front. Going in, Frank said, "What do we need? J&B, vodka?"

"Grapefruit juice," Stick said. "I don't think they'll have it. Maybe."

He asked the clerk behind the counter, a neat little gray-haired man with rimless glasses, and the clerk said, "Yes sir, right over there. All your juices."

Stick got four big cans and brought them to the counter. Frank was ordering the liquor. Stick went over to the cooler and pulled out a case of Stroh's, the brand the young executives were drinking. Walking back to the counter with it, where the clerk was waiting, he saw Frank up by the front of the store.

"We got everything?"

"I'll be right back," Frank said. He went out the door.

There were three bottles of J&B and three top-priced Smirnoff on the counter. The clerk was putting them one at a time into an empty liquor case.

"That be it?" the clerk said.

"I guess a couple bottles of tonic," Stick said. He got potato chips and Fritos from a rack, a can of mixed nuts. The clerk was coming back with the tonic. He stopped, his eyes wide open behind the rimless glasses. Stick looked around.

Frank was coming toward the counter with a grin on his face, his Colt Python in one hand and Stick's Smith & Wesson in the other.

"What the fuck," Frank said. "Right?"

Stick almost said his name. It was right there—*Frank, you dumb shit.*

But they were into it already and it wasn't something you could call off and say, "Oops, just a minute, let's start over." Or tell the guy you were just kidding.

No, he had to take the poor scared-shitless clerk into the back room and tie him up with masking tape and paste a strip of it over his mouth, while Frank, the dumb shit, was out there cleaning the cash register. Stick didn't say a word to the clerk. He laid him on the floor and patted his shoulder, twice, telling the guy with the touch to be calm and not to move.

He still didn't say anything out in the store again. He picked up the cardboard case and took it to the car, got in and waited while Frank brought out a case of scotch and a case of Jack Daniel's and put them on the back seat.

Leaning in he said, "You think while we're at it we should grab some more beer?"

Stick, waiting behind the wheel, said, "Get in the fucking car."

When Frank's door slammed, Stick took his time pulling away from the curb and working the T-bird into the stream of traffic, his eyes going to the mirror to watch the headlights coming up behind them.

"I'd say we got five, six hundred," Frank said. "You missed the wad in the guy's pocket. I got it, I went back there for the cases. Let's see, plus a couple hundred worth of booze, just like that. Not bad for a quick trip to the store, huh?"

Stick didn't answer.

"You're not going to talk to me now?" Frank said. "Is that my punishment? For Christ sake, you saw the guy, the place is empty. You can't pass up something like that, it's too good."

ELMORE LEONARD

"We're in a car," Stick said, "in your name. The registration, the plates."

"All right—this one time, it's an exception. There it is, you got to make up your mind that instant. So it's done and nobody saw us."

"How do you know?"

"Because I didn't see anybody. You got to see somebody for them to see you."

"Somebody could've been coming in," Stick said. "They see Twogun in there, for Christ sake, and they get out. But the car's sitting there, right? And they could've gotten the number."

"All right—we get home, we report it stolen."

"Frank, a dozen witnesses up there, they know we went out. The guy in the store, it'd take him one second to pick us out of a lineup."

"Hey, Ernest," Frank said, "don't be so fucking earnest, all right? It was a spur-of-the-moment thing. It's over, it's done. You want to live by the book all the time, is that it?"

"You wrote the book, ten rules for success and happiness," Stick said. "I didn't."

Neither of them said anything else until they reached the apartment building and Stick turned into the private parking area.

"There's a spot, right by the door."

"I already saw it," Stick said. He eased the T-bird into the space, turned off the ignition and the headlights.

Frank opened his door and paused. "You know something?"

Stick waited. "What?"

"I been thinking. I bet we end up with Karen and Jackie," Frank said. "I mean if Marlys doesn't show."

"That's what you been thinking, huh?"

"Yeah. Which one you want?"

334

17

There weren't as many people, though it was still smoky and smelled of incense and the noise level was high. Somebody had taken off Loretta Lynn and put on one of Frank's Montavanis. The quiet, good-looking Ron had passed out on Stick's bed, smelling like he'd thrown up. Stick came out to the bar and looked around as he made a drink.

Arlene wasn't there. Or the junior executive who'd been admiring her jewelry.

Frank came over to make a drink. "The place's thinning out. We'll have to get it going again."

Stick didn't say anything. He wasn't angry, he was tired. He wasn't upset about the guy passed out on his bed, he wanted to go sit down someplace where it was quiet. He thought of Arlene again. He'd like to get with her and fool around a little. Except she wasn't here.

"I don't think Marlys's coming," Frank said. "We better get a couple before they're all taken." He looked around the room, his gaze going past Mary Kay on the sofa. "I don't know, it's getting pretty thin."

He knew Sonny had left. He didn't see Donna or Arlene. Jackie was smashed. Karen—maybe.

Gordon, Donna's boyfriend, came over with two empty glasses.

"Where's Donna," Frank asked him, "in the can?"

"She left," Gordon said. "I told her I'd be down in a little while. It's my Saturday, but I'm having a very interesting conversation with Karen."

"It's your Saturday?"

"Every other Saturday I spend the night with Donna," Gordon said.

"What if you felt like doing it on a Tuesday night?"

Gordon was intently measuring an ounce and a half of vodka into each glass. He used the stainless-steel shot glass and had been measuring ounces and a half for over four hours.

"Sometimes Tuesday night," Gordon said, "if there's a special reason. See, Donna doesn't work on Wednesday."

"She rations it, huh?" Frank said. "She afraid she's going to run out?"

"No, she's got an idea about not overdoing anything. See, Donna's very parental. Usually she's into her critical parent. She uses *should* a lot. You *should* do this, you *shouldn't* do that. Then on Saturday, every other Saturday, she allows herself to get into her nurturing parent. Now Karen"—Gordon looked over to where she was sitting on the floor against a pile of orange and yellow pillows, still in her bikini—"Karen is very visceral. She feels and acts instinctively and has quite a lot of natural child in her."

"You're going to find out," Frank said, "she's got a lot of mama in her, too."

Gordon held the can of grapefruit juice poised over the glasses. He seemed interested and a little surprised.

"Are you into transactional analysis?"

"Uh-unh," Frank said, "but I've been into Karen." He looked around to get Stick's reaction. Stick wasn't there.

* * *

There were two Arlenes looking at him, the one holding the door partly open, wearing a man's white shirt over her bikini, and a life-size cutout of her on the other side of the room, the one Arlene pouting, the other smiling in her silver Hi-Performance Cams outfit and white boots.

Arlene said, "I don't know if I want to talk to you. I don't see you all week, you don't call—"

"I came by here, twice, you weren't home," Stick said.

"You don't pay any attention to me, you're busy talking to the other girls, putting your arms around them."

"How about you and the guy on the floor?"

"You told me to be nice to him."

"Is he here?"

"He got sick."

"Arlene," Stick said, "I haven't been feeling too good myself all week. I went to see a doctor, he checked me over, gave me a prescription—"

Arlene was showing a little concern. "What's wrong with you?"

"I went to the drugstore, gave the prescription to the pharmacist?"

"Yeah?"

"He said, 'You want this filled?' I said, 'No, it's a holdup note in Latin, you dumb shit.'"

She laughed and he was in.

Sitting down next to Mary Kay, alone on the sofa, Frank said, "Honey, you cook any good?"

Mary Kay looked at him with filmy eyes.

"Why?"

"I'm making conversation. You tell me what you like and I'll tell you what I like. Move over a little." He pulled an LP out from under him and sailed it at the hi-fi.

"If you want to talk, why don't you talk about something real," Mary Kay said.

"Okay. How do you like that Montavani? Nice, uh?"

"It sounds like cafeteria music."

"What do you like, then?"

337

"Nothing you've got, I looked. Country-western and Montavani."

"What're you," Frank said, "you get a little high, you like to argue?"

"I'm not arguing, I'm telling you what I don't like."

"You're a nurse, RN. I thought you were very sympathetic, got along with people, like to make them happy and all."

"Where'd you hear that?"

"Really," Frank said quietly. "I bet you are sympathetic . . . kind. I can see it in your eyes, you care about people."

"I tried," Mary Kay said. "I used to knock myself out being nice. And you know what you get? You get stepped on. If you're nice to people, they're nice to you? That's a lot of crap. They use you, give you the worst jobs. 'Sullivan, take care of One-oh-four—' "

"Who's Sullivan?"

"I'm Sullivan. 'Right away, Sullivan. One-oh-four's painting his wall with shit again.' That's what I get all night, things like that."

"This person," Frank said, "actually paints with it?"

"Smears it on the wall. Sometimes he eats it."

"Jesus," Frank said. He took the smudged glass from her hand. "Here, let me freshen you up." He fixed both of them a drink—Mary Kay's in a clean glass—came back and sat down again, close to her.

"You forgot the salt."

"You shouldn't use salt. It's not good for you." Frank laid his arm along the back of the couch and let his hand fall lightly on Mary Kay's shoulder.

"Listen, let me tell you something," he said, using his quiet tone again. "People who care, people who feel, are nice to one another. They make each other happy."

"I heard that," Mary Kay said. "All my life I heard it. And if you don't mind my saying, or whether you mind or not—"

"Wait, don't say it, Mary Kay." He turned her face gently and stared at her with his nice-guy expression. "All right?" Her lips were parted; there was a fresh pimple scar at the corner of her mouth. "You have to trust people, Mary Kay. No matter what kind of deals you've been handed, you have to go on trusting and believing."

"In what?"

"In yourself, in your own right to . . . have a good time and enjoy life. People need people." Frank paused, trying to think of the words to the song. "People who need people . . . lonely people needing people—" He was improvising now. "You know what I mean? They share their loneliness and find something."

"I get so tired of it," Mary Kay said.

"I know," Frank said. He was pretty tired himself, but he moved in closer. "I know."

"Why do I have to smile all the time and be nice when I don't feel like it?"

"You don't, honey. You should do what you feel like doing."

She snuggled against him, closing her eyes. "God, I get tired. The same thing all the time. Sometimes my face aches from smiling when I don't even want to."

"Listen, Mary Kay, how'd you like to stretch out and get comfortable?"

"Hmmm?"

"Go to your place, where it's quiet. What do you think?"

"I don't know if I could make it down the stairs, I'm so tired."

"Well, I guess I could help you," Frank said.

Mary Kay sighed. "You're a nice person, you know that?"

"I try to be," Frank said.

There was one picture Stick especially liked, Arlene kneeling with her back arched, winking as she kissed the knob of a Hi-Performance Four-Speed Shifter. There were shots of Arlene at the Nationals and at hot-rod shows and conventions. Arlene said the SEMA show was her favorite. Stick said he guessed it would be. He didn't ask her what See-Ma meant. He fixed them a couple more drinks and brought them over to the couch where Arlene was holding open the big album and got to see pictures of her posing with "Big Daddy" Don Garlits, Tom "Mongoose" McEwan, and Don "The Snake" Prudhomme.

She pointed them out and named them. She said she also had their autographs on a pair of her panties as a joke, if he wanted to see them. Stick said he'd look at anything she showed him. All right, then.

The second album she got out wasn't as big as the first one and there weren't any shots of Hi-Performance machinery in it or silver outfits or white boots, either. It was Arlene in her birthday suit, skinny hips, perky boobs, and all, like a little girl posing for exotica. Stick said they were really cute pictures of her and found out her friend was a camera nut and owned three Nikons that cost about a thousand dollars each.

He wondered if she showed him the nude pictures on purpose. Whether she did or not they were working.

When she went in the bathroom to take a leak—that's what she said, "Be right back, I got to take a leak"—Stick picked up the two drinks and headed for the bedroom. He heard the toilet flush and the door open and then Arlene's voice out in the other room.

"Hey, where are you?"

He let her find him, lying on the bed in his striped shorts with the two drinks on the night table. Arlene said, "I suppose you want me to take my rings off."

The next thing she said was, "You always perspire a little, don't you?"

"Not always," Stick said. "Sometimes I do, I don't know why. It doesn't have anything to do with, you know, the enjoyment of it."

"I wondered."

Then neither of them said anything for a little while, lying next to each other in the darkness, touching but not holding. The light from the hall reached the bed, and if he turned his head he could see their outline, in shadow, on the wall close by. He liked her. He liked the way she moved, skinny little thing. She was funny. And she was smarter than she sounded. She sounded goofy, but it was just that she let it come out and didn't try to act or be someone else. He liked her a lot.

Arlene said, "I wondered, it made me think of it, something else."

"What?"

"If you were sweating that time—in the bar."

"What bar?"

"In Hazel Park."

"I don't remember any bar—" He stopped.

"The one a couple of blocks from the Hazel Park track."

Stick sat up. He knocked a glass off the night table getting the light on. She was looking up at him, eyes wide open, her hands clutching the sheet to her tightly.

"Oh, God, I shouldn't have said anything, should I?"

"Wait a minute, I'm not sure what you're talking about. Some bar I was supposed to've been at? You thought you saw me?"

"I saw you," Arlene said. "You and Frank, you took the money from him, I thought, God, they're cops. And then you locked us in the room."

"You were at the bar?"

"I had on this scarf, over my hair? You looked right at me once, I thought sure, I thought, Oh, God, but I guess you were busy, you looked right at me but didn't see me. I didn't know whether to say anything or not. Then in the room"—Arlene started to smile and she giggled—"it was really funny, everybody was opening bottles and drinking and the woman was trying to stop them. She kept hitting the poor guy—"

"Who were you with?"

"Just my friend."

"Arlene," Stick said, as gently as he could, "did you tell him you knew us?"

The telephone rang in the living room.

She frowned. "Who's that? I know he's out of town." She was up, climbing over him—

"Arlene—let it ring."

—running naked out of the room.

"Arlene—"

He listened and heard her saying, "Really? But isn't it kinda late? . . . No, but it's pretty short notice."

She'd been in the bar, seen the whole thing, and admitted it to him. Christ almighty.

"No, no, I didn't mean *that*. Hon, you know I'd love to

come. . . . Yeah, okay. . . . God, I'll have to move. . . . Okay, 'bye."

Arlene came back in the room, hurrying, not looking at Stick.

"I'm going to Chicago. Calls up practically in the middle of the night—gets the big urge, I *have* to come. He's sending the company plane over."

"Arlene," Stick said, "hold still a minute, okay?" He watched her come out of the closet with a suitcase and clothes over her arm.

"He's at the APAA convention. God, I didn't know it was the APAA. Who's he had in the booth? Some girl, must be from Chicago. But what would she wear?"

"Arlene, did you tell him about me and Frank, that you knew us?"

She looked at him briefly. "You got to get out of here, I'm being picked up. Why didn't he take me when he went? The prick. No, I shouldn't say that, he's been very nice to me."

"I'll drive you," Stick said. "We can talk in the car."

She was in the closet again, getting a green pantsuit and the shiny silver costume. "One of his hot-rodders is on the way over. God, the way they drive. He doesn't believe anybody should get to the airport more than ten minutes early. It means they don't have anything to do."

"Arlene, did you tell him our names?"

"Why would I do that?"

"Say yes or no, will you?"

"No, of course not."

He felt a little relief, just a little. It was funny, in a way, watching her run around the room naked, taking things out of the dresser and throwing them in the suitcase.

"Did you tell anybody else?"

She was out of the room again.

"Like the police!"

He heard the bathroom door close and lock and the water turned on. Stick put on his pants and shoes. He couldn't believe it. Carrying his shirt he went into the hall and stood close to the bathroom door.

"Arlene?"

"Hon, I can't talk now, I'm doing my eyes."

"You didn't tell anybody else?"

"God, I almost forgot. Look in the front closet, see if there's something hanging there, from the cleaner's."

Stick hesitated, then went into the living room, putting his shirt on.

The front doorbell rang.

Almost immediately the bathroom door opened.

"Get in the bedroom."

Her eyes, vividly lined and framed in silver-green, were wide open. She ran in and put on the green pantsuit before running back out to open the door. Stick waited.

He heard her say, "Larry, hi, you're a doll." She laughed at something Larry said. "No, no, get in the car, I'll be right out."

Arlene came into the bedroom with a dry cleaner's plastic bag, finished packing in less than half a minute, and picked up the suitcase.

"Arlene—"

"I'll talk to you when I get back," Arlene said and rolled her eyes at him. "God."

The front door closed and there was silence. Stick made himself a drink, Canadian Club, because her friend didn't have bourbon. He drank it and smoked a cigarette and went back to Arlene's bed for the night.

18

"I put a stack of plastic glasses on the bar," Frank said, "they use the good ones, have to go and *find* them so they can put their cigarettes out in the glasses—plastic ones're sitting right there."

Stick passed him, going out to the kitchen with a couple of ashtrays.

"I'm surprised you got anything in there at all," Frank said and picked up a glass. "Look at the cigarette butts. Potato chips all over, ground in the carpet, drinks spilled—like they're raised in a fucking barn."

Stick came out of the kitchen. He felt like moving, doing something, and kept picturing Arlene running around naked, packing the suitcase.

"Next morning always looks depressing," Stick said. "Especially with the sun out." He could remember hangovers in the Florida sun. He went through the open doors to the balcony and began gathering empty beer cans. "Nobody's down at the pool yet."

"And they aren't at church," Frank said. "Where you suppose all the partygoers are?"

"Throwing up," Stick said. "Hugging their toilets."

"You get the guy out of your bed all right?"

"He opened his eyes, didn't know where he was."

"You didn't come back, huh?"

"This morning," Stick said, "about half past seven." He didn't want to mention Arlene just yet—Arlene seeing them in the bar—so he said, "I noticed you weren't home."

"You want to know where I was?"

"With the nurse," Stick said. "I figured you were both about due."

He came in and dropped beer cans into an open grocery bag on the floor. "She any good?"

"The quiet ones," Frank said. He was resting, taking a break with a beer and a cigarette. "You know what they say about the quiet ones."

"I know what they say," Stick said, "I just don't know as it's true."

"Take my word, buddy."

"You promise to marry her?"

"We're engaged," Frank said. "I notice you went out, you must've made some arrangements."

Stick brought in more beer cans from the balcony. He didn't say anything. He let Frank believe whatever he wanted.

"Well, let's see," Frank said. "Karen was with the talker. Jackie was smashed. If you got her kitty outfit off, you might as well've put her jammy-jams on, she was through for the evening, and I can't see you doing a number on some broad's out practically cold, at least I hope you wouldn't. Arlene was already gone when we got back—was it Arlene?"

"You got another cigarette?"

"Last one. Look on my dresser. It must've been Karen, then. She got rid of the talker and you met her at her place."

Stick went into his bedroom; he might as well get his own. He was thinking maybe he should wait until Arlene got back and talk to her again. He didn't know what she really thought about it. Say she didn't tell her friend who they were, fine; but what did she think about it, seeing two guys she knew holding up a bar? She was nutty. It was hard to imagine what she might think. She might even think it was cute.

He could hear Frank in the living room.

"How you like doing it by the numbers? Now the other. Do the thing with the boobs. That Karen—she's too much. Now the one where we stand on our heads."

Stick got a pack of cigarettes from his dresser.

Tell him, he was thinking. You got to tell him sometime.

He opened the pack going out to the front room.

"She too much?"

"I wasn't with Karen," Stick said. "Arlene."

Frank raised his eyebrows, a little surprised. "Arlene— yeah? Not much there but I can see it could be very active, a good workout. Right?"

"She's a nice girl," Stick said.

"Almost all of them are," Frank said. "But is she any good?"

"What're you asking me something like that for?"

"You just asked me the same thing, for Christ sake."

"Okay, let's drop it," Stick said, "get the place cleaned up."

"You hear that? Honest to God," Frank said, "the way you think. You don't sound like a broad, but—I don't know—it's like you think like one, with a broad's mentality. I don't mean that as an insult—"

"You don't, huh?"

"No, it's just you've got a different way of looking at things."

"Wait'll I get a beer," Stick said. "We can sit down and argue for a change."

"We're supposed to be at Sportree's, four o'clock," Frank said.

That stopped it. Stick looked at Frank sitting there with his beer, Frank staring at him, waiting, sort of a little challenge in his expression.

Stick thought, Well, screw him. And then he thought, No, why fight about it?

He said, "What's that, the cocktail hour? Drinks are half price?"

"He's arranged a meeting, a special presentation," Frank said, "I think you're going to be quite interested in."

"Shop at Hudson's and be happy," Stick said. "Am I warm?"

"That's all you are," Frank said. "Shop at Hudson's and make enough to be happy for a year is the way it goes. It's all worked out. He's going to show you how we knock down the biggest department store in town and find happiness. Show you how it's no more trouble than a supermarket."

"Nothing to it, huh?"

"Not if you know what you're doing."

Stick said to himself, I'm not going to get pissed off. I'm not going to get in a dumb argument. I'm not going to say anything, no, nothing at all about Arlene.

He said to Frank, "Okay, let's go, then."

"One more thing," Frank said. "They're all going to be black. At least I think they are. Now, it's okay to call a Negro a Negro. Like with Jewish girls, they know what they are. But don't refer to them as niggers, okay?"

Fuck you, Stick said to himself. He said to Frank, "I'll try not to."

19

They were in Sportree's apartment, upstairs over the bar, and Frank was telling them how Stick had shot the two muggers in the Northland parking lot.

Stick was uncomfortable, he didn't like it at all. Three colored guys and a colored girl listening to Frank describe how he'd killed two other colored guys, not telling it the way it actually happened but making him sound like a gunman: The two guys come up and try to take the bag, my partner here doesn't say a word, fuck no, pulls out his piece, .38 chief's special, and blows the two guys away.

Blows them away—Christ, he shot one of them in the back.

Sportree would nod as he listened and sometimes smile, but you couldn't tell what he was thinking. Or sometimes what any of them were thinking. There was Sportree in some kind of funny loose open shirt and trading beads. Marlys cool in a bare midriff, showing a dark little navel. And the two guys Sportree had brought in for the job.

Leon Woody, with a beard and moustache, looked like an Arab. He sat quietly, with one leg crossed over the other. He'd smile a little with a gentle gaze that held as long as he wanted it to. Leon Woody reminded Stick of Sportree. There was something African, mysterious, about them. Nothing was going to hurry or surprise them.

The other one, Carmen Billy Ruiz, was Puerto Rican. His eyelids were heavy with scar tissue and his mouth looked puffy and sore drawing on his Jamaican tailor-made. A long time ago he had been a welterweight with a seventeen-and-seventeen record, then a sparring partner for Chico Vejar, then for Chuck Davey after Davey whipped Vejar. In 1955, in Detroit, he shot and killed a store clerk during a holdup and spent the next seventeen years in Jackson. (Carmen Billy Ruiz said *diez-y-siete* was a bad fucking number; don't mention it in front of him.) He resented the fact Stick had killed two men and said through a smoke cloud, while Frank was telling the story, "What is this shit? He put away a couple of kids." Leon Woody and Sportree looked at each other—Stick noticed this—and Leon Woody said, "Billy, be nice and let the man finish. Then you can tell how many you put away."

Stick was glad, God, he was glad he wasn't going to have any part of this. They could say anything they wanted. He'd listen and nod and seem to go along, and when they were through, that was it. He didn't know these guys or owe them a thing. Be nice, like the man said, and play along.

He nodded yes, he'd have another bourbon, yes please, when Marlys picked up his glass. Marlys was doing the drinks and constructing big Jamaican cigarettes with four pieces of paper each for Billy Ruiz and anybody who wanted one. The redheaded black girl who played the piano wasn't around. Unless she was in the bedroom. Or Sportree could've gotten rid of her for the meeting.

There wasn't any doubt Sportree was in charge. He sat on the couch with Marlys next to him, looking over his shoulder, and sheets of drawing paper on the coffee table that showed the floor plan of several different sections of Hudson's downtown store—including the administrative offices, with dotted lines leading to exits—and a plan of the exterior with adjacent streets indicated.

"We start with the outside," Sportree said and looked at Stick. "You—you here on Farmer Street on the back side of the building, in the bar, right here. You see the Brink's truck turn in the alley that run through the building. You know what I'm saying?"

"I know the alley you mean," Stick said. "It's like a tunnel."

"That's right," Sportree said. "They come in off Farmer, alley bends in there, they pick up the load and come out on the south side the building. Before that, soon as you see it coming, you make the call."

"What's the number?"

"You get the number when I'm through."

Sportree looked at Frank. "You by the telephone outside the men's room, north end of the toy department, fourteenth floor. You been there to see it?"

Frank nodded.

Sportree's gaze moved to Leon Woody. "You watching Frank. You got the doll box, huh, in the Hudson bag."

"Little Curly Laurie Walker's box," Leon Woody said.

Sportree began to smile and shook his head. "Come on, shit—Curly Laurie Walker. That her name?"

"Little redhead girl, three foot tall, she do everything but bleed," Leon Woody said. "Billy try to jump her. I give her to my little girl so she be safe."

"What was that?" Billy Ruiz said. "What'd you say?"

Marlys was laughing and slapped her leg. "I can see him doing it, stoned on his herb."

Billy Ruiz was frowning, puzzled. "See what?"

"Man, let's pay attention," Sportree said. "Okay? You got one minute. Bang on the door the men's room, Billy comes out in his uniform." He looked at Ruiz. "We get that tomorrow, bus driver suit, I know where we can get one. With the holster it be good enough, get you in the office. Okay, so the three of you take the stairs, here, by the exit sign. You go up to the office floor."

"How long's it take them, the Brink's guys?" Frank asked.

"About five minutes," Sportree said. "It varies."

Marlys looked up from the drawings. "You know the man down at the door, he's like a porter? He calls up the office when they come, then we know to expect them in a few minutes. He doesn't call and some dudes walk in with uniforms on, we know they not from Brink's."

"So we get to the office just before the Brink's guys," Frank said, "giving us, say, four minutes."

"Say three," Sportree said, "to get in and get out. They see Billy in the bus driver suit and the gun, they open the door. You two go in behind him, put the people on the floor, take the sacks, put them in the doll box, and get the fuck out, down the stairs to the toy department. You go in the stock room and put the box on the shelf where all the curly what's-her-name little jive-ass doll boxes are, in the back. The box is already marked." He looked at Leon Woody. "You been in there?"

"Yesterday."

"And they still got enough little curly-ass doll boxes?"

"Whole shelf full. I put it there and see Billy get out of his bus suit."

"All right," Sportree said, "about that time the bell's going to ring and they'll be security people all over the store, at every door and exit. The police, First Precinct, could be there before you get to the ground floor, and then it's time to be cool. First thing, dump your pieces in a trash bin, someplace like that. Then split up and circulate. They want to search you going out, that's fine, you just a dumb nigger, you don't know what the fuck is going on at *all*. They let you out, you go home. Two days later, this man here"—he looked at Stick—"goes up to the stock room and gets the doll box with the mark on it. He goes because nobody's seen him before, clean-looking white gentleman. Tell me you see something wrong." He waited.

Frank and Leon shook their heads.

Billy Ruiz said, "How much we going to get?"

"No way of knowing," Sportree said. "I told you, I give you a guarantee, five K off the top. You said beautiful. You want something else now?"

"I want to be with him, carry it out," Billy Ruiz said. "I don't want somebody giving me some shit later—we didn't do so well, here's a hunnert bills. Fuck that shit, man, right now."

Stick saw Sportree and Leon Woody look at each other again. "Hey, we trust each other," Sportree said to Billy Ruiz. "Nobody going to cheat nobody. You hear Frank saying anything? Leon? No, we all in this."

"This guy, he picking up the money, I don't even know him," Billy Ruiz said.

"He don't know you, either." Sportree looked over at Stick and back to Billy Ruiz. "You saying you want to pick it up, Billy? You don't trust nobody?"

"I go with him," Billy Ruiz said.

Stick saw the exchange between Sportree and Leon Woody again, their gaze meeting, each one knowing something.

"All right, Billy," Sportree said. "You go with him."

After that they sat around a little while. Sportree went out to the kitchen for something and Frank followed him. Marlys went over to the hi-fi and picked up a record sleeve. Stick looked over at Leon Woody sitting there quietly with his legs crossed. There was something he wanted to ask him. It wasn't important, but if he got the chance, if the guy happened to look over.

Billy Ruiz said to Marlys, "Hey, Mamma, play some of that Al-ton for me, okay?"

Marlys, reading the record sleeve, had her back to them. "You want some Alton Ellis and his Caribbean shit? I'll give you some Stevie," Marlys said. "Be grateful."

"He's all right, his soul," Billy Ruiz said. "It's very close."

"Close about a thousand miles," Marlys said. "Stevie can fake that reggae boogie shit better than Alton can do it straight."

Leon Woody was smiling, listening to them. Stick didn't know what they were talking about. He waited until the music came on. Leon Woody looked over at him, maybe to see what he thought of it.

"You have a little girl?" Stick said.

"Yeah, little eight-year-old. She small, not much bigger than the doll." Leon Woody smiled faintly. "Sportree has trouble with that name, don't he?"

"I got a little girl seven," Stick said. "She's going to be in the second grade next month."

"Is that right? Yeah, they cute that age, aren't they?"

Stick said yeah, they sure were. After that, he couldn't think of anything to say.

It was getting dark when they left. Frank drove. He was up, excited about what they were going to do. He tried to appear calm, but it showed in the way he took off from lights and wheeled the T-bird through traffic.

Stick said, "That Carmen Billy Ruiz—where'd he get a name like that?"

"He's Puerto Rican," Frank said. "He was a fighter once. Fought Chuck Davey—you remember him?"

Stick said, "What I meant to say—where'd they get him, for Christ sake. He could get you in trouble, not even trying."

Frank said, "Don't worry about it. Sportree's going to handle him."

"Is that what he's going to do?" Stick said, "because I'll tell you something, I don't see him doing anything else."

"He's been going down there—he's the one put the whole thing together." Frank looked over at Stick. "Now that you've seen it, what do you think?"

"What do I *think?* I think it looks like amateur night."

"Come on—"

"Come on where? You got a guy with a little girl used to steal TV sets. You got a crazy Puerto Rican living on dope and a guy runs a bar telling you what to do. A bus driver's suit— you imagine that crazy fucking guy walking in in a bus driver's suit? Is he going to have one of those change things on him?"

"He knows what he's doing," Frank said, "Sportree. Listen, that's why I took it to him. Everything he gets into, it goes. He doesn't touch something he doesn't make out."

Stick said, "What's he touching? He's sitting home watching the fucking ball game while you clowns are running around the store with a doll box. I thought you said it was your idea."

"It was, the basic idea, yeah, when I find out Marlys's working in the office. But it was Sportree worked it out. You got any doubts or questions, talk to him about it."

"I'm talking to *you.* I don't even know the guy, what do I want to talk to him for, like I work for him now or something? We got a nice thing going, two grand a week, we can't even spend it all, you want to go hold up a department store."

"You know for how much?"

"He said you didn't know."

"He told Billy we didn't know. We're talking about a minimum, I mean *minimum,* a hundred grand."

"You're crazy," Stick said. "It's all charge accounts there, and checks."

"Uh-unh, not the downtown store. Half the people go there are colored. You think they all got charge accounts?"

"I don't know—" Stick said.

"I know you don't. Listen, fourteen floors of cash registers, every floor the size of a city block. People come in, buy all kinds of things, some on charge, some pay with a check, and a bunch of them, man, a bunch of them, have to pay strictly cash, because that's all they've got."

"Anybody ever do it before?"

"Not the whole thing," Frank said, "that any of us can remember. Ten years ago, maybe more than that, a guy got twelve hundred from a cashier on the mezzanine. All small stuff."

"Small stuff like what we've been doing," Stick said, "and getting away with. Now all of a sudden you want to do the whole fucking thing at once."

"I'll talk to you when you calm down," Frank said. "It's staring you in the face and you can't even see it."

"Relax, huh?"

"Right. Relax and think about it. We walk in—it's waiting there in little gray sacks—and pick it up. Christ, you're outside, what're you worried about?"

"I'm outside—till I go in with that crazy Puerto Rican."

"I told you, what're you worried about him for? I talked to Sportree, he said, 'Don't worry about Billy.'"

"I'm not worried, because I'm not going to have anything to do with it," Stick said. "Nothing."

20

Stick lined up four pay phones on Farmer Street, behind the
J. L. Hudson Company.

He did this after he'd given in and told Frank okay, but this
was the last one, and found out this part of the plan hadn't been
thought out at all. What if he went in the bar to call and some
guy was using the phone? What if he went in the doughnut
shop or the drugstore, the same thing? What if all of a sudden
the Brink's truck comes and everybody around there decided
to make phone calls? Sportree hadn't planned it at all. He'd
gone through the motions. If they made it, fine; if they didn't,
well, it wasn't his ass, he wasn't out a thing.

Stick didn't like relying on other people he didn't even
know.

He didn't like Arlene knowing about them—Christ, just to
add a little more to it—and not knowing where Arlene was and

what she was thinking. She hadn't been home all week and he hadn't told Frank about her yet.

He told himself he was dumb. He should've stayed out of this, not learned anything about it. If he wasn't afraid of Frank and he didn't owe him anything, then why was he doing it?

Maybe he felt he did owe him something. Frank could've put him in jail, but he didn't. Shit no, Frank needed him.

He should've left for Florida. Right after shooting the two black guys, the next morning, he should've left and not said a word to Frank.

Now he was into something with three more black guys. Christ, everybody on the street, half the people anyway, seemed to be black. He wondered where everybody was going—if they had someplace to go. Or if they were out of work and just walking around downtown. It was a nice day, mid-seventies, the sky fairly clear. Maybe because some auto plants were shut down. What do you want, a job or a clear sky? He looked across at Hudson's—old, dark-red building filling the block and rising up fifteen floors, then narrowing into a tower that went up another five stories. He wondered where they kept the flag they displayed across the front of the building on some of the U.S. holidays, the biggest American flag ever made.

The Brink's truck was coming south on Farmer, the way Sportree had said it would. Stick went inside the bar on the corner. Nobody was using the phone. He stepped into the booth and made the call.

When the phone rang, Frank turned from the wall, ripped off the sheet of paper that said OUT OF ORDER, and picked up the receiver.

"Toy department."

That was all he said. A moment later he hung up and nodded as he turned.

Leon Woody was playing with a game called Mousetrap, watching the little metal ball rolling through a Rube Goldberg contraption that set off a chain reaction of things hitting things that finally dropped a plastic net over the mouse. Leon Woody left the counter, carrying a big greenish Hudson's shopping bag with a doll box inside, and walked down the main aisle to the Men's Room.

Frank watched him go inside. He started down the aisle.

Leon Woody came out of the Men's, followed by Carmen Billy Ruiz in the Air Force–blue bus driver's suit and peaked cap. Frank was ten feet behind them when they went through the door beneath the exit sign.

The stairway took one turn to the fifteenth floor. None of them said anything; the sound of their steps filled the stairwell. Leon Woody opened the door and stepped back to let Billy Ruiz go ahead of him. Billy hesitated.

Leon Woody said, "Take out the piece, hold it flat against your leg, you dig? Go past the elevators, down on the right side. That's this hand here. You see the door, credit department. Don't say nothing. Nod your head, they say anything to you."

Frank, waiting on the stairs, watched Billy Ruiz take out the gun he had given him, Stick's .38 chief's special. He could feel his own, the big Python, in the pocket of his safari jacket. The store was air-conditioned, but it was hot in the stairwell. Leon Woody glanced back at him and went through the door.

Frank hurried to catch it before it closed—like he didn't want to be left behind. He went out on the fifteenth floor, cutting diagonally across the main aisle, past the bank of elevators. Billy Ruiz was thirty feet ahead, taking his time. Leon Woody paused by the optical department to look at glasses frames. Frank came up next to him.

"What's he doing?"

"He's all right," Leon Woody said. "Be cool."

They moved on, past theatrical display boards and ticket windows, past the travel service and portrait studio. There were no customers anywhere. Billy Ruiz turned into the credit department. They were fifteen feet behind him now. A face appeared at a teller's window. The door next to the window opened. Billy Ruiz went through. Leon Woody sprinted the last few yards and caught the door. Frank went in behind him, pulling the Colt Python.

He heard Billy Ruiz say, "Turn around, everybody. I mean *everybody*, get down on the floor."

Frank saw their faces briefly, their eyes with the startled expressions, two older women and a young man. Marlys wasn't in the room. They got down on their hands and knees, the women awkwardly, and lowered themselves to the carpeting. Billy Ruiz covered them, holding the .38 straight out and down. Leon opened the doll box without taking it out of the shopping bag and set it on a table against the wall where five gray-canvas sacks were waiting. Leon looked at them a moment, then walked over to a door with a frosted-glass window and opened it a little at a time, looking in.

Marlys's eyes rose from her typewriter, but her fingers continued to move over the keys for another few moments. The door beyond her desk was open to an office where a man sat half turned from his desk, talking on a phone and gesturing with his free hand. They couldn't hear his voice. Leon Woody stepped away from the frosted-glass door. Marlys came out, closing it behind her, and Leon nodded toward the sacks.

Frank watched her walk over to the table. She paused, then touched three of the sacks and looked up at Leon Woody. When Leon nodded, she walked back to her office, went in, and closed the door. Like that, not a word.

Leon dropped two of the sacks into the doll box, then the three Marlys had indicated. Frank watched him, not understanding. What difference did it make which ones went in first? He wanted to touch Leon's arm, get his attention, frown at him or something.

He heard Billy Ruiz say, "Jesus!" Like he was sucking in his breath.

Frank looked over and saw him raising the .38—it didn't make sense—raising it up to an angle above his head.

Leon Woody yelled at him, "Hold it!"

And Frank didn't know what was going on, until he looked up, in the direction the .38 was pointing, and saw the window above the row of file cabinets and the guy outside, strapped in a safety harness with a cloth over his shoulder and a squeegee in his hand, standing on the window ledge.

The guy had been there all the time and they hadn't seen him, concentrating on the three people getting down on the floor. The guy standing there, leaning out away from the window, trying to get away from it, fifteen floors up and no place to hide.

Frank wanted to run—seeing the guy staring at them scared to death—get the hell out of here and keep running, forget it, call it off, the whole thing, like it hadn't happened.

Leon Woody said, very quietly, "Shit . . . man seen the whole show. I don't know where my head's at." And he shook it from side to side, almost as if to make sure he was awake. He said then, "Billy—"

Billy Ruiz shot the guy twice, through the glass, shattering the pane, and they saw the red spots blossom on his white T-shirt and his head snap back, maybe screaming—there was a sound, a woman screaming—the guy straining against the harness before his feet slipped from the ledge and his legs and hips dropped away and they could see only the top half of him in the shattered window, his head hanging forward, motionless. The woman inside the room was still screaming.

Billy Ruiz went for the door and Leon said, "Walk, man, don't run. Same way we came." Frank was right behind him, then stopped as Leon shoved the Hudson's shopping bag into his arms and took the Python in both hands.

"Let me have it."

"What for?"

"I'll get rid of it."

"Where you going?"

"Hey, be cool, we all going together."

Frank didn't understand, but he couldn't argue. He let go of the gun and held the Hudson's bag in front of him, his arms around it. It wasn't as heavy as he had thought it would be.

There were a few shoppers down toward the end of the aisle, by display cases. None of them seemed to be looking this way. The rest of the aisle was empty.

The three of them were close together going through the exit door to the stairway. Then Frank had to stop. Holding the box in front of him, he almost piled into Leon Woody standing at the top of the stairs looking down, waiting. Past him, Frank could see Billy Ruiz reaching the landing where the stair made its turn.

"Go on, for Christ sake."

Leon Woody didn't move or say anything. He raised the Colt Python, aiming it down, and shot Billy Ruiz between the shoulder blades, the explosion filling the stairwell as Billy Ruiz was slammed against the wall and slid partway down the rest of the stairway.

Leon Woody moved now. Frank watched him, his profile, bending over Billy Ruiz. He told himself to drop the box or throw it at him and get out, back through the door. He knew he wouldn't make it, though. Leon Woody was looking up, the Python in his hand pointing at him but not aimed at him.

"Come on, man," Leon Woody said, "what you waiting for? You know where to put it, back behind. It's already marked. Then go down the fourth floor, get the escalator. Maybe I see you outside."

Frank watched him go through the door to the toy department. By the time Frank got there, stepping over Billy Ruiz, not looking at him, Leon wasn't anywhere around.

The voice inside Frank Ryan wasn't in condition; it had gone to fat and was pretty weak when it told him he had fucked up and the whole thing was an awful mistake. The voice did get through, and in those words, but Frank barely heard it and it didn't take much to smother the voice completely. A couple of scotches on the rocks.

Stick said, "Well?"

Frank stood at the bar, between two of the bamboo stools, holding onto the drink. He heard the faint sound of a girl laughing, coming from the patio below, then silence again.

"Well what? It's done."

"I never saw so many police cars," Stick said. "I would say within ten minutes of the time I called, no more than that, they're all over the place, completely around the store, and these guys are running in with their riot guns."

"Don't tell me," Frank said. "They're waiting at the bottom

of the escalator, four of them with their guns out. Anybody looks suspicious, 'Would you mind stepping over here?' They're going through packages, searching people, even women."

"How'd you get out?"

"How'd I get out? I walked out. What're they going to find on me? 'Hey, what's going on, Officer?' And they give you something about a routine investigation—five hundred cops in the place, shotguns, riot outfits, everything, it's a routine investigation."

"You ditched your gun all right?"

"Leon took care of it."

"How come Leon?"

Stick was sitting forward in his chair, holding a can of beer between his hands. He watched Frank go over to the coffee table to get a cigarette.

"Weren't you carrying it?"

"I carried the doll box," Frank said. Lighting the cigarette gave him a little time. He walked back to the bar and took a drink of scotch.

"Yeah? So you gave him your gun?"

"We had a little problem." The whole thing would be in the evening paper—Frank realized that—still, he wanted to tell it the right way, like there was really nothing to it, or Stick was liable to go through the ceiling.

"What kind of problem?"

"Billy shot a guy."

"Jesus—I *told* you."

"Wait a minute, a witness," Frank said. "A guy washing the window."

"Christ almighty—"

"We look up, the guy saw the whole thing, sees Marlys, so Billy had to shoot him."

"I told you. Christ, didn't I tell you? That guy's going to fuck the whole thing up, not even trying?"

"Will you wait a minute?" Frank said. "Take it easy, okay? and listen." He paused to make sure his voice would sound calm. "Billy pulled something else."

Stick was staring at him, waiting.

"He tried—we're going down the stairs—he tried to grab the box from me. See, he wants the whole thing, probably had it planned all the time and that's why he was going to settle for five. He shoots a couple times and misses, luckily, Christ, and Leon, he's got the Python, he shot him and that was it."

"You left him there?"

"He was dead, for Christ sake."

Stick shook his head slowly and let his breath out and shook his head again. He said, "Oh, boy—well, how do you like the big leagues?"

"We still did it," Frank said. He was being earnest now. "We got the money, five sacks, waiting there in the stockroom."

"Hey, Frank, come on—"

"I'm not shitting you, we got it, it's there. Everything went according to the book except the thing with Billy Ruiz. Okay, Billy's out of it, put his five K back in the pot, you never liked the guy, anyway."

"Frank, you got two dead men—you want to go back in there for the walkie dolly box?"

"I look at it this way," Frank said, getting into it and feeling more at ease, in control. "Whether two guys are dead or not, the money's sitting there waiting. The two guys don't change anything—you think Sportree, Leon Woody's going to say, Yeah, well let's leave it, then? Bullshit. This is armed robbery, man, and you know what I'm talking about, you go in with a gun and sometimes you have to use it or else you'd carry a fucking water pistol, right? When it's you or him, buddy, you know who comes first or you're in the wrong business. Listen, I saw you blow away two guys in that parking lot. You ought to know what I'm talking about better than I do."

"It's different now," Stick said. "We're not talking about armed robbery, ten to a quarter, we're talking about murder, maybe life."

"I can't argue with you," Frank said, "or quibble about the degree. Yeah, it's different now. But the odds, the odds are the same. You go in, look around, take your time. You don't like the feel, you smell something isn't right, you walk out. Nobody's going to blame you for being careful. You don't like it, get out. If it looks okay, pick up the box. Anywhere along the line something doesn't look right, dump the box, get the fuck out. But remember one thing, my friend, Ernest Stickley, Junior, there's over a hundred grand in the box and it's no heavier than you're carrying the doll in it, a present for your little girl."

There was a silence. Stick took a sip of beer. "I'll think about it," he said.

"What's there to think about? Your part, what you said you'd do, hasn't changed any."

"I said I'd think about it."

Frank put on an act of being calm, in control. He said, "Take your time. But if you turn chickenshit before day after tomorrow, let me know, okay? I'll go get it myself."

Leon Woody came in while Frank was at Sportree's, the two of them sitting in the living room upstairs. Frank saw Marlys in the doorway for a moment: she looked in, didn't nod or say anything and kept going down the hall. Leon Woody said, "How you doing?" and sat down. Frank frowned, looking over at Sportree sitting there in his Afro-Arabian outfit and a big Jamaican smoke held delicately between his fingers.

"She upset about the man wash the windows," Sportree said.

"How upset?"

Sportree shook his head. "Uh-unh, little girl's fine."

"I can't keep up with you," Frank said. "Last week, no, the week before, it was the redheaded girl plays the piano."

"Yeah, she still playing, she happy," Sportree said. "The one I'm worried about is your friend, if he's got his shit together on this thing."

"Well, you say don't worry about Marlys," Frank said. "It's the same thing, you don't have to worry about Stick. I remind him he said he'd get it and he will, I'm sure of it."

"I like a man like that," Sportree said. "Can take his word. I mean if it's true."

"I don't know, I'm saying the same thing to him all the time. I'm in the middle of you two guys, I trust both of you, naturally, so I just assume you trust each other."

"You like him," Sportree said, "hey, then I like him. You

give me a Stick, I give you a Leon Woody." He looked over at Leon, who nodded but didn't say anything.

"And take away a Billy Ruiz," Frank was saying. "That was a setup, wasn't it? You knew he wasn't coming out."

"No, he could've made it. It was up to Leon. I told Leon to use his judgment."

"But what for? I mean if you don't trust the guy, what'd you bring him for?"

"Let me explain something to you," Sportree said. "See, Billy's fine for how you use him. Say to him, Billy, here two hundred-dollar bills. You keep one, if you can make that policeman over there eat the other one, tied on your hog. He'd try it, think it was easy money. But see, Billy was very, very dumb. He could go one two three four, no trouble. But something happen he had to go one three seven five, shit, you don't know what the man was going to do. So I told Leon, Hey, you come to where you got to travel light, then dump the excess baggage, man. See, another thing, if Billy was picked up, you got to hold your breath all the time he in there. They could punch him, he wouldn't say a word. As I told you, I trust him. But that man, he so fucking dumb they be getting things out of him he don't even know he telling."

"I guess so," Frank said, "but Christ, killing him like that—I wish we could've got rid of him some other way, put him on a plane to San Juan or someplace."

"Not easy, is it?" Sportree said, in his Afro-Arabian robe, the Jamaican toke between his fingers, watching the gray smoke curl up. "Sometime we have to make sacrifices."

Leon Woody was at the window, watching Frank's T-bird pull away, making sure. Sportree was smoking. He yelled out, "Hey, baby!"

Marlys came in behind the three-foot doll box she was carrying, smiling back there, and placed it on the coffee table by Sportree.

"Little Curly Laurie. You want to know how much she got in her box?"

"Tell us," Sportree said.

"Exactly eighty-seven thousand four hundred and twenty-five."

Sportree smiled in his Jamaican smoke. "You have any trouble?"

"Walked out with it in the bag, Leon's waiting," Marlys said. "I didn't see anybody giving me looks, but I wouldn't want to do it again."

"Divide three into eighty-seven," Sportree said, "you would."

Leon, coming over from the window to sit down, said, "Now this Stick goes in tomorrow, comes out with the box still there, marked. Frank pick him up, they come here all smiling—what do we say then?"

"We say—they open the box," Sportree said, "two sacks in there. Two? Open them, checks. Checks? What's this shit, checks? Where the money sacks? He looks at us, huh? We look at Frank. Hey, Frank? You put the box there the day before yesterday? Frank say yeah, he put it there. He start to look at his friend. His friend start to look at him. One put it there, the other pick it up. But what do they have? Bunch of checks made out to the J. L. and Hudson Company. Somebody begins to say—they looking at each other—Hey, fuck, what is this? What's going on, man? They don't know shit what's going on."

"So maybe they go after each other," Leon Woody said. "One say, You put it there, five sacks in it, or not? The other say, You pick it up, but you don't come out the store with everything."

"That's the way I like to see it," Sportree said. "Now after a while, sometime, they going to look at us. We can look back at them, our eyes saying what is this ofay shit going on? Somebody trying to fuck somebody? Or we can look back at them and not say anything. Frank say to me, You wouldn't be pulling something, would you? Not wanting to come right out and accuse me, you understand? Finally I say to him, Frank, maybe everybody better forget about the whole thing and not think of hurting each other, because if anybody gets hurt, you know who it's going to be. And none of us can go to the police, can we? Because we all in it. So why don't we quit talking about it, dig? And you all go home."

Leon said, "You think he do it, huh, go home and be good?"

"Why would a man want to die at his age?" Sportree said.

Stick got two sets of Michigan plates off cars parked on the roof of the Greyhound bus station and wrapped them in the morning edition of the *Free Press* that ran two follow-up stories on Hudson's robbery.

There was a graduation-looking photo of a smiling, dark-haired guy, the window washer, and a twenty-year-old shot of Carmen Billy Ruiz in a boxing pose, on the front page, wrapped around the license plates. On page three there was a photo of the window washer's wife and two small children, and on the sports page a column devoted to Billy Ruiz's seventeen-and-seventeen record and how he had been Chuck Davey's sparring partner. Davey, now of the Chuck Davey Insurance Agency, Southfield, recalled that Billy Ruiz liked to eat ice cream—he ate ice cream all the time—but was not much of a puncher.

The two sets of license plates went in the trunk of the T-bird to be transferred to Stick's suitcase. He might use them on the way to Florida, he might not, but extra plates were good to have. He'd pick up a car that afternoon sometime.

He'd decided, finally, to tell Frank his plan and Frank had said, Wait'll you see your cut and you're holding it in your hand before you start talking about leaving.

Stick said don't worry, he was taking his cut, he wasn't going up to the toy department for nothing; but this was the end of it. After, he'd go home get his bag and if Frank would drop him off at a shopping center he'd appreciate it.

Frank said, "What about your share in the bank deposit box?" Stick said, "We can pick it up after, or you give me the same amount out of your cut from the Hudson's deal and keep all what's in the bank." That was all right with Frank. He said, "All right, if that's what you want to do. You'll get down there, play on the beach with your little girl, and I'll probably see you in about a week." He said, "If I'm in Hawaii or Acapulco or someplace, I'll leave word with the lady, the manager." Frank was in a pretty good mood.

That was about all that was said between them that morning in the apartment and driving downtown. It didn't seem like much after being together three months. Frank drove up to the rooftop parking lot over the bus station and waited for him while he got the license plates. Then drove him around to the Woodward Avenue side of Hudson's and said, "I'll see you in about fifteen minutes."

That was the last they saw of each other for six days.

Stick took an escalator up as far as he could and then a local elevator to the fourteenth floor. It still took him less than five minutes. He located the stock room first, in an arcade that connected with another section of the store. He roamed through the toy department then for a few minutes. There were only a few customers around—one guy very intently fooling with some kind of a target game, a young guy in jeans with fairly long blond hair—and hardly any salespeople.

He watched the stock-room door another couple of minutes. Nobody went in or came out. He said, "Okay," let his breath out slowly, walked over, and pushed through the door.

Frank had said the third aisle over. But he hadn't said which side. The sectioned metal shelves reached almost to the ceiling and it looked like there were boxes of dolls on both sides, all the way down to the end.

America's Little Darling, Baby Angel, Playmate for a Princess, Baby Crissy, Crissy's Cousin Velvet, Jean Marie, Tender Love . . . Christ, Shirley Temple . . . Rub-a-Dub Dolly, Saucy, Wendy, Cutie Cleaner, Cathy Quick Curl, Peachy and her Puppets, Beautiful Lee Ann the Dancing Doll . . . there, Little Curly Laurie Walker. She wasn't bad-looking.

The one he wanted had a little red dot near the bottom of the box. Which wasn't on any of the ones in front. He had to pull them out one at a time to look at the boxes in the row behind. Then two at a time, Christ.

It was in the third row, the fifth one. Stick got it up to the front and shoved boxes in to fill the space. He picked it up.

Frank was right, it wasn't heavy at all. He wondered if he should look inside, make sure.

That was when he glanced to the side.

It was strange, recognizing the guy in the quick glance and wanting to do something with the box, not knowing the guy, but knowing who he was—even if he did have long hair and jeans on—and knowing, shit, it was too late.

"Drop it and put your hands on the shelf, man, right now."

The guy had a big gun like Frank's, some kind of a mag, the same guy who'd been fooling with the target game.

Stick didn't have anything to lose. He said, "What's going on? What is this, a holdup?"

"It sure looks like it to me," the guy said. He had a little leather case open in his other hand, showing a badge.

Another guy, in a suit, came around the corner from the other side, at the end of the aisle, and that was it.

Stick said, "I was in here looking—I thought it was the Men's Room."

"You piss on dolls?" the young man said. "Man," and whistled. "Hey, Walter, he says he thought it was the Men's Room."

The one in the suit was next to him now. He said, "I can see why he'd think that. All the toilets."

"No, I mean I was looking for a doll for my little girl. Then I had to go to the Men's Room. I came in here, I saw it wasn't, of course"—Stick was giving the young guy a nice grin he knew already wasn't going to do him any good—"but then I saw these dolls, see, and started looking at them . . . for my little girl."

"You like the one with the red dot on it best?" the young guy said.

"You can read me my rights if you want," Stick said, "I'm not saying another word."

368

21

Stick remembered a time once in Yankton, South Dakota, standing around back of the chutes at a rodeo, watching the contestants drawing the bulls they'd ride.

He remembered one especially, a skinny guy with his big scooped-brim hat and tight little can, spitting over his hip and saying, "If I cain't ride 'im, I'll eat 'im." He lasted about three and a half seconds on a bull named Candyman and came back through the dust limping and hitting his big curly hat against his chaps.

The young guy, the cop, reminded him of one of those bull riders or a saddle bronc rider. Long hair, no hips, faded jeans, boots. It was the badge and the foot-long .44 mag under his left arm that made him something else, a Detroit police officer.

Frank had said it, you couldn't tell the cops from the hackers and stalkers anymore.

Stick kept his eyes on the young guy while they were at the First Precinct police headquarters, but didn't say anything to him or answer any of his questions. Shit no, he was standing mute. He didn't say anything getting fingerprinted and photographed and the only thing he said at the arraignment was not guilty. They set a bond of five thousand dollars and asked him if he wanted it. He said no. They asked him if he had counsel. He said no. They asked him if he wanted the court to appoint counsel for him. He said no. He'd sit it out and take his chance at the examination. If he didn't say anything, if he didn't call anyone for bond money, if he didn't talk to a lawyer or to the young guy even about the weather, he knew they couldn't do a thing to him—not for picking up a doll box, even if it did have a red dot on it.

Stick sat in the Wayne County jail with all the colored guys awaiting trial. He had never seen so many colored guys. He didn't say much to them and got along all right. The place smelled—God, it smelled—and the food was awful, but he'd been here before. He'd make it.

It was funny, sitting in jail he remembered the ice machine at the motel in Yankton and the sign on it that said: WE CANNOT PROVIDE ICE FOR COOLERS. He remembered thinking at the time, But how do they know if they don't try?

He remembered going into the place next to the motel, walking up to the two girls at the bar, and saying, "Good evening, may I buy you ladies a drink?" One of them said, "You dumb bunny, we work here." He said, "Oh, then would you bring me a drink?" And she said, "Certainly, sir, what would you like?"

Sitting in the Wayne County jail. He remembered telling Frank, coming out the last time, they didn't serve cocktails in there.

Most of all a Porter Waggoner song kept going through his head, about a hurtin' behind his left eye and a tiny little bee buzzin' around in his stomach. Porter was all tore down because of too many good, good buddies and bad, bad gals.

Stick didn't know about the gals, but the buddies were something to think about.

Every once in a while he'd think about the doll box, too. He had only held it a moment, but he remembered, in that moment, the box was a lot lighter than he'd expected it to be.

And he kept thinking about the cop who'd arrested him, the young guy. He could tell the guy was eager.

The young cop's name was Cal Brown.

Once he said to a superior, "But look, I've learned that already. I know it. Responsi*bil*ity? Having people under you? Giving them paychecks and shit? I had sixty guys under me and I kept them fucking *alive*. I've done that, man, what, when I was twenty-three."

He had been a combat infantry officer in Vietnam and had been with the police department seven years, since trying out with the San Diego Chargers as a free-agent wide receiver and ruining one of his knees before the season started.

Today he was having lunch at the Hellas Café on Monroe with Emory Parks, the young little fat black assistant from the prosecutor's office. Cal Brown ordered the stuffed grape leaves, feta cheese salad, and a glass of retsina. Emory Parks ordered roast lamb and lima beans and hot tea. They were waiting for the food to come. Emory Parks was fooling with his tea bag. Cal Brown was hunched over the table on his elbows.

"You read up on it yet?"

"I haven't had time, man. I probably won't read it till we're in court."

"You met the guy before, three months ago. Three and a half."

"Refresh my memory."

"Ernest Stickley, Junior, auto theft. Charge dropped at the exam, no positive ID."

"Shit," the little prosecutor said, "you know how many Ernest Stickley, Juniors, there are?"

"This one was in on the Hudson's thing."

"You'd like to believe that."

"His roomie," Cal said, "the guy he lives with in a four-hundred-and-fifty-dollar-a-month apartment out in Troy—listen to this part—is the same guy who was the eyeball witness to the auto theft and lost his memory."

Emory Parks stopped fooling with his tea bag. "Is that so?"

"Interesting?"

"Where's this boy Stickley now, out?"

"In. Passed on the bond, passed on the free lawyer. He gives you his name, rank, and serial number and raises his hand when he has to go to the bathroom."

"What's he arraigned on?"

"Larceny from a building. Conspiring."

The little prosecutor frowned now. "Larceny? Shit, you got a murder in there, haven't you?"

"Murder? We got two murders. We got all fucking kinds of numbers going. That's why we're talking. Listen—the gun used on the window washer? Same one killed the two guys out at Northland. In the parking lot."

"Well, you don't need him for that. Man did the community a favor, as I recall."

"That's not my question. Right now I'm giving you facts, okay? One of the guys killed at Northland—I don't remember which one—had a piece of grocery bag in his hand, and a few bills. From a store that'd been knocked over about an hour before. But the guys that knocked over the store weren't black."

"This one, Stickley—you show his picture out there?"

"With the Southfield police. Manager says no, he never saw him. One of the checkout girls, she cocks her head, well, maybe. She couldn't say for sure."

"So you got to stay with Hudson's, which is better anyway."

"Not necessarily," Cal said. "Yes, it's better, but I mean there're other possibilities, at least two dozen robberies out there, all armed, same everything, two guys come in, very polite, but no bullshit. We can go that way, right? Follow it up and probably get a conviction."

"You mean hand it to all the little police departments out there, they ain't cutting their grass they can work on it, and the first one off his ass and gets an ID gets an armed robbery bust. That saves you some work, doesn't it?"

"Look," Cal said, "since I'm buying the fucking lunch, don't tell me things I know, okay?"

"Excuse my friend," the little prosecutor said to the waitress putting their plates in front of them. "He likes to talk dirty, he wasn't insulting the food."

The waitress looked at him but didn't change her expression. She either didn't know what he was talking about or didn't care. It was 1:30 and the place was crowded.

Cal didn't look at his stuffed grape leaves. He said, "We can send this clown out to the country. There're a dozen circuit courts he can get lost in."

"Or?" Emory Parks was starting on his lamb and lima beans.

"Let me tell you the rest. A different gun was used on Billy Ruiz. We found it in a trash thing, a Colt Python three-five-seven."

"Belonging to whom?"

"Guy out in Bloomfield Hills. Registered—you listening?"

"I can eat and still listen, Calvin. It's a trick I learned."

"The Colt's registered to this guy and"—Cal paused—"you ready? So is the thirty-eight they used on the window washer."

"That's impressive." Emory Parks nodded, chewing his lamb. "You're keeping it neat, but you're still out in suburbia with the two guns."

"They were stolen three and a half months ago, in May," Cal said. "Stickley was acquitted in May. The two dozen or so robberies that all smell alike go back to May. Two guys get in the business, liquor stores, supermarkets, doing pretty well— you follow me?"

"And they decide it's time to go big time."

"And they get greedy, right? and go for the big banana."

"Bring some friends in."

"Bring *some*body in. A white guy and two gentlemen of the Negro persuasion go into the Hudson's office. Not Stickley, though, an unknown male Caucasian, Billy Ruiz, and another black gent with an unhappy childhood. One of whom shot Billy Ruiz in the back on the way out. Why?"

"Shit, anybody'd shoot Billy Ruiz in the back if they got the chance. That's not the question. Ask the right one," the little prosecutor said. "No, let me ask you one. How'd you know the money was still there, in the box?"

"Not the money, checks. Just checks."

"Not the money?"

"Let me tell it," Cal said. "We're looking all over the fucking store, top to bottom, and we find a little something—this is the next day—in Billy Ruiz's street clothes. They're in another trash thing, on the same floor we found the Python."

"Something in his clothes."

"In a pocket. A little toy soldier, thing's two inches high, costs nine and a half bucks. No sales slip. Where's it from? The toy department. One floor below the office. What was Billy Ruiz doing in the toy department? We start looking, two o'clock in the morning—this is the second day after, now—we found the doll box with the checks in it."

"The question," the little prosecutor said, "what would he want with just checks?"

"He comes in the *second* day after," Cal said. "Keep that in mind. What if he thought the money was there, too?"

"I see that," the little prosecutor said. "Like maybe somebody's fucking somebody over."

"Like maybe somebody came in the day before," Cal said, "and picked up another dolly box with a mark on it, but they don't tell Mr. Stickley. He's supposed to come out, they open the box and they say, Yeah—giving him the dead eyes—now where's the real stuff? But he doesn't come out. He looks around and he's got a forty-four mag in his ass. He doesn't know he wasn't picking up the money, because he doesn't know what was in the box."

"And you haven't told him."

"Not yet. That's why we're having the lunch."

The little prosecutor paused. "The store, they haven't released the news yet that any money is missing."

"They don't want to advertise for any repeat business."

"How much?"

"In the neighborhood of eight-seven."

The little prosecutor smiled. "And you got this boy for larceny from a building, which I doubt will even get to trial. He says, 'I didn't know what was in the box besides a doll,' and you didn't let him look, or walk out with it."

"We figured, we were *sure* he'd be identified in the office."

"You haven't mentioned what his roommate was doing that day. What *do* they do, both of them?"

"Yes indeedy," Cal said, "how do these two pay the rent? Stickley, unemployed, drives a cement truck when he isn't behind the wheel of a stolen vehicle. Frank J. Ryan, that's his roomie, is a car salesman. Last place of employment, Red Bowers Chevrolet. You ready to hear it again? Three and a half months ago."

"You got a sheet on him?"

"Frank's been a clean liver up to now, or else he's never been caught. He's a dude, with the hair and the mod suit and shit. I present myself at the apartment with a search warrant and tell him his buddy's been arrested. 'Oh, my,' he says, 'I don't believe it. Stick? But he's a nice guy.' I'm thinking, Not Johnny, he was always such a good boy, good to his mother."

"What'd you find?"

"The search revealed nothing unusual or incriminating other than nine hundred bucks under the sink in an Oxydol box. Clever? Ryan goes, 'Gee, how did that get there?' I said to him, 'Don't you ever do the dishes?' He goes, 'Oh yeah, Stickley won it at Hazel Park, but he never knew where he'd put it.'"

The little prosecutor kept his plate neat and didn't let anything touch. He moved a few lima beans away from his mashed potatoes before slicing off a piece of lamb. He said, "Why don't you have the Hudson's people take a look at him?"

"Because the only one they saw—the only face—was Billy Ruiz. The other two, all they're sure of, one was black, one white."

"Well, maybe there's some liquor store and supermarket people out there can identify Ryan as well as Stickley."

"That could be," Cal said, "but then I wouldn't have anything, would I?"

"Your grape leaves are going to get cold."

Cal started eating and neither of them spoke while Emory Parks finished his roast lamb and poured himself more tea. He said, "I agree we should save them for the Hudson's job and get a murder conviction, besides find the money. We're building a new Renaissance Center, getting downtown all fixed up, we can't have this kind of shit going on. Doesn't look good, does it?"

"It fucks up our image," Cal said, "not to mention people getting killed."

"All right, you got two male Caucasians," Emory Parks said, "but no lead on the brother. What I've been wondering, if somebody might've bankrolled this deal."

"Bankroll? What's to bankroll? They get a secondhand bus driver suit from the Goodwill."

"How about the people in the office?"

"That's a possibility. They knew when to walk in. Two, the check sacks were sealed, hadn't been opened. So we assume they knew the money sacks from the check sacks. I don't want to sound racially biased, Emory, but there's a cute little black chick up there that's sort of caught our eye."

Emory Parks was thinking again.

"You didn't tell me where this Frank Ryan was the day of the robbery."

"He said he was home sleeping, but he thinks Stickley went out for a while in the morning. That afternoon, they got three broads can swear they were out sitting by the pool."

"Must be nice to be unemployed," Emory Parks said. He looked thoughtful again.

"I talked to the broads," Cal said, "asking them what they knew about the two guys. Every one of them: Oh, they're business consultants. They have something to do with sales training or something like that. Nice guys, and they throw keen parties. I go back to Ryan. What's this I hear you're a business consultant? He says oh, that was just a little patio bullshit they handed the girls one time. They didn't want the girls to know they were unemployed. Oh, is that why you throw these big parties? He said they'd bought a lot of stuff one time and had a little bit left. The little bit, two cases of booze. There was one girl"—he took a small notebook out of his pocket and turned a few pages—"Arlene Downey. I asked her if she knew the two guys. Yeah, she knew them, but just slightly. I asked her if she knew what they did for a living. Right then, just for a second, her expression—like the light went on and her mother caught her doing it on the couch. Then she was evasive, had been out of town a lot, hadn't seen much of them."

Emory Parks was smiling a little. "Right there, aren't they? But you can't quite reach them. I think . . . what you're going to have to do . . . first thing, tell Ryan his partner needs somebody to post his bond. I think, playing Mr. Innocent Nice Guy, he'll run down there and do it."

"Yeah," Cal said. "I think he would. He knows I know he's got some money. Yeah—"

"Then you got the two of them looking at each other, the one guy facing a conviction. What's the other guy going to say to him?"

"He's going to say, Jesus, it's a shitty deal, but hang in there, man. It's like, Gee, I'm sorry you got leukemia, but there isn't anything I can do about it."

"And what's Stickley thinking, feeling his temporary freedom? He's already served time, he knows what it's like in there."

"He's thinking, Why me and not them? See," Cal said, "the trouble is I can't mention the money to him, let him know he's been fucked over. We can't let that out yet to anybody."

"You don't have to tell him," Emory Parks said. "His buddies, maybe his roommate if he's one of them, they don't know what's in Mr. Stickley's head. They don't know what he knows or doesn't know. He was in jail, they couldn't touch him, they hold their breath. But if he's out—can they take a chance letting him go to trial? Won't the cops try and plea-bargain with him? They already shot poor Billy Ruiz. They going to take a chance on this cat telling stories about them?"

"It's interesting," Cal said.

"It's not only interesting," the little prosecutor said, "it's all you got. Unless you find out one of them's been jumping that cute little black chick in the office. Then you got a lead on something else."

"Listen," Cal said, "I think I've got enough to work on for a while. Yes sir, I believe this could open it up."

"If you plant a little seed with this Stickley before you turn him loose."

"Yeah"—Cal was nodding—"make sure he realizes what a shitty deal he's getting."

"Not only a shitty deal, make him realize life can be dangerous out there. Man disappears for a time, they find him in the trunk of a car out at the airport. Say to him he ought to be very careful where he goes, where he meets his friends."

"Yeah," Cal said, "get him to reconsider who his friends are, who can do him the most good."

"That's it." Emory Parks smiled then. "You're going to take all this back to Thirteen hundred and Walter's going to say, 'You've been talking to that fat little nigger again, haven't you?' And you'll say, 'Well, I just picked at his brain a little.' "

"Your ass," Cal said. "I'll tell him I figured it all out myself. You got a free lunch, you fat little nigger, what more do you want?"

22

"Why don't you just not say anything?" Stick said. "If you don't talk for a while, it's okay with me."

"Look, I'm sorry," Frank said. "You think I'm blaming you, for Christ sake? I'm trying to find out how it happened."

"How it *hap*pened? I reach for the box and the guy, the cop, puts a fucking gun in my face is how it happened. They're waiting there—this great idea—they know exactly where it was."

"But how could they?"

"How do I know? They found out or somebody told them—shit, I don't know. This fucking great idea—I should be in Florida right now, I'm facing a robbery conviction."

"Conspiring to commit larceny from a building," Frank said.

"At the moment. But the cop, you know what the hotshot

cop says? 'Maybe at the exam we'll change it to robbery armed. And if we do that, we might as well go all the way to murder, right?' "

"The guy's blowing smoke up your ass. I think they'll go in on the larceny thing and get it thrown out."

"Yeah, well I'll tell the judge that, you don't think I'll get convicted. I'm facing the fucking thing and you're sitting home with your nice thoughts."

They walked along in silence, away from the Wayne County jail building down St. Antoine toward the parking structure. It was four in the afternoon, warm and sunny. They had walked down this street once before—it seemed a long time ago—on their way to the Greek place, the Bouzouki.

Frank said, "You want a drink?"

"I want to take a shower and change my clothes," Stick said.

Frank was silent again. Everything he said came out wrong, not the way he intended it, or Stick would turn it around. He didn't know what to say to him, but he kept trying anyway. Walking along in silence, Stick next to him, was worse.

"There was a cop, a hippie-looking guy," Frank said, "he was out a couple of times. Came with a search warrant the first time. I said, You don't need that, we got nothing to hide. He found the dough under the sink. I told him it was our nest egg, we'd won it at the track."

"He talk to anybody else there?"

"He talked to everybody. The ladies told him we're consultants."

"How about Arlene? He talk to her?"

"I don't know, I guess so."

"She was away," Stick said, "in Chicago or someplace."

"She's back now. I've seen her a couple of times."

"But you don't know if he talked to her."

"You afraid he told her something? What's the guy know? There's one little piece in the paper about you. It said you'd been arrested, but it was only speculated, in connection with the Hudson's thing. See, they're not playing it up because they don't have a case against you. They start bragging they got the guy and then you walk out, they don't look so good."

"Who'd you talk to?" Stick said. "I mean the girls there."

"I talked to Karen and I talked to Jackie. They say, What's this with your buddy? I told them it was all a dumb mistake. You walk in, you're going to buy a doll, send to your little girl, they think you look suspicious for some reason and they arrest you. They get it cleared up, you'll be out, we'll all be laughing about it," Frank said. "Don't worry about the girls, they don't know anything."

"Arlene does," Stick said.

"What? There's nothing anybody could tell her."

"I'm saying Arlene knows about us."

It took Frank a moment. He almost came to a stop. "Wait a minute, you mean *you* told her something?"

"I didn't tell her anything," Stick said. "The bar in Hazel Park, we took the money from the guy? She was there."

"Come on—"

"Sitting at the bar with her friend."

"Jesus Christ—you sure?"

"Am I *sure*? She told me, she's sitting there. We push her in the room with everybody, we didn't even see her."

"But—she didn't go to the cops?"

"I think we'd of heard."

"Then what's she doing? She want something?"

"I don't know. I'm going to have to talk to her."

"You don't *know*? You discuss this with her—when was that?"

"Just before she left. I haven't seen her since that night."

"Jesus Christ," Frank said. "That's all we need."

Stick felt a little better. Frank wasn't his calm, casual self anymore.

"Latest development," Detective Calvin Brown said into the phone, "I didn't get to him soon enough. While we're having the lunch, his roomie put up the bond."

He took a sip of coffee as he listened to the little prosecutor and put the cup down on the metal desk in the little gray partitioned room that was called his office: Criminal Investigation Division, fifth floor, 130 Beaubien.

"It could be all right," the little prosecutor said, "if the man's been thinking and he realizes they could be worried about him and that's why they wanted him out. But you don't know, do you, the extent of his imagination."

"I don't know," Cal said. "He sounds like a country boy, but I really don't know."

"You don't want to find him dead before he has a chance to learn who his true friends are, do you?"

"No, I sure don't."

"Then you better see about talking to him pretty soon. Maybe go so far as to mention some money being taken. I've been thinking about that."

"I have, too," Cal said. "I just wanted to hear you say it."

"This other Ryan, man used to work with me a long time ago," Leon Woody said. "His name was *Jack* Ryan. We work for this man was in the carpet-cleaning business? Get in a house, we see some things we like, we have a window un-locked, come back at night. He was a nice boy, Jack Ryan."

Sportree came in from the kitchen with a drink in each hand. Frank Ryan thanked him as he took his and waited as Sportree handed the other drink to Leon Woody and went out again.

"No, I don't think I ever heard of him," Frank said.

"He wanted to be a baseball player."

"Is that right?"

"Play in the major leagues. Nice boy, but he couldn't hit a curve ball for shit."

"I guess it's pretty hard," Frank said, "you don't have an eye."

Sportree came in with a drink for himself and sat down.

"See, what I'm thinking," he said, "man was in the joint once, he sure don't want to go back."

"There's no reason he will," Frank said, leaning forward now, sitting on the couch. "All they got on him, he might've been *think*ing about robbing the place. How do they prove he knows there's money in the box?"

"I'm thinking I don't know what he's thinking," Sportree said. "Maybe he believes they can put him away. He does, he might want to tell them things, give them some names, huh? And they tear up his piece of paper."

"He wouldn't tell them *any*thing," Frank said. "I know he wouldn't."

"Thing that bothers me most," Sportree said, "man was in the joint. See, he think different after that. He finger his mama to stay out in the fresh air."

"Look," Frank said, "if they had something on him, it'd be different. If they were really going to hit him and he saw he was going to take the whole shot. But he knows if he waits them out, keeps his mouth shut, they're going to have to let him go. All he did, he picked up a box."

"*The* box."

"Yes, and they assumed things too quick, he'd been in on the hit and somebody in the office would identify him. Otherwise they'd have let him walk out with it and then nailed him. But they were too eager, little too sure of themselves."

Sportree looked over at Leon Woody.

"That'd be nice he don't say nothing," Leon Woody said, "and they say to him, Thank you, we sorry we bothered you, man, let him go. That'd be nice. But the way I see it, they going to take him down in the basement and whip the shit out of him and pull his fingernails out 'less he start to talk to them."

"Come on," Frank said, "they don't, they can't get away with that stuff anymore."

"Hey shit, they don't," Leon Woody said. "If he the only one they got, they going to do something with him, drop him out a window on his head, he don't start to talk to them. Say he try and run away."

Frank looked at Sportree. "How about I bring him around, you talk to him?"

"Might be an idea."

"I think you should," Frank said. "You got any doubts at all, talk to him. You trust me, don't you?"

"You not arrested," Sportree said. "Not yet."

"I mean wouldn't you trust me? If it was me instead of him? It's the same thing. I give you my word the guy won't talk."

Sportree said, "He knows about Billy getting hit, don't he?"

"I told him Billy wanted it all for himself and it was something had to be done."

"You make up a story, you not too sure of him either."

"No, it was so he'd go in and get the box, not change his mind."

Sportree and Leon Woody sat in silence, staring at him.

Frank shook his head. "Hey, come on, what're you thinking about? You're not sure you can trust the guy, you want to kill him, for Christ sake?"

"Frank," Sportree said, "we known each other a long time, longer than you known him. He start mentioning names, your name's going to be on the list, too. Everybody's name. Next thing, they got us in there for murder. Something a dead man did, and we didn't even make it, did we? Got nothing. But nothing is better than being in there for murder, and the only way we can have some peace of mind is to know your friend isn't going to tell them anything. You agree?"

"But he won't," Frank said. "I give you my word he won't talk."

There was a silence, and again they stared at him. Leon Woody took a sip of his drink. Sportree's fingers fooled with his trading beads.

"I'll bring him here," Frank said.

Sportree nodded. "I be anxious to see him."

23

"I thought we were coming right back," Arlene said, "but we went to St. Louis for the Gateway Nationals and I spent three days in the courtesy trailer passing out beer and soft drinks. Least it was air-conditioned. God, it was so hot and dusty at the track you wouldn't have believed it. But the only times *I* had to go out was when they gave out an award and I'd pose with Larry Huff and Chuck Hurst and Bob Amos and those guys. I got a lot more pictures. Oh, God, but there was a terrible accident. This pro stocker went out of control about nine hundred feet down the track, went through the guardrail, flipped over—fortunately there weren't many people in the stands that far down—"

"Arlene."

She stopped.

"Have you told anybody about seeing us?"

"What?"

"You know what I mean."

"I shouldn't have mentioned that to you, should I?"

"You did," Stick said. "I've been a little anxious wondering if you told anybody."

"I haven't. Honest to God, I haven't told a soul."

She was afraid of him and afraid of showing it. He saw it in her expression again, in her eyes, as he had seen it, momentarily, when she had opened the door and he was standing there. Then covering up quickly with a smile that must have ached: Come on in, stranger. Gosh, it's been a while, hasn't it? And getting rapidly into what she had been doing the past two weeks. Busy, God, she'd never been busier.

They were alone in her apartment in the quiet of a sunny afternoon. Arlene had come up from the pool a few minutes before—Stick had watched her from the balcony—and she was still in her lavender little two-piecer with her beads and rings and damp, tight-curly red hair, looking fragile and afraid. He wanted to touch her, put his arms around her, and feel the calm settle in her body as she realized there was nothing to be afraid of. But he knew he had to approach her gradually, that if he raised his hands she might scream and run from him.

"I believe you," Stick said. He tried a little smile and meant it. She was still tense but trying not to show it, standing in the middle of the room with the photographs and the life-size cut-out of her in her silver Hi-Performance Cams outfit. They were both awkward standing there, not knowing what to do with their hands. Arlene touched a Maltese cross hanging from a thin gold chain and held on.

"How about the guy you were with? You didn't tell him you knew us?"

"Honest to gosh, I really didn't."

"Why not?"

"I don't know. . . . Well, I knew he wouldn't want to get involved, and you know, his wife finds out he was there with somebody. So I didn't say anything."

"Why didn't you tell the police? Leave him out of it."

"Well"—she made a face, frowning—"it's hard to explain. You want to sit down and have a drink or something? I don't know why I told you before. Maybe because I'd had all those drinks and wasn't feeling any pain, but I could sure use one now."

Stick made her a Salty Dog and then changed his mind and fixed one for himself, something to sip on. They sat down on the couch, Stick anxious but covering it pretty well, showing her she didn't have anything to worry about. He remembered telling Frank about Arlene knowing. It popped into his mind with the realization, an instinctive feeling, he shouldn't have; he should have waited at least, talked to Arlene first. Dumb, telling Frank because he had wanted to give him something to worry about. Would Frank tell the others? He said no, there wasn't any reason for him to tell them. But it continued to come into his mind, wondering about it and not being sure. Arlene sitting there, not knowing—he wanted to hold her.

"I liked you," Arlene said. "I mean I *like* you. The way it happened, it was funny, and it wasn't like you were robbing the bar, you were taking it from, you know, taking it from the one who did rob the place, like it was his then, and taking it wasn't a bad thing, it served him right. It was *fun*ny." She smiled a little. "God, I can still see it."

"Well, did you wonder," Stick said, "if we did it all the time? I mean, if that was what we did?"

"I didn't think about it."

"You must've, a little."

"I didn't. I said it wasn't any of my business. I thought—this may sound funny—I thought if you wanted to tell me, it was up to you."

"But if I had, then what would you think?"

"Well, I'd think that . . . you trusted me. You felt close enough that you could tell me something like that and know you didn't have to worry about it."

"You mean you wouldn't care?"

"Well, it isn't I wouldn't care. It's—see, I *have* thought about it and I always think, well, there's a reason. Like you have to have money for something. You need it desperately and nobody'll loan it to you, so you're just doing it for, whatever the reason is, and you're not going to do it anymore after."

"Arlene, I've held up a lot of places."

"Don't tell me, okay?"

"See, I can say I did need the money, as desperately as anybody needs it who doesn't have any. But I stole it."

"Why do you keep saying that? I don't want to know, okay?"

"You know about the Hudson's robbery?"

"Oh, God. Don't." She squeezed her eyes closed with an expression of pain.

"I was in on it," Stick said. "That's why I got arrested. It wasn't a mistake."

He told her about it, describing what he did, his part in the robbery, trying not to minimize or make excuses, telling it quietly and seeing her eyes open to watch him with an expression that gradually lost its tension as her face, with its delicate features, became composed and her eyes took on an expression of calm awareness, as though she were looking into him and seeing more than a man involved in a robbery, someone else inside the man. He was aware of this as he spoke, feeling an intimacy between them that was different, softer yet stronger than what he had felt making love to her, and he knew why he was telling her about himself. He needed her.

He said, "I don't know what to do."

She moved to him on the couch, still looking into his eyes, and took his face in her hands and kissed him, then put her arms around him and drew him against her body.

They were in the darkness now, in her bedroom, lying beside each other. He had slept and was awake, staring at the ceiling, at a faint reflection of light from the other room.

He said, "Can you go away for a while, till we see what happens?"

"Why?"

"Maybe some race or a convention coming up?"

"I'm not going to do that anymore." She sounded a little mad and surprised. "God, what do you think I am?" When he reached over and touched her she waited a moment and said, "Don't you love me?"

"I really do."

"Say it."

"I love you." He made his voice softer and said, "I love you—I never loved anybody so much."

He felt funny hearing himself and felt her breath come out in a little sigh as she turned to cling tightly against him and that part was good. He could feel her and knew by the touch who it was, the firm little body against his. He felt good. But God, he ought to take one thing at a time and save the best, put it someplace where it wouldn't get hurt. He knew he loved her. Like waking up and being somewhere else. He could hardly believe it.

"I'm not going to stay here," Arlene said. "I'll move out tomorrow, the stuff's not mine anyway. But I'm not going away—unless you want to and we go together."

"I got to stay for the pretrial thing, I can't jump bail. You get brought back with handcuffs on and they got you cold."

"Okay, I'll get another apartment then," Arlene said, "something cheaper. I've got enough to live on for at least a month."

"I can help you out there."

"No, I'll get another job if I have to. Tell you the truth, I'm awful sick of that silver outfit." She paused a moment. "It's funny, I just feel different with you."

"Everything could work out," Stick said. "They drop the charge and we get out of here and that's it. Clean living from now on. I'm liable to even get a job, too."

Arlene laughed, a muffled sound close to him that he liked. "That'd be nice of you," she said.

They held onto each other in the darkness. Pretty soon he'd get up and see if the car was downstairs. If it wasn't, he'd pick up a car somewhere, one last time. Everything could work out, that was true, it was possible.

As long as he stayed alive.

When Emory Parks walked into Cal Brown's drab gray partitioned office on the fifth floor, Cal looked surprised first, then turned on a little grin, and Emory knew he had something good to tell him.

"I saw Walter downstairs."

Cal's grin faded. "He told you?"

"He was in a hurry. He said, 'Stop up and see the boy if you get a chance.' All right, boy, what you got?"

Cal was happy again. He said, "The guy out in Bloomfield Hills with all the firearms? He got broken into again last night."

"They know where to go, don't they?"

"Maybe not *they* this time," Cal said. "One gun was taken, a Walther P-38, nine millimeter. The family was upstairs sleeping, didn't hear a thing."

"It could've been somebody else."

"You want to bet?"

"You're going to assume it's one of the whities. All right, if it makes you happy, but which one?"

"I like Mr. Stickley."

"That's a good first choice," the little prosecutor said. "But what if Mr. Ryan's in with the brothers—assuming there's more than one brother, which I'm inclined to believe—"

"Me, too," Cal said.

"—and they say to him, 'Hey, man, he's your roomie, you do it.' Then Mr. Ryan might have to get himself a weapon."

"I don't like it that way," Cal said. "Then it isn't divided up right. I want to see Frank and Ernest on the same team. I mean if the brothers are going to fuck over one of them, why not both?"

"You know what?" the little prosecutor said. "I believe you just said the magic word. *Both.* Why not? It wouldn't be any harder to take two whities as one, would it?"

Cal smiled. "But the whities have a gun now. Somebody's been doing some thinking and I like it."

"You talk to them yet?"

"It's on my list of things to do," Cal said. "I want to talk to one of the young ladies out there, too, Miss Arlene Downey, the one that was a little edgy. I've been looking into their friends and acquaintances through the computer, a nifty little machine, and you want to hear a it's-a-small-world story? Miss Arlene Downey, we find, was a witness to a holdup a month ago, the Saratoga Bar in Hazel Park. And the Saratoga Bar? Why it's on the list of twenty-five or so that fit the style of our friends Frank and Ernest."

"It certainly is a small world," the little prosecutor said. "You don't suppose she's working with them?"

"I don't know," Cal said, "but I'm sure anxious to find out."

24

"I go down to get the car last night," Frank said, "it's not there. I thought maybe I forgot where I parked it. I looked all over. Christ, I thought, I parked it right in front, it's gone. I thought somebody stole it and I got to call the police."

"You call them?"

"No, I go back out this morning, it's there. This afternoon it's gone again. Then just now—I don't know what the hell's going on."

"I had the other set of keys," Stick said.

"Why didn't you tell me? I'm thinking, Am I going crazy or what?"

"I got to get permission?"

"Save me some trouble, that's all. Where'd you spend the night?"

"With a friend."

"I didn't know you had any." Stick didn't smile and Frank said, "I'm kidding. What's the matter with you?"

"I didn't think it was funny."

"How about this one? We were so poor when I was a kid if you didn't wake up Christmas morning with a hard-on you didn't have anything to play with."

"You been talking to Barry."

"I just saw him outside. He was asking about you."

"How about Sportree, he been asking, too?"

He slipped it in and caught the startled look on Frank's face.

"Well, sure, he asked about you. He called me, in fact. He said, Why don't you make the bond on your friend? You want him sitting in jail?"

"Wanted me out, huh? In case I start getting too friendly with anybody? I can hear him: 'We don't know your friend, man. We don't know where his head's at on this thing.' He wants to talk to me?"

"Naturally he's concerned," Frank said. "Right, because he doesn't know you. But listen, I was the one suggested the two of you have a talk. He wasn't anxious or anything, he said maybe that was a good idea."

"I'm supposed to go down there? He must think I'm out of my fucking mind."

"As a matter of fact," Frank said, "put your mind at ease, he's not too hot on you coming to his place. And he's not going to come here, for obvious reasons, or anywhere the police or somebody might see you together."

"How about down by the fucking river late at night?" Stick said. "Jesus, he must think you're as dumb as I am. Or you think the same way he does, I don't know."

"I'm standing in the middle," Frank said. "I know both you guys, but I can't convince either of you to trust me, take my word. He doesn't care where you meet. He said you name the place you want to. He doesn't care at all, long as it's, you know, private, away from where you could be seen."

"You going to be there?"

"If you want me to, sure."

"I mean does Sportree want you to come along or am I supposed to show up alone?"

"*I* suggested it. I said *I'd* bring you. Why? What difference does it make?"

"I'm trying to find out what side you're on," Stick said.

"What *side* I'm on? For Christ sake, what're you talking about *sides*, there aren't any *sides*."

"Frank," Stick said quietly, "the guy wants to kill me."

"Come on—"

"Listen to me!" Stick waited, getting himself in control again. "I say two words, Sportree . . . Leon, they're in the can for murder, maybe life. He can't take a chance."

"What about me? I can say the two words. He want to kill me, too? He could've done it. I was with him."

"Maybe you are with him," Stick said. "Or he knows you stand to lose as much as he does, or he doesn't give a shit. I don't know, but I'm the one going to trial. I'm the one stands to lose if they can build something against me, and I'm the one stands to gain if I was to mention names."

Frank waited, staring at him. "They make you an offer?"

"Not yet, but I can see it coming. I wasn't in on the hit, they know that. So maybe they reduce it to some kind of accessory or shoplifting or throw it out altogether. They want somebody for murder, Frank. And they know I know who did it."

"Are you saying—let me get this straight." Frank walked over to the bar and poured himself a scotch. "Are you saying you're willing to make a deal with them? Cop down to shoplifting or some fucking thing?"

"No, I didn't say that," Stick said. "I'm going to ride it and keep my mouth shut and not get anywhere near that witness stand and I think I have a pretty good chance of making it, if they stay with the larceny thing. If they don't, well, tough shit, I've thought it over, I went in with my eyes open, nobody forced me, I still won't say a word. But Sportree, Leon, they're not going to hold their smoke in waiting to see what I do. Leon shot Billy Ruiz, you were standing there."

"He tried to take it all, sure, Leon didn't have any choice."

"Frank, don't shit me. A very reliable source, that hot-dog

cop, one of the first things he told me, Billy Ruiz was shot in the back. They didn't need him anymore and it's that simple. You make up a story he tried to take the goods, why? Frank, you're either with them or your head's all fucked up and you don't know what you're doing."

Stick watched him drink his scotch and pour another one.

"I don't know," Frank said. "I have some doubts, yeah. It's, well, it didn't work out. It looked easy, but things happened, things you couldn't plan on. You said we should've left it alone, stay with what we're doing. Okay, I have to agree with you, it got all fucked up and complicated. But it could've worked and we could've had an awful lot of money."

Stick said, "It never had a chance, Frank. You know why? Because you thought you knew this guy, but you don't."

"Take my word," Frank said, "okay? You don't trust him, then trust me."

"No," Stick said, "you take *my* word. Tell Sportree and Leon I've already shot two colored guys, so I know how to do it. They're always saying, Be cool. Well, tell them to be cool."

Arlene did a dumb thing. She was expecting some glossies taken at the Gateway Nationals and she wanted them, just to have, the last shots of her taken in the silver outfit. So she rented a box in the Royal Oak post office and told the lady manager of the Villa Monterey to forward her mail there. She thought it was safe because she'd just be a number, with no name.

That's how Cal found Arlene, in three steps, from the manager to the post office to the name and apartment address in Clawson.

Arlene opened the door, thinking it was Stick. She could feel her expression change. God.

Cal smiled and said, "How you doing, Miss Downey?" He had his notebook open in his hand and looked down at it.

"There's something here I wanted to ask you. About this holdup you were a witness to?"

25

The young guy, the cop, was straddling the leg-rest part of the lounge chair with his boots on the cement deck. Hunched forward in skinny faded Levi's and a corduroy sport coat and tie. Stick couldn't tell where he was carrying his gun.

He was relaxed, his hands folded in front of him, facing Frank, and seemed to be interested in whatever Frank was saying. Frank was lying back in his chair scratching his belly, being cool, his sunglasses raised to the hot four o'clock sky.

Stick watched them from the balcony. He went into the living room and walked to the Formica table and back to the balcony a few times, pausing to look down over the railing. They were the only ones at the pool. On the fifth pass, Stick said, "Shit," and went into his bedroom. He could either hide under the bed or put on his new bright blue swimming trunks. He put on the trunks.

"I believe you two know each other," Frank said. He'd had enough to drink to be relaxed or able to fake it; or else the guy, for some reason, wasn't scaring him. "He was just mentioning a friend of ours," Frank said to Stick walking up to them, "Arlene Downey."

"I thought she moved," Stick said. He pulled a chair around and sat down facing Cal Brown, showing him he didn't have anything to hide.

"That's what I told him," Frank said. "I haven't seen her around."

"Yeah, she moved," Cal said. "She's got an apartment in Clawson. But see, that's not the point. I'm not looking for her, I already talked to her. About twenty minutes ago."

Stick had his knees up in front of him, a barrier between him and the policeman.

"How's she doing?"

"She'll be okay, I think. The thing that's bothering her is that holdup she saw in a bar not too long ago. It's stuck in her mind."

"I don't believe I heard about that one," Frank said. Stick kept staring at the guy. It was coming now.

"She said it was two guys. They take the bills off this first guy that went in with a shotgun. Weird, huh? A shotgun."

"What're you trying to say?" Stick said.

"Okay." Cal straightened up a little, looking over at Stick. "Everything I say is off the record. Everything you say, same thing. No recorders, no bullshit. You know who I am, I know who you are. Let's talk things over."

"So talk," Frank said.

"All right, first thing," Cal said. "We could bust you on a couple dozen robbery armed. Listen, shit, just the cars you used could get you a hundred years apiece."

"What's he talking about?" Frank said.

"The two spades in the Northland parking lot, you can have them," Cal said. "It reminds me of an old saying, Don't ever shit a shitter. Don't ever try and hustle a couple of ace hustlers either, especially right after a job. But what I don't understand, on the Hudson's thing—"

"What Hudson's thing?" Frank said.

"The J. L. Hudson Company Hudson's thing," Cal said. "Is why you want to take just checks. What're you going to do with them? You got some guy named Hudson you're going to lay 'em off on?"

Frank didn't move. His face remained raised to the sky. But his eyes were open now behind the sunglasses.

"That's all they got in that one, just checks?"

"That's all your buddy was picking up," Cal said. "Two Brink's sacks in the doll box."

He waited, letting the silence lengthen.

"This was the second day after, right? What I been wondering, a theory of mine, is what if somebody went in there the next day, right after, and switched some other sacks to another box? Boy, that would sure fuck over the guys left with just the checks, wouldn't it?"

"I didn't read in the paper," Frank said, "about it being just checks in the box. I think—I believe it said whatever was stolen was recovered."

"Well, they don't like to publicize anything that'd make them look bad, or look dumb, you might say."

"You mean there's some money that was stolen, hasn't been found, recovered?" Frank said.

"Well, actually, I'm not at liberty to say. Normally there'd be seventy-five, a hundred thou in the cash sacks. And considerably more than that in checks." Cal grinned. "But the checks aren't worth shit in comparison, are they? And if you don't even have the checks, you ain't got nothing at all."

Stick said, "You want to come right out and say what you're trying to say?"

"I can spell it for you," Cal said. "It's a-s-s-h-o-l-e-s. That's what your associates, your black buddies, are making you look like."

"This is wild," Frank said. "Shit." He was sitting up now, pulling himself up and taking off his sunglasses to look at the guy. "You give us all this like we're supposed to know what you're talking about. Our black *buddies*—what black buddies?

Who? Give us some names. Shit, you start to make accusations, give us some proof. What? You're talking about the Hudson's thing?"

"Frank—"

Stick waited. He looked from Frank to the policeman and said, "What's the deal?"

Cal Brown took his time. He put on a pleasant, innocent, sort of a surprised expression as he looked at Stick. He said, "Deal? Who's talking about a deal? I'm just telling you how I see it. The question is, do you want to go to Jackson for a while or do you want to take a chance on getting shot in the head by your buddies? It's entirely up to you, man."

There was a silence. Cal waited. He said then, "Well—" and got up to go, starting to move off, timing it, stopping and looking at Stick.

"I almost forgot. Your pretrial exam's been moved up."

It caught Stick by surprise. "How come nobody tells me?"

"I'm telling you," Cal said. "Day after tomorrow, nine o'clock. Frank Murphy Hall of Justice."

Frank was still in his trunks, pacing now, following the route from the balcony to the Formica table and back again. Stick had on a shirt, unbuttoned. He sat at the table with a cup of coffee, looking at it, looking at the wall, looking at Frank when Frank got in the way. Frank had a scotch on the bar and would stop off there every few minutes. He had two cigarettes going, one on the bar, one in an ashtray on the balcony he'd forgotten about.

"You didn't look in it at all?" Frank said.

"I didn't have time," Stick said. "I told you I thought it felt light."

"Five sacks went in the box, I saw them. Marlys came out—" Frank stopped. "Jesus, I'm standing there—Marlys *told* him. She pointed to three sacks, he put the other two in first. I watched him do it. The whole thing was set up, Billy Ruiz, everything. Leon, Marlys, somebody goes in the next day, takes out the three sacks, leaves the ones with the checks— Jesus."

"The cop spelled it right," Stick said, "didn't he?"

"We show up the next day," Frank said, "we got checks, that's all we got, checks. Sportree says, 'What's this shit?' Turns it fucking around on us. We say—we don't know what to say. We can't believe it."

"Your old buddy," Stick said. "He gives it to you, he puts it in all the way, doesn't he?"

"The son of a bitch," Frank said. "Like we're a couple of little kids. I'd like to have that Python right now—or get my hands on one."

"Don't do anything dumb," Stick said. "They're not going to let you walk in there with a gun. Take it easy. As your old buddy would say, be cool."

"I'm going to cool him," Frank said, "the son of a bitch, sitting back, all that time blowing smoke at us."

"Sitting back ready. I'm not trying to talk you out of anything," Stick said. "I'm saying you got to be careful and do it right. Put yourself in his place. If he's smart enough to pull this deal, he's not going to let you walk in and take it away from him. One advantage, he doesn't know what we know and he must think we're pretty dumb to begin with. I'm saying put yourself in his place and look at it as he sees it before you run out and do anything dumb. See, that's what's bothering you right now. You don't like the idea of him laughing at you, thinking you're dumb. Like when I swiped the car from you out there. You don't want to prove he's right, so let's think on it a while."

"We walked into places thirty times," Frank said, "no problem. How about once more? What's the difference?"

"The difference, they were guys in aprons and A&P coats. This guy's a pro. He's into, Christ, probably everything you can think of. He has people *killed*."

"And he thinks we're a couple of hicks," Frank said. "That's what I keep thinking about."

"I know you do, and maybe there's a way to use it, if you know what I mean. But it's something we'd have to give some thought to. Remember, I'm going to court the day after tomorrow and I might not be around for a while. We'll have to wait and see." Stick got up from the table and took his cup into the kitchen. When he came back in he said, "I'm going to see Arlene. Hang onto that scotch bottle till I get back."

He spent the night at Arlene's, patting her, saying, "Come on, it's okay," telling her as calmly as he could not to worry, the cop didn't know anything—that's the way they were, they showed their badge and were very official and serious and tried to scare you into admitting things, but it was all fake. Arlene said she hadn't told the cop anything. Good. Thank God, good, she hadn't slipped him anything, not knowing she was doing it. He got Arlene calmed down and lay there in the dark most of the night staring at the ceiling, hoping Frank was in bed and not out looking for a gun. He had a pretrial exam to face that could be the first step to putting him away and he had to worry about Frank and Arlene and the jazzy colored guy that had really fucked them over and they hadn't even felt it. It was a terrible mess, but it was also kind of interesting, exciting. He was getting to the point, feeling it, that he didn't have much to lose and maybe a lot to gain. What he had to do, lying there in the dark, was consider his options. Like:

Run.

No, don't run. Maybe don't move at all. Don't even look around. Forget about the money, somewhere between seventy-five and a hundred grand, the cop had said, implied. He believed the cop. So write it off.

To what?

The principle: Don't ever do business with a colored guy, especially one who's smarter than you are.

The funny thing was he still kind of liked the guy, Sportree—Maurice Jackson, his real name—Sportree in Detroit's black ghetto "Valley" and out on West Eight Mile. He admired him, the way he pulled it, and really didn't blame him. Why not? Sportree didn't give a shit about them one way or the other. Shit, if you're going to knock down a department store, get involved in murder, what was surprising about fucking over a couple of poor dumb white boys? Sportree didn't owe them anything.

They owed him something, though.

He sure hoped Frank was in bed.

He knew how Frank felt because he felt the same way. You could admire a guy's method, but you didn't have to grin and look dumb when the guy was putting it to you. You could *act* dumb, yes, if it helped the cause. And the cause was him and Frank, nobody else anymore. Except Arlene, but that was different.

All right, the options.

Sit tight. Don't say a word. Hope the larceny charge is dropped and go back to pouring cement and drinking beer and watching TV. Thank God you made it through and promise never to do it again.

Or, go for the prize. Get the fucker, sitting there blowing his Jamaican smoke.

Take the Luger P-38 and put it in the guy's face and say, "Give me the money, man. Be cool, man." All that *man* shit. "Be cool or else you're a dead nigger."

That sounded pretty good lying in the dark. Next to him, Arlene moved and he could hear her breathing.

Make sure Leon Woody was there and give him some of it. See it? The Luger, a good-looking, mean-looking, no-bullshit handgun. "Hey, man, you know what we do down in Oklahoma to guys like you?"

No, keep it straight. Who gives a shit where you came from or what they do in Oklahoma? He didn't even know what they did.

Keep it personal. He liked both of them. Leon Woody, too, with his little girl, he seemed like a nice guy and couldn't picture him shooting Billy Ruiz in the back.

He respected them.

But he also wanted them to respect him. And that was the whole thing. His only option.

It was about 4:30 in the morning by the time he figured out a way to do it that might work.

At 7:30 he woke up Arlene and said, "Come on, you're moving to a motel. And this time don't leave a forwarding address, okay?"

* * *

"They're sitting there in their swimming trunks taking a *sun*bath," Cal said. "These two assholes, it hadn't even entered their heads something was funny."

He was talking to his superior now, Detective Lieutenant Walter Shea, in the lieutenant's office at 1300.

"How about the stolen gun?" Walter said. "Somebody's been doing some thinking."

"I'm pretty sure it was for protection," Cal said. "Stickley's. In case the blackies came after him. But now things are different, a little more interesting."

"You didn't search his place, then."

"What do I want to find the gun for? I'd have to arrest him."

"I'm grateful you're telling me all this," Walter said, "so I won't feel my twenty-seven years were wasted."

Cal nodded politely. "Yes, sir, I can use all the experienced advice I can get."

"Emory suggest you go for a deal?"

"What's to make a deal about? I think they realize now they don't have anything to sell. Names, yes. Except that if Frank Ryan starts naming names, somebody's going to name his name right back. Because I'll bet you eighty-seven thousand bucks he was in the office when the window washer got it."

"So where are we?"

"Still watching," Cal said. "But I think the clowns are about ready to come out and put on a show."

26

"You tell him my court date's tomorrow," Stick said, "so if he's worried and wants to talk, it's got to be today."

"You were right there, you should've picked up two of these." Frank was sitting hunched over, examining the Walther, hefting it, feeling its weight, looking at its Luger profile in his hand. The box of cartridges was on the coffee table.

"Why would I get one for you?" Stick said. "I don't even know what fucking side you're on. I believe you told me more'n once you knew him a hell of a lot longer than you'd known me."

"That's what we should do," Frank said, "get in an argument. It just seems like, I don't know, we need more time to get ready."

"If he's setting up a hit on me, it's got to be today," Stick said. "Tomorrow I'm on the stand, you know that."

"But he doesn't know it," Frank said.

"Right. That's why he's going to have to move fast once you tell him and he finds out, I mean if he still wants me. I'll tell you something else I've been thinking," Stick said. "If he wants me, I bet he wants you, too. Why not? He's not going to split with you, he's already jacked you out of a cut. But if you found it out—he doesn't know what you'd do. So if he sets me up, why not set you up, too? Two birds. Two dumb fucking dumb white birds. I bet he says he wants you to be there."

Frank called Sportree and told him about Stick's court date.

Sportree said, "Yeah? Hey, yeah, I'd like to talk to him, as I told you. Let me get back to you."

Frank hung up.

Stick said, "He calls back, then we wait, then we call him back."

Frank said, "Jesus, I hope it works."

Stick said, "You hope it *works?* If it doesn't work, we're fucking dead."

"He didn't say anything about me being there."

"Wait," Stick said.

Sportree called back in twenty minutes. He said, "How about I meet both of you—"

Holding the phone, Frank looked over at Stick.

"—but I prefer you didn't come here, your friend going to court and everything, you understand?"

"Where?" Frank asked.

"How about—I mean you sure you can do it, nobody following you—how about this motel, call the Ritz Motel, out Woodward near that hospital, almost to Pontiac. Look for Leon's car, light blue '74 Continental. Make it nine o'clock."

"Just a minute." Frank put his hand over the mouthpiece and looked at Stick. "He wants to meet at a motel out by Pontiac, tonight."

"We walk in and Leon or some jig steps out of the can shooting," Stick said, "while Sportree's home watching Redd Foxx. I thought he was going to say some back alley, or an empty building. Tell him we'll meet him in front of the police station, talk in the car."

"Come on," Frank said. He was nervous holding the phone with Sportree on the other end.

"Tell him we'll think it over and get back to him. That's good enough."

Frank told him.

Sportree said, "Hey, don't be too long. I send somebody to pick you up."

Frank hung up. "He says he'll send somebody for us."

"I bet he will. One thing we know," Stick said, "no, two things. He can't take a chance doing it at his place. He's got too much going on there. And we're not going to get in with a gun. So you see any other way?"

"No, I don't guess so."

"Let's get going, then."

"Okay," Frank said. He laid the Luger on the coffee table and got up. "What're you going to wear?"

A half hour later Frank called him again from the Graeco-Roman lobby of the Vic Tanny on Eight Mile Road, almost directly across from Sportree's Royal Lounge.

"We decided it'd be better if we came to your place," Frank said.

"I *told* you," Sportree said. "Man could be followed, he bring 'em here. You want to get me in the shit? Frank, hey, use your head."

"No, we decided," Frank said. "Get Leon there so he can listen. We'll leave now and be very careful of tails and be there in about a half hour."

"Frank, listen to me—"

Frank hung up. He reached into the big pocket of his safari jacket for a pack of Marlboros.

"He doesn't like it."

"I bet he doesn't," Stick said. Stick was wearing his light green sport coat he'd bought in Florida. The right side hung straight, tight over his shoulder, with the Luger filling the inside pocket. They lighted cigarettes and stood by the showcase window, looking out across the parking lot and the flow of traffic on the wide, parkway-divided lanes of Eight Mile. It was a long way over there to Sportree's and the traffic was getting heavier. They concentrated on the cars that, every once in a while, pulled into Sportree's side lot.

A young guy with a build came over from the counter in his tight Vic Tanny T-shirt and tight black pants and asked them if they were members. Frank said they were thinking about joining but were waiting for a friend. The Vic Tanny guy invited them to make themselves comfortable and when their friend came he'd be happy to show them around and describe the different membership plans.

"It might not be a bad idea," Frank said. "Work out two, three times a week, get some steam or a sauna."

"I could never do push-ups and all that shit," Stick said. "I don't know, it sounds good, but it's so fucking boring. The thing to do, just don't eat so much."

"I don't eat much," Frank said.

"You drink too much. You know how many calories are in a shot? What you put away, those doubles, it's a couple of full meals."

"What do you do, count my drinks?"

"I can't," Stick said. "I can't count that fast."

"Jesus—" Frank said and stopped, looking out the window. "There we are. Light blue '74 Continental. Son of a bitch, how does he afford a car like that?"

"Maybe he lives in it," Stick said.

They watched the car pull off Eight Mile into Sportree's parking lot. A half minute later Leon Woody appeared, coming around front to the upstairs entrance, and went in.

Frank said, "What if there's a guy in the lot parks the cars?"

"I haven't seen anybody," Stick said, "but if there is, we go home and think of something else quick—"

"Maybe we should give it a little more time. I told him a half hour." Frank looked over at the Vic Tanny guy behind the counter, talking on the phone now. "Let's let him give us the tour. Maybe there's some broads in the sauna."

No parking-lot attendant, no one coming in behind them or going out. There was nothing to it. Frank pulled the T-bird into an empty space next to Leon's light blue Continental. They got out. Frank waited, standing by the rear deck of the T-bird.

Stick walked around the right side of Leon's car and opened the front door. He looked at Frank.

Frank nodded.

Stick took the Luger out of his coat pocket, felt under the seat to make sure it was clear and there was enough room, and slipped the Luger under there, carefully, and closed the door. He opened the rear door and reached in to feel under the front seat, closed the door and nodded as he walked out to where Frank was waiting.

"You're sure?" Frank said.

"You can reach it from both sides."

"I mean that we'll take his car. Shit, or if we're going anywhere."

"I can't see Sportree driving, exposing his plates," Stick said. "I can't see him letting us drive, meet them. What if we made a stop at the hardware store?"

"If we go anywhere," Frank said. "That's the big *if*."

"No, we're going somewhere," Stick said. "That's the only thing I'm sure of. Probably after it gets dark. And we're going to make it easy for him by acting as dumb as he thinks we are, playing into his hands and giving him a *reason* for taking us out, so he won't have to use force."

They were walking out of the lot toward the front.

"There's an old Indian saying," Stick said: "You can't judge a guy until you've walked a mile in his moccasins. I haven't been able to do that, but last night, all night long, I imagined being in that fucker's red patent-leather high-heel shoes, remembering everything I could about him—the way he talked, the way he moved, how he's kept himself out of the whole deal. He's not going to have a lot of noise in his place and get blood on his carpeting. We're going somewhere."

"And I'm supposed to offer to drive," Frank said.

"Don't forget that."

"And what if they say okay?"

"We're fucked," Stick said.

* * *

Leon Woody opened the door. He said, "How you doing?" and stepped inside. Sportree was in the doorway leading to the kitchen, pointing a pump-action shotgun at them.

Frank said, "What're you doing?" getting fear and amazement in his voice and not having to fake much of it.

"I want to make sure we still friends," Sportree said. "Leon's going to check you out, if that'd be all right."

"I don't get it," Frank said. Stick liked the dumb look on his face.

Leon did a good job. He felt every part of them where a gun or a knife could be hidden, and felt their coats, under the arms and the lining as well as the pockets. They let him, not saying anything, Frank staring at Sportree.

"Look like they still friends," Leon said.

Sportree turned with the shotgun and went into the kitchen. He came back out with two bottles, glasses, and a bowl of ice, saying, "Since you all're here." When they were sitting down and had their drinks, Sportree looked over at Stick.

"What kind of deal they make you?"

"As a matter of fact," Stick said, "they haven't said a word about a deal. They haven't made an attempt, physically, to get anything out of me either. The way it stands, I'm going to the exam tomorrow with no reason to say a word about anything that's not any of their business. All they got on me, I lifted a doll box off a shelf. If I was conspiring to walk out with it, they have to prove it."

Sportree got a Jamaican out of a gold-leaf box and lit it, looking at Stick.

Leon Woody said, "They know you part of something else."

"They got to prove that, too," Stick said.

"They ain't going to let you go."

"Then they'll have to make up something, and they'd still have to prove it."

"You saying you pure and they ain't nothing to worry about?"

"I'm saying I've played this straight so far," Stick said, "but I'm not saying you don't have anything to worry about. There seems to be a discrepancy in how many Brink's sacks were in the doll box originally and how many were there when I picked it up."

"Say what?" Leon Woody sounded a little surprised without changing his bearded African expression.

"Five went in," Stick said. "Three came out sometime before I got there."

"How you know that?" Sportree asked him.

"Because I can add and subtract," Stick said. "I think two from five is three. There were two sacks in the box when I looked in it, right before they stuck the gun in my face."

"This comes as something new," Sportree said, at ease with his cigarette. "You never mention it before."

"I wasn't there," Stick said. "I didn't know how many sacks went in. Frank and I are talking yesterday, not till yesterday he mentions five. I said, 'Five? There were only *two.*' "

Sportree smiled and shook his head, his gaze moving to Frank.

"What'd you think, Frank, he said that?"

"What'd I *think?*" He had a good on-the-muscle edge to his tone. "First I couldn't believe it. Then I thought, Shit, somebody's fucking somebody. Guy I thought was a friend of mine."

"Oh, my," Sportree said, shaking his head again. "It can get complicated, huh? People get the wrong idea." He looked at Stick. "What the police think?"

"I don't know what they think," Stick said. "They didn't discuss it with me. Maybe they think it's still in the store somewhere, I don't know. The thing is, we know it isn't." He kept his gaze on Sportree.

"Yeah, maybe they think it is," Sportree said, squinting in the smoke, thoughtful. "But I doubt it. See, that's why we have to be so careful—you coming here—man, they could be watching every move you make."

Frank said, still on the muscle, "I think we're getting off the subject, how we got fucked by a guy I thought was a friend."

"Frank, did we know Stick was going to get arrested?" Sportree waited, patient, like he was speaking to a child.

"No."

"So he'd come up here with two sacks, wouldn't he?"

"Yeah."

"What do you think I was going to do?"

"I don't know—shit, I don't get it at all. But you took the three sacks."

"As a precaution," Sportree said. "Marlys walked out with them in a box the next day. This was something I thought of after. If she can do it, fine. If they too many cops around, we wait to do it like we planned it. But see, then we have two chances and two's better than one."

"How come," Frank said, "you didn't call us after, say you had it?"

"Frank, you never give us your number till the other day. Unlisted, right? Marlys went out there to look for you. Said she couldn't find you. Probably out with those chicks."

"Shit."

"Come on, Frank, ain't no scam. We get it, man, we busy counting. Shit, you want to know what eighty-seven thousand look like? You and him supposed to come by the next day. Only he get arrested."

"*I* came by," Frank said, "the day after. You never mention it. Shit, we're sitting here talking, you already got it."

"Hey, man, listen to me. I'm telling you now, ain't I? Because I know I can trust him. But he's in jail, good friend of yours, I don't know what he's going to say. I don't know you two been talking or not. So I keep quiet till the smoke begin to settle and I see where I'm at, see where you and him are at. Okay, now everything's cool. He don't say a word tomorrow, he walk out and we split the kitty."

"Not tomorrow," Stick said, "right now. I can still go to trial. I could get ninety days, shit, a year, I don't know. I don't want to come out and not find anybody around."

"We be here," Sportree said. "Man, nobody's going nowhere."

"Today," Stick said. "Right now. I take care of mine, you take care of yours."

"I'd just as soon do it now," Frank said. "I get nervous

thinking about that much money sitting someplace, not making any interest."

Sportree grinned. "How you know it's not in the bank?"

"Shit," Frank said. "Where is it, under the bed?"

Sportree's finger caressed the little bebop growth on his chin, thinking, making up his mind. He looked over at Leon Woody.

"You can understand they want to see it."

Leon didn't say anything.

"Well, we might as well drive out there, make them happy. All right with you?"

"They own as much of it we do," Leon said. "I feel better, though, we wait till it gets a little dark. People won't see us walking in and out of places."

Sportree looked over at Frank. "We can relax here a while, have something to eat—"

"Where we going?" Stick asked.

Sportree grinned. "We all going together, man. You'll see."

27

In the parking lot, walking past the cars, Frank and Stick were following Leon Woody. Stick thought Sportree was right behind them. But when he glanced around, Sportree wasn't there, he hadn't turned the corner.

Leon was walking toward his light blue Continental. Frank said, "Hey, Leon, I'll drive."

Leon looked around. "How you going to drive, man, you don't know where we going?"

"You tell me," Frank said.

Stick was thinking, Shit. He wanted Sportree to be here.

But it was all right. Sportree came around the corner, some kind of coat or jacket over his arm. Leon waited for him. He said then, "Frank say he want to drive."

Sportree looked happy, going out for the evening to have a

good time. He said, "Shit, Leon drive. Then we come back, have a drink, get your car. Frank, you ride up with Leon, me and the Stick here will sit in the back."

Stick saw it, Sportree and Leon looking at each other, quick little look in the dreamy African eyes, telling each other something. They never let down, Stick thought.

They went on North Woodward as far as Norwalk Freight Lines, past the semi's lined up in the dim-lighted yard, and U-turned around the island and came back south a few blocks to the Ritz Motel, VACANCY in orange on the big, bright-lighted Las Vegas sign. There were heavy-duty truck cabs in there, Macks and Peterbilts, and a couple of vans and a few new-model cars with Michigan plates. The swimming pool was lighted and empty in the half rectangle; most of the units were dark. Leon Woody let the Continental glide quietly into a parking space in the far corner of the rectangle, in front of Number 24, away from the motel office. Leon cut the ignition.

Sportree said, "Hey, shit, listen." And Leon turned the key back on so Sportree could hear the radio.

Leon got out, taking the motel key out of his pocket. Frank got out. Stick waited in the back seat with Sportree.

" 'Feel Like Making Love,' " Sportree said. "Bob James, hey, shit. Idris, listen to Idris, huh?" Sportree sat there listening. Stick sat there. Sportree wouldn't get out of the car. It was pretty good, it melted over Stick with a nice beat, but it wasn't Merle Haggard and Stick wasn't sure how long he could sit there.

Sportree said, "That's a number, you know it? Man used to arrange for Aretha." He opened the door and finally got out of the car, then reached into the front for the key and turned off the ignition.

Stick waited.

Sportree looked back at him. "You coming? You don't seem too anxious."

Stick said, "What? I dropped my cigarettes."

When Sportree turned, Stick reached under the seat. Jesus, where was it? His hand touched the grip and he got it out, stuck it in the waist of his pants, and pulled the jacket down over it.

They went inside, into Number 24, a big room with a double bed and two twins and a refrigerator that had a cooking range and sink on top. Stick knew it wasn't going to take too much time. There wasn't anything to talk about, nothing to look at, no faking anything. No, it'd be done quick. Sportree had the poplin jacket over his arm. He looked around, as if picking a place to sit down, but he didn't. Frank was standing there, too, waiting for it. Leon Woody went into the bathroom and closed the door.

Stick said to himself, Here it is.

In the bathroom, Leon Woody took a Colt .45 automatic out of the medicine cabinet and wrapped a towel around it loosely. He flushed the toilet.

Stick was ready. When he saw Leon come out with the towel wrapped around his hand, around something in his hand, Stick pulled the Luger, pointed it at him, at the white, surprised look in Leon's eyes, and shot him in the face. Stick turned the Luger on Sportree and shot him twice in the body, dead center, above the jacket falling away and the revolver in Sportree's hand. Sportree made a grunting sound, the wind going out of him, and fell back against a chair, turning it over and going down as he hit the wall.

Stick said to himself, I don't believe it. You've killed four colored guys.

"Jesus Christ," Frank said. "Holy Christ almighty."

Stick got down on one knee over Sportree and took the car keys and another ring of keys from his side pocket. Frank was saying, Jesus Christ.

"We'll leave them," Stick said, "we might as well. And take Leon's car."

"We got to get our car," Frank said.

"You bet we do," Stick said, "and that ain't all. It's got to be in his apartment someplace."

Marlys was in the bedroom with the air conditioning going, lying on top of the bed in a short little slip she used for a

nightgown, reading *Viva* and listening to Stevie coming out of
the bedroom speaker. She heard the door to the apartment
open and close and looked over the top of the magazine, waiting.

"Hey, I'm in here. Where you been?"

She was looking at the magazine again when Stick came in,
the Luger in his hand, not pointing it, holding it at his side. He
saw her slender dark legs extending from the slip, her ankles
crossed.

"Hey—"

Marlys jumped and sat up quickly, swinging her legs over
the side of the bed.

"What you want?" Not about to take anything from him.

"A doll box," Stick said.

"Where's Sportree? You come walking in here—what kind
of shit is this?"

They heard Frank call from the other room, "I found it.
Come on." He appeared in the bedroom doorway with the Little Curly Laurie Walker box under his arm and smiled at the
girl. "Hi, Marlys."

"I think you better put that back and talk to Sportree,"
Marlys said. "I mean if you have any sense at all."

"I think he'd want us to have it," Frank said.

Marlys frowned at him. "What you talking about?"

"You're going to find out anyway," Frank said. "He died.
And you know something? You could, too."

They didn't say anything walking out to the parking lot or
while Frank dropped the doll box in the trunk of the T-bird—
not until they were driving away from the place, in the night
traffic on Eight Mile.

Stick said, "Slow down."

Frank said, "Jesus, the steering wheel of Leon's car, you had
your hands all over it."

"I wiped it off," Stick said, "the keys just in case, the door
handles, different places we might have touched."

Frank kept watching the rearview mirror. He said, "I'm trying to see how we could've messed up. What do you think?"

"I think we're halfway home," Stick said. "But we got to make one stop."

"You think she'll do it?"

"She said she would."

"I don't know—bringing her in."

"You got somebody else in mind?" Stick looked over at him. "I think we're lucky the way it's working out. She's a good one, which is pretty nice, since we sure as shit can't take it home and that hot-dog cop drops in to visit again. I don't see any other way."

28

Stick was at the Frank Murphy Hall of Justice, fifth floor, before nine the next morning, and found out examinations would be held in Judge Robert J. Columbo's courtroom. He told the clerk who he was and sat in the seats with the waiters and spectators two and a half hours, listening to examinations: a rape, a complicated dope-related shooting, and a felonious assault, watching the little fat black prosecutor, whom he remembered from the time before. The judge didn't say much; he seemed patient, sitting back in his chair against the light wood paneling, but would interrupt in a relaxed way when the defense attorneys took too much time, and he kept it moving.

When the judge took the envelope from the clerk and called Stick's number, he walked in through the gate and was sworn in, gave his name, sat down at the table facing the witness stand, and didn't say a word after that.

The young guy, the cop, took the stand, told about arresting
Ernest Stickley, Jr., in the storeroom of the J. L. Hudson Company toy department, and identified Stick as the one. There
was no mention of the holdup. After Cal Brown had testified,
was questioned, and stepped down, the little prosecutor talked
to the judge for several minutes in conference, then turned and
walked away from the bench shaking his head, knowing it was
going to happen, but making a show of being surprised after
His Honor asked him if he actually wanted to bring this one to
trial; he had said yes, and His Honor had said he didn't. He
dismissed the charge and called a noon recess.

Frank was there in the audience, getting up now with the
rest of the people, starting to move toward the door. Stick was
coming through the gate to join the crowd. Frank was grinning
as he caught Stick's eye, and Stick grinned.

Cal Brown was waiting. He held the gate as Stick swung it
open and said, "Be good now." He was grinning, too. Everybody seemed happy.

Cal watched them move out through the courtroom doorway, seeing their Caucasian heads among the pimp hats and
naturals.

The little prosecutor came over to watch, too. He said,
"Now, about the real business."

Cal said, "Their place was searched while they were here. I
was hoping we'd come up with a P-38, like the one caused the
death of the brothers and was stolen from that guy's house in
Bloomfield, and of course I was hoping we'd find the eighty-
seven. Nothing."

"What if they run out on you?"

"We got somebody watching their place. The two guys'
clothes, the money still there in the Oxydol box and about a
grand in an old beat-up suitcase—they run, they're going home
first."

"You hope."

"That's all I got is hope," Cal said, "that somebody fucks
up."

Stick called Arlene from a phone booth on the first floor of
the Frank Murphy Hall of Justice. When she answered he said,

"I'm out. No shit, it's all done, no trial. . . . Okay, call Delta, it'll have to be that five-something flight, five forty-five, I think, nonstop to Miami. Make the three reservations—your name, Mr. E. Stickley, Mr. F. Ryan. . . . Sure, you can use real names, we haven't done anything. . . . No, you won't have any trouble this time of year. Find out how much and take enough out of the box to cover it and fifty or a hundred for yourself, for magazines and gum and. . . . Right. Take a cab out to Metro. Pick up, pay for all three tickets but only pick up your own. Leave the other two at the Delta counter with our name on it. You got a suitcase that'll hold it? . . . Good, put it all in the suitcase, nothing else in with it, and burn the box. . . . In the bathtub, I don't know, someplace you won't burn the goddamn motel down. Then, listen, check the suitcase through with your own stuff. Don't carry it on, you know, they look at everything. . . . That's right. . . . No, we'll see you in the Miami airport. You get there, check the suitcase in one of those boxes, you know, and meet us in the bar in the Miami airport near the Delta counter. It's way down at one end. At Metro, waiting for the plane, you see us, don't say anything or act like you recognize us at all. . . . No, shit no, we won't be sitting together. . . . I know. . . . Listen, I can understand, I'm a little nervous, too, but don't worry. There isn't anything to worry about. . . . Right, a few more hours it'll be over. . . . I do, too. . . . You'll hear me say it plenty. . . . All right. Arlene? I love you. . . . 'Bye."

Frank dropped his cigarette and stepped on it. "It took you long enough."

"I wanted to go over it again."

"She got it cold?"

"I don't see how we can miss," Stick said.

"I don't know, I think maybe we ought to put it in the car and just go."

"How far?" Stick said.

Burning the doll box made a mess, left a tubful of black ashes that dissolved under the shower spray but left a dark, smeary-looking stain in the tub. Arlene wished she had some Ajax. The bath soap just seemed to smear it around more. The maid would probably think she'd been awfully dirty, greasing a car or something.

The money—God, $87,000 and a little more, in all kinds of bills—was stacked neatly in the small light blue suitcase, with a few inches to spare. She thought about laying one of her photograph albums on top—it would fit perfectly—but she remembered what Stick had said. Just the money. So she'd have to jam her albums and manila envelopes of photographs in with her clothes.

You don't need them anymore, she thought.

Or the silver costume.

The pictures would be fun to look at later, years later. Here's mommy when she was a model. Here's mommy at the Indy Nationals. Cute?

The NHRA Grand Nationals were going to be in Los Angeles this year. September 5-6-7. She could picture it on posters and in ads that ran in hot-rod magazines. They'd get some other girl. In Los Angeles that probably wouldn't be hard at all.

The silver costume didn't take up any room; it didn't even have to be folded, it was so skimpy. The boots were soft and rolled up and could be stuck down at the corners.

The life-size cutout—smiling at her—God, what was she going to do with it?

She had made Stick bring it along with all her stuff. He'd said, Why? What did she need it for? She remembered she had been surprised at him asking and had said she just wanted it, that's all.

She would have to leave it now and she wondered what they'd do with it and if they'd be mad. Well, they could just throw it out. She saw her life-size reinforced cardboard image cracked and folded in a trash can, her face looking out. She was glad she was getting out of here. She hated being alone and thinking so much. God, how did a person stop thinking when they wanted to?

Arlene finished packing, called a cab, and paid the motel bill. When the cab came she walked out with her purse, following the driver carrying the two suitcases, and closed the door on the smiling life-size cutout in the silver costume.

The lady, the manager of the Villa Monterey, said she wished she could take a vacation sometime. Frank said well, they'd been working pretty hard and needed a chance to take it easy and recharge the old batteries. The lady, the manager, said she'd have thought they got enough rest sitting around the pool every day. Sitting, yes, Frank said, but they were always thinking, and thinking was hard work. He paid her four-fifty in advance for the next month, September, and she smiled and said she hoped they had a nice time.

Stick, waiting there, was glad she wasn't a talker. He was starting to get awful antsy.

Cal Brown had volunteered and taken over the watch. Surveillance of suspects.

He was parked across from the Villa Monterey and down a hundred feet in a dark brown Chrysler Cordoba they had taken off a smack dealer the week before. Cal was in love with the car, his first time in it, and he was trying to think of ways to keep it for his own personal-official use.

He watched them come out of the Villa Monterey with their suitcases and open the trunk of the white T-bird. The one guy, Stickley, with a cardboard suitcase, looked like he was going somewhere to pick sugar beets. The other one, Ryan, had on a suit that glistened in the afternoon sun.

Well now, Cal Brown said to himself. Hit them now or wait? He had warrants in his pocket for search or arrest, with the dates left blank.

Is the eighty-seven in the suitcase?

No. Probably not.

So why hit them now?

Are they going to pick it up and keep going?

Probably. Yes.

Might you need more help than just yourself, rather than maybe blow it and get your head cut off, not to mention other parts?

Bet your ass.

But he did not turn on the newly installed radio until he had followed the white T-bird for fifteen minutes and finally they hit the Southfield Freeway, going south.

He said into the mike, after describing the cars and their location, "Get me some very quiet state police backup. Give them my code and let me have theirs. We could be heading for the Ohio line, but I got a feeling we're going to turn off on Ninety-four."

That's what they did, south of the Veterans Hospital, took the off ramp down through the tight curve to the right, past the sign that said AIRPORT. It was about twenty minutes from here, out the old Willow Run Expressway.

Cal got on the mike again. "We'll need two men at each terminal, International, North Terminal, and West. Give them descriptions. They're to watch for the suspects and keep them under surveillance, but are not to collar them unless they attempt to put their luggage on a flight. I'm going to be right behind them—but just in case."

The T-bird crept along in the dimness of the cement structure, past the lines of cars that seemed to extend without end, up one lane and down another, from the first to the third level.

Stick was driving. He said, "Come on, let's go up on the roof."

Frank said, "I don't *want* to park it on the roof. Twice I parked up there, I come back, my wheel covers're gone."

"They can take the wheel covers anyplace you park," Stick said. "Right in front, in the no-parking zone, they can take your fucking wheel covers."

"There's more chance up there," Frank said. "Sitting up there away from everything a couple of weeks."

Stick said, "You worried about the car, then come back in a couple of days and get it. How long you think it'll take us to make the deposits? Say eight banks, North Miami to Lauderdale. You drive it in a half hour, less."

"Maybe we'll want to rest a while. *Maybe?* Christ, I'm tighter now than when I went in that fucking store."

"What I'm really saying," Stick said, "what difference does it make how long we leave it or if it gets stripped or not or even gets stolen, so what? Buy a new one."

"I like this one," Frank said. "I don't want to see it get damaged."

"Then come back tomorrow." Stick paused. "Wait a minute. What're we arguing about?"

"I don't want to park it up on the roof," Frank said.

Arlene paid the cabdriver and turned around to see a porter picking up her two suitcases. The porter asked her, What airline, ma'am? Arlene said thank you, but she'd take the bags herself, they weren't heavy. The porter, without a word, set them down and turned away as she picked them up. Arlene was afraid to let the bags out of her sight. She had never been so tense. She went through the automatic doors that opened in front of her, beginning to angle toward the right as she entered the terminal, knowing Delta was over there, the counters running the length of the right wall. She had come in and walked over that way before, going to Atlanta and Daytona Beach for NASCAR races.

But this time Arlene stopped.

Directly in front of her, high above the American Air Lines counter, was a giant black rectangle with white lighted letters and numbers that listed departures. It was strange the way her gaze saw, not a list of flight numbers and cities, but only one.

LOS ANGELES.
FLIGHT 41.
5:30 P.M.
ON TIME.

She looked over at the clock high above the Delta counter. A quarter to five.

Arlene thought of her friend in Bakersfield. She thought of the Grand Nationals coming up, the week after next. She thought of Hollywood. That was strange, Hollywood. She thought of the silver costume. And she thought of her age, twenty-six. In a month, twenty-seven. Why'd she think of that?

Arlene walked over to the American counter.

Frank and Stick came across the enclosed overpass that joined the parking structure to the main entrance that was on the second level of the West Terminal, Detroit Metropolitan. They had walked from the parked T-bird, carrying their bags, about two hundred yards.

Frank said, "You got the keys?"

Stick said, "What keys?"

"The *car* keys."

"Jesus Christ," Stick said.

Maybe he wouldn't be coming back with Frank in a couple of weeks. Let him get the car by himself, he loved it so much.

They crossed the roadway and passed the cars being unloaded and the porters and the hand trucks—none of the porters offered to take their bags—and entered the terminal through the automatic doors.

"I don't see her around," Stick said.

Frank's gaze followed Stick's, studying the people walking around and waiting, most of them waiting at counters, some sitting down in the rows of seats. The place didn't seem very busy.

There were several lines at the Delta counter. Frank picked the shortest line, behind two people. Stick waited with him a minute, then stepped over to a line of three people. Frank gave him a look. Ten minutes later Frank was still behind the two people. Stick was at the counter. Frank came over. He said to the reservations clerk, "Mr. Ryan and Mr. Stickley. I believe you're holding a couple of seats for us. The Miami flight."

The clerk stepped over to a machine, punched a few keys, waited while the thing clicked back at him, and punched a few more. He did it again and stepped back to them saying, "Yes, you're confirmed on Flight Eleven-eighty, departing at five forty-five from Gate Twenty-nine. Will you be checking your luggage through?"

"Yes, we will," Frank said.

Behind him, Stick said, "I don't see her anywhere."

Frank said, over his shoulder, "She's probably at the gate already, picking her seat."

The clerk was holding up an American Air Lines ticket envelope, looking at it. He said, "I see this was left for you. It has your names on it." He handed the envelope to Frank.

Stick saw the names, written in ink, as Frank took the envelope. *Mr. E. Stickley, Mr. F. Ryan,* one above the other.

The clerk said, "If you'll put your luggage up here please—" He was holding the luggage tags.

Frank shoved the American Air Lines envelope into his inside coat pocket and reached down for his suitcase. Behind him, Stick was picking up his ratty-looking bag. Behind Stick, somebody said, "Just a moment, please."

They both looked around. Frank said, "What?"

There were two of them, thirty-year-old guys in neat summer-weight suits, no hats. They looked like pro football players. No they didn't, they looked like cops.

One of them had his badge case open already, giving them a look at his shield. He said, "State police. I'd like you, please, to pick up your suitcases and go around the counter over there to that door you see marked AUTHORIZED PERSONNEL ONLY."

"What is this?" Frank said, indignant. "What for?"

The state policeman said, "Pick up your bag, buddy, *now.*"

"I just want to know what's going on, for Christ sake. I mean what is this? You accusing us of something, or what?"

Frank stopped as Cal Brown came in and walked up to the two state cops and showed them his credentials. They nodded and said something to him.

Stick was watching. He said mildly, "I hope this doesn't take too long. We got a flight to make."

Cal Brown turned to them sitting at the metal table in the bare, brightly fluorescent-lighted room, and gave them a nice smile.

"You got a flight, I got two warrants," he said, taking them out of his jacket, giving them a flash of the mag holstered under the jacket, and holding the warrants up for them to see. "This one's for search. You mind?"

"If we miss the flight, you got to pay for it," Frank said.

"No, the airline'll put you on another one free of charge," Cal said. "I mean if you're going anywhere."

Stick said, "If you want to look in our bags, go ahead. I mean maybe if we hurry up, we can get it done. What do you think?"

They watched as the two state cops came over and opened their suitcases and began going through them, taking out each item of clothing separately and feeling it.

Frank sat back and lighted a cigarette. He said, "I hope, when you're through, you guys put it all back the way it was."

Stick said to Cal, "You mind I ask what you're looking for?"

"Yeah, I do," Cal said.

They unrolled socks and looked inside shoes and studied their toilet kits very closely. The one going through Stick's bag took out a wad of bills and looked over at Cal. Cal shook his head. Frank stared at the money, then at Stick, but he didn't say anything to anybody, not until the two state cops were finished.

"Is that it, Officers?"

Cal Brown said, "Now if you'll stand up please, gents, and empty your pockets—lay whatever you have on the table."

"Come on," Frank said, "pat us down if you want. You think we're carrying guns, for Christ sake, on an *air*plane?"

"Get up," Cal said.

Stick took out his wallet, the car keys, a pack of Marlboros, matches, and a comb.

Frank started with his coat. He took his sunglasses case and the American Air Lines envelope out of his inside coat pocket. He pulled out his wallet and a clean, folded handkerchief.

Cal looked at the American envelope. Why, if they were flying Delta— He picked it up.

Stick was watching him. Frank was digging for loose change in his pants pocket.

Cal took a piece of paper out of the envelope. He unfolded it and a locker key fell to the table. He looked down at the key, then at Stick, then at the piece of paper for a moment, and handed it to Stick.

Stick looked at the two words written in ink in the neat, slanting feminine hand.

I'm sorry.

He kept looking at the words.

Cal handed the locker key to one of the state cops, who studied the number on it as he walked out.

Frank was frowning, not knowing what was going on. "What's it say?"

Stick handed him the note. He said to Cal, "Maybe somebody left that, we got it by mistake, you know?"

"With your names on it?" Cal said.

Walking through the terminal, the two state cops were behind them carrying their bags. Cal was right in front of them, holding tight to the small, light blue suitcase. No one they passed stopped or turned around or seemed to notice that the two in the middle were handcuffed together.

They went through the automatic doors and down the sidewalk, away from the entrance, to wait for the police car to pull up.

Frank said, half whispering against his shoulder, trying not to move his mouth, "Of all the ones, all the broads that'd jump at the chance, I mean *jump*, you pick that turkey. Christ, and I let you, I go along. What'd you say, the great judge of broads? 'She's a good one.' Your exact words, 'She's a good one.' "

"She didn't mean this to happen," Stick said. "It's not her fault."

"Whose fault is it, mine? What'd I say? Let's put it in the car and go, take the swag and run, man, and not get anybody else in the act. Remember that? Hey, remember the rule? Don't tell anybody your business. Nobody. Especially a junkie. Shit, especially a broad. One you pick."

The police car was pulling up to them.

"What do you think I went to the trouble to think up all those rules for? You remember the ten rules? We act like businessmen and nobody knows our business. You remember that?"

Stick said, "Frank, why don't you shut the fuck up?"

MR. MAJESTYK

1

This morning they were here for the melons: about sixty of them waiting patiently by the two stake trucks and the old blue-painted school bus. Most of them, including the few women here, were Chicano migrants, who had arrived in their old junk cars that were parked in a line behind the trucks. Others, the Valley Agricultural Workers Association had brought out from Phoenix, dropping them off at 5:30 A.M. on the outskirts of Edna, where the state road came out of the desert to cross the U.S. highway. The growers and the farm workers called it Junction. There was an Enco gas station on the corner, then a storefront with a big V.A.W.A. sign in the window that was the farm labor hiring hall—closed until next season—and then a café-bar with a red neon sign that said BEER-WINE. The rest of the storefronts in the block were empty—dark, gutted structures that were gradually being destroyed by the desert wind.

The farm workers stood around on the sidewalk waiting to be hired, waiting for the labor contractors to finish their coffee, finish talking to the foremen and the waitresses, and come out and point to them and motion them toward the stake trucks and the blue-painted school bus.

The dozen or so whites were easy to spot. Most of them were worn-out looking men in dirty, worn-out clothes that had once been their own or someone else's good clothes. A tight little group of them was drinking Thunderbird, passing the wine bottle around in a paper bag. A couple of them were sipping from beer cans. Two teenaged white boys with long hair stood off by themselves, hip-cocked, their arms folded over tight white T-shirts, not seeming to mind the early morning chill. They would look around casually and squint up at the pale sky.

The Chicanos, in their straw hats and baseball caps, plaid shirts, and Levis or khakis, with their lunch in paper bags, felt the chill. They would look at the sky knowing it was near the end of the season and soon most of them would be heading for California, to the Imperial and San Joaquin valleys. Some of them—once in a while for something to do—would shield their faces from the light and look in the window of the hiring hall, at the rows of folding chairs, at the display of old V.A.W.A. strike posters and yellowed newspaper pages with columns marked in red. They would stare at the photograph of Emiliano Zapata on the wall behind the counter, at the statue of the Virgin Mary on a stand, and try to read the hand-lettered announcements: *Todo el mundo está invitado que venga a la resada—*

Larry Mendoza came out of the café-bar with a carry-out cup of coffee in each hand—one black, one cream and sugar—and walked over to the curb, beyond the front of the old blue-painted school bus. Some of the farm workers stared at him—a thin, bony-shouldered, weathered-looking Chicano in clean Levis and high-heeled work boots, a Texas straw funneled low over his eyes—and one of them, also a Chicano, said, "Hey,

Larry, tell Julio you want me. Tell him write my name down at
the top." Larry Mendoza glanced over at the man and nodded,
but didn't say anything.

Another one said, "How much you paying, Larry? Buck
forty?"

He nodded again and said, "Same as everybody." He felt
them watching him because he was foreman out at Majestyk
and could give some of them jobs. He knew how they felt,
hoping each day to get their names on a work list. He had stood
on this corner himself, waiting for a contractor to point to him.
He had started in the fields for forty cents an hour. He'd
worked for sixty cents, seventy-five cents. Now he was making
eighty dollars a week, all year: he got to drive the pickup any
time he wanted and his family lived in a house with an inside
toilet. He wished he could hire all of them, assure each man
right now that he'd be working today, but he couldn't do that.
So he ignored them, looking down the sidewalk now toward
the Enco station where the attendant was pumping gas into an
old-model four-wheel drive pickup that was painted yellow, its
high front end pointing this way. Larry Mendoza stood like
that, his back to the school bus and the farm workers, waiting,
then began to sip the coffee with cream and sugar.

The Enco gas station attendant, with the name *Gil* stitched
over the pocket of his shirt, watched the numbers changing in
the window of the pump and began to squeeze the handle of
the nozzle that curved into the gas tank filler, slowing the rota-
tion of the numbers, easing them in line to read three dollars
even, and pulled the nozzle out of the opening.

When he looked over at the station he saw the guy who
owned the pickup stepping out of the Men's Room, coming
this way across the pavement—a dark, solemn-faced man who
might have passed for a Chicano except for his name. Vince
Majestyk. Hard-looking guy, but always quiet, the few times
he had been here. Vincent Majestyk of MAJESTYK BRAND
MELONS that was lettered on the doors of the pickup and made
him sound like a big grower. Shit, he looked more like a picker
than a grower. Maybe a foreman, with his khaki pants and blue
shirt. From what the station attendant had heard about him,

the guy was scratching to get by and probably wouldn't be around very long. Comes in, buys three bucks worth of gas. Big deal.

He said, "That's all you want?"

The guy, Majestyk, looked over at him as he walked past the front of the pickup. "If you're not too busy you can wipe the bugs off the windshield," he said, and kept going, over toward the school bus and the farm workers crowding around.

The gas station attendant said to himself, Shit. Get up at five in the morning to sell three bucks' worth. Wait around all day and watch the tourists drive by. Four-thirty sell the migrants each a buck's worth. Shit.

Larry Mendoza handed Majestyk the cup of black coffee and the two of them stood watching as Julio Tamaz, a labor contractor, looked over the waiting groups of farm workers, called off names and motioned them to the school bus. There were already men aboard, seated, their heads showing in the line of windows.

"We're almost ready to go," Mendoza said.

"Good ones?" Majestyk took a sip of coffee.

"The best he's got."

"Bob Santos," the labor contractor called out. "And . . . Anbrocio Verrara."

"They're good," Mendoza said.

"Luis Ortega!"

A frail old man grinned and hurried toward the bus.

"Wait a minute," Mendoza said. "I don't know him. He ever picked before?"

Julio Tamaz, the labor contractor, turned to them with a surprised look. "Luis? All his life. Man, he was conceived in a melon field." Julio's expression brightened, relaxed in a smile as he looked at Majestyk. "Hey, Vincent, nice to see you."

Mendoza said, "That's thirty. We want any more'n that?"

Majestyk was finishing his coffee. He lowered the cup. "If Julio's got any like to work for nothing."

"Man," Julio said, "you tight with the dollar. Like to squeeze it to death."

"How's my credit?"

"Vincent"—Julio's expression was sad now—"I told you. What do I pay them with?"

"All right, I just wondered if you'd changed your mind." He took a fold of bills out of his pants pocket and handed them to the labor contractor. "Straight buck forty an hour, ten hours' work for a crew of thirty comes to four hundred and twenty. Don't short anybody."

Julio seemed offended now. "I take my percent. I don't need to cheat them."

"Larry'll ride with you," Majestyk said. "He finds anybody hasn't slipped honeydew melons before, they come back with you and we get a refund. Right?"

"Man, I never give you no bums. These people all experts."

Majestyk had already turned away and was walking back to the Enco station.

The attendant with the name *Gil* on his shirt was standing by the pickup.

"That's three bucks."

Majestyk reached into a back pocket for his wallet this time. He took out a five-dollar bill and handed it to the attendant, who looked at the bill and then at Majestyk. Without a word he turned and leisurely walked off toward the station. Majestyk watched him for a moment, knowing the guy was going to make him wait. He walked off after the guy and followed him into the station, but still had to wait while the guy fooled around at the cash register, shifting bills around in the cash drawer and breaking open a roll of coins.

"Take your time," Majestyk said.

When the bell rang he turned to see a car pulling into the station: an old-model Ford sedan that was faded blue-purple and rusting out, and needed a muffler. He watched the people getting out, moving slowly, stretching and looking around. There seemed to more of them than the car could hold.

The station attendant was saying, "I'm short of singles. I'll have to give you some change."

There were five of them, four men in work clothes and a young woman, migrants, looking around, trying to seem at ease. The young woman took a bandana from her head and, raising her face in the sunlight, closing her eyes, shook her hair from side to side, freeing it in the light breeze that came across the highway stirring sand dust. She was a good-looking girl, nice figure in pants and a T-shirt, in her early twenties, or maybe even younger. Very good-looking. Not self-conscious now, as though she was alone with whatever was behind her closed eyes. Two of the men went to the pop machine digging coins out of their pockets.

Beyond the girl the blue-painted school bus passed the station and the state road intersection, moving east down the highway.

"Here you are," the attendant said.

Majestyk held out his hand and the attendant dropped eight quarters into his palm, four at a time.

"Three, that's four and five. Hurry back and see us now."

Majestyk didn't say anything. He gave the guy a little smile. He had enough to think about and wasn't going to let the guy bother him. When he turned to the doorway he had to stop short. The girl, holding the bandana, was coming in and their eyes met for a moment—nice eyes, brown—before she looked past him toward the attendant.

"Is there a key you have to the Ladies' Room?"

The attendant's eyes moved past her, to the four men outside, and back again. "No, it's broken, you can't use it. Go down the road someplace."

"Maybe it's all right now," the girl said. "Have you looked at it? Sometimes they get all right by themselves."

The attendant was shaking his head now. "I'm telling you it's broken. Take my word for it and go someplace else, all right?"

"What about the other one?" the girl said. "The Men's Room."

"It's broken too. Both of 'em are broken."

"See, we go in separately," the girl went on. "The men, they come out, then I go in. So you don't have to call the cops, say we're doing it in there."

"I can call the cops right now." The attendant's voice was

louder, irritated. "I'm telling you both toilets are broken. You got to go someplace else."

"Where do you go?" the girl said. She waited a moment, not looking around but knowing the four men were close to the doorway now, and could hear her.

The attendant said, "I'm warning you—"

And the girl said, "Maybe you never go, uh? That's why you're full of shit."

The migrants grinned, some of them laughed out loud and there were words in Spanish, though the girl continued to stare at the attendant calmly, almost without expression.

The attendant turned to a counter and came around with a wrench in his hand, his jaw set tightly. Majestyk reached over to put a hand on the man's arm.

He said, "When did the toilet break? Since I used it?"

"Listen, I got to do what I'm told." He pulled his arm away from Majestyk and lowered his voice then, though the tension was still there. "Like anybody else. The boss says don't let no migrants in the toilets. He says I don't care they dancing around like they can taste it, don't let them in the toilets. They go in there, mess up the place, piss all over, take a bath in the sink, use all the towels, steal the toilet paper, man, it's like a bunch of pigs was in there. Place is filthy, I got to clean up after."

"Let them use it," Majestyk said.

"I tell you what my boss said. Man, I can't do nothing about it."

"What're they supposed to do?"

"Go out in the bushes, I don't know. Mister, you have any idea how many migrants stop here?"

"I know what they can do," Majestyk said. He turned from the attendant to the nice-looking Chicano girl, noticing now that she was wearing small pearl earrings.

"He says for all of you to come inside."

"I want them out of here!"

"He says he's sorry the toilets are broken."

"They're always broken," the girl said. "Every place they keep the broken toilets locked up so nobody steal them."

Majestyk was looking at her again. "You come here to work?"

"For the melons or whatever time it is. Last month we were over at Yuma."

"You know melons, uh?"

"Melons, onions, lettuce, anything you got."

"You want to work today?"

The girl seemed to think about it and then shrugged and said, "Yeah, well, since we forgot our golf clubs we might as well, uh?"

"After you go to the bathroom." Majestyk's gaze, with the soft hint of a smile, held on her for another moment.

"First things first," the girl said.

"Listen, I don't say they can't use them," the attendant said now. "You think I own this place? I work here."

"He says he works here," Majestyk said.

The girl nodded. "We believe it."

"And he says since the toilets are broken you can use something else." Majestyk's gaze moved away, past the attendant and the shelves of lube oil and the cash register and the coffee and candy machines, taking in the office.

"What're you doing?" The attendant was frowning, staring at him. "Listen, they can't use something else. They got to get out of here."

Majestyk's gaze stopped, held for a moment before coming back to the attendant. "He says use the wastebasket if you want," and motioned to the migrants with his hand. "Come on. All of you, come on in."

As two of the migrants came in hesitantly behind the girl, grinning, enjoying it, and the other two moved in closer behind her, the attendant said, "Jesus Christ, you're crazy! I'm going to call the police, that's what I'm going to do."

"Try and hold on to yourself," Majestyk said to him quietly. "You don't own this place. You don't have to pay for broken windows or anything. What do you care?"

The phone was on the desk in front of him, but the Enco gas station man with *Gil* over his shirt pocket, who had never been farther away from this place than Phoenix, hesitated now, afraid to reach for the phone or even look at it. What would happen if he did? Christ, what was going on here? He didn't know this guy Vincent Majestyk. Christ, a cold, quiet guy, he didn't know anything about him except he grew melons. He'd hardly ever seen him before.

"How do you want it?" Majestyk said to the attendant.

Watching him, the migrants were grinning, beginning to glance at each other, confident of this man for no reason they knew of but feeling it, enjoying it, stained and golden smiles softening dark faces and bringing life to their eyes, expressions that separated them as individuals able to think and feel, each one a person now, each one beginning to laugh to himself at this gas station man and his boss and his wastebasket and his toilets he could keep locked or shove up his ass for all they cared. God, it was good; it was going to be something to tell about.

"Let them use the toilets," Majestyk said to the attendant. "All right?"

The attendant held on another moment, as if thinking it over, letting them know he was not being forced into anything but was making up his own mind. He shrugged indifferently then and nodded to two keys that were attached to flat pieces of wood and hung from the wall next to the door.

"Keys're right there," the attendant said. "Just don't take all day."

2

The girl rode with him in the pickup and the four men followed in the Ford sedan that needed a paint job and a muffler, heading east on the highway toward the morning sun, seeing the flat view of sand and scrub giving way to sweeps of green fields on both sides of the highway, citrus and vegetable farms, irrigation canals and, in the near distance, stands of trees that bordered the fields and marked back roads and dry washes. Beyond the trees, in the far distance, a haze of mountains stood low against the sky, forming a horizon that was fifty miles away, in another world.

The girl was at ease, though every once in a while she would turn and look through the back window to make sure the car was still following.

Finally Majestyk said, "I'm not going to lose them."

"I'm not worried about that," the girl said. "It's the car. It could quit on them any time, blow a tire or something."

"They relatives of yours?"

"Friends. We worked the same place at Yuma."

"How long you been traveling together?"

The girl looked at him. "What are you trying to find out? If I sleep with them?"

"I'm sorry. I was just curious, I didn't mean to offend you."

When she spoke again her tone was quiet, the hostility gone. "We go to different places, help organize the farm workers. But we have to stop and work to pay our way."

"You're with the union?"

"Why? I tell you, yes, then you don't hire us?"

"You sure get on the muscle easy. I don't care if you're union or not, long as you know melons."

"Intimately. I've been in the fields most of my life."

"You sound like you went to school though."

"Couple of years. University of Texas, El Paso. I took English and History and Economics. Psychology 101. I went to the football games, learned all the cheers. Yeaaa, team—" Her voice trailed off and she added, quietly, "Shit."

"I never went past high school," Majestyk said.

"So you didn't waste any time."

He looked at her again, interested, intrigued. "You haven't told me your name."

"Nancy Chavez. I'm not related to the other Chavez, but I'll tell you something. I was on the picket line with them at Delano, during the grape strike."

"I believe it."

"I was fifteen."

He glanced at her and waited again, because she seemed deep in thought. Finally he said, "Are you from California?"

"Texas. Born in Laredo. We moved to San Antonio when I was little."

"Yeah? I was at Fort Hood for a while. I used to get down to San Antone pretty often."

"That's nice," Nancy Chavez said.

He looked at her again, but didn't say anything. Neither of

them spoke until they were passing melon fields and came in sight of the packing shed, a long wooden structure that looked like a warehouse. It was painted yellow, with MAJESTYK BRAND MELONS written across the length of the building in five-foot bright green letters.

As the pickup slowed down, approaching a dirt road adjacent to the packing shed, the girl said, "That's you, uh?"

"That's me," Majestyk said.

The pickup turned off the highway onto the dirt road and passed the front of the packing shed. There were crates stacked on the loading dock, the double doors were open; but there was no sign of activity, the shed stood dark and empty. Next to it was a low frame building with a corrugated metal roof that resembled an army barracks. The girl knew what it was, or what it had been—living quarters for migrants. It was also empty, some of its windows broken, its white paint peeling, fading gray.

The farmhouse was next, another fifty yards down the road, where three small children—two boys and a little girl—were standing in the hard-packed yard, watching the pickup drive past, and a woman was hanging wash on a clothesline that extended out from the side of the house. The children waved and Nancy put her hand out the window to wave back at them.

"Are they yours, too?"

"My foreman, Larry Mendoza's," Majestyk said. "That's my house way down there, by the trees."

She could see the place now, white against the dark stand of woods, a small, one-story farmhouse with a porch, almost identical to the foreman's house. She could see the blue school bus standing in the road ahead and, off to the left beyond the ditch, the melon fields, endless rows of green vines that were familiar to the girl and never changed, hot dusty rows that seemed to reach from Texas to California, and were always waiting to be picked.

"You must have a thousand acres," she said. "More than that."

"A hundred and sixty. The man that owned this land used to have a big operation, but he subdivided when he sold out. This is my second crop year, and if I don't make it this time—"

When he stopped, the girl said, "What?"

She turned to see him staring straight ahead through the windshield, at the school bus they were approaching and the men standing in the road. She could see the car now, a new model of some kind shining golden in the sunlight, parked beyond the bus. Beyond the car was a stake truck. At the same time she was aware of the figures out in the melon field, at least twenty or more, stooped figures dotted among the rows.

She said, "You have two crews working?"

"I only hired one," Majestyk said.

"Then who's out there working?"

He didn't answer her. He pulled up behind the bus and got out without wasting any time, feeling a tenseness now as he walked past the bus, past the faces in the windows, and saw Larry Mendoza's serious, concerned expression. His foreman stood with Julio Tamaz by the front of the bus, both of them watching him, anxious. Only a few of Julio's crew had gotten out. The rest of them were still inside wondering, as he was, what the hell was going on.

He was aware of the two men standing by the gold Dodge Charger that was parked on the left side of the road—long hair and Mexican bandit moustaches, one of them wearing sunglasses. A skinny, hipless guy with a big metal belt buckle, bright yellow shirt and cowboy boots, watching him, seeming unconcerned, lounged against the rear deck of the Charger with his arms folded. There was another guy he had never seen before standing by the stake truck that, he noticed now, had a horn-type speaker mounted on the roof of the cab.

"We get here," Larry Mendoza said, "this guy's already got a crew working."

Julio Tamaz said, "What are we supposed to do, Vincent, go home? Man, what is this?"

Majestyk walked over to the ditch, behind the Charger, and stood looking out at the field, at the men standing among the rows with long burlap sacks hanging from their shoulders. Only a few of them were working. All of them, he noticed, were white. And all of them, that he could make out clearly, had the same worn-out, seedy look, skid row bums taken from the street and dropped in a melon field.

But not my melon field, Majestyk was saying to himself. He turned to the skinny dude with sunglasses lounged against the car.

"I don't think I know you."

He watched the guy straighten with a lazy effort and come off the car extending his hand.

"I'm Bobby Kopas. Come out from Phoenix with some top hand pickers for you."

Majestyk ignored the waiting hand. "I don't think I've ever done business with you either. What I know for sure is I never will."

Bobby Kopas grinned at him, letting his hand fall. "'Fore you say anything you might be sorry about—how does a buck twenty an hour sound to you? Save yourself some money and they're already hard at it."

"I hire who I want," Majestyk said. "I don't hire a bunch of winos never slipped melons before."

Kopas glanced over at the bus, at Larry Mendoza and Julio and Nancy Chavez. "I don't know—you hire all these Latins, no white people. Looks like discrimination to me."

"Call them out and get off my land," Majestyk said.

"These Latins buddies of yours? What do you care who does the job, long as it gets done?"

"I just told you, I hire who I want."

"Yeah, well the thing is you want me," Kopas said. "Only it hasn't sunk in your head yet. Because everything is easier and less trouble when you hire my crew. If you understand what I'm saying to you."

There it was, a little muscle-flexing. Hotshot dude trying to pressure him, sure of himself, with two strong-arm guys to back him up. Majestyk stared at him and thought about it and finally he said, "Well, you're making sounds like you're a mean little ass-kicker. Only you haven't convinced me yet it's true. Then again, if you say anything else and I don't like it, I'm liable to take your head off. So maybe you ought to consider that."

Majestyk stared at him a moment, as Kopas began to say, "Now hang on a minute, dad—" but that was all. Majestyk turned away, ignoring him, looking out at the field again and began yelling at the winos.

"Come on, time to go home! Leave anything you picked or messed up and haul ass out, right now! Come on, gents, move it!"

The few that were working stopped, straightened, and now all of the men in the rows were looking this way, not sure what to do. Kopas saw them. He had to stop them before they moved. He turned to the guy behind him and nodded toward the stake truck. The guy took off. The other one, standing by the truck, saw him coming and quickly got into the cab.

"You hear me?" Majestyk yelled out. "Time to go home. Man made a mistake. You come to the wrong place." As he began to say, "Come on, move!" his words were drowned out by a blast of rock music, intense hard rock, the sound of electrified, amplified guitars wailing out over the melon fields.

Majestyk looked toward the truck, at the horn speaker mounted on the cab. His gaze shifted to Bobby Kopas. He saw him grinning and saw the grin fade as he moved toward him. He saw him get around to the side of the Charger, reach in through the open window and come out with a pump-action shotgun. Kopas put the gun under his arm, pointing down slightly, holding it with both hands, and Majestyk stopped.

Nancy Chavez, staring at Bobby Kopas, came away from the bus. She said, "Man, what're you going to do now, shoot us?"

"I'm gonna talk to him and this time he's gonna listen," Kopas said. "That's what I'm gonna do."

She was moving toward him, taking her time. "Buck twenty an hour—you going to shoot people for that? Man, you need another hit of something."

"He threatened me," Kopas said, "and all your people heard it. But I'll tell you, he ain't gonna threaten me again."

Staring at him, moving toward him, Nancy Chavez said, "I don't know—guy brings wine heads out, plays music for them. He must be a little funny."

Majestyk was past the trunk of the car, two strides from the muzzle of the shotgun.

"You say you come from Phoenix? What do you do there, roll drunks and hire them as pickers?"

Kopas kept his eyes on him, holding onto the shotgun. "I'm telling you, keep back. Stay where you are."

"Mean little ass-kicker like you," Majestyk said. "What do you need a gun for?"

"I'm warning you!"

Majestyk stepped into him as he brought the shotgun up, grabbing the barrel with his left hand and drove his right fist hard into Bobby Kopas's face, getting some nose and mouth, staying with him as Kopas went back against the car door and slammed the fist into him again, getting his sunglasses this time, wiping them from his face, and pulling the shotgun out of his hands as Kopas twisted and his head and shoulders fell into the window opening.

The other one with the hair and heavy moustache who had been with Kopas was coming back from the truck, coming fast, but not in time. He stopped and raised his hands, three yards away, as Majestyk put the shotgun on him.

The loud rock music continued, the wailing guitars wailed on, until Majestyk stepped into the middle of the road, raised the shotgun and blew the horn speaker off the top of the stake truck.

The sound stopped. Majestyk looked at the man with his hands half raised. He pumped a shell into the chamber of the shotgun and walked past him to the truck. When he opened the rightside door he could hear the radio music again, the rock guitars. The man sitting behind the wheel stared at him.

"Get those wine heads out of my field," Majestyk said, and slammed the door.

He came back to the Charger, nodded toward Kopas hanging against the door and said to the one with his hands raised, "Put him inside and get out of here." He waited, seeing the blood coming out of Kopas's nose, staining his yellow shirt, as the guy pulled Kopas around, opened the door and eased him onto the seat.

"You got the key?" When the guy nodded Majestyk said, "Open the trunk."

He had to wait for him again, for the guy to walk back and unlock it. As the trunk lid swung up, Majestyk stepped over, threw the shotgun inside and slammed it closed. He stood one stride away from the guy with the hair and the heavy moustache who was staring at him and maybe was on the verge of doing something.

Majestyk said, "Make up your mind."

The guy hesitated; but the moment was there and passed. He walked around to the driver's side and got in the car.

Majestyk walked up on the other side to look at Kopas holding a handkerchief to his face. He said, "Hey," and waited for Kopas to lower the handkerchief and look out at him.

"You want my opinion, buddy, I think you're in the wrong business."

3

He was arrested that afternoon.

Nancy Chavez saw it happen. She was crouched in the vines working a row, slipping the ripe honeydew melons off, gently turning the ones that would be ready in a day or two, pushing them under the vines so they would not be exposed to the sun. Her sack, with the rope loop digging into her shoulder, was almost full. A few more melons and she would carry it over to the road and hand it up to Vincent Majestyk in the trailer that was hooked to the pickup truck. Maybe they would talk a little bit while he unloaded the sack and she got a drink of water from the canvas bag that hung from the side of the trailer. He had been curious about her, admitting it, and she was curious about him. There were questions in her mind, though she wasn't sure she could come right out and ask them. She wondered if he lived alone or had a wife somewhere. She wondered if he knew what he was doing, if he could harvest a hundred and sixty acres within the next week, sort and pack the melons and get them to a broker. Even for a late crop he was running out of time.

When her sack was full and she looked up again, straightening, the squad car, with blue lights flashing, was standing in the road by the pickup truck. She saw the two policemen, in khaki uniforms and cowboy hats, talking to Majestyk in the trailer. When he came down and one of them took him by the arm, he pulled his arm free and the other policeman moved in close with his hand on his holster. What the hell was going on?

Nancy Chavez dropped the sack and started across the rows. Some of the other pickers were watching now and Larry Mendoza was coming out of the field, not far away from her. She hurried, but by the time she and Mendoza reached the road, Majestyk was in the squad car and it was moving off, blue lights spinning, raising a column of dust that thinned to nothing by the time the squad car reached the highway and turned left, toward Edna.

"What's going on?" Nancy Chavez said. "They arresting him?"

Larry Mendoza shook his head, squinting in the sun glare. "I don't know. But I guess somebody better go find out."

"Is there somebody at his house maybe you better tell?"

"No, there's nobody lives there but him."

"He isn't married?"

"Not anymore."

The squad car was out of sight but Mendoza was still staring in the direction of the highway. "Those were sheriff deputies. Well, I guess I better go find out."

"If there's anything you want me to do," the girl said, "don't be afraid to tell me. Go on, we'll take care of the melons."

The Edna Post of the County Sheriff's Department had been remodeled and painted light green. Everything was light green, the cement block walls, the metal desks, the chairs, the formica counter—light green and chrome-trimmed under bright fluorescent lights. They took Majestyk into an office, sat him down against the wall and left him.

After a while one of the arresting officers came back in with a file folder, sat down at a desk where there was a typewriter and began to peck at the keys with two fingers. The deputy's name was Harold Ritchie. He was built like a running guard, had served four years in the Marines, including a combat tour in Vietnam, and had a tattoo on his right forearm, a snake coiled around a dagger, with an inscription that said *Death Before Dishonor.*

Looking down at the typewriter, as if reciting the words from memory, he said, "This warrant states that you have been arrested on a charge that constitutes a felony, assault with a deadly weapon. You may choose to stand mute at this time and of course you have a right to counsel. You can call a lawyer or anybody you want. You are allowed one phone call—"

The deputy paused, looking up, as a man in a lightweight summer suit came into the office and closed the door behind him.

The man said, "Go on. Don't let me interrupt."

His tone was mild, his appearance slightly rumpled. For some reason he reminded Majestyk of a schoolteacher, a man who had taught high school English or civics for at least thirty years, though he knew the man was a policeman.

"After which," Ritchie continued, "you will be released on bond, if you choose, or held here till you're taken to the county seat for your pretrial examination."

The deputy looked up, finished. The mild-appearing man came over to the desk, his gaze holding on Majestyk.

"My name is Detective Lieutenant McAllen. Do you understand your rights under the law?"

"I can keep my mouth shut, and that seems about it," Majestyk said.

"You can tell your side of it if you want. Feel free."

"A man I never saw before tried to force me to use a crew I didn't need."

"So you hit him with a shotgun."

"I hit him with a fist."

"The complainant says he was offering you a business proposition. Instead of a simple no thanks, you assaulted him with a shotgun."

"It was his, not mine," Majestyk said. "Man was trespassing on my land."

"Lieutenant"—the deputy was holding the file folder; he handed it, open, to McAllen—"four years ago in California he got one to five for assault. Served a year in Folsom."

McAllen studied the folder a moment before looking up. "Vincent A. Majestyk. What're you, a Polack?"

Majestyk stared at him in silence. The lieutenant was looking at the folder again.

"He grows melons," the deputy said. "Generally keeps to himself. I mean he hasn't given us any trouble before this."

"But sometimes you like to mix it up," McAllen said. "You use a gun the time in California?"

"I was in a bar. A man hit me with a beer bottle."

"Sitting there minding your own business, he hit you with a bottle."

"We were arguing about something. He wanted to go outside. I told him to drink his beer."

"So he hit you and you hit him back. If it was your first offense, how come they put you away?"

"The guy was in the hospital a while," Majestyk said. "He came to the trial with a broken collarbone and his jaw wired up and some buddies of his that said I started it and kicked his face in when he was on the floor."

"But you never did such a thing."

"I've already been tried for it. You want to do it again?"

"Served your time and now making an honest living. You married?"

"I was four years. My wife divorced me while I was in prison."

"Run out on you, huh? How come? Didn't you get along?"

"You want to talk about my marriage? Find out what we did in bed?"

McAllen didn't say anything for a moment. He stared at Majestyk, then turned to leave, dropping the folder on the desk.

"I think you better talk to a lawyer."

"Lieutenant, I got a crop of melons to get in." He saw the man hesitate and turn to look at him again. "Let me get them picked, I'll come back right after."

McAllen took his time. "That's what you're worried about, melons?"

"I get them in and packed this week or I lose the crop. I'm asking for a few days, that's all."

"The court'll set a bond on you," McAllen said. "Pay it, you can go out and pick all the melons you want."

"Except if I put up bail I won't have any money left for a crew. And I can't pick a hundred and sixty acres by myself."

McAllen was thoughtful again, studying him. He said, "I don't know anything about you but the fact you've been arrested for assault and have a previous conviction. So I don't have any reason to feel sorry for you, do I?"

"I give you my word," Majestyk said. "I'll come right back."

"And even if I did feel sorry for you, if for some reason I believed you, the law doesn't happen to make any provision for your word," McAllen said. "That's how it is." He turned and walked out.

Larry Mendoza waited three and a half hours on the bench by the main desk, looking up every time one of the deputies came out of an office. They would stand around drinking coffee, not paying any attention to him. Finally they told him no, it was too late to see his friend now, he'd have to come back tomorrow. They told him the charge was felonious assault and the bond was set at five thousand, which would cost him five hundred, cash, if he wanted to go to the county seat and get a bondsman to put up the money. Or wait a couple of days for the examination. If the court set a trial date and appointed a lawyer, maybe the lawyer could get the bond lowered.

Christ, he didn't know anything about bonds or examinations. He didn't know what the hell was going on—how they could arrest a man for throwing somebody off his property who didn't belong there. It didn't make sense.

When he got back Julio had already picked up his crew and was gone. He asked his wife, Helen, and Nancy Chavez and the four men who were with her—the group of them sitting on the front steps of his house in the shade—if it made any sense.

Nancy Chavez said, "Cops. Talking to cops is like talking to the wall. They don't tell you anything they don't want to."

Of course not, it didn't make sense. Christ almighty, who ever expected cops to make sense? All they could do was keep working, do that much for him while he was in jail, then all of them tell at the examination, or whatever it was, what happened and maybe, if the judge listened, he would see it didn't make any sense and Vincent would get off. Maybe.

Helen Mendoza let Nancy use her kitchen and gave her some green beens and beets to go with the Franco-American spaghetti she fixed for her friends and herself. Larry Mendoza said why didn't they stay in Vincent's house while he was in jail. Vincent wouldn't mind. In fact he'd want them to. Nancy Chavez said all right, for one night. But tomorrow they'd get the migrant quarters in shape, clean up the kitchen and a couple of rooms and stay there. They had cots and bedding in the car. For a week it wouldn't be so bad. They'd lived in worse places.

Larry Mendoza went back to the Edna Post the next day, Saturday. They searched him good and put him in a little closet of a room that had a table, two chairs facing each other and a metal cabinet. He waited about a half hour before a deputy brought Majestyk in and closed the door. The deputy waited outside. They could see him through the glass part of the door.

"Are you all right? Christ, it doesn't make any sense."

"I'm fine," Majestyk told him. "Listen, what we got to think about's the crop. You're here visiting me, you should be working the crew.

"Man, we're worried about you. What if they put you in jail?"

"I'm already in jail."

"In the penitentiary. For something that don't make any sense."

"We're going to court Monday," Majestyk said. "I'll see if I can talk to the judge, explain it to him."

"And we'll be there," Mendoza said. "Tell them what happened."

"I'll tell them. You'll be out in the field."

"Vincent, you need all the help you can get. You got to have a lawyer."

"I need pickers more than I do a lawyer," Majestyk said, "and they both cost money."

"The deputy says the court will appoint one."

"Maybe. We'll see what happens. But right now, today and tomorrow, the melons are out there, right? And they're not going to wait much longer. You don't get them in we'll lose a crop, two years in a row."

Mendoza was frowning, confused. "How can something like this happen? It doesn't make any sense."

"I don't know," Majestyk said. "If it isn't a drought or a hailstorm it's something else. Skinny little dude comes along thinking he's a big shooter—"

"Bobby Kopas," Mendoza said. "This morning Julio says he saw the guy's car parked at a motel."

"Where?"

"Right here, in Edna. He's still hanging around."

"I can't think about him," Majestyk said. "I would sure like to see him again sometime, but I can't think about him. I do— I'm liable to get it in my head to bust out of here."

Mendoza reached across the table to touch his arm. "Vincent, don't do anything foolish, all right?"

"I'll try not to," Majestyk said.

4

Monday morning, early, they brought Majestyk and four other prisoners out of the jail area to a tank cell, near the back entrance, that was used for drunks and overnighters. There were no bunks in here, only a varnished bench against two of the light green cement block walls, a washbasin, and a toilet without a seat. The fluorescent lights, built into the ceiling and covered with wire mesh, reflected on the benches and waxed tile floor. For a jail the place was clean and bright; that much could be said for it.

The food wasn't too good though. A trusty, with a deputy standing by, slipped the trays in under the barred section of wall, next to the door. Five trays, for Majestyk, two Chicanos, a black guy, and a dark-haired, dude-looking guy in a suit and tinted glasses who hadn't said a word all morning.

One of the Chicanos passed the trays around and went back to sit with the other Chicano, probably a couple of migrants. The black guy was near the corner, where the two benches met. The dark-haired guy looked at his tray and set it on the bench next to him, between where he was sitting low against the wall and where Majestyk sat with his tray on his lap.

Stiff-looking fried eggs and dried-up pork sausage, stale bread, no butter, and lukewarm coffee. Majestyk ate it, cleaned the tray, because he was hungry. But he'd have a word for the deputy when he saw him again. The one with the tattoo. Ask him if they ruined the food on purpose. Christ, it was just as easy to do it right. Where'd they get the idea food had to be stiff and cold?

He looked down at the tray next to him. The guy hadn't touched anything. He sat with his shoulders hunched against the wall, smoking a cigarette. Long dark wavy hair that almost covered his ears and a two-day growth of beard. Striped collar sticking out of the rumpled, expensive-looking dark suit. Shirt open, no tie. No expression on his face behind the lightly tinted wire-frame glasses.

Looking at him, Majestyk said, "You going to eat your sausage?"

The guy drew on his cigarette. He didn't look at Majestyk. He moved his hand to the tray, behind it, and sent it off the bench to hit with a sharp metal clatter, skidding, spilling over the tile floor.

The two Chicanos and the black guy were poised over their trays, eyes raised, but watching only for a moment before looking down again and continuing to eat.

"You're not going to eat it," Majestyk said, "then nobody does, uh?"

The dark-haired guy was lighting a fresh cigarette from the butt of another, the pack still in his hand.

He said, "You want it? Help yourself."

"I guess not," Majestyk said. He looked at the guy as he put the pack of cigarettes in his coat pocket. "You got an extra one of those?"

The guy didn't say anything. He drew on his cigarette and blew the smoke out slowly.

"I'll pay you back when I get out," Majestyk said. "How'll that be?"

The guy turned now to look at him, and another voice said, "Hey, you want a smoke?"

The black guy was holding up a cigarette package that was almost flat.

Majestyk put his tray on the bench and walked over to him. They both took one and Majestyk sat down next to the black guy to get a light.

"Man, don't you know who that is?"

"Some movie star?"

"That's Frank Renda." The black guy kept his voice low, barely moving his mouth.

"He looks like an accordian player," Majestyk said, "used to be on TV."

"Jesus Christ, I said Frank Renda."

"I don't know—I might've heard of him."

"He's in the rackets. Was a hit man. You know what I'm saying to you? He shoots people, with a gun."

"But they caught him, huh?"

"Been trying to for a long time," the black guy said. "Other night this off-duty cop pulls up in front of a bar, some place up on the highway. He sees a man come out. Sees Renda get out of his car, walk up to the man, and bust him five times with a thirty-eight."

"Why didn't the cop shoot him?"

"Didn't have to. Renda's gun's empty."

"He doesn't sound too bright. Pulling a dumb thing like that."

"They say he wanted the man bad, couldn't wait."

Majestyk was studying Renda. Maybe he was dumb, but he looked cool, patient, like somebody who moved slowly, without wasted effort. He didn't look like an accordian player now. He looked like some of the guys he had seen in prison, at Folsom. Mean, confident, hard-nosed guys who would give you that look no matter what you said to them. Like who the fuck are you? Don't waste my time. How did guys get like that? Always on the muscle.

"They got him this time," the black guy said. "Gonna nail

his ass for ninety-nine years—you ask him is he gonna eat his sausage."

Because of Renda they brought the five prisoners out the back way to the parking area, where the gray county bus and the squad cars were waiting. Get them out quick, without attracting a lot of attention. But a crowd of local people had already gathered, along with the reporters and TV newsmen who had been in Edna the past two days and were ready for them. A cameraman with a shoulder-mounted rig began shooting as soon as the door opened and the deputies began to bring them out in single file, the two Chicanos first, startled by the camera and the people watching, then the black guy. They held up Renda and Majestyk in the hallway inside the door, to handcuff them because they were felons. A deputy told them to put their hands behind their backs; but the deputy named Ritchie told him to cuff them in front—it was a long ride, let them sit back and enjoy it.

When Renda appeared, between two deputies, the TV camera held on him, panning with him to the bus, and a newsman tried to get in closer, extending a hand mike.

"Frank, over here. What do you think your chances are? They got a case against you or not?"

Renda held his head low, turned away from the camera. A deputy stuck out his hand, pushing the mike away, and two more deputies moved in quickly, from the steps by the rear door, to stand in the newsman's way and restrain him if they had to. This left Majestyk alone at the top of the steps. He watched them put Renda aboard the bus. Four, five deputies standing now with their backs to him. He watched the newsman with the mike come around and mount the steps. The newsman turned, facing the bus, and the TV camera swung toward him.

Majestyk was close enough to hear him and stood listening as the TV newsman said, "Today, Frank Renda is being taken to the county seat for pretrial examination on a charge that will undoubtedly be first-degree murder. Renda, a familiar name in organized crime, has been arrested nine times without a conviction. Now, it would appear, his luck has finally run out. The prosecutor's office is convinced Renda will stand trial, be convicted of the murder charge, and spend the rest of his life in prison. This is Ron Malone with TV-Action News coming to you from Edna."

Majestyk walked down the steps past the newsman, came up behind the deputies standing by the bus door and said, "Excuse me."

The two deputies nearest him turned, with momentary looks of surprise. One of them took his arm then and said, "Get in there."

He got in, moved past the driver and the deputy standing by him, and took a seat on the left side of the bus, in front of the black guy, who leaned forward as he sat down and said over his shoulder, "You get on TV? Your mama'll be proud to see you."

Renda sat across the aisle, a row ahead of him. The two Chicanos sat together on Renda's side, two rows closer to the front. When the door closed and the bus began to move, circling out of the parking area with a squad car leading and another following, the deputy standing by the driver moved down the aisle to take a seat in the back of the bus. Both he and the driver, Majestyk noticed, were unarmed.

He said to himself, How does that help you? And settled back to stare out the window at the familiar billboards and motels and gas stations, the tacoburger place, the stores that advertised used clothing, *Ropa Usada*. Railroad tracks ran parallel with the highway, beyond a bank of weeds. They passed the warehouses and loading sheds that lined the tracks, platformed old buildings that bore the names of growers and produce companies. They passed the silver water tower that stood against the sky—EDNA, HOME OF THE BRONCOS—and moved out into miles of fences and flat green fields, until the irrigation ditches ended and the subdued land turned color, reverted to its original state, and became desert country.

Looking out at the land he wondered when he would be coming back. When, or if he would be coming back. He said to himself, What are you doing here? How did it happen? Sitting handcuffed in a prison bus. His fields miles behind him. Going to stand trial again. The chance of going to prison again. Could that happen? No, he said to himself, refusing to believe it. He could not let it happen, because he could not live in a prison again, ever. He couldn't think about it without the feeling of panic coming over him, the feeling of being suffocated, caged, enclosed by iron bars and cement walls and not able to get out. He remembered reading about a man exploring a cave, hundreds of feet underground, who had crawled into a seam in the rocks and had got wedged there, because of his equipment and was unable to move foward or backward or reach the equipment with his hands to free it. Majestyk had stopped reading and closed the magazine, because he knew the man had died there.

Prison was for men like Frank Renda—sitting across the aisle with his own thoughts, slouched low in his seat, staring straight ahead, off somewhere in his mind. What was he thinking about?

What difference did it make? Majestyk forgot about Frank Renda and did not look at him again until almost a half hour later, when the land outside the bus had changed again, submitting to signs and gas stations and motels, and the empty highway became a busy street that was taking them through a run-down industrial area on the outskirts of the city.

He noticed Renda because Renda was sitting up straighter now, stretching to see ahead, through the windshield, then turning to look out the windows as the bus moved along in the steady flow of traffic. The man had seemed half asleep before. Now he was alert, as though he was looking for a particular store or building, a man looking for an address written on a piece of paper. Or maybe he had lived around here at one time and it was like revisiting the old neighborhood, seeing what had changed. That was the feeling Majestyk had. He was curious about Renda again and continued to watch him and glance off to follow his gaze. Through the windshield now—to see the intersection they were approaching, the green light and the man standing in the middle of the street, caught between the flows of traffic.

MR. MAJESTYK

Later, he remembered noticing the man moments before it happened. Maybe ten seconds before—seeing the man in bib overalls holding a paper bag by the neck, a farmer who'd come to town for a bottle of whiskey, guy from the sticks who didn't know how to cross a busy street and got trapped. He remembered thinking that and remembered, vividly, the man in bib overalls waiting for the lead squad car to pass him and then starting across the street, weaving slightly, walking directly into the path of the bus.

There was a screeching sound as the driver slammed on the brakes and the tires grabbed the hot pavement. Majestyk was thrown forward against the seat in front of him, but pushed himself up quickly to see if the man had been hit. No, because the driver was yelling at him. "Goddamn drunk—get out of the way!"

He saw the man's head and shoulders then, past the hood of the bus, the man grinning at the driver.

"Will you get the hell out of the way!"

The deputy who'd been in the rear was coming up the aisle, past Majestyk, and the driver was standing now, leaning on the steering wheel.

The man in the overalls, whose name was Eugene Lundy, was still grinning as he took a .44 Colt magnum out of the paper bag, extended it over the front of the hood, and fired five times, five holes blossoming on the windshield as the driver hit against his seat and went out of it and the deputy was slammed backward down the aisle and hit the floor where Majestyk was standing.

Lundy drew a .45 automatic out of his overalls, turned and fired four times at the squad car that had come to a stop across the intersection. Then he was moving—as the doors of the squad car swung open—past the front of the bus and down the cross street.

Harold Ritchie knocked his hat off getting out of the lead squad car, swinging out of there fast and drawing his big Colt special. He put it on Lundy, tracking with him, and yelled out for him to halt, concentrating, when he heard his partner call his name.

461

"Ritch!"

And he looked up to see the panel truck coming like crazy on the wrong side of the street, swerving around from behind the bus to take a sweeping right at the intersection. Ritchie jumped back out of the way, though the truck had room to spare. He saw one of the rear doors open and the bottle with the lighted rag for a wick come flying out and he was moving to the right, running hard, waving an oncoming car to keep back when the bottle smashed against the rear deck of the squad car and burst into flames. Five seconds later the gas tank exploded and instantly the entire car was on fire, inside and out.

Ritchie was across the street now, waving at the traffic, yelling at cars to stop where they were. He didn't see his partner or know where he was. From this angle he could see the second squad car close behind the bus and the driver-side door swing open.

In the same moment he saw the station wagon coming up fast from behind. He saw the shotgun muzzles poke out through the side windows and heard them and saw them go off as the station wagon swerved in, sheared the door off the squad car, and kept coming, beginning a sweeping right turn around the bus.

Ritchie raised his big Colt special, steadying it beneath the grip with his left hand and squeezed off four shots into the station wagon's windshield. The first two would have been enough, because they hit the driver in the face and the wagon was already out of control, half through the turn when the driver slumped over the wheel and the wagon slammed squarely into the burning squad car.

One of the men in the back seat of the wagon tried to get out the left side and Ritchie shot him before he cleared the doorway. But then he had to reload and the two who went out the other side of the wagon made it to a line of parked cars before Ritchie could put his Colt on them. He still didn't know where his partner was until he got to the station wagon, looked out past the rear end of it and saw his partner lying in the street.

Watching from the bus, Majestyk recognized Ritchie, the

one with the tattoo who looked like a pro lineman. He was aiming and firing at two men crouched behind a parked car— until one of them raised up, let go with a shotgun and they took off, running up the street past a line of storefronts. Ritchie stepped out from behind the station wagon, fired two shots that shattered two plate-glass windows, then lowered his Colt and started after them, waving his arm again, yelling at the people on the sidewalk and pressed close to the buildings to get inside, to get the hell off the street.

Now there were no police in front of the bus.

The moment Renda moved, Majestyk's gaze was on him, following him up the aisle past the two Chicanos huddled low in their seat. He watched Renda—who did not bother to look at the dead driver lying on the floor—reach past the steering wheel and pull a control level. The door opened. Renda approached it cautiously, looking through the opening and down the cross street a half block to where Eugene Lundy and the panel truck were waiting. He seemed about to step out, then twisted away from the opening, dropping to his hands and knees, as two shots drilled through the pane of glass in the door panel.

Majestyk's gaze came away and he looked down at the deputy lying in the aisle. He was sure the man was dead, but he got out of his seat and reached down to feel for a pulse. Nothing. God, no, the man had been shot through the chest. Majestyk was about to rise, then hesitated as he saw the ring of keys hanging from the deputy's belt. He told himself to do it, *now*, and think about it later if he had to. That's what he did, unhooked the ring and slipped the keys into his pants pocket. As he rose, turning toward the rear of the bus, he saw the black guy, only a few feet away, staring at him.

Neither of them spoke. The black guy looked away and Majestyk moved down the aisle to the back windows.

The second squad car was close behind, directly below him. He could see the deputy behind the wheel, his face bloody, talking excitedly into the radio mike. The next moment he was out of the car with his revolver drawn, moving around the back end of it to the sidewalk. Majestyk watched him. The deputy ran in between two cars that were facing out of a used car lot, then down behind the row of gleaming cars with prices painted on the windshields to where his partner was covering the door of the bus from behind the end car in the line.

Majestyk made his way back up the aisle in a crouch, watching the used car lot through the right-side windows. He saw both deputies raise their revolvers and fire.

With the closely spaced reports Renda dropped again away from the door and behind the first row of seats.

Halfway up the aisle Majestyk watched him.

Renda was looking at the two Chicanos now who were also crouched in the aisle, close to each other with their shoulders hunched.

After a moment Renda said, "Come on, let's go. We're getting out of here."

When they realized he was speaking to them the two Chicanos looked at him wide-eyed, frightened to death, and Renda said again, "Come on, move!"

One of the Chicanos said, "We don't want to go nowhere."

"Jesus, you think we're going to talk it over? I said we're going." Renda was reaching for them now, pulling the first one to his feet, then the other one, pushing them past him in the narrow aisleway.

The other Chicano said, "Man, I was drunk driving—I don't run away from that."

And the Chicano who had spoken before was saying, as he was pushed to the front, "Listen, please, they see us coming out they start shooting!"

"That's what we're going to find out," Renda said.

He crowded them, jamming them in the doorway, then put a foot behind the second man—as the man said, "Please, don't! We don't want to go!"—pushed hard and the two Chicanos were out of the bus, stumbling, getting to their feet, starting to make a run or it.

Majestyk watched the two deputies in the used car lot swing their revolvers over to cover them and was sure they were going to fire. But now the two Chicanos were running toward them with their hands raised high in the air, screaming, "Don't shoot! Please! Don't shoot!" And the deputies lowered their revolvers and waved them into the used car lot.

Renda was watching, crouched by the open door as Majestyk came the rest of the way up the aisle.

"Go out there, you give yourself up or get shot," Majestyk said.

Renda looked over his shoulder at him. He watched Majestyk step over the dead driver and slip into the seat, lean against the steering wheel and reach with both hands to turn on the ignition.

"What're you doing?"

Majestyk didn't answer him. He put the bus in gear, began to ease it forward a few feet, then braked and shifted into reverse.

The two deputies in the used car lot saw it happen. They moved the two Chicanos out of the way and returned their attention to the bus—in time to see it start up abruptly in reverse and smash its high rear end into the grille of their squad car. The bus moved forward—God almighty—went into reverse and again slammed into the car, cranked its wheels and made a U-turn out of there, leaving the radiator of the squad car spewing water and the two deputies watching it pick up speed, back the way they had come. They wanted to shoot. They were ready, but at the last moment had to hold their fire because of the people in cars and on the sidewalk, on the other side of the street.

Then the two city police cars were approaching the intersection from the south—off to the left—their sirens wailing, and the two deputies ran out to the sidewalk, waving their arms to flag the cars down.

Majestyk heard the sirens, the sound growing fainter, somewhere behind them. He headed west on the street they had taken into town, turned north on a side street, then west again a few blocks up. Finally he slowed down and eased the bus into an alley, behind a row of cinder-block industrial buildings that appeared deserted. He pulled the lever to open the door and looked around at the black guy.

"Here's your stop."

"Man," the black guy said, "you know where you going? If they don't shoot you?"

Renda was in the aisle, moving toward the black guy. "Come on, Sambo, move it. And take them with you."

Majestyk helped the black guy lift the bodies of the driver and the deputy and ease them out through the narrow doorway. Renda told them to hurry up, for Christ sake, but Majestyk paid no attention to him.

As he got behind the wheel again the black guy, standing outside, said, "Man, what did you do?"

Majestyk looked at him. For a moment he seemed about to say something, then closed the door in the black guy's face and took off down the alley.

Move out fast and try to get to high country before the police set up road blocks and got their helicopters out. That's what he had to do. Keep to the back roads, working north, get far enough away from the highway and find some good cover.

That's what he did. Found an old sagging feed barn sitting out by itself on a dried-up section of pasture land, pulled the bus inside, and swung the double doors shut to enclose them in dim silence.

Majestyk remained by the crack of vertical light that showed between the doors, looking out in the direction they had come, seeing the dust settling in the sun glare.

Somewhere behind him in the gloom Renda said, "You move, don't you? I figured you for some kind of a local clown, but you move."

Majestyk didn't say anything.

"What'd they bust you for?"

"Assault."

"With what?"

"A shotgun."

"Assault, shit, that's attempted murder. They were going to jam you the same as me."

"Maybe," Majestyk said.

"Maybe? What do you think you're going to do about it?"

"I got an idea might work."

"Listen," Renda said, "we get to a phone we're out of the country before morning. Drive to Mexico, get some passports, we're gone."

His back still to Renda, Majestyk pulled the deputy's keys out of his pocket. He'd almost forgotten about them, hurrying to get out of there, maybe hurrying too fast and not thinking clearly. He would have to slow down a little. Not waste time, but make sure he wasn't doing anything dumb. He listened to Renda as he began to study the keys and select one that would fit his handcuffs.

"I got friends," Renda was saying, "as you noticed, huh? It was set up in a hurry and they blew it. All right, I call some more friends. They get us out of the country, someplace no extradition, and wait and see what happens. I got enough to live on, I mean high, the rest of my life. It won't be home, shit no, but it won't be in the fucking slam either. I couldn't make that. Couple of weeks I'd be sawing my fucking wrists." He paused. "What're you doing?"

Majestyk didn't say anything and Renda came over to him, his face brightening as he saw the keys.

"Jesus, it keeps getting better. You not only move, you think. Give me those, hold your hands up." As he tried the keys in Majestyk's handcuffs he said, "Figure if you take a long chance, get me out of there, it'd be worth something, huh? Okay, you do something for me, I do something for you. Maybe fix it so you can go with me."

Renda snapped the handcuffs open. As Majestyk slipped them off Renda handed him the keys and raised his own hands to be unlocked.

"How's that sound?"

"I think you got it ass-backwards," Majestyk said, returning the keys to his pocket. "I'm not going with you, you're going with me."

He found an old hackamore that did the job. Looping it around the link of the handcuffs, he could pull Renda along by the length of rope, yank on it when Renda resisted, held back, and the cuffs would dig into his hands.

Leaving the feed barn, hauled out into the sunlight, Renda put up a fight, yelling what the fuck was going on, calling him a crazy insane son of a bitch. So he belted Renda, gave him a good one right in the mouth that quieted him down, and brought him along. But, God, he didn't like the look in the man's eyes. The man wanted to kill him and would probably try. So his idea had better turn out to be a good one and come off without any hitches.

All afternoon and into the evening he led Renda by the hackamore, forcing him to keep up as they moved through the brush country, following dry washes and arroyos that gradually began to climb, reaching toward the high slopes. Majestyk, in his work clothes and heavy work boots, had little trouble; he seemed at home here. He seemed to know what he was doing, where he was going. Renda, in his tailored suit and thin-soled shoes, stumbled along, falling sometimes, getting his sweat-stained face and clothes caked with dust. Majestyk judged the man's endurance and let him rest when he felt he was near the end of it. Then would pull him to his feet again and they would continue on, through brush and pinyon thickets, climbing, angling across high slopes and open meadows.

He brought Renda more than ten miles this way, up into the mountains, and at dusk when they reached the cabin—a crude one-room structure that was part timber and part adobe—he had the feeling Renda would not have gone another ten yards.

"We're home," Majestyk said.

Renda looked at the place with a dull, lifeless expression. "Where are we?"

"Place I use sometime. Mostly in hunting season."

Inside, he found a kitchen match on a shelf, feeling for it in the dark, and lighted a kerosene lamp that hung from the overhead.

"We got coffee and canned milk. Probably find some soup or some beans. I haven't been up here since spring."

Renda was looking around the room, at the two metal bunks with bare mattresses, the wooden table and two chairs, the cupboard with open shelves that showed a few cans and cobwebs, but were nearly empty. Renda went to the nearest bunk and sat down. Majestyk followed him over, taking the keys from his pocket.

"Hold up your hands."

The man sure looked worn out. Renda raised his arms slowly, too tired to move. But as soon as Majestyk freed one of his hands, Renda came off the bunk, pushing, chopping at Majestyk with hard jabs. It took him by surprise, Renda's fists stinging his face, and he had to back off and set himself before he could go after Renda, jabbing, feinting, then slamming in a hard right that stunned him and dropped him to the bunk. Majestyk put a knee on him and got him handcuffed to the metal frame before he could move again.

It took something out of him. Majestyk had to sit down on the other bunk and rest, get his breath.

There was a silence until Renda said, "All right. What do you call this game?"

Majestyk looked over at him. "You'll find out."

"Tomorrow night," Renda said quietly, "we could be in L.A. Stay at a place I know, get some broads in, booze, anything you want to eat or drink, get some new clothes. A couple days later we're in Mexico. Get a boat, some more broads. I mean like you never seen before. Cruise around, anything you want, it's on the house. You ever have it like that? Anything you want?"

"I been to L.A." Majestyk said. "I been to Mexico and I been laid."

"Okay, what do you want?"

"I want to get a melon crop in. That's what I want to do." Renda gave him a puzzled look and he added, "I grow melons."

"Hire your work done."

"I hope to. But I got to be there."

"I'll tell you something," Renda said, taking his time. "I've killed seven men with a gun, one with a crowbar, and another guy I threw off a roof. Five stories. Some people I didn't kill but I had it done. Like I can have it done for you, even if I get put away and they let you off. Any way you look at it, you're dead. Unless we go out of here together. Or, we make a deal."

"What kind of deal?"

"Put a price on it. You take the cuffs off, I walk away. What's it cost?" Renda watched him closely. "If you think it's going to be hot out there, all right, you'll have dough, you can go anywhere you want." He paused. "Or if you feel like taking a chance, turn yourself in, you can tell them I got away. Serve some time, come out, the dough's waiting. How much?" He paused again. "You don't know what your price is, do you? Afraid you might be low. All right, I'll tell you what it is. Twenty-five."

"Twenty-five what?"

"Twenty-five thousand dollars."

It was Majestyk's turn to pause. "How would we work it? I mean how would I get the money?"

"You call a Phoenix number," Renda said. "Say you got a message for Wiley. You say where you want the money delivered and where I can be picked up. It's all you have to do."

Majestyk seemed to be thinking about it. He said, "Twenty-five thousand, huh?"

"Tax free."

"Could you go any higher than that?"

Renda grinned. "Getting greedy now. Like what's another five or ten."

"I just wondered."

"Twenty-five," Renda said. "That's your price. A nice round number. Buy yourself a tractor, a new pair of overalls. Put the rest away for your retirement." He waited a moment. "Well, what do you think?"

"You say I call somebody named Wiley," Majestyk said. "What's the number?"

5

The Papago Trading Post was a highway novelty store in the desert, about three miles below and east of the hunting cabin. Big red-painted signs on and around the place advertised AUTHENTIC INDIAN SOUVENIRS . . . ARROWHEADS . . . MOCCASINS . . . HOMEMADE CANDY and ICE COLD BEER. There was a Coca-Cola sign, an Olympia sign, and a Coors sign.

Majestyk came down from the cabin about nine in the morning and approached the store from about three hundred yards up the highway, reading the signs and listening for the sounds of oncoming cars. Nobody passed him. He reached the store and went inside.

Beyond the counters displaying the trinkets and souvenirs, the Indian dolls and blankets, and sayings carved on varnished pieces of wood—like, *"There's only one thing money can't buy.*

Poverty"—he saw the owner of the place sitting at a counter that was marble and looked like a soda fountain. The man was about sixty, frail-looking with yellowish gray hair. He was having a beer, drinking it from the can.

Approaching him Majestyk said, "I got a flat tire a couple of miles back. No spare."

"That's a shame," the owner said.

"I wonder if I could use your phone. Call a friend of mine."

"Where's he live?"

"Down at Edna."

"That's two bits call Edna."

Majestyk watched him raise the wet-glistening beer can to his mouth.

"I don't have a spare. The truth is, I don't have any money on me."

"Have to trust you then, won't I?"

Majestyk smiled at him. "You trust me for a can of that too?"

When he got his Coors, a sixteen-ounce can, he took it over to the wall phone with him, looked up a number in the Edna directory, and dialed it. He kept his back to the man at the counter. When a voice came on he said, quietly, "I believe you have a Lieutenant McAllen there? . . . Let me speak to him, please."

He waited, looking over at the counter where the owner of the place was watching him, then turned his back to the man and hunched over the phone again.

"This is Vincent Majestyk. You remember we met a few days ago?" He paused, interrupted, then said, "No, I'm downtown in a hotel. Where do you think I am? Listen, why don't you let me talk for a minute, all right?" But he was interrupted again. "Listen to me, will you? I got Frank Renda . . . I said I got him. . . . You want to listen or you want me to hang up? . . . Okay, I got Renda and you got an assault charge against me. Drop it, tear it up, kick it under the rug, and I'll give you Frank Renda."

With the loud sounds coming from the receiver he held the phone away from him, covered the speaker with his hand, and looked over at the owner of the place.

"He's sore cause I took him away from his breakfast." He turned and put the phone to his ear again, waiting to break in.

"Yeah, well nothing's free in this world," Majestyk said finally. "You want him, that's the deal. . . . No, I'll deliver him. You come here you're liable to say you found us. But I bring him in it's me doing it and nobody else. . . . Yeah. Yeah, well it's nice doing business with you too."

He hung up, took a sip of beer, but didn't move away from the phone. "Put another call on there, okay?" he said to the store owner. "Phoenix. And maybe a couple more beers, to go."

He finished dialing, waited, and as he turned to the wall said, "I got a message for somebody named Wiley. You understand? All right, get a pencil and piece of paper and write down what I tell you."

It was a little after twelve, the sun directly above them, when the sports car appeared on the county road. They had been waiting since eleven-thirty, partway up the slope that was covered with stands of pinyon pine. In that time this was the first car they had seen.

"That's it," Renda said. He started to rise, awkwardly, still handcuffed.

Majestyk motioned to him. "Keep down." He watched the sports car, a white Jaguar XK, go by raising a trail of dust on the gravel road, finally reaching a point where it passed from sight beyond the trees.

"That's the *car*," Renda said.

Majestyk continued to watch the road, saying nothing until the car appeared again, coming slowly from the other direction.

"All right, let's go."

By the time they reached the road the Jaguar was approaching them and came to an abrupt stop. An attractive young girl with short blond hair and big round sunglasses got out and stood looking at them over the open door.

Majestyk stared, taken by surprise. He hadn't expected a girl. The possibility had never entered his mind.

"Who's that?"

"That's Wiley," Renda said. He started toward the car and called to the girl, "You got the money?"

"I already gave it to him," the girl said. "God, Frank, you're a mess."

"What do you mean you gave it to him? Come on, for Christ sake, where's the money?"

She was frowning as she raised the sunglasses and placed them on her head. "I was told to stop at the store on the highway and pay the man three dollars and eighty-five cents, and that's what I did. It's the only money I was told to bring."

Renda turned to Majestyk, who was walking toward the Jaguar now, looking at it closely.

"What are you pulling? What kind of shit are you *pulling!* We made a deal—twenty-five grand!"

"It doesn't look like you'd fit in the trunk," Majestyk said. "So I guess maybe you better drive, Frank. Keep your hands on something. Wiley can squeeze in behind the seats." He looked at Renda then. "You can get in by yourself, or I can help you in. Either way."

"I must have missed something," Wiley said. "Is it all right if I ask where we're going?"

Majestyk gave her a pleasant smile. "To jail, honey. Where'd you think?"

Wiley was three years out of Northwestern University, drama school; two years out of Universal City, a little television; one year out of a Las Vegas show-bar, topless; and six months into Frank Renda.

Until recently she had been amazed that life with him could be so—not boring, really—uneventful. Living with a real-life man who killed people had sounded like the trip to end all trips. It turned out to be mostly lying around swimming pools while he talked on the phone. Frank was fun to watch. He was a natural actor and didn't know it. He played roles constantly, from cool dude to spoiled child, and looked at himself in the mirror a lot, like almost every actor she had ever known. It was interesting watching him. Still, it was getting to be something of a drag until, four days ago, when she fingered the guy in the bar for him. No, it wasn't exactly a finger job. What she did was sit at the bar, keeping an eye on the guy. When it looked like he was getting ready to pay his check, she got up and walked out of the place, letting Frank know the guy was coming, giving him a minute or so to get ready. She didn't know what Frank had against the guy; she didn't ask him. This was real-life drama. She stood off to the side and watched Frank calmly shoot the guy five times. Wow. From about ten feet away. The guy was a great dier. It was really a show, cinéma vérité. Until the cop came from out of nowhere and jammed his gun into Frank's back. She got out of there, took a cab back to her apartment and waited, the next four days, close to the phone.

More true-life adventure now, scrunched behind the bucket seats of an XK Jag, driving down a back-country dirt road, her handcuffed boyfriend with both hands on the top arc of the steering wheel, and a solemn-faced, farmer-looking guy staring at him, watching every move he made.

"Left when you get to the blacktop," Majestyk said. "That'll take us to the highway."

Renda braked. As he began to turn onto the county road he lost his grip and had to grab the steering wheel and crank it hard to keep from going into the ditch. Wiley was thrown hard against the back of Majestyk's seat. He glanced around as she straightened up, holding onto the seat.

"Hey, are you trying to put me through the windshield?"

Renda's eyes raised to the rearview mirror and the reflection of Wiley's face. Their eyes met briefly before he shifted his gaze to the road again. Perhaps a minute passed before he glanced at Majestyk.

"All right, you got a new game. What's it cost?"

"Three dollars and eighty-five cents," Majestyk said. "You paid and you're in."

"Come on, cut the bullshit. How much you want?"

"Nothing."

"I explained it as simply as I could," Renda said. "We make a deal or you're dead. I get sent away, you're still dead."

"I've already made a deal."

ELMORE LEONARD

Renda glanced at him again. "You think the cops can keep
you alive? They'd have to live with you the rest of your life.
Can you see that? Never knowing when it's going to happen?"

When Majestyk didn't answer, Wiley said, "He's kind of
weird, isn't he?"

Renda's eyes raised to the rearview mirror and met Wiley's
gaze.

When he looked at the road he saw the curve approaching,
waited, started into the curve and braked sharply to reduce his
speed. Again Wiley was thrown against Majestyk's seat.

"Hey Frank, take it easy, okay?"

He glanced at her reflection. She was ready.

Coming out of the curve and hitting the straightaway, Renda
accelerated to almost seventy, held it for a quarter of a mile,
then raised his right foot and mashed it down on the brake
pedal.

Wiley already had her hand on the latch to release the backrest of Majestyk's seat. It was free as the car braked suddenly
and she threw herself hard against it, her weight and the momentum slamming Majestyk into the dashboard.

"Frank, under the seat!" She screamed it.

"Get it, for Christ sake!"

Renda was accelerating with his left foot, bringing his right
foot up and over the transmission hump to kick viciously at
Majestyk, jammed between the seat and the dashboard, as
Wiley reached beneath the driver's seat, groped frantically, and
came up with a Colt .45 automatic in her left hand.

"Shoot him! Shoot the son of a bitch, will you!"

"I don't know how!"

"Pull the fucking trigger!"

Majestyk pushed against the seat back, lunging at Wiley.
Renda hit the brakes again, bouncing Majestyk off the dashboard. But he was able to push off from it, twisting around
enough to get a hand on the girl's arm just as she fired and the
automatic exploded less than a foot from his head.

Renda was kicking at him again. "Christ, shoot him!"

He kicked at Majestyk's ribs, got his heel in hard a couple of
times, kicked again and this time his heel hit Majestyk's belt

buckle, slipped off and hit the door handle as Wiley pulled his arm free and put the automatic in Majestyk's face. The door opened and she saw him going out, fired, saw his expression and fired twice again, saw the window of the swung-open door shatter, but he was gone, out of the car, and she knew she hadn't hit him.

The XK Jag was two hundred feet up the road before its brake lights flashed on. The car made a tight turn, backed up on the narrow blacktop, and turned again to come back this way.

Majestyk heard the sound of the engine. He was lying face-down on the shoulder of the road, propped on his elbows, dazed, staring at gravel and feeling it cutting into the palms of his hands. His vision was blurred and when he wiped his eyes saw blood on the back of his hand. He heard the engine sound louder, winding up, coming toward him. When he raised his head he saw the headlights and the grille, low to the ground, the nose swinging toward the gravel shoulder, coming directly at him.

With all of his strength he threw himself to the side, rolling into the ditch, as the Jag swept past. A moment later he heard the tires squealing on the blacktop and knew he had to get out of here, pushing himself up now, out of the weeds, climbing the bank away from the road and ducking through the wire fence, as the Jag made its tight turn and came back and this time stopped.

Majestyk was running across the open scrub, weaving through the dusty brush clumps, by the time Renda got out of the car and began firing at him with the automatic, both hands extended in the handcuffs. Majestyk kept running. Renda jumped across the ditch, got to the fence, and laid the .45 on the top of a post, aimed, and squeezed the trigger three times, but the figure out in the scrub was too small now and it would have to be a lucky shot to bring him down. He fired once more and the automatic clicked empty.

Seventy, eighty, yards away, Majestyk finally came to a stop, worn out, getting his breath. He turned to look at the man standing by the fence post and, for a while, they stared at one another, each knowing who the other man was and what he felt and not having to say anything. Renda crossed the ditch to the Jag and Majestyk watched it drive away.

It seemed easier to get out of jail than it was to get back in.

He got a ride in a feed truck as far as Junction, after walking a couple of miles, then sitting down to rest and waiting almost an hour in the sun. When the driver asked what'd happened to him he said he'd blown a tire and gone off the road and was thrown out when his pickup went into the ditch. The driver said he was lucky he wasn't killed and Majestyk agreed.

At Junction he went into the Enco station and asked the attendant, the one named Gil, for the key to the Men's Room. The attendant gave it to him without saying anything, though he had a little smile on his face looking at Majestyk's dirty, beat-up condition. In the Men's Room he saw what a mess he was: blood and dirt caked on his face, his shirt torn up the back, his hands raw-looking with imbedded gravel.

It was four-thirty that afternoon when he walked into the Edna Post of the County Sheriff's Department and asked the deputy behind the desk if Lieutenant McAllen was around. The deputy, ignoring his face, asked him what it was he wanted to see the lieutenant about.

"I want to go to jail," Majestyk said.

He waited on the bench thinking, Christ, trying to get back in. He was still sitting on the bench twenty minutes later when McAllen walked up to him and stood there, not saying anything.

"I had him," Majestyk said.

"Did you?"

"I guess you want to hear what happened."

"I think I can see," McAllen said.

6

Getting Renda to Mexico was no problem. A young guy who brought reefer in two or three times a month flew him down in his Cessna, landing on a desert airstrip not far from Hermosillo. Renda spent two nights in a motel while the rest of it was being worked out. On the morning of the third day an Olds 98 with California plates and a house trailer attached—with Eugene Lundy behind the wheel and Wiley curled on the back seat reading a current best-selling novel—pulled up in front of the motel. Renda, wearing work clothes and a week's growth of beard, walked out of his room and got in the trailer. The Olds took off and didn't stop again until they were on the coast road south of Guaymas and Lundy thought maybe Frank would want to get out and stretch his legs, exercise a little, breathe in the salt air, and throw a couple of stones at the Gulf of California. Wiley said to him, "You don't know Frank very well, do you?"

He didn't come out of the trailer or bother to look up when the door opened. He was sitting in back on one of the bunks, smoking a cigarette.

Wiley said, "Hey, do you love it? I think it's great."

Behind her, Lundy said, "Air-conditioned, you got plenty of vodka, scotch, steaks, and beer in the ice box and"—he took an envelope out of his pocket and handed it to Renda—"twenty-five hundred cigarette money."

Wiley was opening cabinets and doors. "There's a shower in the john. Even a magazine rack."

"Tonight we'll be in Mazatlan," Lundy said. "We can stay there or go on down to Acapulco, it's up to you."

Renda looked up at him. "Regular vacation. You having a nice time?"

"Listen, I think I could use a rest. That stunt, hitting the fucking bus, that took some years off me."

Renda watched him turn to the refrigerator and take out a can of beer.

"Where is he?"

"You want one?"

"I said where is he!"

Lundy, about to pop open the can, looked over at Renda. "The guy? He turned himself in. Last I heard they're still holding him at Edna."

Wiley came in to stretch out on the opposite bunk. "Kind of tight fit, but all the comforts of home."

"We're not at home," Renda said. "He is."

"He's in jail, Frank." Wiley's tone was soft, approaching him carefully. "You're free. We can go anywhere you want."

"There's only one thing I want," Renda said. "Him."

Lundy opened the can and took a swig. "He gets out, we can have somebody take care of that."

Renda shook his head. "Not somebody. I said *I* want him. I want him to see it and know it's me. Put the gun in his stomach and look at him. Not say anything, just look at him and make sure he understands."

"You still have to wait," Lundy said.

Renda didn't say anything. He was still picturing it, putting the gun in the melon grower's stomach.

"All right, let me ask you," Lundy said. "What do you do, walk in the jail, ask them for a visitor's pass? How do you get close to the guy?"

"You get him out of jail."

"You get him out. How?"

"Find the guy he hit," Renda said. "Tell him to drop the complaint. It was all a mistake, a misunderstanding."

"What if the guy doesn't want to drop it?"

"Jesus, I said *tell* him, not ask him."

"Maybe pay him something?"

"That's up to you. See what it takes."

"You mean you want me to do it? Go back there?"

"I'm talking to you, aren't I?"

"I just wanted to be sure."

"You're going to go back and set it up," Renda said. "Find the guy made the complaint and get that done. Get some people if you see we need them. Call me, I come up. We go in and get out fast. No bullshit screwing around. Arrange it, I walk up to him, and it's done."

Lundy took a sip of beer, getting the right words ready in his mind. "I keep thinking though, what about the cops? They'll be looking for you, watching your house, the apartment."

"Christ, you think I'm going to go home? We'll stay someplace else. Call Harry, tell him to arrange it."

"I mean right now, why take a chance?"

"I told you why."

"I'm not against it," Lundy said. "I'm just thinking, we're this far. Why change your mind all of a sudden?"

"I didn't change it. I hadn't made it up yet. But the more I think about it—I know it's what I'm going to do."

"I was going to lie on the beach," Wiley said, "and read my book."

Lundy waited a moment. "You know, Frank, there's a lot of guys'd do it. I mean guys the cops aren't waiting to flag."

Renda said, "Hey, Gene, one more time. I said I want him. I

never wanted anybody so bad and I'm going to do it strictly as a favor to myself. You understand? Am I getting through to you? *I'm* going to do it, not somebody else. Before I take any trips or lay on any beach I'm going to walk up to that melon grower son of a bitch, I'm going to look him in the eyes, and I'm going to kill him."

Harold Ritchie was a pallbearer at his partner's funeral. Bob Almont, good guy to ride with in a squad car, and god*damn* he'd miss him. Shot down in the street by some creepy son of a bitch. Ritchie hoped it was the one he'd shot coming out of the station wagon. He went to Bob Almont's house after the funeral, with Bob's close friends and a few relatives that'd come from Oklahoma. They sat around drinking coffee and picking at the casserole dishes some neighbors had brought over, while Evelyn Almont stayed in the kitchen most of the time or sat with her two little tiny kids who didn't know what the hell was going on. After a couple of hours of watching that, it was a relief to get back to the post.

The deputy at the counter tore off a teletype sheet and handed it to him. "What you asked for. Just come in."

He read it as he walked over to Lieutenant McAllen's office, knocked twice, and walked in. McAllen was sitting at his desk.

"You're right," Ritchie said, "Phoenix had a sheet on him. Robert L. Kopas, a.k.a. Bobby Kopas, Bobby Curtis. Two arrests, B and E, and extortion. One conviction. Served two years in Florence."

"I could feel it," McAllen said. "The guy's up to something."

"Changed his mind and dropped the charge. The way I read it," Ritchie said, "he's decided it'd be more fun to get back at the guy himself."

"Maybe. But is he smart enough? Or dumb enough to try it? However you want to look at it." McAllen paused. "Or did somebody put him up to it?"

Ritchie was nodding. "That's a thought."

"Yes, it is, isn't it?" McAllen said. "You got any more on Majestyk?"

"On my desk. I'll be right back." Ritchie went out and returned within the minute with an open file folder in his hands, looking at it.

"Not much. He lived in California most of his life. High school education. Truck driver, farm laborer. Owned his own place till he went to Folsom on the assault conviction. Here's something. In the army three years, a Ranger instructor at Fort Benning."

McAllen raised his eyebrows. "An instructor."

"Combat adviser in Laos before that," Ritchie went on. "Captured by the Pathet Lao, escaped and brought three enemy prisoners with him. Got a Silver Star." Looking up at McAllen he said, "Man doesn't fool, does he?"

"Well, he's a different cut than what we usually get."

"Doesn't seem afraid to take chances."

"Doesn't appear to." McAllen was thoughtful a moment. "Let's talk to him and find out."

He said to Majestyk, "You look better than the last time I saw you."

"Thank you, but I'd just as soon wear my own clothes." He was dressed in jail denims with white stripes down the sides of the pants. The scrapes and cuts on his face were healing and he was clean-shaven. "What I'd like to know which nobody'll tell me, is when I'm going to court."

"Why don't you have a seat?" McAllen said.

"I've been sitting for four days."

"So you're used to it," McAllen said. "Sit down."

He watched Majestyk take the chair then picked up a pack of cigarettes and matches and leaned over to hand them across the desk.

"Have a smoke."

As Majestyk lighted a cigarette, McAllen said, "I guess what you want most is to get out of here."

He waited, but Majestyk, looking at him, said nothing. "Well, I think it might be arranged."

Majestyk continued to wait, not giving McAllen any help.

"The guy you hit, Bobby Kopas?" McAllen said finally. "He dropped the charge against you."

When Majestyk still waited, McAllen said, "You hear what I said?"

"Why'd he do that?"

"He said he thought it over. It wasn't important enough for him to waste a lot of time in court. You think that's the reason?"

"I met him once," Majestyk said. "I can't say I know him or what's in his head."

"He's got a record. Extortion, breaking and entering. Does that tell you anything?"

"You say it, I believe it."

"I'm saying he could have a reason of his own to see you walking around free."

"Well, whatever his reason is, I'll go along with it," Majestyk said. "If it means getting my crop in."

"You can stay if you want," McAllen said.

"Why would I want to?"

"Because Frank Renda's also walking around free."

Majestyk saw him waiting for his reaction and he said, "Why don't you just tell me what you're going to anyway, without all the suspense."

McAllen looked over at Ritchie and back again. He said, "The eyeball witness who saw Frank Renda commit murder was an off-duty police officer."

"I heard that."

"He was a member of this department."

Majestyk waited.

"He was killed during Renda's escape. Shot dead. So there's no witness. The gun Renda used—is alleged to have used—can't be traced to him. That means there's no case."

"If you want him so bad," Majestyk said, "why don't you arrest him for the escape?"

"Because there's no way to tie him in with the attempt. His lawyer made that clear and the prosecutor had to agree. Technically—and tell me how you like this?—he was kidnapped. We can stick you with that if we want. Or let you go. Or, we can hold you in protective custody."

"Protective custody against what?"

"Frank Renda. What do you think he's going to do when he finds out you're on the street?"

"I don't know. What?"

"He might've already found out. Though right now we don't know where he is or what he's doing."

Majestyk took a drag on the cigarette and let the smoke out slowly. "Are you trying to tell me my life's in danger?"

"You should know him by now. What do you think?"

"Why would he risk getting arrested again? I mean just to get me."

"Because it's his business. Now you've given him a personal reason to kill," McAllen said. "And I can't think of anything that would stop him trying."

"You're that sure."

"He might even think it would be easy. Get careless again, like he did the last time."

"Something's finally starting to get through," Majestyk said. "You'll let me go if I'll sit home and act as your bait."

"Something like that."

"Maybe even you'd like him to shoot me, so you can get him for murder."

"That entered my mind," McAllen said, "but we'll settle for attempted."

"Attempted, huh? And if he pulls it off, you try something else then?"

"I believe you're the guy who wanted to make a deal," McAllen said, "so you could get your melons picked. All right, go pick them."

"And where'll you be?"

"We'll be around."

"He could send somebody else."

"He could." McAllen nodded. "Or he could wait a few months, or a year. Shoot you some night while you're sleeping. Or wire your truck with dynamite. One morning you get in and turn the key—" McAllen paused. "No, you're right, we don't know for certain he'll try for you himself, just as we can't guarantee we'll be able to stop him if he does. It's a chancy situation any way you look at it. But remember, you got yourself into it. So, as things stand, it's the best offer I can make."

"Well then"—Majestyk got up from the chair, stubbing out the cigarette—"I guess there's no reason for me to hang around, is there?"

7

It was still cool at 6:00 A.M., the vines were wet and darkened the pants legs of the pickers as they worked along the rows with their burlap sacks. Somebody said it was insecticide, the wetness, but most of them knew the fields had not been sprayed in several days and that moisture had settled during the night. Their pants and the vines would be hot and dusty dry within an hour. The sun, which they would have all day, faced them from the eastern boundary of the fields, above a tangle of willows that lined an arroyo five miles away. The sun seemed that close to them.

Larry Mendoza stood by the pickup truck counting the stooped, round figures in the rows. He had counted them before, but he counted them again and got the same number. Twelve, including Nancy Chavez and the ones from Yuma—

thank God for them. But he wasn't going to get any crop in with twelve people. Some of them had never picked before—like the two Anglo kids he'd been able to get because nobody else wanted them.

He saw one of them stretching in his white T-shirt, rolling his shoulders to work the ache out of his back, and Mendoza yelled at him, "Hey, how you going to pick melons standing up!"

He crossed the ditch and went out into the field, toward the white T-shirt that said *Bronco Athletic Dept.* and had a small numeral on it, 22, in a square.

"I was seeing how much I had in the sack," the white Anglo kid said.

"Fill it," Larry Mendoza told him. "That's how much you put in. Then you stand up."

"I'm getting used to it already."

A colored guy he had hired that morning, who was working the next row, was watching them. Mendoza said to him, "You need something? You want some help or something?"

The colored guy didn't answer; he turned and stooped over and went back to work. At least the colored guy had picked before, not melons, but he had picked and knew what he was doing. The Anglo kid, with his muscular arms and shoulders and cut-off pants and tennis shoes—like he was out here on his vacation—couldn't pick his nose.

"This one"—Mendoza took a honeydew from the Anglo kid's sack—"it's not ready. Remember I told you, you pick the *ripe ones.* You loosen the other ones in the dirt. You don't turn them so the sun hits the underneath, you just loosen them."

"That's what I been doing," the Anglo kid said.

"The ones aren't ready, we come back for later on."

"I thought it was ripe." The Anglo kid stooped to lay the melon among the vine leaves.

Larry Mendoza closed his eyes and opened them and adjusted the funneled brim of his straw hat. "You going to put it back on the vine? Tie it on? You pick it, it stays picked. You got to keep it then. You understand?"

"Sure," the Anglo kid said.

Sure. How do you find them? Mendoza asked himself, turning from the kid who might last the day but would never be
back tomorrow. Walking to the road his gaze stopped on another big-shouldered, blond-haired Bronco from Edna and
yelled at him, "Hey, whitey, where are you, in church? Get off
your knees or go home, I get somebody else!" Christ, he wasn't
paying them a buck forty an hour to rest. He yelled at the guy
again, "You hear me? I'll get somebody else!"

"Like it's easy," Nancy Chavez said. She was going over to
the trailer with a full sack of melons hanging from her shoulder. Pretty girl, thin but strong-looking, with a dark bandana
and little pearl earrings.

"I may have to go to Mexico," Mendoza said. "Christ, nobody wants to work anymore. And some of the ones I got don't
know how."

"Teach them," the girl said. "Somebody had to teach you."

"Yeah, when I was eight years old." He went over to the
pickup truck and got in. "Now I got to tell Vincent. He don't
have enough to worry about."

"Tell him we'll get it done," the girl said. "Somehow."

Majestyk came out through the screen door of his house to
wait on the porch. When he saw the pickup coming he walked
out to the road. Larry Mendoza moved over and Majestyk got
in behind the wheel.

"How'd you sleep?"

"Too long."

"Man, you need it."

Majestyk swung the pickup around in a tight turn. When
they were heading back toward the field that was being
worked, on their right now, Mendoza said, "I try again this
morning, same thing. Nobody wants to work for us. I talk to
Julio Tamaz, some of the others. What's going on? What is this
shit? Julio says man, I don't have a crew for you, that's all."

"He can get all he wants," Majestyk said.

"I know it. He turn some away, says they're no good. I hire
them and find out he's right."

As they approached the trailer, standing by itself on the side
of the road, Mendoza saw the girl with the dark bandana and

pearl earrings coming out of the field again with a sack of melons. He glanced at Majestyk and saw him watching her.

"That one," Mendoza said, "Nancy Chavez. She wasn't here, we wouldn't have any good workers at all. She got some more friends drove over from Yuma. She picks better than two men. But we got to have a full crew, soon, or we never get it done."

Mendoza got out by the trailer. He slammed the door and said through the window, "I hope you have better luck than me."

"Least I'll find out what's going on," Majestyk said. He could see the girl by the trailer, unloading her melon sack. That was something, she was still here. She didn't know him or owe him anything, but she was still here.

Harold Ritchie was leaning over the fender of the State Highway Department pickup truck, holding a pair of binoculars to his eyes. He was looking across the highway and across a section of melon field to where the dust column was following Majestyk's yellow truck all the way up the side road.

"It could be him this time," Ritchie said. "Hang on."

He was speaking to another deputy who was sitting inside a tool shed by a police-frequency two-way radio. It was hotter than hell inside and the door was open so he could get some air. The shed hadn't been built for people to sit in, but it was the best they could do. Besides the shed, there was a mobile generator, a tar pot, some grading equipment, a pile of gravel, a portable toilet that looked like a rounded phone booth without windows, wooden barricades and lanterns and a sign that said ROAD CONSTRUCTION 500 FT., though nothing was going on. The only ones here were Ritchie and the deputy operating the radio, both of them in work clothes.

"Yeah, it's him," Ritchie said now, lowering the glasses and watching Majestyk's pickup come out of the side road without stopping and swing onto the highway. "Jesus Christ, I could arrest him for that," Ritchie said. "Tell them he just drove out in his truck, yellow four-wheel-drive pickup, heading toward Edna. I'm getting on him right now."

Ritchie slid behind the wheel of the State Highway Department truck and took off after him.

Majestyk parked across the highway from the blue school bus and the stake truck and the old junk cars the migrants would return to later in the day. In the stillness he could hear the juke box out on the street. Tammy Wynette, with a twangy Nashville backup, telling about some boy she loved who was in love with somebody else.

Majestyk followed the sound of the music to the café-bar and had the screen door open when the State Highway Department truck slowed down at the Junction intersection and came coasting by. He gave the truck a little wave before he went inside.

A waitress was serving Julio Tamaz and another Chicano labor contractor their breakfast. They were sitting at a table, the only customers in the place. Another woman, wearing a stained white apron, was sweeping the floor, moving chairs around, banging them against the formica tables. The two men didn't look up as Majestyk approached them. They were busy with the salt and pepper and pouring sugar and cream. Julio was dousing his fried eggs dark brown with Lee & Perrins.

"Julio?"

He looked up then, with a surprised expression he had prepared as Majestyk walked over.

"Hey, Vincent. They let you out, huh? Good."

Majestyk pulled a chair out but didn't sit down. He stood with his hand on it, as though he had changed his mind.

"How come I can't hire a crew?"

"Man, you been away, in jail."

"Larry Mendoza hasn't. Last two mornings you turned him down. How come?"

"It's the time of the year. I got too much business." He poked at the eggs with his fork, yellow appearing, mixing with the brown. "Other people need crews too. They ask me first."

"All right," Majestyk said, "I'm asking you right now for thirty people tomorrow morning. Buck forty."

Julio kept busy with his eggs and didn't look up. "I got

crews signed more than a week. Vincent, you too late, that's all."

Majestyk watched him begin to eat his eggs before turning his attention to the other man at the table. He was already finishing, wiping the yolk from his plate with a piece of toast.

"How about you?" Majestyk said. "You get me a crew?"

"Me?" With the same helpless tone as Julio's. "Maybe in ten days," the labor contractor said. "I can't promise you nothing right now."

"In ten days my crop will be ruined."

"Like Julio says, other people ask first. We can't help that."

"What is this, stick-up time? You want more money? What?"

"It's not money, Vincent." Julio's tone was sad as well as helpless. "How can we get you people if we don't have any?"

Majestyk pulled the chair out a little farther. This time he sat down and leaned over the edge of the table on his arms.

He said quietly, "Julio, what's going on?"

"I tole you. I got too much work."

"You'd drive to Mexico if you had to. Come on, somebody pay you, threaten you? What?"

"Listen," Julio said, intently now, his voice lower, "I got to work for a living and I can't do it in no goddamn hospital. You understand?"

"I'm beginning to. You could help me though."

"I'm not going to say any more. Man, I've said enough."

Majestyk stared at him a moment. Finally he said, "Okay," got up and walked away from the table.

Julio called after him, "Vincent, next season, uh?"

That contractor at the table with him, eating his piece of toast, said, "If he's still around."

Coming out of the place into the sunlight he was aware of the State Highway Department truck parked across the street and the deputy sitting in the cab, watching him. Tell him you're going back home, Majestyk was thinking. Put his mind at ease. He started for the street, through the space between the back of the school bus and the stake truck, when the voice stopped him.

"You looking for a crew?"

He saw Bobby Kopas then, leaning against a car with his arms folded, a familiar pose, a tight lavender shirt; sunglasses and bandit moustache hiding a thin, bony face. The car, an Olds 98, was at the curb in front of the school bus. Someone else was inside, a big-shouldered man, behind the wheel.

"You want pickers, maybe I can get you some wine heads," Kopas said. He straightened, unfolding his arms, as Majestyk walked over to him. "You touch me, man, you're back in jail by lunchtime."

Majestyk stared at him, standing there close enough to touch. All he had to do was grab the front of that pretty shirt and belt him. It would be easy and it would be pure pleasure. But the deputy was across the street and Majestyk didn't have to look over to know he was watching them. He wondered if Kopas knew the man in the State Highway Department truck was a cop.

"You dropped the complaint," Majestyk said. "Why? You want to try and pay me back yourself?"

"I do you a favor—Jesus, after you like to broke my nose, you think I'm pulling something." Kopas gave him the hint of a grin. "Man, I'm being a good neighbor, that's all."

"What'd you say to Julio Tamaz and the other contractors? You pay them off or threaten them? How'd you work it?"

The little grin was still there. "Man, I hope nobody's telling stories on me, giving me a bad name."

"They didn't say it was you. I'm saying it."

"Why would I do a thing like that?"

"So I'll lose my crop."

"I think you must be a little mixed up," Kopas said. "Don't know where your head's at. Here you are standing in deep shit and you're worried about a little dinky melon crop."

"You've been talking to somebody," Majestyk said.

"Who's that?" Kopas said, giving him the grin.

"I can fix it you'd have a hard time smiling again."

Kopas tensed and the grin vanished. "Listen, I'm not kidding. You even make a fist, man, you're back in jail."

"Are you working for him?"

"Who's that?"

"He get you to drop the complaint?"

"I think I'm tired of talking to you," Kopas said. He moved to the car door and opened it, then looked back at Majestyk.

"I'll tell you one thing though. Somebody's going to set your ass on fire. And I'm going to be there to see it."

The Olds started off as Kopas got in and slammed the door.

Majestyk caught a glimpse of the driver's profile—looking at Kopas, saying something—and for a moment he thought he knew the man or had seen him before. But the car was moving away and it was too late to get another look at him and be sure. Big shoulders, curly hair. Maybe he was one of the guys who had been with Kopas a week ago, the day it began. Or a different one. The car was different.

What difference did it make? He had enough people to think about without bringing in new ones. Faces to remember. Frank Renda's. Telling him he was going to kill him. Now Kopas and Renda. The man had already started to make his move. He didn't waste time. He found Kopas and hired him. That was plain enough. Now they were beginning to play a game with him. Let him know they were coming. Give him something to keep him awake nights. He thought of telling the deputy in the State Highway Department truck. Get him after them, quick, before they turned off the highway somewhere. Maybe they would lead him to Renda.

But Renda didn't have any reason to hide. He was free.

And what does the cop do, arrest them? For what?

No, whatever's going to happen is going to happen, Majestyk thought. So go home and pick your melons.

8

"I'm not shittin' you," Kopas said. "I was thinking of dropping the complaint anyway, so I could take care of the son of a bitch myself."

Eugene Lundy wasn't listening to him. He was staring straight ahead, over the hood of the Olds 98, at the vacant land of dust-green mesquite and sun glare and bugs rising with the airstream and exploding in yellow bursts against the windshield. Like somebody was spitting them there.

"Load up the pump gun and wait for him," Kopas said. "Or stick it in his window some night. See him sittin' on the toilet. *Bam.* Scatter the motherfucker all over the room."

Lundy was counting the bug stains, more than a dozen of the yellow ones: some kind of bug flying along having a nice time and the next thing sucked into the wind, coming up fast over the hood and wiped out, the bug not knowing what in the name of Christ happened to him. Maybe they had been butter-flies. Seeing the bugs suddenly, there wasn't time to tell what they were.

"I got to piss," Kopas said.

Lundy looked at the speedometer and up again. He was holding between seventy and seventy-five down the country road that rose and dropped through the desert, seeing no other cars, no people, not even signs.

"Man, I'm in pain," Kopas said. "All you got to do is stop the car."

"We're almost there," Lundy said. "I'm not going to stop twice."

"How long you think it's going to take me, an hour? All I want to do is take a piss."

"Hold it," Lundy said.

Maybe they were all different kinds of bugs, but all bugs were yellow inside. Like all people were red inside. Maybe. Lundy had never thought about it before. His gaze held on the stained windshield as he waited for a bug to come up over the hood.

He felt so good his eyes were watering, and kept going like he was never going to stop. Jesus, what a relief. Son of a bitch Lundy made him hold it twenty minutes, refusing to stop the car. He'd finally pleaded with him, Christ, just slow down, he'd piss out the window, but the son of a bitch wouldn't even do that. A very cold son of a bitch who didn't say much, sitting on two pieces under his seat, a Colt .45 automatic and a big fucking Colt .44 mag. He had asked the guy if he had been in on the bus job and the guy had looked at him and said, "The bus job. Is that what you call it?" And that was all he'd said.

Bobby Kopas zipped up his fly and walked around to the front of the Olds where Lundy was standing, squinting up at the sky.

"Hurry up and wait," Kopas said. "I never seen a plane come in on time in my life. Not even the airlines, not once I ever went out to the airport. Everybody sitting around waiting.

Go in the cocktail lounge you're smashed by the time the fucking plane arrives. You ever seen a plane come in on time?"

Staring at the sky and the flat strip of desert beyond the road, Lundy said, "Why don't you shut your mouth for a while?"

Christ, you couldn't even talk to the guy. Kopas moved around with his hands in his pockets, kicking a few stones, looking around for some shade, which there wasn't a bit of anywhere, squinting in the hot glare, squinting even with his wraparound sunglasses on. The glasses made him sweat and he had to keep wiping his eyes. Lundy stood there not moving, like the heat didn't bother him at all. Big, heavy son of a bitch who should've been lathered with sweat by now, like a horse.

They heard the plane before they saw it, the faraway droning sound, then a dot in the sky coming in low, the sun flashing on its windshield. The Cessna passed over them at about a hundred feet. As it banked, descending, coming around in a wide circle, Lundy finally spoke. He said, "Wait here," and walked out into the desert.

Kopas was excited now. He wanted to appear cool and make a good impression. He put his hands on his hipbones and cocked one leg, pointing the toe of the boot out a little. Like a gunfighter. So the guy was big time. He'd act cool, savvy, show the guy he wasn't all that impressed.

He watched the plane come to a stop about a hundred yards away. Lundy, going out to meet it, was holding up his arm, waving at the plane. Big jerk.

Renda came out first and then the girl—white slacks and a bright green blouse. Even at this distance she looked good. Blond, nice slim figure. Now they were coming this way and Lundy was talking to them, gesturing, probably telling Renda how the murder charge against him had been dropped. Renda wouldn't have known about it, though the pilot might have told him. As the plane started its engine to take off, the prop wash blew sand at them and they hunched their shoulders and turned away from the stinging blast of air. Lundy was talking again. Renda stopped and they all stopped. Renda was saying something.

Then Lundy was talking again. As they came up to the road Kopas heard Lundy say, "You could have rode up here bare-ass on a white horse, nobody would've stopped you."

"What about the bus thing?" the girl asked him.

She was something. Maybe the best-looking girl Bobby Kopas had ever seen.

"There's nothing they can stick you with," Lundy said. "The bus, nothing. They tried to, naturally. There're three cops involved and they don't like that one bit. But what're they going to stick you with? You didn't shoot the cops. You didn't take the bus. The guy did, Majestyk. But they don't even jam him for that. You see what I'm getting at?"

Kopas had never heard Lundy talk so much.

The good-looking girl said, "God, nothing like a little dumb luck."

"Luck, bullshit," Renda said. "Timing. Make it happen. And never run till you see you're being chased."

"With a fast lawyer available at all times," the girl said. She didn't seem to be afraid of him.

"They had to let him go," Renda said. "I could see that right away, the cops coming up with this great idea. Don't stick him with the bus, no, let him go so I'll show up and try for him."

"That's the question," Lundy said. "What're the cops doing?"

"No, the question is what's the guy doing? Is he sitting still for it or what?"

"He's around," Lundy said. "We just saw him."

Kopas stepped out of the way as they approached the Olds. He set a grin on his face and said, "Probably home by now waiting on you, Mr. Renda."

Renda looked at him. Christ, with the coldest look he'd ever gotten from a person. Like he was a thing or wasn't even there. Christ, he'd been arrested, he'd been in the can. He wasn't some lightweight who didn't know what he was doing.

He said, "Mr. Renda? I wonder if I could ask you a favor." Renda was looking at him again. "I know it's your party, but—after you finish the son of a bitch—you mind if I put a couple of slugs in him?"

Renda said to Lundy, "Who's this asshole?"

"Bobby Kopas. Boy Majestyk hit."

"You pay him to drop it?"

"Five hundred."

"Then what's he doing here?"

"He's working for us," Lundy said, "to see nobody works for Majestyk. So there won't be a crowd hanging around there. He knows the guy's place, back roads, ways in and out. I thought he might come in handy."

Kopas thought he could add to that. He said, "I been watching that Polack melon picker since they let him out. He doesn't fart that I don't know about it."

The girl said, probably to Lundy, "Is he for real?"

Kopas wasn't sure what she meant. He kept his eyes on Renda, who was staring at him, and tried not to look away.

"You're telling me you know him pretty well?" Renda asked.

"I know he's a stuck-up son of a bitch. Got a two-bit farm and thinks he's a big grower."

"How long's he lived here?"

Kopas grinned. "Not much longer I guess, huh?"

"I ask you a question," Renda said, "you don't seem to want to answer it."

Jesus, that look again. "Well, I'm not sure how long exactly he's been here. Couple years, I guess. I just got into this labor business recently, when I seen there was money in it."

"Show me where he lives," Renda said.

"Yes sir, any time you say."

"Right now."

"Frank," Lundy said, "your lawyer got the house, it's all set. Up in the mountains, nobody can bother you or know you're there. I thought maybe you'd want to go up to the house first, you know, take it easy for a while."

Renda said, "Gene, did I come here to take it easy? I could be home, not at some place in the mountains. But I'm not home."

"I know you're anxious," Lundy began.

"Gene, I want to see the guy's place," Renda said. "I want to see it right now."

* * *

The two Anglo kids in the white T-shirts quit at noon and Mendoza paid them off. That left nine. So Majestyk went out in the field and picked melons all the rest of the day with Nancy Chavez and her friends from Yuma. Maybe next year he could stand around and watch, or sit in an office like a big melon grower. Sit on the porch and drink iced tea. That would be nice.

He wasn't used to this. He could feel the soreness in his back, and each time he reached the end of a row it would take him a little longer to straighten up. All day, dirty and sweaty and thirsty—drinking the lukewarm water in the canvas bag. Tomorrow he'd get a tub of ice and some pop, cover it with a piece of burlap. He'd forgotten how difficult and painful stooped labor was. Around 5:30, after eleven hours of it, the pickers began to straggle out of the field and unload their last melon sacks at the trailer parked on the road.

Majestyk was finishing a row, finally, when Nancy Chavez crossed through the vines and came toward him, a full sack hanging from her shoulder.

She said, "I've been watching you. For a grower you're pretty good."

"Lady, I've picked way more'n I've ever grown." He got up with an effort, trying not to show it, and the girl smiled at him. As they moved off toward the trailer, where Mendoza and two of his small sons were emptying the sacks and stacking the melons, Majestyk said, "I meant to ask if you ever sorted."

"All the time. It's what I do best."

"Maybe you could start things going in the packing shed tomorrow. If you'd like to."

"Whatever you say."

"We ever get it done, I'd like to pay everybody something extra."

"You worried we won't take it?"

"I just want you to know I appreciate your staying here and all."

"Don't mention it. You're paying, aren't you?"

"Are the quarters all right? They haven't been used in a while. Couple of years at least."

"They're okay," the girl said. "We've lived in worse."

They were approaching the trailer and he wanted to say something to her before they reached it and Mendoza might hear him.

"You want to have supper with me?"

She turned her head to look at him. "Where, your house? Just the two of us, all alone?"

"We can go down the highway you want. I don't care."

They were at the trailer now. She handed up her sack to Mendoza before looking at Majestyk again.

"For a man needs a job done, where do you get all this free time? You want to pack melons, why don't we start?"

"You mean tonight?"

"Why not?"

"They'd keep working?"

"For money. You make it when you can." She said then, "If you don't want to ask them, I'll do it. We'll eat, then go to the packing shed and work another half shift. All right?"

"Lady," Majestyk said, "you swing that I'll marry you and give you a home."

She seemed to be considering it, her expression serious, solemn, before saying, "How about if I settle for a cold beer after work?"

"All you want."

"Maybe a couple."

She gave him a nice look and walked away, up the road toward the migrant quarters. Both Majestyk and Mendoza, on the trailer, stood watching her.

Mendoza said, "You like a piece of that, huh?" He looked down at Majestyk's deadpan expression and added quickly, "Hey, I don't mean nothing. Take it easy."

Majestyk handed him his sack. "You hear what she said? They'll start packing tonight."

Mendoza emptied the sack and came down off the trailer while his sons stacked the melons. "You must live right," he said. "Or maybe it's time you had some good luck for a change." He nodded toward the migrant quarters, fishing a cigarette out of his shirt pocket. "Those people, they're twice as good as what Julio brings up. Good people. They work hard because they like you. They don't want to see you lose a crop."

"I don't know," Majestyk said. "Maybe we can do it."

"We'll do it, Vincent. Don't get anybody else mad at you, we'll do it."

"We're coming to it now," Kopas said, over his shoulder. "On the right there. That's his packing shed."

Renda and Wiley were in the back seat. Lundy was driving, slowing down now as they approached the yellow building with MAJESTYK BRAND MELONS painted on the side.

"See," Kopas said. "Puts his name up as big as he can get it. Down the end of that road we're coming to his house. Way down, where you see the trees."

Renda was studying the road, then hunching forward to look across the field at the road, at the trailer and the figures in the road and the three old cars parked in front of the migrant living quarters.

He sat back again. "You said nobody was working for him."

"No crews," Kopas said. "He picked up a few migrants, that's all."

"They're people, aren't they?"

"Some claim they are. I don't." Christ, he knew right away he shouldn't have said it. It slipped out, talking smart again and not answering his question direct. He waited, looking straight ahead, knowing it was coming. But Renda didn't say anything for a moment, not until they were passing the sign that said ROAD CONSTRUCTION 500 FT., passing the barricades and equipment, the portable toilet and the State Highway Department pickup truck.

He said then, "Go up to the next road and turn around."

Lundy's eyes raised to the rearview mirror. "You want another look at his layout? That's all there is, what you saw."

"Gene," Renda said, "turn the fucking car around."

They had to go up about a mile to do it. Coming back, approaching the road repair site again, Renda said, "How long's that been there?"

Kopas wasn't sure what he meant at first and had to twist around to see where he was looking.

"That road stuff? I don't know, a few days."

"How long!" Renda's voice drilled into the back of his head and Kopas kept staring at the barricades and equipment as they approached, trying to remember, trying to recall quickly how many days.

"They been there as long as I been watching his place. I'm sure of that."

Now they were even with the site, going past it. Kopas was looking out the side window and saw the guy in khaki work clothes getting into the pickup truck. It was a close look at a face he'd seen somewhere before, but only a quick glimpse, and he was turning to look back when Renda's voice hit him in the head again.

"It's *cops!* Jesus, don't you know a cop when you see one!"

Kopas was turned, trying to see the guy, but it was too late. Looking past Renda, trying not to meet his eyes, he said, "You sure? I thought if there was any cops around I'd recognize them."

And he remembered as he said it and turned back around to stare at the windshield. Christ yes, the guy was a deputy. He'd seen him in Edna, at the station. He'd seen him in the pickup earlier today, across the street, when he was talking to Majestyk.

Kopas gave himself a little time, trying to relax and sound natural, before he said, "Well, I figure after a while they get tired waiting, they'll pick up and leave."

Nobody said anything.

"Then we can run off those Mexicans he's got. No sweat to that."

There was a silence again before Renda said, "Pull over."

Lundy looked up. "What?"

"Pull over, for Christ sake, and stop the car."

Lundy braked, bringing the Olds to a gradual stop on the shoulder of the road. They sat in silence, waiting for Renda.

"Hey, asshole. Get out of the car."

"Me?"

Kopas turned enough to look over his shoulder. Renda was staring the way he had stared before—as if not even seeing him—and he knew the man wasn't going to say anything.

503

"What did you want me to do?"

"Get out," Lundy said. "That's all you have to do."

Kopas grinned. "Is this a joke or something?"

Nobody was laughing. The girl had a book open and was reading, not even paying any attention.

Kopas said to Lundy, "I mean I left my car in Edna, where you picked me up. That's a six-mile hike just back to Junction."

Lundy didn't say anything.

Kopas waited another moment before he got out and turned to the car to close the door. He saw the window next to Renda lower without a sound.

"Come here," Renda said.

Kopas hunched over to look in the window. The girl was still reading the book.

"You hear me all right?"

"Yes, sir, fine."

"The way you come on," Renda said, "I don't like it. I don't know you a half hour you start talking shit out the side of your mouth. I say I don't want anybody working for him, he's got a dozen people living there. The cops set up a fucking grandstand to watch the show, you don't know they're cops. What I'm saying, I don't see you're doing me a lot of good."

"Mr. Renda, I been watching, seeing he doesn't run off."

"I'll tell you what," Renda said. "You go home, maybe we'll see you, maybe not. But listen, if it happens don't ever talk shit to me again, okay? Don't ever tell me what I'm going to do."

"I sure didn't mean anything like that, Mr. Renda."

But that was the end of it and he knew it. The window went up, the Olds drove off and Bobby Kopas was left standing there, six miles from Edna, feeling like a dumb shit who'd blown his chance.

9

Renda's lawyer was a senior partner in a firm that represented a number of businessmen and business organizations who shared related or complementary interests. Renda's lawyer looked out for his clients, helping them any way he could, and liked to see them help one another, too. For example, he had a client, a mortage broker, who was spending twelve months in the Federal Penitentiary at Lewisburg for willfully conspiring to defraud the United States government. All right, the mortgage broker had a hunting lodge–weekend funhouse up in the mountains that he wasn't using. Frank Renda, he was informed, wanted some solitude, a place to rest where no one would bother him. So Renda's lawyer arranged for Frank to lease the place from the mortgage broker for only six hundred dollars a week.

That was all right with the lawyer, Frank wanting a place in the mountains. But it wasn't all right if he was going to sit up there on his ass worrying about a 160-acre melon grower when he should be attending to his commercial affairs: his restaurant linen service, his laundry and dry cleaning supply company, his modeling service, and his string of massage parlors. That's where the money was to be made; not in shooting people.

The lawyer knew Frank Renda very well—his moods, his inclinations—so he knew it was sometimes hard to get through to him, once he had made up his mind. He began calling Frank at the mortgage broker's hunting lodge an hour after the Cessna was scheduled to drop him in the desert. There was no answer at the place until late afternoon, and then he had to wait another ten minutes before Renda came to the phone.

Wiley handed it to him, the phone and a scotch, and went over to a bearskin couch where her reading glasses and her novel were waiting.

Renda stood looking around the room, at the Navajo blankets and mounted heads of antelope and mule deer, the shellacked beams and big wagon-wheel chandelier, antique guns and branding irons. Christ, western shit all over the place. He had never met the mortgage broker friend of his lawyer, but he could picture the guy now: little Jewboy with a cowboy hat, string tie and high-heeled boots, and horn-rimmed glasses and a big fucking cigar.

He said into the phone, "Yeah."

His lawyer's calm, unhurried voice came on. "How are you, Frank? How was the trip?"

"Great, and the weather's great if it doesn't rain or snow. Come on, Harry, what do you want?"

"You like the place all right?"

"It looks like a fucking dude ranch."

"I called a few times this afternoon." The tone was still calm, unhurried. "Where've you been?"

"On the can," Renda said. "I come here to get away, I'm in the fucking place ten minutes and the phone starts ringing."

"I'm not going to bother you," the lawyer said. "I want to let you know how the situation stands."

"I thought I was clear."

"You are at the moment. Technically you're free on a five-thousand-dollar bond, pending your appearance at an investigation in ten days. It's a formality, something to inconvenience us. Though there is the possibility they'll try to dream up a lesser charge."

"No they won't," Renda said. "They don't want to touch me unless it's for the big one."

"I'm glad you understand that," the lawyer said. "So you know this is not the time to do anything"—he paused—"that would bring you under suspicion. Frank, they want you very badly."

"What else is new?"

"You must also have figured out why they released the melon grower."

Renda didn't say anything.

"All right," the lawyer said, "then let me mention that you have business matters that need your attention."

"Anything I was doing can wait."

"And you have business associates," the lawyer went on, "who may not feel like waiting. It's been my experience that the general reaction is one of impatience with anyone who puts his personal affairs ahead of the . . . common good, if you will."

"I've got something to do," Renda said. "I think they understand that. If they don't, tough shit."

"All right, you're saying you're going to do what you want," the lawyer said. "I want it on record that I'm advising you to wait—"

"You got your machine on?"

"Getting every word. As I was saying, I want it on record that I'm advising you to wait. I'm suggesting that any dealings you might have with the melon grower would be extremely ill-timed."

"Harry," Renda said, "don't fuck with me, okay? I need you, I'll call you."

He hung up.

Wiley rested her book on her lap and looked over the top of her reading glasses.

"What did he want?"

"The usual shit. Lawyers, they talk and talk, they don't say anything."

"I'll bet he told you not to do anything hasty," Wiley said. He didn't answer. She watched him sit down with his scotch and take a drink, sipping it, thinking about something.

She tried again. "After all, you pay him for his advice."

He looked over at her. "And you know what I pay you for. So why don't you shut the fuck up?"

"You don't pay me."

"It's the same thing."

She was starting to annoy him. Not too much yet, but she was starting. He had dumped a wife who had bored the shit out of him, talking all the time, buying clothes and showing them to him, and now he had a girl who was a college graduate drama major, very bright, who read dirty books. Books she thought were dirty. He said to himself, Where are you? What the fuck are you doing?

Five years ago it had been better, simpler. Get a name, do a study on the guy, learn his habits, walk up to him at the right time, and pull the trigger. It was done. Take a vacation, wait for a call, and come back. L.A., Vegas, wherever they wanted him. Now it was business all the time. The boring meetings, discussions, planning, all the fucking papers to sign and talking on the phone. Phones all over the place. He used to have one phone. It would ring, he'd say hello, and a voice would give him the name. That was it. He didn't even have to say good-bye. Now he had six phones in his house, four in the apartment. He took Librium and Demerol and Maalox and even smoked reefer sometimes, which he had never done before in his life or trusted anybody who did. A hundred and fifty grand plus a year to talk on the phone and sign the papers. He used to take a contract for five grand and had got as much as ten when it was tricky or the guy had a name.

That's what he missed. The planning and then pulling the trigger, being very steady, with no wasted motions. Then lying around after, drinking all the scotch he wanted for a while and thinking about how he'd pulled the trigger. He was good then. During the last few days he had caught himself wondering if he was still good and would be good enough to hit the melon grower clean. He hadn't hit the guy coming out of the bar very clean and that was probably why it was on his mind. He hadn't hit anybody in a while and had taken the job because he missed the action and had talked them into letting him hit the guy, who wasn't anybody at all to speak of. But he had been too *up*, too anxious to pull the trigger and experience the feeling again, and he hadn't blueprinted the job the way he should have. Christ, an off-duty cop sitting there watching. Empty the gun like a fucking cowboy and not have any left for the cop. Or not looking around enough beforehand. Not noticing the cop. Like it was his first time or like his fucking brains were in his socks. They could be wondering about him right now. What's the matter with him? Can't he pull a simple hit anymore?

No, they wouldn't be thinking that. They didn't know enough about it, how you made it work. They'd think it was dumb luck the cop was there and dumb luck the cop was killed and couldn't finger him. So the two canceled each other out and he was okay.

Except somebody had talked to the lawyer and that's why the lawyer had talked to him. It wasn't the lawyer's idea to call—he realized that now without any doubt. The lawyer wouldn't do anything unless he was getting paid to do it or somebody had told him to. Their lawyer, *they*, were telling him not to go after the melon grower. Because they thought he was wasting time or because it might involve them in some way or because they didn't have anything against the guy. The guy had not done anything to the organization. If he had, sure, hit him. They could pay him to do it and he wouldn't think any more about it. That was the difference. He *was* thinking about it and this time they couldn't pay him to hit the guy. He wouldn't take it. That was the thing. He couldn't get the melon grower out of his head he wanted to hit him so bad, and he wasn't sure why. Not because the guy had belted him a couple of times; though that could be reason enough. No, it was the way the guy had looked at him. The way he talked. The way he pulled that cheap cool shit and acted like he couldn't be bought.

How do you explain that to them?

Look, I *want* to hit the guy. I got to. I want him—listen, I never gave a shit about anybody before in my life, anybody I hit. It was never a personal thing before like this one.

Or try this.

Listen, if nobody gives a bunch of shit about this, if you let me hit him, then I'll give you the next one, anybody you want, free.

He said to himself, For Christ sake, you going to ask permission? You want the guy, do it.

And he yelled out, "Gene."

Wiley looked up from her book.

Lundy came in from wherever he had been with a can of Coors in his hand.

Renda said to him, "How many we got?"

Lundy wasn't sure at first what he was talking about, if he meant beers or what. But as he looked at Renda, he understood and said, "You and me for openers. I don't know when we're going, so I don't have anybody here. I thought after we talk about it, you know, see what you got in mind, I make a call and we get whatever we need."

"I think we need a truck," Renda said. "Good-size one. I'm not sure, but just in case we got to haul some people."

Lundy nodded. "Bobby Kopas's got one. Stake truck, open in back."

"All right," Renda said, then immediately shook his head. "No. Shit, I don't want him around. Get the truck tell him you're going to borrow it you'll bring it back, and get . . . four, five guys who know what they're doing."

"For when?"

"Tonight," Renda said. "Let's get it done before the fucking phone starts ringing again."

There was enough light in the packing shed to work by, but it was a dreary, bleak kind of light, like a light in a garage that didn't reach into the corners. A string of 100-watt bulbs, hanging beneath tin shades, extended the length of the conveyor that was bringing the melons in from the dock outside. The sound in the packing shed was the steady hum of the motor that drove the conveyor.

Most of the crew were outside, unloading the trailer. Nancy Chavez and Larry Mendoza's wife, Helen, did the sorting and were good at it, their hands deftly feeling, rolling the melons on the canvas belt, pulling out the ones that were badly bruised or overripe. Majestyk and Larry Mendoza were at the end of the line, packing the melons in cardboard cartons that bore the MAJESTYK BRAND label. Two other men in the crew were stacking the cartons, building a wall of them as high as they could reach.

By the time the trailer was unloaded it was almost ten o'clock. There were still melons on the conveyor, but Majestyk shut it down and said that was enough for one night, more than he'd expected they'd get done.

Mendoza came along the line to where his wife was standing and said, "I don't know, Vincent, but I think we're going to do it."

Nancy said, "If we can keep the grower working instead of goofing off, laying around in jail."

Majestyk was tired, but he felt good. He felt like talking to her and getting to know her. He said, "I remember—it seems to me somebody mentioned having a beer after work."

Nancy looked across the conveyor at him. "You still buying?"

"Sure, I'm going to be rich in about a week." He said to Mendoza, "Larry? How about you and Helen?"

"No, me and mama got more important things to do," Mendoza said, and slapped his wife on the can, making her jump a little and grin at them. "We're going to bed."

Nancy was still looking at Majestyk. "Maybe you'd rather do that." As she saw him begin to smile, she added quickly, "I mean if you're tired."

Majestyk said, "Come on, let's go get a couple of cold ones." He was still smiling at her.

Harold Ritchie watched the headlights of the pickup approaching the highway and said to the deputy over by the tool shed, "Now where in the hell's he going?"

"If it's him," the deputy said.

"I guess I'm going to have to find out, aren't I?"

Ritchie walked over to the State Highway Department truck, grabbed the door handle and looked around again. "'Less you want to this time. You been sittin' all day."

"You can talk plainer than that," the deputy said. "I'm about to go sit again. I think I got me some bad enchiladas or something."

He waited until Ritchie drove off before he went into the tool shed and radioed the Edna Post to let them know what was going on—which would be relayed to Lieutenant McAllen probably sitting home reading the paper or watching TV, a nice, clean, lighted bathroom down the hall from him, empty, nobody even using it.

Walking over to the portable toilet he was thinking, hell, he should've tailed the pickup this time, probably could've stopped at a gas station somewhere, or a bar. Unbuckling his belt, the deputy stepped inside the toilet and closed the door.

Less than a hundred yards east of the construction site three pair of headlights popped on.

The stake truck came first, followed by the two sedans, picking up speed, the truck reaching forty miles an hour by the time it got to the barricades, swerved in and sideswiped the portable toilet, the right front fender glancing off, scraping metal against metal, but the corner of the stake body catching it squarely, mashing into the light metal as it tore the structure from its base, carried it with forward momentum almost to the tool shed before it bounced end over end into the ditch. The stake truck kept going and turned into the road that led to Majestyk's place.

The two sedans, Lundy's Olds 98 and a dark-colored Dodge, came to a stop by the barricades, the Olds bathing the battered toilet in its headlight beams.

Renda and Lundy, and a third man with a machine gun under his arm, got out of the cars and walked into the beam of light. When Lundy got the twisted door of the toilet open, straining to pull it free, the third man aimed his machine gun into the opening. Lundy pushed him aside, reached in with one arm and when he straightened again looked at Renda.

"Dead."

"Must've got hit by a truck," Renda said.

* * *

Pushing open the screen a little, Mendoza could see the stake truck in front of the migrant quarters and hear the low rumble of its engine. Just sitting there. Nobody had got out of the truck. Nobody had come out of the migrant quarters. They were all inside or around someplace close by because their cars were there, the three old junk heaps. When the two pair of headlights came down the road from the highway and passed the migrant quarters, Mendoza moved away from the doorway. He was wearing only his jockey shorts—maybe he should hurry up and put some clothes on. But the cars weren't coming to his place. They kept going.

Behind him his wife whispered, "Who are they? Do you know them?"

He knew. He was pretty sure he knew. But he said to her, "Stay with the children."

When she stepped into the doorway to look out he pulled her back because of the slip she wore as a nightgown. It showed dull white in the moonlight and he was afraid they would see her, even though he knew they were all the way to Vincent's house by now.

She said again, "Who are they?"

"I don't know," Mendoza answered. "But they don't have any business with us and they're not friends I know of. Go to bed."

She lingered, but finally moved away from him. When he heard the springs and knew she was in bed again, he pushed open the screen door carefully and went outside, holding the door to close it, so it wouldn't make noise. On the steps of the porch, looking down the road, he could see the headlights of the two cars in front of Vincent's house. He didn't know if they were waiting or if they had gone inside. He said, God, why don't they leave? He's not there, they can see that, so go on, get out of here. Vincent was with a girl, talking, drinking beer. He could be gone for hours, having a good time; stay out late he could still get up early and work. They didn't know him.

He saw them in the headlights for a moment and faintly heard the car doors slam, then went into the house again as the cars came back this way. He was sure they were going to pass his house, leave, and when the cars turned in—coming straight at his house before stopping close to the porch—he couldn't believe it and began backing away from the screen door, but not soon enough. The headlights were blinding and he knew they could see him. He could hear the engines idling. Some men, three of them, dark shapes were coming up on the porch. When they came into the house he still couldn't see them because of the headlights.

One of them walked past him. He heard his wife's voice. "What do you want?" Frightened. He didn't hear the children.

Renda said, "Where is he?"

Mendoza thought of his wife and three children in the bedrooms, behind him. What was he? A guy standing in his underwear who just got waked up out of a sound sleep. How was he supposed to know what was going on?

He said, "I don't know. You mean Vincent Majestyk? Isn't he at home?"

He had never seen Eugene Lundy before and didn't see his features now, only a big shape that stepped up close to him. The next thing he knew he was hit in the mouth with a fist and felt the wall slam against his back. The man reached for him then and held him against the wall so he wouldn't fall down.

"Where is he?" Renda said again.

"I don't know," Mendoza said. "Believe me, I knew I'd tell you."

"He go into town?"

"I don't know," Mendoza said. "Honest to God, I thought he was home in bed."

Renda waited, knowing he was wasting time. The guy was probably telling the truth. He said, "Bring him along. And his wife."

They brought everybody out of the migrant quarters, pushing them to hurry up, making them stand in front of the place, in underwear or just pants, barefoot, squinting in the glare of the truck's headlights. Mendoza and his wife were pushed into the group by the men with guns in their hands who stood out of the light. The migrants waited, everyone too afraid to speak or ask what was going on.

Finally Lundy, who stood with Renda next to the truck, said to them, "We're looking for the boss. Who wants to tell us where he's at?" Lundy waited, giving them time. In the silence they could hear the crickets in the melon field. "Nobody knows, huh?" Lundy said then. "Nobody heard where he was going or saw him leave?"

Quietly, to Lundy, Renda said, "We got a dead cop and we're running out of time. Get rid of them."

Renda walked off into the darkness, toward the packing shed. He heard Lundy tell them, "You all've got two minutes to get in your cars and drive away from here and never come back." He heard one of the migrants say, a weak little voice with an accent, "We been working, but we haven't been paid yet. How we suppose to get paid?" And he heard Lundy say, "Keep talking, I'm going to start busting some heads. Now you people all get the hell out of here. Now."

The doors of the packing shed were open. Renda went up the steps to the loading dock and looked inside. He could make out the conveyor and the melons on the canvas belt. He was curious about the place—as if the place might be able to tell him something about the man who owned it. Feeling along the wall inside the door, he found the light switch. Outside there was a sound of engines trying to start and finally turning over.

Lundy and the one with the machine gun came in. Renda was staring at the wall of cartons, the melons that had been sorted and packed that evening.

"Man's been busy," Lundy said.

"I said to him what do you want?" Renda continued to stare at the wall of melon cartons and Lundy and the one with the machine gun looked over at him. "He said I want to get my melons in," Renda went on. "That's all he wanted. Get his melons in."

Lundy couldn't believe it when he saw Frank pull out his .45 automatic—Christ almighty—and start firing it at the stacked-up melon cases, firing away, making an awful racket in the place, until his gun was empty.

Renda looked at them then. He seemed calm. His voice was, and said, "What're you waiting for?"

Lundy always did what he was told. It didn't have to make sense. He took out his big magnum and opened up at the cartons. Then the other one with the machine gun let go and the din was louder than before. They tore up the cartons, lacing them with bullet holes. Renda took the machine gun from the guy, turned to the conveyor, and shot up all the melons left on the canvas belt, blew them apart, scattering pieces all over the shed.

Christ, Lundy thought. He hoped Frank felt better now.

Kopas had been told they'd probably drop his truck off later that night, somewhere near the county road intersection west of Edna, where there was that Enco station on the corner and the café. Kopas asked what time. Lundy said, when they got back. But if they had to take some people somewhere—and Kopas had a hunch he meant the migrants—then he wouldn't get his truck back until morning.

But the migrants had cars. They could run them off in their own cars and not have to take them anywhere. So Kopas was pretty sure the truck would be back tonight.

He hung around the café-bar that evening, going outside and looking up the highway every once in a while. Being sure they had gone to Majestyk's place, he was anxious to know if they had killed him. If they hadn't been able to for some reason —and if Renda was with them—he was anxious for Renda to see him again. Renda might decide he was a handy man to have around after all: he was alert, waited, did what he was told.

When Majestyk and the girl arrived, he was in the Men's Room of the café-bar. He came back into the room that was about half full of Chicanos and spotted Majestyk and the girl right away, sitting in a booth along the wall. He didn't see the two deputies at the bar—Ritchie and a deputy who had met him here—didn't notice them because they were in work clothes, and all Kopas was thinking about was getting out of there before Majestyk looked over. He glanced at the booth again as he went out the door—leaving the light and the smoke and the loud country steel-guitar beat inside—and saw Majestyk listening to something the girl was saying, giving her his full attention. Good.

He was more excited now than earlier in the day when he was out in the desert, the plane was taking off, and he was waiting to meet the famous Frank Renda. He saw Majestyk's pickup, parked a short way down from the café. He had a thought and began looking at the other cars, on both sides of the highway, and there it was, the State Highway Department truck. It was parked at the Enco station by the pumps; the station closed for the night.

Kopas started putting things together in his mind. They hadn't gotten Majestyk because Majestyk was inside. Also a cop was in there, or around someplace. He was more anxious now than ever. He went across the highway and across the county road to wait there at the intersection, moving around, wanting them to hurry up and come before the guy left. About fifteen minutes passed. He was so anxious for them to come that, when he saw the three pair of headlights approaching, he knew it was them and couldn't be anyone else. The thing now was he had to act cool and hold down his excitement.

Lundy, slowing down for the intersection, saw the figure on the corner. He recognized the shirt, bright in the headlights, and the sunglasses and the curled-brim Texas hat. He said to Renda, next to him, "There's Bobby. He looks like he's got to take a leak or something."

Kopas was there as the car came to a stop, hunched down to look in the side window. He said, as calmly as he could, "Mr. Renda . . . man you want's inside that place over there, having a beer."

Renda said, "Alone?"

"With a girl. One works for him."

"Where's the cop sitting?" Renda asked.

The good feeling was there and it was gone as he felt his confidence begin to drain out of him. Kopas straightened and, with a squinting, serious expression, looked over toward the State Highway Department truck parked at the gas station.

He said, "I'm not exactly sure yet, Mr. Renda. But you want me to, I'll find out."

He was not aware of the country music or the two deputies at the bar or the other people in the place. Not right now. His hand was on the bottle of beer, but he was not drinking it. He was looking at the girl's eyes, at the pearl earrings and the way her dark hair was parted on the side, without the bandana, and had a silver clip holding it back, away from her face.

Nancy said, "Do you mind my asking about her?"

"No, it's all right." Majestyk paused. "I don't know, I guess people change. Or else it turns out they're somebody else all the time and you didn't realize it. Do you think it's hard to know people?"

"Not always," Nancy said. "Was she blond, with blue eyes?"

"Most of the time blond. You put your hair up in rollers? You have very pretty hair."

"Once in a while I have. Why?"

"I picture my wife, I see her with rollers. She was always fooling with her hair, or washing it."

"You have any kids?"

"Little girl, seven."

"And you miss her."

"I guess I do. I haven't seen either of them in two years. They moved to Los Angeles."

A silence began to lengthen and Nancy said, "Are you thinking about them?"

"No, not really."

"What are you thinking about?"

"I'm thinking I'd like to know you better."

"Well, I'll fill out a personnel form," Nancy said. "Read it over, see if I pass."

"Always a little bit on the muscle." He was staring at her as he said, "You're very pretty."

"No, not very. But I suppose not bad-looking either. Not somebody you'd kick out of bed, huh, if that's what you've got in mind."

"Why don't you try and relax a little," Majestyk said, "and be yourself. Find out what it's like."

"You want to go to bed with me. Why don't you say it?"

"I'd like to hold you."

"See how close we can get?"

"Sometimes, hard as you try, you can't get close enough," he said. "You know that?" She didn't answer, but he knew by her expression, the soft smile, she was aware of the feeling. Wanting to lie very close to someone, holding each other, not saying anything, because they wouldn't have to use words to say it.

He said, "Let's go home, all right? Go to my house."

There was no need to make him wait. Or, as he said, to be on the muscle. She was aware that they knew each other, each other's feelings. She knew she could relax with him and be herself. Still she hesitated, she supposed out of habit, before saying to him, "All right, your house." She smiled then as he smiled. "But first I'll go to the Ladies'—if it isn't locked."

"If it is," he said, "I'll kick it open."

He watched her cross the room—and the men looking up at her as she passed their tables—to the little hall that led back to the kitchen and the rest rooms.

He saw a man come away from the jukebox and turn into the hallway and knew, even before the man with the hat and the sunglasses looked over his shoulder and grinned at him, it was Bobby Kopas. Majestyk started to slide out of the booth, rising. Then stopped, and sat down again as he felt the pressure of the hand on his shoulder.

"How you doing, buddy?"

Majestyk looked up, then past Renda toward the bar. "There're two cops sitting over there."

Renda took his time. He slid into the seat where Nancy had been and looked at Majestyk before saying, "If there weren't, you'd already be dead."

Majestyk's eyes went to the hallway again. Kopas was still there, watching.

"Leave the girl alone, all right? She doesn't have anything to do with this."

"I don't give a shit about the girl," Renda said. "As long as she stays in the can, out of the way. I got something to tell you. You probably already know it, but I want to make sure you do. I'm going to kill you."

"When?" Majestyk said.

"I don't know. It could be tomorrow. It could be next week." Renda spoke in a normal tone, quietly, without the sound of a threat in his voice. "You could hide in the basement of the police station, but I'm going to get you and you know it."

Majestyk raised the beer bottle and took a drink. Putting it down again his hand remained on the bottle and he seemed to study it thoughtfully before looking at Renda again.

"Can I ask you why?"

"I told you why. We make a deal or you're dead. The fact I got off has got nothing to do with it. You jammed me. You tried to, and nobody does that."

"I don't guess I can talk you out of it then, huh?"

"Jesus Christ—"

"Or there's anything I can do about it?"

"You can run," Renda said. "I'll find you. You can live at the police station. But you got to come out some time. There's no statute of limitations on this one. Whether I kill you tonight or a year from tonight, you're still going to be dead."

Majestyk nodded and was thoughtful again, fooling with the beer bottle. He said, "Well, I guess I got nothing to lose, have I?"

He raised the bottle in his left hand, but it was the right fist that did the job, hooked into Renda's face, in the moment he was distracted by the bottle, and slammed him back against the partition. There was no purpose in hitting him again or hitting him with the bottle. There was little satisfaction in it; but he was letting the guy know he wasn't a goat tied to a post. If Renda wanted him he was going to have to work for it.

The people at the next tables saw the blood and the look of pure astonishment on Renda's face. They saw the expression begin to change as he touched his face, a dead expression that told nothing, but stared at Vincent Majestyk as he got up from the table.

They heard Majestyk lean over, his hands on the table, and

say to the man he had hit, "Why don't you call the cops?" They watched him walk away as the man sat there.

Bobby Kopas didn't like it at all, what was happening now. Majestyk coming toward him. Renda, in the booth, who could stand up any second and start blasting the guy. The two cops at the bar, trying to see past the people at the tables who were standing now.

But nothing happened. Kopas stepped back as Majestyk came into the hallway and went past him—didn't even look at him—to the Ladies' Room. He didn't do anything. Renda didn't. Nobody did. Majestyk pushed open the door to the Ladies' Room and said to the girl who was standing there, "Let's go home."

It could have been a good night. Then there was no chance of it being even a pretty good night. They got back to the place to find no one there. Not even Mendoza and his family. Majestyk saw the flares and the flashing lights across the field, on the highway. The lights were there for some time before he went over and found out a deputy had been killed. Hit and run it looked like.

Harold Ritchie blew up when he saw Majestyk. He said, "Goddamn it, you're the one started this!"

Majestyk said to him, "Listen, an hour ago I had fourteen people at my place counting my foreman and his family. Now everybody's gone, chased off while you're sitting in a bar drinking beer."

"And a man was killed and we don't know who done it because I had to watch *you!*" Ritchie yelled at him.

There was no point standing on the highway arguing with a sheriff's deputy in the pink-red flickering light of the flares that had been set around the area.

Majestyk went home. He told Nancy what had happened, then told her to sleep in the bedroom, he'd sleep on the couch in the living room. When she objected he said, "I'm not going to argue with you. You're sleeping in there."

She didn't say any more and he didn't either. It wasn't until the next morning they found out what had been done inside the packing shed.

10

When Nancy came into the shed, Majestyk was opening the cartons that were stitched with bullet holes and stained where juice from the melons had seeped out. She looked at the open cartons scattered about the floor, at the chunks of melon, yellow fragments, on the conveyor line.

"If he can't have you, he'll take your melons," the girl said. "How does it look?"

"Some are all right."

He walked past her, out to the loading dock, and stared at his empty fields and the pale morning sky. Some were all right. Spend a half day to sort them, maybe have one load to deliver to the broker. Most of the crop was still on the vines. If he could get it in he would at least break even and be able to try it again next year. If he could get the crop in. If he could get a crew. And if Renda would forget the whole thing and leave him alone.

But that was not going to happen, so he'd sit here and wait and watch the crop rot in the field.

Unless you could finish it somehow, Majestyk thought, and had a strange feeling as he thought it. Instead of waiting, what if there was something he could do to get it over with?

When he saw the figure walking in from the highway he knew it was Larry Mendoza—the slow, easy way he moved—and went down to the road to meet him. As Mendoza approached he held up his hand, as if to hold Majestyk off, knowing what was in his mind.

"Don't say nothing, Vincent. I live here, I work here. I took my wife and kids to her mother's, so they'd be out of the way. Now, what are we doing?"

"They hurt you," Majestyk said, staring at Mendoza's bruised, swollen mouth. "I'm sorry, Larry. I should have been here."

"No." Mendoza shook his head. "Getting that beer was the best thing you ever did."

"They asked you where I was and you wouldn't tell them," Majestyk said. "So they roughed you up."

"Not much. I only got hit once. Nobody else was hurt."

"You don't know if Frank Renda was one of them?"

"No, I never seen him, picture or nothing."

"Did you talk to the police?"

"Sure, a cop stop me in town, take me in. They ask some questions, but what do I tell them? Some men come, I don't even know who they are. I don't even *see* them. They tell us leave or get our heads busted. That's all. Come on, Vincent, we got some work, let's do it."

"If you'll do one thing for me, Larry," Majestyk said. "I think we got enough good melons for a load. Take the trailer into the warehouse and leave it there. You can come back later sometime, and get your personal things, your clothes and stuff."

Mendoza frowned. "What the hell are you talking about? I'll

bring the trailer back, we'll pick melons and load it again. You retiring already, or what?"

"I can't ask you to stay here," Majestyk said.

"Then don't ask. I'll get the trailer."

As he started away Majestyk said to him, "Larry . . . it's good to see you."

When he returned to the packing shed Nancy had already begun the sorting, separating the undamaged melons and placing them in fresh cartons. She looked up as he came in.

"Lots of them are still good, Vincent. More than I thought."

"Larry's going to take a load in," Majestyk said. "He'll drop you off in town."

"What am I going to town for?"

He realized, by her expression, he was taking her by surprise. "To get a bus," Majestyk said. God, he sounded cold and impersonal, but went on with it. "There's no reason now for you to stay. I'll pay you, give you money for the others in case you run into them." She came to her feet slowly, as he spoke.

"Last night you want to hold me," Nancy said, "see how close we can get. Today you want me to leave."

"Last night—that seems like a long time ago." He still didn't like his tone, but didn't know what to do about it. "I must've been nuts, or dreaming," he said, "believe the man'd sit and wait for me to get my crop in."

"All right, if you feel he's going to come back," the girl said, "then why don't we both leave?"

"Run and hide somewhere? He'd find me, sooner or later."

"So face it and get it over with, huh?" There was a sound of weariness in her tone. "Big brave man, has to stand alone and fight, no matter what. Where'd you learn to think like that?"

"You're not going to be here, so don't worry about it."

"Now you're mad."

"I don t have time to worry about it."

She said then, "I'll tell you something, Vincent. I've been in a car that was shot at and the man sitting next to me killed. Another time, a truck chased a bunch of us down a road, trying to run us over. And once I was in a union hall when they threw in a fire bomb and shot the place up. I don't need anybody looking out for me. But if you want me to leave, if you don't want me here, that's something else."

He had to say it right away, without hesitating. "All right, I don't want you here."

"I don't believe you."

She was holding him with her eyes, trying to make him tell what he felt.

"I said Larry'll drop you off. Get your bag and be ready when he leaves." He stared at her, fought her eyes, until finally she walked past him, out of the shed.

They were lifting the battered portable toilet onto a flatbed truck with a hoist when Lieutenant McAllen arrived. He had them set the toilet back on the ground and looked at it, not touching it or saying anything until he turned to Harold Ritchie.

"How's it written up? Hit and run?"

"That's about all we can call it for the time being," Ritchie said.

McAllen nodded. "What're they going to do with it?"

"Scrap it, I guess. 'Less the road people want to bump it out."

"You think maybe it ought to be dusted first?"

"Well, we could. But there's people been handling it."

"I'm interested in the door," McAllen said. "Like maybe someone pulled it open, at the time I mean, to see if the man was alive or dead. There could be some prints along the inside edge."

"I guess there could be at that," Ritchie said.

"Let's bring it in and do it at home," McAllen said. "I think that'd be better than having a lot of people hanging around here, don't you?"

Ritchie was looking past McAllen, squinting a little in the glare. "Here comes his truck." As McAllen turned, Ritchie raised his binoculars. "Pulling a trailer load of melons. Going to market, like he didn't have a goddamn trouble in the world. No, it ain't him," Ritchie said then, as the truck reached the highway. "It's his hired man, Larry Mendoza, and looks like . . . some Mexican broad."

* * *

Mendoza paid attention to his driving, concentrating on it, and would keep busy looking at the trailerload of melons through the rearview mirror, because he didn't know what to say. The girl, Nancy, didn't say anything either—staring out the side window, her suitcase on the seat between them—but he was aware of her, could feel her there, and wished she would start talking about something.

He tried a couple of times to get it going, asking her if she thought she would run into her friends. She said probably, sooner or later. He asked her if she thought all the migrant farm workers would ever be organized and paid a living wage. She said again probably, someday.

It was too hard to make up something, to avoid thinking about Vincent and what was going on. So Mendoza didn't say any more until they crossed the state road intersection and he pulled to a stop opposite the café-bar.

He said then, "You don't mind waiting?"

"No, it's all right. I can get something to eat," she said, opening the door and putting a hand on her suitcase.

"Sure, get a beer, something to eat. The bus always stops there, so don't worry about missing it."

She said, "Thanks, Larry, and good luck."

"Good luck to you, too."

She closed the door and walked around the front of the truck. As she started across the highway, Mendoza said, "Nancy—"

She paused to look back at him.

"If he didn't have this trouble going on—"

"I know," she said.

"Come back and see us, all right?"

She nodded this time—maybe it was a nod, Mendoza wasn't sure. He watched her reach the sidewalk and go in the café-bar.

He drove on, into Edna, thinking about the girl and Vincent, the kind of girl Vincent ought to have. Especially Vincent. He didn't refer to Chicanos as Latins or look down at them in any way. It was easy to tell when someone looked down, even when he pretended to be sincere and friendly. Mendoza didn't busy himself with the trailerload of melons now, looking through the rearview mirror. He thought about Vincent and the trouble he was in, wondering what was going to happen. He didn't notice the Oldsmobile 98 following him.

Just past the water tower that said EDNA, HOME OF THE BRONCOS, Mendoza turned off the highway, crossed the railroad tracks, and drove along the line of produce warehouses and packing sheds. At a loading dock, where a man was sitting eating a sandwich, his lunch pail next to him, Mendoza came to a stop and said out the side window, "Where's your boss? Man, I got a load of top-grade melons."

The man on the loading dock wasn't in any hurry. He took a bite of his sandwich and chewed it before saying, "He's out to lunch. You'll have to wait till he gets back."

"What if I unload while I'm waiting?"

"You know he's got to check them first," the man on the dock said. "Go sit down somewhere, take it easy."

Well, if he had to. But he wasn't going to wait in the hot sun, or in the pickup that would get like an oven. And he wasn't going to sit with the guy on the dock and have to talk to him— he could tell the guy had it against Chicanos. So Mendoza got out of the truck and walked around the corner of the warehouse where there was a strip of shade about five feet wide along the wall.

He sat down with his back to it, tilted his straw down over his eyes and settled into a reasonably comfortable position. He pictured himself there as someone might come along and see him. Goddamn Mexican sleeping in the shade. Make him wait and then call him a lazy Mex something or other. He yawned. He was tired because he had gotten only about four hours sleep last night at Helen's mother's house, all of them crowded in there, two of the kids in bed with them. He wouldn't mind taking a nap for about a half hour, till the broker got back from his lunch.

His eyes were closed. Maybe he had been asleep, he wasn't sure. But when he opened his eyes he saw the front end of the Olds 98 rolling toward him—creeping, like it was sneaking up on him—from about thirty feet away.

Mendoza got up so fast his hat fell off. What the hell was going on? The whole wall empty and a car coming directly at where he was standing. Like some kind of joke. Somebody trying to scare him.

But he knew it wasn't a joke when he saw Bobby Kopas, the skinny, hunch-shouldered hotshot guy, coming along the wall toward him. He knew there would be another guy coming from the other side. Mendoza turned enough to look over his shoulder and there he was. It was too late to run. The car kept coming and didn't stop until it was only about three feet from him. Kopas and the guy on the other side came up to stand by the front fenders. He could smell the engine in the afternoon heat.

Kopas said, "Larry, I believe you were told to shag ass and don't come back. Ain't that right?"

"I was just helping out my friend a little bit, deliver some melons," Mendoza said.

"We give you a chance to run, you don't even take it."

"No, listen. I'm just doing this as a favor. I get rid of the load I'm gone, you never see me again."

"Larry," Kopas said, "don't bullshit me, okay?"

"Honest to God, I'm going to drop the melons and keep going."

"In the Polack's truck?"

"No, I told him I leave it here, so he can pick it up."

"Is that a fact? When's he coming?"

"I don't know. Sometime. Maybe tomorrow."

"How's he supposed to get here?"

"Hitchhike, I guess. He don't worry about that."

"Larry, you're shittin' me, aren't you?"

"Honest to God, ask the man in the warehouse, around on the dock. Come on, let's ask him. He'll tell you."

"You aren't going nowhere," Kopas said. "You had your chance, Larry, you blew it."

The man behind the wheel of the Olds 98 hit the accelerator a couple of times, revving the engine. Mendoza looked at the car and at Kopas again quickly.

"Listen—what did I do to you? I worked for the guy that's all."

He saw Kopas step away and knew the car was coming as he stood with his back against the wall and no room, no direction, in which to run. He had to do something and jumped up, trying to raise his legs, but the car lunged into him, the bumper catching his legs and flattening him against the wall, holding him against it as he screamed and fell against the hood and then to the ground as the car went abruptly into reverse. He remembered thinking—the last thing as he tensed, squeezing his eyes closed—now the wheels were going to get him.

The hospital in Edna had an emergency room and eighteen beds, but it was more an outpatient clinic than a hospital and looked even more like a contemporary yellow-brick grade school.

For almost a year Majestyk had thought it was a school. He had never been in the hospital before today—before the squad car picked him up and delivered him, blue lights flashing, to the emergency entrance where an ambulance and another squad car were waiting. Inside, the first person he saw was Harold Ritchie, the deputy coming toward him from the desk where a nurse's aide sat typing.

"Where's Larry?"

"Round the corner. I'll show you."

"What'd they do to him?"

"Guy at the warehouse—there was only one guy anywhere near where it happened—didn't see a thing. Not even the car."

"What'd they *do* to him?"

"Broke his legs," Ritchie said.

He was lying on a stretcher bed covered with a sheet, his wife with him, a curtain drawn, separating them from the next bed where a little boy was crying. A nurse, with a tray of test tubes and syringes, was drawing a blood sample from Mendoza's arm. Majestyk waited. Helen saw him then and came over and he put his arms around her.

"Helen . . . how is he?"

He could feel her head nod against his chest. Her voice, muffled, said, "The doctor say he's going to be all right. Vincent, you know what they did?"

He held her gently, patting her shoulder. "I know." He held

her patiently because she needed his comfort, letting her relax and feel him close to her and know she was not alone. He heard Mendoza say, "Vincent?" and went over to the bed.

"Larry—God, I'm sorry."

"Vincent, I left the melons there."

"Don't worry about the melons."

"That's what I was going to say to you. Staying alive is more important than melons. Did you know that?" He seemed half asleep, his eyes closing and opening slowly.

Majestyk leaned in close to him. "Larry, who were they? You know them?"

"I think the same car as last night, the same people. And your friend, Bobby Kopas, he was there. Vincent, they not kidding. They do this to me, they going to kill you." Mendoza's face tightened as he held his breath, then let it out slowly before relaxing again. "Jesus, the pain when it comes—I never felt nothing like it."

"You want the nurse?"

"No, they already gave me something. They getting ready, going to set my legs."

"Larry, you're going to be all right. The doctor said so."

"I believe him."

"You go to sleep and wake up, it's done. You'll feel better."

Mendoza kept his eyes open, staring at Majestyk. He said, "You want me to feel better, Vincent? Tell me you'll go away. Hide somewhere. There's nothing wrong doing that. Or, sure as hell, you going to be dead."

Harold Ritchie was in the waiting room, arms folded, leaning against the wall. He came alive when he saw Majestyk going past, heading for the door.

"Hey, what'd he say? He tell you anything?"

Majestyk kept going, pushing through the door.

Outside, he saw Lieutenant McAllen getting out of a squad car. He heard McAllen say, "Wait a minute!" And heard himself say, "Bullshit," not looking at the man or slowing down until McAllen said, "If you will, please. Just for a minute."

He waited for McAllen to come to him.

"Where you going?"

"Pick up my equipment."

"We'll drive you."

"I can walk."

McAllen paused. "I'm sorry about your hired man."

"He wasn't my hired man. He was my friend."

"All right, he was your friend." McAllen's tone changed as he said it, became dry, official. "I believe you know a deputy was killed last night, run over or beaten to death possibly, about the same time your migrants left. We'd like to locate them, talk to them."

"Why don't you talk to Frank Renda instead?"

"Because if we brought him in for questioning he'd be out in an hour, and we wouldn't be any farther ahead."

"Where does he live? I'll talk to him."

"You would, wouldn't you?"

"Right now. Soon as I get a gun."

"We'll handle that," McAllen said. "The Phoenix police are watching both of his places, his house, his apartment. So far he hasn't been to either."

Majestyk stared at him. "You mean you don't know where he is? Christ, I was sitting with him last night. So were two of your deputies."

"They had to stay with you," McAllen said. "They radioed the post, but by the time a car got there Renda was gone. We know somebody's given him a place to stay. Probably in the mountains. But who, or where the place is, we don't know that yet."

"You don't know much of anything, do you?"

"I know I have a warrant with your name on it, and I can put you back in jail if you're tired of this."

"Or I can sit home and go broke," Majestyk said. "Why don't you just keep the hell out of the way for a while?"

"We pull out, you know what'll happen."

Majestyk nodded, as though he was thinking about it. "Well, let's see now. So far he's run off my crew, shot up a week's crop of melons and broke my friend's legs. So please don't give me any shit about police protection. Keep your hotshots and their flashing lights away from my property and maybe we can get this thing done and I can go back to work."

McAllen paused, studying Majestyk, as if trying to see into

his mind, to understand him. He said, "Still worried about your melons. You're not going to get them picked if you're dead."

"And if I'm dead it won't matter, will it?"

"You want to bet your life against a melon crop—" McAllen paused again. "All right, you're on your own."

"I have been," Majestyk said, "from the beginning."

McAllen watched him walk off, down the drive toward the main street. He was thinking. The man seems simple, but he's not. He's easy to misjudge. He knows what he wants. He's willing to take risks. And he could already be planning something you haven't thought of yet. Mr. Majestyk, he was thinking, I'd like to know you better.

Ritchie had been waiting a few yards off to the side. He walked over now.

"We pulling out?"

"Let's let him think so," McAllen said, "and see what happens."

11

The broker acted like he was doing him a favor, buying the trailerload of melons and waiting around after quitting time while Majestyk unloaded the cases himself because the warehousemen had gone home. He asked Majestyk how his hired man was. Majestyk told him Larry Mendoza was his friend, not his hired man. The broker said it must've been an accident. Mexican sleeping there in the shade, car comes along doesn't see him, rolls over his legs. Those people were always getting hurt with broken beer bottles and knives, the broker said. Now they were getting hurt while they slept. Majestyk didn't say anything. It was hard not to, but he held on and finally the broker went into his office. Later, when he picked up the check, he didn't say anything either. It was getting dark by the time he got out of there, heading home with the empty trailer.

Home. Nobody there now. A dark house at the end of a dirt road.

As he turned off the highway onto the road he looked at the rearview mirror, then out the side window to see the car that had been following him for several miles continue on. An Oldsmobile, it looked like.

He could hear crickets already in the settling darkness, nothing around to bother them. The packing shed was empty, Mendoza's house, the melon fields—driving past slowly, looking out at the dim fields the way he had looked at fields and rice paddies from the front seat of a jeep a dozen years before, feeling something then, expecting the unexpected and, for some reason, beginning to feel it again, now.

Majestyk drove up to within fifty yards of his house at the end of the road, stopped, turned the key off, put it in his pocket and waited a few moments, listening. When he got out he reached into the pickup bed for a wrench and used it to free the trailer hitch, crouched down between the pickup and the trailer where he could inch his gaze over the melon rows and study the dark mass of trees beyond his house. Pine trees. He didn't know what kind of trees he had watched twelve years ago, lying in the weeds not far from a Pathet Lao village after the H-34 helicopter had gone down, killing the pilot, the mechanic, and the ten Laotian soldiers. No, the trees were different. Only the feeling inside him, then and now, was the same.

Lundy cut his lights as he turned off the highway, hoping to hell he didn't get hung up on a stump or something. Once the road got into the trees it was all right. It was so narrow brush and tree limbs scraped the car on both sides, and the ruts were deep enough that he could feel his way along in the darkness and not worry about going off the road. He came up next to the Dodge parked in the small clearing, got out, and moved through the trees to where Bobby Kopas was watching the house.

Hearing him, Kopas looked over his shoulder. "He just come home."

"Who do you think I been following?" Lundy said. "Where is he?"

"By the truck. See him?"

It was about forty yards across a pasture to the house with its dark windows, and about the same distance again down the road to the pickup truck and trailer. Lundy held his gaze on the front end of the truck.

"I don't see him."

"Unhitching the trailer. He *was.*"

"Well, where's he now?"

"Goddamn it, he was there a minute ago."

"He go in the house?"

"I'd have seen him."

Lundy looked around, getting an uneasy feeling. "Where're the others?"

Kopas pointed with his thumb. "Down there in the trees. So's to watch the side and back of the place."

"Later on," Lundy said, "we'll bring some more people in, seal him up." He looked at Kopas. "If he's still here."

"He's here. We can't see him is all. Down in behind the truck."

"I hope so," Lundy said. "You imagine what Frank would do to you if the man slipped out?"

He moved through the melon rows to the irrigation ditch and again, smelling the damp earth close to his face, experienced a feeling from the time before. It was easier this time because he wasn't carrying the M-15 and the sack of grenades. He wouldn't mind having the M-15 now, or the .30–.30 Marlin in the house or the 12-gauge Remington. The shotgun would be best, at night, at close range. He had thought of the gun when he thought of scouting the house and decided against it. He could be caught in the open too easily. It was better to look around first, make sure, and not approach the house until it was full dark. He reached the end of the irrigation ditch and came up behind the pump housing. From here, in the deep shadows he was able to walk into the trees.

It had been midsummer when the pesticide tank truck came in through the back road to spray his outlying fields. Studying the trees he had remembered the road. It was a point to reach and follow, to help him keep his sense of direction. He remembered the clearing, too, and approached it through the dense trees and scrub as he had approached the village, smelling the wood smoke from a hundred meters away. He stopped when he heard the voice.

"I mean the man's got to be around, hasn't he? His truck's here. How's he going to go anyplace less he's in his truck?"

He knew the voice. There was another voice then, lower, and the sound of a car door slamming.

"Hey, I forgot to tell you—this afternoon, right after I got back—"

The familiar voice was drowned out by the car engine starting. Majestyk moved back into the trees. He waited. When the Olds 98 rolled past him he was close enough to touch it.

The deputy at the road repair site, sitting by the radio in the tool shed, said to the Edna Post, "His truck's still over there. Haven't seen nothing or heard a sound, so I judge he's home safely."

"Harold's about to leave," the voice coming over the radio said. "He wants to know what you want on your hamburgers."

"Mustard and relish," the deputy said.

"Mustard and relish, out."

"Out," the deputy said and flicked the switch off.

He heard the car coming and waited until it passed before stepping outside with the binoculars. So he saw only the taillights of the Olds, the lights becoming little red dots before they disappeared. He raised the binoculars putting them on Majestyk's house, inching them over to the trees and back again. It was too dark to see anything. Dark already, the melon grower was probably in bed, and here he hadn't even had his supper yet.

There were five of them watching the house. He came on them one at a time as he circled through the trees, passing them, seeing dark silhouettes, hearing a muffled cough. The last man was looking out of the trees toward an equipment shed and past it, across the yard, to the back of the house, Majestyk knew he could take the man from behind if he had to, with his hands. But he told himself no, as he had told himself the time before, circling the perimeter of the Pathet Lao village and almost running into the sentry—a young man or a boy who wore a cap with a short visor and held a Chicom machine gun across his skinny knees. He remembered the profile of the boy's face in the moonlight, the delicate features, and remembered wondering what the boy was thinking, if he was afraid, alone in the darkness. He could have shot him, cut his throat or broken his neck with his forearms. But he backtracked into the rain forest and waded for miles through a delta swamp so he wouldn't have to kill the boy. Maybe he had lost too much time and it was the reason they captured him the next morning as he slept, opening his eyes to see the muzzle of the Chicom in his face. He wasn't sure it was the reason he was caught; so he told himself it wasn't. They were on patrol and had stumbled across him.

There had been five of them then, as there were five now. They tied his arms behind him with hemp and looped it around his neck, to lead him back to the village or to another village. He was filthy and smelled from wading through the swamp. At a river he remembered was the Nam Lec, he asked if he could wash himself. One of them untied him and took him, with his Chicom, to the edge of the water. The rest sat on the bank ten yards away and began rolling cigarettes, leaning in toward the match one of them held, and the one guarding him was turned to watch them. Almost in one motion he grabbed the man by his collar, pulling him into the river, chopped him across the face with the side of his hand, took the Chicom away from him and shot two of the Pathet Lao with a single burst as they scrambled to raise their weapons. The three that were left he brought with him, thirty miles to the fire post at Hien Heup.

They gave him a Silver Star and a seventy-two-hour pass, which he spent in the bar at the Hotel Constellation in Vientiane. He told the story to a friend of his, another combat adviser sergeant, saying it didn't make sense, did it? Fall asleep and have to work your ass off to get out of a bad situation and they give you a medal. He remembered his friend saying, "You think people set out to win medals? They're just guys who fuck up and get lucky, that's all."

He was still glad, when he thought about it, he had not killed the sentry.

The one here, watching the back of the house, was nothing to worry about. Majestyk came out of the trees fifty yards down from the man, crossed at an angle so that the equipment shed would give him cover, and reached the side of the house without being seen. Then over the rail to the porch, where he waited a good minute, listening, before going in through the screen door.

In the dark he moved across the room to the cabinet where he kept his deer rifle and automatic shotgun, placed them on a long table behind the sofa that faced the front door, and went back to the cabinet for shells and cartridges. He began loading the shotgun first, thinking, You could go out the same way and take them one at a time. Except Bobby Kopas would be last and he'd run. Get them all together somehow. And Frank Renda, get him out there. That would be too much to ask, to have Renda waiting for him in the woods and not see him coming.

The sound was faint, the squeak of a floorboard, but clear in the silence. He came around with the shotgun at his hip, almost in the same moment he heard the sound, and put it squarely on the figure in the bedroom doorway.

"Don't shoot me, Vincent."

Nancy. He knew it before she spoke, seeing her size and shape against the light from the bedroom window, though not able to see her face. Her voice sounded calm.

"How'd you get here?"

"On the bus. It was going by—I went up to the driver and told him to stop. I told him I forgot something."

"You must've forgot your head. You know what you walked into?"

She didn't say anything. She had never heard this tone in his voice. Not loud, quiet, but God there was a cold edge to it, colder than it had been when he told her to leave.

"There are five men out there," Majestyk said. "With guns.

They're not going to let me leave and they're not going to let you leave either. You got nothing to do with this, but now you're in it."

She said to him quietly, "So I guess you're stuck with me, Vincent."

After a moment, when he came over to her and put his hand on her shoulder, turning her in the doorway so that the light showed part of her face, she knew his tone would be different.

"Why did you come back?"

"I don't know," she said, and that was partly true. "Maybe see what it's like to be on the same side as the grower. That's a funny thing, Vincent. All my life I've been fighting against the growers. Now, this is different."

"You like to fight?" He kept watching her, making up his mind.

"You don't know me yet," Nancy said. "I like to do a lot of things."

He raised the barrel of the shotgun. "You know how to use this?"

"Show me and I will."

"How about a deer rifle?"

"Aim it and pull the trigger. Isn't that all you do?" She waited, looking up at him.

"I don't want you to be here," he said then, "but I'm glad you are. You understand what I mean?"

"You don't have to say anything. If I didn't know how you feel I wouldn't be here."

"You're that sure?"

She hesitated. "I hope so."

"You do have to leave yourself open, don't you? Take a chance."

"That's what it's all about."

"We'll have to talk about it again, when we have more time."

"Sure, it can wait." She smiled at him, even more sure of herself now.

"I'm going outside," he said. "Bring the truck up closer to the house—case they get it in mind to pull some wires."

"Are we going to make a run?"

"I don't know what we're going to do yet. First thing, I'll show you how to work the rifle." She followed him to the table and watched him as he began to load the Marlin. "If anybody tries to come in," he said, "shoot him. Don't say, 'Put up your hands' or anything like that, shoot him."

"All right, Vincent."

He handed her the rifle and picked up the shotgun again. "But make sure it isn't me."

Wiley was on the bearskin couch with her book. She looked up, over her reading glasses, at Lundy and said, "Gene's here."

Renda didn't pay any attention to her. He was on the phone again. Lundy had never seen a guy who was on the phone as much as Frank. The first time he ever met him—after doing seven on the robbery armed conviction and getting out and going to see him with the note his cellmate had given him— Frank was on the phone. It seemed like he had been on it ever since.

Right now he was listening, standing by the bar making a drink, the phone wedged in between his shoulder and his jaw. He put the scotch bottle down, picked up his drink, took some of it, then put the glass down hard and said, "What the fuck you talking about—I got back *yes*terday. Where's the wasted time? What if I was still in Mexico? You going to tell me everything would stop? Shit no." He listened again, moving about impatiently. "Look, it's a personal matter—you said so yourself. It's got nothing to do with the organization. I get it done and we get back to business. Not before."

He slammed the phone down and picked up his drink again. "Fucking lawyers. You don't know if they're working for you or you're working for them."

Wiley said, "I think your friends are worried you might get them involved."

"That's what I need, some more opinions."

She went back to her book as he turned to Lundy.

"What's he doing?"

"He picked up his trailer," Lundy said, "and went right home."

"Alone?"

"He *was*. But Bobby says there's a girl there. Come before he got back. I don't know," Lundy said, "man's waiting to get shot he's got some tail with him."

Put yourself in his place, Renda was thinking, and said, "The cops could've told him don't worry and he feels safe. Thinks, with all that's happened, I won't come for him right away."

"Whenever we do it," Lundy said, "we can't just walk in. The cops could be there waiting."

"You see any?"

"No, but they could've slipped in when it got dark. Be all over the place."

"I don't have time to fool around," Renda said. "They're starting to pressure me, give me some shit, tell me forget about the guy or hire it done."

Lundy agreed with them 100 percent, but he said, "You want to hit him yourself you got to wait for the right time, that's all."

"I don't *have* time! Can't you get that in your head?" He took a drink of scotch and calmed down a little. "How many guys you got there?"

"Five. In the trees by his place. There's a back road takes you in there." He watched Frank put his glass down and go over to a window that looked out on a dark patio and swimming pool.

When Renda turned to him again he said, "If it can take you in, nobody sees you, it can take him out, can't it?"

"If there's no cops in his house."

"All right, you watch his place. He tries to move during the night, stop him. We see who comes out in the morning. We don't see any cops around we grab him, put him in a car, take him out in the desert."

"What about the girl?" Lundy said.

"What girl?"

"The one with him."

"If she's with him she goes too."

Looking at the page in her book, Wiley wondered what the

girl looked like. She wondered if the girl knew she might get killed. Or if the melon grower knew it. Yes, he'd know it, but she wasn't sure about the girl.

Lundy was gone. Frank was at the bar again making another drink. He was drinking too much, taking more pills than he ever had before.

Wiley said, "Do you every worry about—that you could get caught by the police? Or shot? Or killed?"

"Are you going to give me some more opinions?"

"I was just curious. Is that all right?" He didn't answer her and she said, "The guy really didn't mess you up that much, did he? I mean is it worth it? All the trouble?"

He turned from the bar with a fresh scotch.

"Is your book any good?"

"It's different."

"Good and dirty?"

"Dirty enough."

"Then why don't you read it?"

"And shut the fuck up."

"Right," Renda said, "and shut the fuck up."

For several minutes Majestyk stood by the screen door, holding it open a few inches, looking down the road toward the migrant quarters and the packing shed. He thought he had heard a car, not an engine sound but a squeak of springs rolling slowly over ruts. Now all he heard were the crickets. He looked out at his fields, past the pickup, that was parked about twenty feet from the porch now, facing the dirt road and the highway at the end of it. With his shotgun he moved to a side window and looked out at the dark mass of trees. There was no movement, no sound. He left the window.

From the bedroom doorway he could see the girl's profile against the window and the barrel of the Marlin.

"Anything?"

She shook her head. "I have trouble concentrating, Vincent. What I'd like to more than anything is straighten this place up."

"How can you see it in the dark?"

"When I came it was light. I never saw so much stuff not put away. Don't you hang anything up?"

"I haven't had much time for housekeeping. With one thing or another."

"What's that, on the other side of the bed?"

"Don't you know a deep-freeze when you see one? I got it secondhand for twenty-five bucks. Keep deer meat in it."

"I mean what's it doing in here?"

"What's the difference? You got to put it somewhere."

"You need help, Vincent. Well, maybe it's good you have it. They come, we can hide in it."

"They come shooting," he said, "we won't get a chance to hide. But if they *don't* come, soon, I lose a crop. I been thinking. He can wait a week, a year, long as he wants. But I can't wait anymore. So, I figure, I better get it done myself."

"Like turn it around?" She sounded interested.

"If I could spot him, bring him out—"

"Call him up," Nancy said. "Ask him to meet you someplace." There was enough light that she could see his expression, the smile beginning to form, and she said then, "I'm just kidding. I don't mean really do it. Come on, don't. You're just crazy enough to try."

"If he's watching us," Majestyk said, "I don't have to call him. And if he doesn't come tonight—" He paused. "I've got a half-assed idea that might be worth trying."

"God, you are going to turn it around, aren't you? Go after him instead of him after you."

"It's a thought, isn't it? Something he might not expect."

"God, Vincent, sometimes you scare me."

He smiled at her again, feeling pretty good considering everything, and went back into the living room.

12

Bobby Kopas said, "We got him for you, Mr. Renda. Sure'n hell he's in there and there ain't no way he can get out."

Renda stared at the house, at the early morning sun shining on the windows, waiting for some sign of life, wondering what the man was doing, if he was in there. The place looked deserted, worn out and left to rot. He was thinking that it would be getting hot in there. The guy should open a window, let in some air. The guy should be doing something, open the door, take the garbage out, something.

"He tries to go out the road," Lundy said, "we got two people down there in the packing shed. Another boy's over behind that trailer, see it? Case he tries to take off through the melon patch. Two more round the back. We cut his phone wire. I'd say all we got to do is walk up the door and ring the bell."

"If he's there," Renda said. He looked at Kopas. "You seen him this morning?"

Bobby Kopas had been up all night, but he wasn't even tired. He'd been doing a job and hadn't made any mistakes. He said, "I figure he's locked himself in the toilet. Else he's hiding under the bed."

"I still have trouble, don't I," Renda said, "asking you a question?"

"What I meant, Mr. Renda, no, we haven't seen him yet, but he's in the house. His truck's right there. There's no place else he could be."

"And nobody's come by?"

"The girl," Lundy said, "yesterday. She's the only one."

Renda was staring at the house again. It wasn't Sunday. It wasn't a day off. The guy wasn't sleeping in. He should have come out by now. He should have been out an hour ago, working, doing something. So if he was in there he knew what was going on. He felt it or smelled it or had seen somebody.

"I don't like it," Renda said.

Eugene Lundy didn't like it either, not a bit; but it was a living that paid good money and gave him plenty of time to get drunk in between jobs. The thing to do was not think about it too much and just get the job over with. He said, "Well, we can stand here with our finger up our ass or we can go pull the son of a bitch out of there and get it done."

It was good to have people like Gene Lundy, they were hard to find. "That's what we're going to do," Renda said, "but I don't want any fucking surprises. I don't need surprises. Gene, what have we got? What it looks like we've got. The guy in the house. He's got a girl with him. One, maybe two cops over on the highway. Are there more cops somewhere? You say no. All right, then what are the cops doing? Maybe they pulled out. Maybe they said fuck him. Maybe they don't give a shit about the guy and they don't care what happens to him. Except there's still a cop over on the highway. Gene, you're sure, right?"

Lundy nodded. "I saw him go in the tool shed. He's got a radio in there."

"All right," Renda said, "they know I'm going to hit him, they're hanging around. But they're not hanging around very close, are they? What're they doing?"

"Maybe," Lundy said, "they don't give a shit about the guy as you say. I don't know. Maybe they figure you were here, you're not going to come right back, they got a little time. I don't know how they think, fucking cops, but maybe that's what they think."

Renda took a minute, staring at the house. He nodded then and said, "Okay, we'll bring him out. We'll be quiet, go in and bring him out. Walk him back here to the car. And the girl. We'll have to take the girl."

Bobby Kopas had started to think about it too, the actual doing it, and he said, "Mr. Renda, what if he's got a gun?"

"He does, we take it away from him," Renda said. "He tries to use it, then we got no choice." He looked at Lundy. "Do it in the house and get out." He looked at Kopas then. "What I think we'll do—you walk up to the door first, we'll come in behind you."

Bobby Kopas heard it but didn't believe it. He said holy shit to himself and grinned because, Christ, he had never been in this kind of a set-up before and he didn't know how to act, what kind of a pose or anything. He felt like a dumb shit grinning, but what else was he going to do? He said, "Mr. Renda, I never done anything like this before. You know what I mean? I mean I might not be any good at it." Still grinning.

Renda said, "You walk up to the door, we come in behind you."

Majestyk put the two suitcases by the front door and looked at Nancy.

"You ready?"

"I guess so."

"Both bags go in the back of the truck. Save you time, and we might need the one sooner than I'd like."

"All right."

"Once you start, put your foot on it. Don't stop or slow down. Somebody gets in your way, run him over. Five or six miles down the highway you'll see the Enco sign on the corner. The café's right past it."

"Vincent—"

"Listen to me. You get out, take your suitcase, and walk over to the café."

"Vincent, please, you can't do it alone. You need someone."

"Think about what you have to do," he said. "That's enough. More than I have a right to ask."

"Please take me with you."

"I'm not going to argue with you," Majestyk said. "We've discussed it. I'm not going to change my mind now. You get off and I keep going and that's the way it's going to be."

"All right," Nancy said, "but you feel something, Vincent, the same as I do. You can't tell me you don't."

He opened the door and stepped back from it, out of the way. He said, "It's time to go."

They watched her come out with the suitcases and swing them, one at a time, into the back of the pickup. When she got in behind the wheel Lundy said, surprised, "She's taking off in his truck."

"Two suitcases," Renda said. He had to make up his mind right now. Stop her or let her go. The guy could be making her leave, getting her out of the way. Or the guy could be pulling something. He said to Kopas, "She have a suitcase yesterday?"

"Hey, that's right," Kopas said. "She did."

"How many?"

"Just one. Yeah, walked all the way across the field with it."

They heard her voice as she called something to the house. Her arm came out of the window and waved. As the truck started to roll away from the house Lundy said, "She's leaving him there. You believe it?"

Right now, Renda was thinking. Stop her. Yell to the guy behind the trailer. Yell at him to stop her, pull her out of the truck. But even as he made up his mind and screamed it, "Get her! Stop the truck!" it was too late.

Majestyk was out of the house, running, chasing the pickup,

catching the tailgate with his hands and rolling over it into the box as the truck roared off, raising a trail of dust.

Nancy caught only a glimpse of the one by the melon trailer. He was stepping into the road, raising a gun, then jumping aside, away from the front fender, and she was past him, her hands tight on the vibrating wheel, wondering if Vincent was being bounced to death on the metal floor of the box. She wanted to look around, but she kept her eyes on the road, doing fifty now and suddenly seeing the car coming out from the side of the packing shed, coming fast and braking, skidding a little as it reached the narrow road and sat there blocking the way. Nancy cranked the wheel hard to the right, swerved around the front of the car, in and out of the ditch and back onto the road. In the rearview mirror she saw the car back up and make a tight turn to come after her. She was approaching the highway now and would have to slow down.

Turn left and race the five or six miles to Edna. Get out at the café and take her suitcase while he jumped in behind the wheel and before she could say anything he would be gone, leading them up into the mountains somewhere and she would never see him again.

He couldn't do it alone. He needed her. The two of them might have a chance, but he was stubborn and wouldn't listen to her. So she could be meek and do what she was told and never see him after he got in the truck and she walked across the street to wait for the bus. Or—she could forget his instructions, everything he had said, and help him, whether he wanted her to or not. It was simple, already decided. When she reached the highway she turned right instead of left.

He was pounding on the window, yelling at her, "It's the other way! Where in the hell you going?"

She looked over her shoulder and gave him a nice smile, mashed the accelerator, and saw him fall off balance, away from the window.

The deputy at the road construction site saw him raise up again, just as the pickup was going by, and press against the truck's cab, by the back window. The deputy knew it was Majestyk. But he didn't get a good look at who was driving. He thought it was the girl, but he couldn't be sure. The truck went by so fast—west, away from Edna. He was on the radio when the car came out of the road—dark green Dodge, two-door model—squealed out, turning hard, and there wasn't any question in his mind somebody was after somebody.

Thirty seconds later Harold Ritchie was in McAllen's office.

"Renda or some of his people are hot after him. Going east on the highway."

"Now you're talking," McAllen said. "Let's put everything we got on it."

He knew what she was doing now, and knew what he had to do. Lying on his side in the pickup bed he opened his suitcase, took out the stock and barrel of the Remington 12-gauge, got them fitted together and shoved in five loads. It wasn't easy; it took him longer than usual, because of the metal vibrating beneath him and the sway of the truck and the wind. It was hard to keep his balance, propped on an elbow, hard to keep the shotgun steady and the shells in one place.

The crazy girl was having it her way. He saw her face a couple of times, looking over her shoulder through the window, seeing if he was ready.

He needed more time to get the Marlin put together and loaded.

But the dark green car was coming up on them fast. The truck could do maybe eighty, the car a hundred and twenty probably, or more. It wouldn't be long before it was running up their rear end. He looked back again, as they reached the lower end of a grade, and now saw two more cars behind the green one, closing in from about a half to a quarter of a mile away.

Nancy's eyes moved from the outside rearview mirror to the road ahead, the narrow blacktop racing at her, a straight line pointing through scrub and pasture land. On the left side of the road was a stock fence, miles of wire and posts and up ahead, finally, there it was, a side road. Higher posts marked the road. And a closed gate hung across the entrance.

There wouldn't be time to stop and open the gate. She knew that.

There wouldn't be time to load the Marlin. Majestyk realized that now. He put it down quickly, across the open suitcase, and picked up the shotgun again. He had to get turned around, face the tailgate.

He was moving, keeping low, on his elbows and knees—and was thrown hard against the side of the pickup box as the truck left the road and its high four-wheel-drive front end smashed through the wooden gate, exploded through it with the sound of boards splitting, ripped apart by the high metal bumper.

By the time Renda's three cars were through the gate and had come to a sudden stop, the truck was bounding across the desert pasture, making its own trail, running free where the cars couldn't follow.

No one had to say it. The rocks and holes, steepbanked washes and scrub, would rip the underbody of an automobile, tear out the suspension. They sat staring at the dust settling and the yellow speck out there in the open sunlight—Renda in the front seat with Lundy, Kopas in back.

"There's a road over there," Renda said finally. "They got to be headed for something."

"Taking a shortcut," Lundy said.

"There is one," Kopas said, "if I remember correctly. About a mile, county road cuts through there, goes up in the mountains."

The three cars turned in a tight circle and went out through the gate the way they had come in, the dark green Dodge leading off.

Within five miles the county blacktop began to wind and climb, making its way up into high country.

Majestyk felt better now. He had a little time to breathe and knew what he was going to do. The girl had set it up for him, given him the time. She had said he needed her and she was right. When he signaled to her and she stopped, he got out of the box and came up on her side.

"I guess there's no way to get rid of you, is there?"

"I told you before, Vincent, you're stuck with me."

She was the one to have along all right, but he couldn't think about her now. He told her to hold it about thirty-five, let them catch up again. He got back into the rear end and that was the last thing he said to her for a while.

There were a few new melon cartons in the pickup bed, flat pieces of cardboard he put under him for some cushion, soften the damn skid strips on the floor. Then he put the two suitcases at the back end of the pickup box, against the tailgate, and rested the shotgun on them. Lying belly down they were just about the right height. He reached up and pulled the latch open on one side of the tailgate. The other one would hold the gate closed until he was ready.

When he saw the three cars coming again, they were on a good stretch of road, straight and climbing, a pinyon slope rising above them on the right and a steep bank of shale and scrub that fell off to the left, dropping fifty or more feet into dense growth, dusty stands of mesquite.

Now he would have to keep down and rely on Nancy. In the window he saw her look back at him and nod. That meant they were coming up fast. He could hear the car.

Nancy was watching it in the rearview mirror—catching glimpses of the other two cars behind it—letting them come, watching the first car closely to see what it was going to do and trying to hold the truck steady on the narrow road. The car was fifty, forty feet away, crawling up on the truck, overtaking it and beginning to pull out, as if to pass. She held up two fingers in the rear window, a peace sign.

Majestyk was ready. He reached for the tailgate latch, pulled the chain off. The gate dropped, clanged open and there was the dark green Dodge charging at him, a little off to the right. At twenty feet Majestyk put his face to the shotgun, fired three times and saw the windshield explode and the car go out of control. It swerved across the road, sweeping past the tailgate, hit the bank on the right side and came back again—as the two cars behind, suddenly close, braked and fishtailed to keep from piling into the Dodge. The car veered sharply to the left, jumped the shoulder, and dived into the brush fifty feet below.

He fired twice at the second car, the Olds 98, but it was swerving to avoid hitting the bank. The shot raked its side and caught part of the third car, taking out a headlight, as the car rammed into the left rear fender of the Olds, kicked it sideways and both cars came to a hard abrupt stop.

Majestyk gave Nancy the sign, felt the pickup lurch as it shifted and took off, leaving the two cars piled up in the road.

The first thing Lundy did, he went over to the shoulder to look down at the Dodge, at the rear end of it sticking out of the brush. There was no sign of the two guys. They were probably still inside. He couldn't see how they could be alive, but it was possible. Lundy was starting down the bank when Renda called to him.

"Gene, come on." Renda was walking away from the rear of the Olds. The other car was slowly backing up. He said, "We're okay. Let's go."

Lundy began to say, "I was thinking we ought to—don't you think we should take a look?"

"We're going to get in the car, Gene, and not waste any more time. Now come on."

"They could be alive. Hurt pretty bad, caught in there."

"I don't give a shit what they are. We got something to do, right now, before he gets someplace and hides."

Renda didn't say any more until they were in the car, following the road up through the pinyon, looking at side trails, openings in the trees where he could have turned off. But there wasn't any way to tell.

"That goddamn truck of his, he can go anywhere," Renda said. "He knows this country. He told me, he comes up here hunting."

"If he knows it and we don't," Lundy said, "it changes things."

"I don't know, is he running or what? The son of a bitch."

"If he's still on this road," Lundy said, "we'll catch him. Otherwise I don't know either."

There was a game trail nearby where he had sat with the Marlin across his lap and waited for deer: meat for the winter, to be stored in his twenty-five-dollar deep-freeze. He wondered if he would go hunting this fall. If the girl would still be here. If either of them would be here.

He sat with the Marlin now as he had sat before, this time looking down the slope, through the pine trees to the road, the narrow black winding line far below. The cabin was less than a mile from here. He wondered if Renda would think of it and remember how to find it. No, he wouldn't have picked out landmarks and memorized them. He was from a world that didn't use landmarks.

He said to the girl, "Did you ever shoot a deer?"

"I don't think I could."

"What if you were hungry?"

"I still couldn't."

"You eat beef."

"But I don't have to kill it."

"All right, I'll make you a deal. I'll shoot it, you cook it."

"When are we going to do that, Vincent?"

"In a couple of months. We'll have plenty of time. Sit around, drink beer, watch TV. Maybe take some trips."

"Where do you want to go?"

"I don't care. Anyplace."

"We going to get married first?"

"Yeah, you want to?"

"I guess we might as well, Vincent. Soon as we get some time."

Looking down the slope he said, "Here come a couple of friends of ours."

They watched the two cars pass below them on the winding road.

"Now what, Vincent?"

"Now we give them a kick in the ass," Majestyk said.

Renda's three men in the second car, following the Olds, were in general agreement that riding around in the mountains was a bunch of shit. That Frank Renda ought to take care of his own hit, if he wanted the guy so bad. That maybe they should stop on the way back—if they ever got out of this fucking place—and see about the two guys who went over the side.

Though they must be dead; nobody had yelled for help. They were looking out the windows, up and down the slopes, but if the guy wasn't still on the road they knew they weren't going to find him. How could they get to him?

The one in the back seat said, "There shouldn't be nothing to it. Wait for the right time you can set the fucking guy on fire, do it any way you want. This hurry-up shit doesn't make any sense."

"You know what the trouble is?" the driver said. "The guy, the farmer, he doesn't know what he's doing. He shouldn't even still be around."

"That's it," the one in the back seat said. "If he knew anything he'd know enough not to be here. It's like some clown never been in the ring before. He's so clumsy, does so many wrong things, you can't hit the son of a bitch."

"Fighting a southpaw," the driver said. "You ever fight a southpaw?"

"You get used to that," the one in the back seat said. "I'm talking about a clown. Hayseed, doesn't even own a cup."

"So you know where to hit him," the driver said.

"Shit, try and get to the guy."

Talking about nothing, passing the time. The one in the back seat looked out the side window at the dun-colored slopes and rock formations. They were getting pretty high, moving along a hogback, the spine of a slope. He half turned to look out the back window and said, "Jesus!" loud enough to bring the driver's eyes to the rearview mirror and the man next to him around on the seat.

The high front end of Majestyk's pickup was on top of them, headlights and yellow sheetmetal framed in the back window, the guy behind the wheel looking right at them, saying something, and the girl next to him ducking down.

Majestyk pressed down on the gas, caught up and drove the high bumper into the car's rear deck. He saw the car beginning to pull away, pressed the gas pedal all the way to the floor and caught the rear end again, stayed with it this time, fighting the wheel to keep the car solidly in front of him, ramming it, bull-dozing it down the narrow grade, hitting a shoulder and raising dust, hanging with it, seeing sky above the car and knowing what was coming, foot pressed hard on the gas for another five seconds before he raised it and mashed it down on the brake pedal.

The car almost made the turn. It skidded sideways, power-sliding, hit the shoulder, and went through the guardrail turned onced in the air and exploded in flames five hundred feet below.

Majestyk was through the turn, saw the Olds 98 on the road three switchbacks below him, came to an abrupt stop, turned around, and headed back the way they had come, aware of the smoke now billowing up out of the canyon. He was sure Renda heard the explosion and would be coming back. So he'd go up into the pines again and work out the next step.

In the quiet of the cab he heard Nancy say, "I hope you never get mad at me, Vincent."

The Olds 98 came to a stop in the shadow of a high, seamed outcropping of rock. The shadow covered the road that contin-ued in dimness, reaching a wall of rock and brush before bear-ing in a sharp curve to the right.

Lundy got the map out of the glove box and spread it open over the steering wheel. It was quiet in the car, except for the sound of Lundy straightening the map, smoothing the folds.

Renda stared straight ahead, through the windshield. We haven't been out here an hour, he was thinking, and he's killing us. Do you know what he's doing? Do you see it now?

Bobby Kopas fidgeted in the back seat, looking out the win-dow on one side and then the other, bending down to see the crest of the high rocks. It was so quiet. Sunlight up there and shade down here. Nothing moving.

"His hunting country," Renda said. "He brought us here."

"I see where we're at," Lundy said. "The lodge is only about six, eight miles west of here, but roundabout to get to. 'Less we want to go all the way back to the highway, which I don't think is a good idea."

Renda wasn't listening to him. He was picturing a man in work clothes and scuffed lace-up boots, a farmer, a man who lived by himself and grew melons and didn't say much.

"He set us up," Renda said. "The farmboy knew what he was doing all the time and he set . . . us . . . up."

Lundy said, "What do you want to do? Go back the lodge? I don't see any sense in messing around here." He waited, watching Renda stare out the window. "Frank, what do you want to do?"

He didn't know. He realized now he didn't know anything about the man. It was like meeting him, out here, for the first time. He should have known there was someone else, another person, inside the farmer. The stunt the guy pulled with the bus and trying to take him in, make a deal. That wasn't a farmer. He had been too anxious to get the guy and had not taken time to think about him, study him and find out who he was inside.

Lundy said, "There's no sense sitting here."

Renda continued to stare at the wall of rock ahead of them, where the road curved, thinking of the man, trying to remember the things he had said, trying to out-think him now, before it was too late. He didn't see the figure standing on the crest of the rocks, not at first. And when he saw him he was a shadow that moved, a dark figure silhouetted against the sky a hundred yards away, holding something, raising it.

"Get out of here!"

Renda screamed it, Lundy looked up and the rifle shot drilled through the windshield and into the seat between them with a high whining sound that was outside, far away. The second shot tore through the glass two inches from the first and Renda screamed it again, "Get out of here!"

Majestyk put four more .30–30's into the car before it got around the bend and was out of sight. He might have hit one of them but he doubted it. He should have taken a little more time on the second shot, corrected and placed it over to the left more. That's what you get, you don't hunt in a year you forget how your weapons act.

He walked away from the crest, back into the pines where Nancy was waiting by the truck, shaking his head as he approached her.

"Missed. Now I got to bird-dog him."

"Now?" She seemed a little surprised. "How can you catch up with him?"

"I can cross-country, he can't."

"You're really going after him?"

"We're this far," he said and watched her cock her head, then look up through the pine branches.

"I think I hear a plane," she said. "You hear it?"

He heard it. Walking back from the crest into the trees he had heard it. "You'll see it in about a minute," he said. "Only it's not a plane, it's a helicopter."

Harold Ritchie had radioed ahead to cars patrolling the main roads as far as thirty miles east of Edna. They reported, during the next half hour, no sign of a yellow four-wheel-drive pickup, with or without anybody chasing it.

So he must have taken them up in the mountains, Lieutenant McAllen decided, and called the Phoenix Police for a helicopter. Get more ground covered in an hour than they could in a week.

It didn't even take that long. McAllen and Ritchie had been cruising the highway and some of the back roads. They were at the road repair site when the chopper radioed in. There was static and the sound of the rotor beating the air, but the pilot's voice was clear enough.

"Three-four Bravo, this is three-four Bravo. I believe we got him. Yellow pickup truck heading south, in the general direction of county road 201, just west of Santos Rim, God almighty, or else it's a mountain goat. I thought he was on a trail, but there ain't anything there. He's bouncing over the rocks, flying. Heading down through a wash now like it's a chute-the-chute. Look at that son of a bitch go!"

McAllen and Ritchie looked at one another. They didn't say anything.

"On 201 now heading west," the pilot's voice said. There

was a pause. "Hey, we got something else. Looks like . . . an Oldsmobile or a Buick, late model, dark blue . . . about a half mile out in front of the pickup, going like hell. Let me get down closer. This is three-four Bravo out."

Lieutenant McAllen looked up in the sunlight, toward the mountains, then at Harold Ritchie. "You don't suppose—"

"I'd more likely suppose it than not," Ritchie said.

They heard the radio crackle and the helicopter pilot's voice came on again.

"This is three-four Bravo. Looks like they pulled a disappearing act on us. I don't see either one of them now. They must've turned off on a trail through the timber. Hang on I'll give you some coordinates."

"About how far away are we talking about?" McAllen asked Ritchie. "The general area."

"Not far. Take us twenty, thirty minutes, depending on the coordinates he gives us."

"Then we'd still have to find them," McAllen said.

"We get enough cars up there," Ritchie said, "we can do it."

"But can we do it in time?"

Ritchie wasn't sure what he meant. "In time for what?"

"In time to keep him from killing himself," McAllen said.

13

Wiley was bored. She had finished her book. There wasn't anything else to read in the place but business and banking magazines and a few old *Playboys*. It was a little too cold to go in the pool—which wasn't much of a thrill even when it was warm. She was tired of lying in the sun but not tired enough to take a nap. The whole thing, lying around swimming pools, waiting, was getting to be a big goddamn bore.

And the ice in her iced tea had melted. She put the glass on the cement next to the lounge chair, snapped her orange bikini bottom a little higher on her can as she got up and went into the lodge, or whatever it was, that Frank said looked like a dude ranch.

It did look like a dude ranch. All those Indian blankets and animals looking out of the wall. She turned the hi-fi on, got some rock music she liked but didn't recognize and was patting her bare thighs gently, keeping time, when Frank came in the front door. Frank and Gene and the new one, the little smart-ass carrying a shotgun. She hadn't heard the car drive up.

"Well, hey. What's going on?"

The three of them were at the front windows, not paying any attention to her.

"I never seem to catch the beginning," Wiley said. "Will somebody tell me what's going on?"

She moved over a little, her hips keeping time with the music, to be able to look out the window, past Frank and across the open yard to where the long driveway came in through the trees. She didn't see the Olds; then she did—over to the side a little at the edge of the trees, as if hidden there. They were waiting for someone to come up the drive and as she realized this her hips stopped keeping time and she thought of the police.

"You think," Wiley said, "I should start packing or what?"

"He's in the trees," Renda said.

"He could be," Lundy said, "if he saw us turn. But maybe he didn't."

Renda looked over his shoulder at Wiley. "Give me the glasses. Over on the table."

"Would you mind telling me something?"

"Give me the *glasses.*"

He raised the window and got down on his knees, took the binoculars as she handed them to him and rested his elbows on the sill. The trees were close to him now, dark in there but clearly defined as he adjusted the focus, scanned slowly toward the drive, held for a while, trying to see down the length of the dirt road, then back again, slowly. He stopped. From the side of a tree about twenty feet into the woods, Majestyk was aiming a rifle at him.

With the sound of the shot, the glass above his head shattered. Renda dropped below the sill to his hands and knees, in a crouch. There was a silence before he heard the man's voice, coming from the trees.

"Frank, let's finish it. Come on, I got work to do."

Wiley watched Frank crawl from beneath the window and stand up, turning to put his back against the wall. She expected him to yell something at the guy, answer him, but he didn't. He was looking at her with a thoughtful sort of pleased expression; not really happy, but relaxed as he drew a .45 automatic from underneath his jacket. She still didn't know what was going on.

Majestyk handed Nancy the rifle and picked up the shotgun, leaning against a tree, as he saw the front door open.

Wiley came out in her orange bikini. She seemed at ease, even though she was looking around, more curious than afraid. Coming across the lawn she said, "Where are you?"

"Over here," Majestyk said. He saw her gaze turn this way, but was sure she couldn't see him yet.

"Frank's not home," Wiley said. "You want to come in and wait?" He didn't answer now and she turned to go. "Well, it was nice talking to you."

"Wiley—"

She stopped and looked back. "Yeah?"

"Come here."

"I don't know where you are."

"Over here. That's right."

He waited until she was in the trees, more cautious now, and finally saw where they were standing. "What's he doing?" Majestyk said. "He want you to point to me so he can shoot?"

"I told you, he's not home."

"The car's over there."

"It belongs to somebody else."

"Wiley, tell Frank the cops are on the way. Tell him if he wants to settle it he hasn't got much time."

She hesitated. "Police, huh. Listen, this really hasn't got anything to do with me. I just happen to stop by."

"Who else is in there? How many?"

She hesitated again. "Just Frank . . . and two others. God, he's going to kill me."

Majestyk turned to Nancy. "Put her in the truck. Drive back to the road and wait for me there."

Wiley said to Nancy, "I really don't know what's going on. I don't have any clothes or anything."

"Don't worry, I'll give you a nice outfit," Nancy said, and looked at Majestyk again. "Vincent, wait for the police, all right?"

"If they come," he said, "but right now it's still up to him."

They couldn't see her now. There had been a spot of orange in the trees, but now that was gone.

"Where'd she go?" Kopas said. He didn't like it at all. Five people dead, the man out there waiting for them. The man must be crazy, all he'd done.

"He grabbed her," Lundy said. He was holding his big magnum, resting it on the windowsill.

Why would he? Kopas was thinking and said, "Maybe they left. He sees we got him, so he took her and cut out."

"He's there," Renda said, sure of it now, since he had begun to know the man, understand him. "Son of a bitch, we got to suck him out. Or go in after him."

Kopas said, "You mean walk out there?"

Renda looked at him. "If I tell you to."

Majestyk came up to the Olds 98 through the trees, keeping low, and there was nothing to it. The next part he'd have to do and not worry about and if they spotted him and fired he'd have to back off and think of something else. He opened the front door on the passenger side, waited a moment, then slid in headfirst over the seat and pulled the key out of the ignition. Coming out he looked at the backrest of the seat cushion, at the two bullet holes that were hardly noticeable. Just a little more to the left. He wished he'd taken a couple more seconds. It would have saved him a lot of trouble.

They could still come out the front while he worked around through the trees to the back, but it wouldn't do them any good now. They weren't going anywhere, unless on foot, and then it would be even easier.

That's what he did: cut across the open to the blind side of the house and stayed close to it as he made his way around to the patio.

It could work because they wouldn't expect him. Get up to a window or the glass door underneath the sundeck, shove the pump gun in, and wait for somebody to turn around. He moved past the lounge chair Wiley had been using a little while before, his eyes on the window. Even if he had looked down then he might not have seen the iced tea glass, it was so close to the chair. By the time he did see it he had kicked it over—hearing it like a window breaking—and all he saw were the broken fragments and a piece of lemon on the wet cement.

Renda turned from the front window. He stood listening, holding the .45 automatic at his side, then raised it as he started across the room toward the patio door. Lundy followed him.

Kopas waited. He wasn't sure he wanted to go over there. He watched Renda press against the glass panes to look out, trying to see down the outside wall of the house. Kopas knew he'd have to open the door and stick his head out to see anything. He wondered if Renda would open the door, if he'd go out. Christ, it would take guts.

He heard Renda say to Lundy, "You stay here. I'm going up on the sundeck. I spot him I'll yell to you."

Lundy nodded, holding the big mag, and moved in close to the door as Renda came back across the room. Kopas still didn't know what to do. He was sure, though, he didn't like being here with the guy right outside, the guy maybe poking a gun in a window any minute.

That is why he followed Renda to the front hall and up the stairs. The guy couldn't poke a gun into a second-floor window.

Renda went into a bedroom and over to the sliding glass door that opened on the sundeck. He glanced at Kopas as he went out, noticing him, but didn't say anything—like the other times, looking through him as if he wasn't there.

Kopas said, "What you want me to do, Mr. Renda?"

Maybe Renda hadn't heard him. He was out on the sundeck now, looking over the railing at the patio. Kopas raised his shotgun and moved to the open doorway. He didn't go out. He could see most of the patio and the swimming pool, the sun reflecting on the clear green water. He watched Renda go to his hands and knees, trying to see down through the narrow spaces between the deck boards. Renda crawled along this way, coming back to the door before he got to his feet again.

"Son of a bitch, he's under there," Renda said.

But where? Kopas was thinking. The deck was about thirty feet long. He could be right underneath them or he could be down a ways or hiding behind something. He watched Renda move to the rail again, then look over to the left, to where the patio door would be, where Lundy was waiting. He watched Renda lean over the rail and point the .45 straight down—and couldn't believe it when Renda suddenly yelled out.

"Gene, he's going around the side! Get him!"

Majestyk's eyes were raised to the sundeck above his head, his shotgun pointing straight up to where he was pretty sure Renda was standing—where he had heard the movement and where the glint of sunlight between the boards were blotted out.

He didn't know it was Renda, not until he heard Renda's voice, his words clear, startling. And heard something else. A door. Quick footsteps on cement.

He had time—at least three seconds, before Lundy, running alongside the swimming pool, saw him, came to a stop and swung the magnum at him—time to swing the shotgun down and fire and pump and fire again and see Gene Lundy blown off his feet into the swimming pool.

Renda saw that much and knew where the man was down below, knew close enough, and began firing the .45 automatic straight down at the deck boards, concentrating on a small area only a few feet to his left, fired and fired, splintering, gouging the stained wood, and kept firing until the automatic was empty.

He stood listening then. When the gunfire ringing in his ears began to fade, he could hear, very faintly, the sound of hi-fi rock music coming from the main room. That was all. He stepped into the bedroom to reload the .45, still listening, watching the patio—pulling out the clip and throwing it aside, taking another clip from his jacket pocket and smacking it with his palm into the grip.

"Go take a look," Renda said.

Kopas had backed away from the glass doors until the bed stopped him and he felt it against his legs. "Mr. Renda—" He stopped and started over. "The man wasn't running around the side. I was looking, I didn't see him. You told Gene that—you *used* Gene to spot the guy."

Kopas saw him turn and saw his eyes, not looking through him this time but right at him.

"Go downstairs," Renda said, "look out the door. If he's laying there, walk out on the patio. If he isn't laying there, stay where you are."

"I'm sorry," Bobby Kopas said. "I mean I don't even know what I'm *doing* here. I don't give a shit about the guy. Really, it's none of my business. I think I better just—split. You know?" He had to get out, that's all. Just get the hell out of here, though not make it look like he was scared or running. He said, "I'll leave this case you need it," and dropped the shotgun on the bed as he got around the foot of it and headed for the door.

Renda said, "Bobby—"

Kopas kept going.

He was almost to the stairway when Renda came out into the hall.

"Bobby!"

His hand was on the stair rail. Below him was the open front door and sunlight. He didn't hear his name again. He didn't care if he did. He didn't care now if Renda thought he was running. Just get *out*, that's all.

He got halfway down.

Renda shot him from the top of the stairs, hitting him squarely in the back, twice. Lowering the .45 he saw Kopas lying face-down in the front hall, a few feet from the door, and was aware of the hi-fi music again—a slow rock instrumental—coming from the main room.

All right, he'd go down, go through the room to the patio. Look outside.

Or he could go out the front door and walk around. If the guy was alive he wouldn't know which way he'd be coming from, wouldn't know where to look.

But the guy was probably dead. Or at least hit. He must have hit him. So it didn't matter. Renda moved down the stairs, holding his gaze on the archway below and to the right, that led into the main room. He was at the bottom, in the front hall, about to step over Bobby Kopas's legs, when the hi-fi music stopped. It stopped abruptly, in the middle of the rock number.

Renda waited.

There was no sound from the room. Animal heads looking down in silence at—what? Where would he be? Behind something. Renda could see only part of the room from where he was standing, the windows along the front wall. He would have to walk through the archway to see the rest, not knowing where the guy was. He had never done it like this before, walked in, the guy knowing he was coming. Guy waiting with a shotgun. There was a shotgun upstairs. But if he went up the guy could move again and he wouldn't know where. He knew the guy was in the room. But it was a big room. Or he could be outside again, with the shotgun sticking in the window.

He said to himself, This isn't a fucking game. *Get out.*

Renda went through the doorway, ran across the grass to the Olds 98 and got to it, pulled the door open and started to slide in.

The key wasn't in the ignition.

The fucking key wasn't in the ignition! Lundy had it. No, or it was on the floor . . . or on the dash . . . or on the sun visor. Somewhere!

"Frank?"

Renda came out slowly, turning a little to look over the top of the open door.

Majestyk was standing on the front steps of the house, the shotgun cradled in the crook of his left arm.

"You hear it?" Majestyk said.

Renda turned a little more, keeping the car door in front of him. He could hear it now, the faint sound of a police siren.

Majestyk waited.

Behind the door, below the window ledge, Renda shifted the .45 automatic in his left hand. He knew he could do it, hit the guy before he moved. Farmboy standing there not knowing it was over. He said, "You want to think about it?"

Majestyk shook his head. "Last chance, Frank."

Renda brought up the .45 automatic, at arm's length out past the edge of the door and fired, trying to aim now as he fired again.

Majestyk swung the shotgun on him and blew out the window in the door, watched Renda stagger out from behind it, still holding the .45 extended, and shot him again, the 12-gauge charge slamming Renda against the side of the car and taking out the rear-door window. Renda went down to his knees, hung there a moment and fell face-down.

Majestyk was sitting on the front steps with the shotgun across his knees. He watched the three squad cars come barreling in through the trees, watched them pull to nose-diving stops and the doors swing open and the deputies come piling out with riot guns and drawn revolvers. They stopped when they saw him and stood there looking around. Lieutenant McAllen walked over.

"You were right," Majestyk said. "That man was trying to kill me."

McAllen looked at him. He didn't say anything. He kept going and walked over to where Renda was lying, stooped down and felt his throat for a pulse. He looked over at Majestyk again.

But Majestyk was walking away, over toward the pickup that had come in behind the squad cars, where the girl was standing.

McAllen watched him put his hand on the girl's shoulder as he opened the door and heard him say, "We'll get us a couple of six-packs on the way home. Right?" And he heard the girl say, "Right." He watched Majestyk's hand slide down to the girl's can as she climbed into the cab and heard her say, "Hey, watch it!" He didn't hear what Majestyk said to her as he slammed the door, but he heard the girl's laughter.

Then Majestyk was walking around the pickup to the driver's side. He looked over and gave McAllen a little wave.

McAllen didn't wave back or say a word. He heard the girl laugh again and watched the pickup drive off through the trees.